John cinched up the chinstrap on his helmet before stepping out of the Humvee. The faint rays of sunlight on the horizon were no longer strong enough to punch through the haze that still hovered over the street. He inhaled slowly, recognizing the pervasive, acrid smell of cordite and dried blood. The Museum building itself hadn't been damaged in the ambush, but the front steps were a mess of crumbled concrete and shell casings.

It had taken a maddeningly long time to get here. The Army had had its hands full, trying to secure five different sites throughout Baghdad where explosions had occurred almost simultaneously. As critical as John and Rebecca's mission was, it didn't trump ongoing urban warfare. They'd been stuck on base at Balad, the outlook for Jackson getting bleaker by the minute, until word finally had come down that the Museum area was under control—at least for the moment.

Climbing down from the Humvee, Rebecca adjusted her Kevlar vest and studied the other vehicles on the street, many of them scarred, inoperable hunks of twisted metal. "Good God," she said quietly. "If Dr. Jackson was in one of those—"

STARGATE ATLANTIS™

BLOOD TIES

SONNY WHITELAW & ELIZABETH CHRISTENSEN

FANDEMONIUM BOOKS

An original publication of Fandemonium Ltd, produced under license from MGM Consumer Products.

Fandemonium Books
PO Box 795A
Surbiton
Surrey KT5 8YB
United Kingdom
Visit our website: www.stargatenovels.com

STARGATE
ATLANTIS™

METRO-GOLDWYN-MAYER Presents
STARGATE ATLANTIS™
JOE FLANIGAN TORRI HIGGINSON RACHEL LUTTRELL JASON MOMOA
with PAUL McGILLION as Dr. Carson Beckett and DAVID HEWLETT as Dr. McKay
Executive Producers BRAD WRIGHT & ROBERT C. COOPER
Created by BRAD WRIGHT & ROBERT C. COOPER

ISBN: 978-1-905586-08-0
Printed in the United States of America

To the crew of Apollo 1
—SW

To the crews of Challenger STS-51-L and
Columbia STS-107
—EC

With many thanks to Captain Daniel Kenan, USAF, for his scene-setting assistance—and to our families, for letting us chase these stories every now and then.

PROLOGUE

It was his expression, rather than the words on the page, that conveyed to her the significance of this discussion. Elizabeth Weir was a diplomat, and her strengths lay in reading people, not nucleotide sequences. She had an advantage in this case, because she knew her chief medical officer well. In nearly two years of working together in Atlantis, and the months before that in Antarctica during his attempts to operate the Ancient chair, she'd never seen Carson Beckett look so ill at ease.

Upon hearing his explanation, she understood the basis for his apprehension.

"You've just discovered this?" she asked, handing the printout back across her desk.

Carson hesitated in the middle of a nod. "Yes and no," he replied in his soft Scottish brogue. "I originally identified it during our initial efforts to isolate the ATA gene. We received a great deal of assistance from the Human Genome Project, as well as from Allan Wilson's Mitochondrial Eve research. Through their data we determined that the gene required to operate Ancient technology was first introduced into the human population approximately ten thousand years ago."

"Which fits with what we know of the Ancients' evacuation to Earth from the Pegasus Galaxy during that time period." Elizabeth folded her hands on the desk, a habit she'd cultivated to present an air of interest. In this instance it served to mask her anxiety. "I assume you believe that all of this is interrelated?"

"That I do. I didn't come across my earlier data again until just recently, while making some refinements to the retrovirus." Carson paused a moment, his eyes flicking out from Elizabeth's glass walled office to the city's control room, which was minimally manned for the evening shift. His reluctance came as no surprise to Elizabeth. No one was wholly comfortable with the next planned step of the retrovirus project, but life in the Pegasus Galaxy had forced a kind of moral shift on many aspects of the Atlantis expedition. She just hoped in the case of Michael it wouldn't come back to bite them.

The doctor exhaled a disappointed breath. "At the time of the original research, I'd been focused on isolating exactly what gave General O'Neill the ability to use the Ancient database—to the exclusion of all else. I should have recognized the importance of this other finding immediately."

Elizabeth shook her head. "Hindsight, Carson. No one, least of all you, could have been expected to anticipate what we'd find in this galaxy." With an air of reassurance that she hoped would disguise her own concern, she continued, "It's been ten thousand years, and nothing's shown up in Earth's population to suggest any problems. I'd venture to say that no news is good news."

His concerned expression remained fixed in place. "I probably ought to find that more comforting than I do."

Apparently they were of the same mind. Rising and walking over to the glass wall, Elizabeth crossed her arms and gazed out at the empty gate room. "I suppose this adds a new wrinkle to the retrovirus study. As if we weren't raising some complicated ethical questions with it already."

"In a strange way, I'm more resolved to go forward with the project now."

She turned back to see Carson's lips twisted with grim humor. "At the very least," he continued, "we can take solace in the fact that we won't be the first to tread such shaky ground."

If he could handle this new knowledge without undue alarm, then so could she. Giving a single, sharp nod, Elizabeth said, "All right. Send me your report the moment it's finished. I'll move up our regular check-in time with the SGC so we can get this information to them as soon as possible. What, if anything, they can do with it, I have no idea, but they need to know."

"I'll have the report ready by morning. I'd also like to request that anyone examining the Ancient database notify me immediately if any further references to this topic, or to the Ancient responsible for the research, are found." Collecting the file, Carson stood and, attempting to roll the tension out of his shoulders, started toward the door. "Can I assume you don't plan to participate in movie night? I think they're starting in a few minutes."

She couldn't suppress a wry smile. "I think I'll pass. I have it on good authority that Ronon got to choose tonight's feature, and he's been working his way through the Rambo series. I blame John."

"I'm not sorry to miss it myself, then. Say what you will about our lads, at least they're predictable."

"When they choose to be, anyway. Good night, Carson."

After he had left, Elizabeth stepped out of her office. Intending to go to her quarters, she changed her mind in transit and stopped for a moment at the top of the gate room steps. Although Atlantis operated around the clock to accommodate the vagaries of interplanetary time differences, the expedition's current duty schedule was designed to allow most personnel to stand down in the evenings. The spacious chamber that housed the Stargate seemed even larger at night, its lights dimmed to conserve energy, no technicians chatting or securing equipment.

Normally she enjoyed the stillness at the end of the day, taking it as a sign that all was well—or at least as well as was possible. Tonight she found herself feeling unusually exposed to all the threats, both known and unknown, that lurked beyond the silent gate.

She wasn't a scientist, and so she couldn't see Carson's discovery in purely analytical terms. Science could explain—to a certain extent—why and how a Wraith fed on human life;

it couldn't explain the sensation of frozen dread generated by the mere presence of one of the ghastly creatures.

What Carson had found should have been exciting, a leap forward in their understanding of two galaxies and a potential hope for resolving the Wraith issue at last. Instead, she felt unsettled, as if everything they still didn't know was poised to come crashing down on them.

CHAPTER ONE

Stepping out of her rental car, Rebecca Larance squinted through the glare of flashing red and blue lights and breathed deeply, preparing herself for what she knew she would see inside. Despite the early hour and freezing temperatures, the suburban street was alive with the curious and the morbid. Death had visited here, and it was the nature of humans to scrutinize it, as if they could gain some understanding, perhaps a talisman against their own inevitable passing.

Based on the number of vehicles parked haphazardly on the manicured lawn, most of the Colorado Springs Police Department had arrived soon after the fire truck and ambulance. Vehicles from the ME's office were also here. Just one thing was absent.

Rebecca turned her attention to the house—small, neat, middleclass modern. Inside, it would not be so neat, and the ME would probably be cursing. Determining the cause of any death was rarely straightforward, but, like all puzzles, the evidence could be pieced together, most often by reverse engineering a sequence of definable events.

This death, however, would defy that methodical, scientific approach, leaving the ME with no option but to use phrases such as *heart attack due to an abrupt onset of extreme senescence*. The etiology of the death would elude him, just as it had eluded others, because they lacked the tools or understanding to chart the complete desiccation of the victim's body. The heart ceased to beat only because of advanced decrepitude. There was no scientific explanation as to why.

Two uniformed cops were belatedly securing the yard with canary yellow crime scene tape. Several more were directing the inquisitive onlookers—most of whom were dressed in sleepwear and bundled up in overcoats against the cold—to stand back. Firemen were rolling hoses, packing away equipment they'd never used, and climbing back into their trucks. In the near distance a car siren bellowed. Rebecca absorbed the background noise of radios and conversations, a Lilliputian dog yapping from a house across the street, and someone throwing up. She glanced around and noticed a cop bent low between the house and a tree strung with Christmas lights that had yet to be packed away. The forensics team was going to love that: a rookie's regurgitated takeout meal messing up their crime scene.

Through the glare and confusion, Rebecca saw more uniformed cops easing a visibly distraught man toward a car, no doubt to be delivered to neighbors, friends, family—anything to get him away from a site of inexplicable horror.

"Hey, you! Get that car the hell out of here. This is a crime scene."

And a fresh one at that. Rebecca could almost smell the lingering trace of the perpetrator. She resisted the temptation to study the crowd. It would be pointless; he wasn't the type to take nourishment from the fear he engendered in the living. Instead, she pulled her ID from the pocket of her blue leather jacket and angled it so that the cop approaching her could see it in the light from the lamppost. "Who's in charge?"

The cop looked her over once and turned a pointed gaze to her empty car.

"Contrary to popular myth," Rebecca added, "we don't all wear black overcoats and travel in a posse."

"No! I can't leave! She…she…!"

The cop's attention was drawn to the distraught guy—victim's husband, most likely—being helped into the other vehicle. An agonized sob was cut short when the car door was closed behind him. It was more than grief, Rebecca knew, but an emotion that spoke of horror and something more…an edge of desperation and…urgency? A childhood memory briefly mounted an assault, but her well-honed defenses soon shut it down. Still, she watched the car drive away, vaguely uneasy that she'd missed something.

"This way." With another look, this time frankly appraising, the cop led Rebecca up to the front porch and announced her arrival to his clipboard-wielding partner. "FBI."

"Feds, huh?" The second cop, rumpled, weary-looking, and considerably older but clearly just as disturbed by the situation, regarded Rebecca with a mix of suspicion and relief.

Local law enforcement didn't much like it when the feds stepped on their turf, despite—or perhaps because of—the numerous Denver police officers now assigned full time to the FBI's Joint Terrorism Task Force. This crime, though, had nothing to do with terrorism. Fundamentalism and terror, yes, but not terrorism as the world currently defined it.

"Not exactly," she replied, trying to suppress a yawn with a rapidly expelled breath that sounded like a sigh. "I'm a forensic psychiatrist. Your boss called my boss after the second victim, so do me a favor, would you, Officer—" she glanced at the nametag— "Wilson, and save any indignation for him."

"Okay, Dr. Larance, but…look, this is a bad one. Really." Even under the frosted yellow porch light, Wilson's features were gray, and his freckled fingers shook as he filled in her information on his crime scene log.

What was the standard for bad? When could someone say with any certainty that one scene was worse than any other? It was all a matter of perspective. For her, for an investigator, it depended on how much could be read from it. Bad was when the body lay intact and clean, a dozen or more people having come stumbling through. Worse was a DOA, the forensic evidence contaminated by discarded items from EMTs and anyone else involved in the failed attempt at first aid. Best was when the patterns of the killer's mind were still intact. Like now.

"I appreciate the heads-up, Officer Wilson. Mutilated and set on fire in what looks like a satanic ritual. Got it." She lifted her cell phone. "Welcome to the wonderful world of text messaging. Detective Ramirez and the ME inside?"

Wilson nodded and kept writing, taking his time to note her ID number. His partner wandered off to man the plastic tape barricade.

"Tell them I'm here. I'd like to get a look in before the crime scene guys arrive and start stomping all over the place." With their sterile equipment and methodical indifference, they would rapidly dissolve the subtle, persistent scent of fear, and the equally subtle sense of satiation.

Pen frozen mid-stroke, Wilson shot her a peculiar look. The crime lab had bitten heads off over the mess the Sheriff's Department had made of the first cases.

"Kind of ruins the atmosphere for me. You know what they say about profilers," she added with a conspiratorial grin.

A familiar expression settled over his face; contempt born of ignorance, with a hefty dose of good old-fashioned chauvinism thrown in. Rebecca didn't come across it too often, but there were still some old timers who lumped profiling into the same category as Tarot card reading and crystal ball gazing, plus maybe a touch of voodoo—the latter no doubt inspired by the occasional need to interpret artfully macabre displays of human entrails.

Giving no indication that he'd even considered her request, Wilson went back to writing.

Rebecca's patience was pretty much at an end. Enduring a transatlantic flight in a coach class seat beside some guy whose philosophy of personal hygiene didn't include deodorant had been bad enough, but, to add to her misery, he'd had the most vocal case of sleep apnea Rebecca had ever encountered. By the time she'd cleared customs, collected her luggage, and gotten a taxi to her apartment in D.C., she'd seriously entertained the idea of ignoring the order to get her ass out to Colorado Springs. A hot shower and comfortable bed beckoned.

It had been a nice fantasy, but the situation was escalating and the FBI only had so many resources to go around. She'd had just enough time to swap the dirty clothes in her suitcase for clean ones, call a cab—same taxi, same driver—and head back to the airport.

She was about to pull rank when a touslehaired detective with a caffeine-deprived expression emerged from the front door. Ramirez, presumably, had been dragged out of bed for this one. "You the profiler?" he asked, shooting her a hopeful look.

Wilson, who looked more like he'd been dragged out of a marriage, stopped writing and looked up. "By the way," Rebecca told him, "she's not going to take you back, so deal with it."

"I'll take that as a yes," Ramirez said, smirking.

Ignoring Wilson's dropped jaw, Rebecca introduced herself, and said, "Tell me about the vic."

"Jamie Cabal, thirty eight, engineer; three months pregnant. Her husband, Logan, got here about two minutes ahead of the fire trucks. Somehow he managed to keep it together long enough to put out the fire with an extinguisher." Ramirez's dark-eyed gaze slid from Rebecca's and moved across the faces in the nearby crowd.

"Don't bother," Rebecca told him. "Not his style to hang around." A couple of television trucks had arrived and were setting up rooftop cameras, completing the scene.

Ramirez's gaze returned to hers. "His? Witnesses in the D.C. cases all saw a woman."

"That was D.C. This is Colorado. How 'bout we go inside and you can walk me through it?"

Nodding, Ramirez pulled his jacket closer, consigning the temptation to touch anything to deep pockets. Rebecca did the same, mostly to reassure him. Forensics would get nothing of substance from this, not because of ham-fisted cops or sloppy procedures, but because there was little in the way of physical evidence to be found. There never was in these cases, which was why she'd been called in.

"Was it the badly ironed shirt, or the stain on Wilson's tie?" Ramirez asked her when they were inside.

"Both, plus attitude and statistics. Divorce rate for cops in this neck of the woods is off the charts." Framed prints of Air Force planes lined the entryway walls. No sign of kids. "Civilian engineer, huh?"

"The Cabals worked for the military. Victim was a radar technician." Ramirez stepped into the living room. "Couch was on fire," he added unnecessarily. "That triggered the alarm."

Either the fire department was right around the corner, or—

"Fire resistant paint, according to the husband."

Drapes had been too far away to ignite, and the floor was tiled. Carpet was better in some ways than tiles because it did not allow blood to spread; splatter patterns remained fixed. Didn't matter in this instance. There was no blood, not even bodily fluids. Just a desiccated corpse with its chest cracked wide open. Still, the residual malevolence was obviously creeping out the youthful cop standing nearby. "Relax," Rebecca assured him. "The perp got all he came for. He's not coming back."

The cop exchanged nervous glances with Ramirez, who shrugged. On the floor, dressed in the kind of disposable plastic suit that everyone present should have been wearing, the ME was kneeling beside Jamie Cabal's body, poking around inside the open chest cavity like someone digging for treasure. Rebecca turned her attention to the coagulated mass of chemical fire retardant, charred leather, slimy balls of polyurethane—cushions, most likely—and a couple of indefinable lumps mashed together in the middle of the room.

Although accustomed to such sights, Rebecca had never entirely been able to inure herself against the childhood terror this particular smell evoked. No matter; it would not interfere with her job. It never had. "Lungs and liver are over there, on the couch," she observed, pointing. "Heart's been souvenired."

The ME glanced up at her, his thick black eyebrows confined behind his protective glasses, then sat back on his heels to get a better look at the couch. Using the back of one latex-covered wrist to push his glasses further up a bulbous nose, he began detailing what she already knew.

Rebecca paid only scant attention to the ME's familiar monologue. She'd heard it all before, in several languages. Eventually he'd shut up, and then she could be alone in the room, alone with the body, listening to the tale it had to tell. For now, she examined the display.

Something sharp—a single blade, not scissors—had been used to slice into Jamie Cabal's sweater, leaving the shoulders and sleeves in place while the front had been torn away. The remains of a bra, flesh-colored, had been pulled up; the upper abdomen had been sliced open with a single, unhesitating cut that appeared surgically precise. The body itself otherwise was intact, mouth open wide in a permanent silent scream, eyeballs bulging from sunken sockets, the entire corpse neatly displayed inside a turquoise spray-painted symbol on the pale patterned tiles.

"Very controlled," Ramirez said, spouting off a textbook interpretation.

It was the same symbol every time. A slim isosceles triangle, its apex pointing due south, bisected a pair of concentric circles. Between the circles was a repeating set of geometric shapes: eight rounded chevrons and sixteen squares.

Rebecca managed to ignore what sounded like a growing argument outside until Wilson yelled, "Hey, Lieutenant Ramirez!"

Looking up and out between the half-drawn drapes, she saw shadows moving rapidly. Why the hell was a SWAT team being deployed around the house?

Ramirez had barely taken a step when a bunch of military goons in camouflage, helmets and flak jackets came tearing inside through the front and back doors, P-90s pouring light in the already well-lit room. Paying no heed to Ramirez's stream of invective and the ME's demands to know what was going on, the troops swarmed through the house, yelling 'Clear' from every room.

She might have expected the military to poke their noses into this, but a special ops team seemed a tad melodramatic, even for them. Then another man strode into the room, sporting a pair of wire-rimmed glasses, a slightly distracted expression — and, most interesting of all, black Velcro patches where his unit insignia should have been and nothing on his jacket to indicate his rank. Ignoring Ramirez's repeated demands for an explanation, no-rank G.I. Joe brushed past Rebecca, took one look at the body and muttered, "Oh... great."

His tone told her he wasn't altogether shocked. "And you would be?" Rebecca demanded, pulling her hands from her coat pockets and planting them on her hips.

Eyebrows knitted, he barely spared her a glance. "I'm sorry, but this is a matter of national security, which means that anything you've seen here—"

Rebecca's patience finally snapped. She barked out a laugh. "Oh, right. That's a good one. National security." Hoping to tease out information, she added, "You clowns don't have any idea what's going on, do you?"

"I know you," Ramirez said to G.I. Joe. "You work with Colonel Carter—Sam Carter."

Rebecca could hear the resignation in the detective's voice, but she wasn't about to fold so easily. "He got a name?" she asked, directing her question to Ramirez.

"Yeah." Ramirez sighed. "Jackson."

"Dr. Daniel Jackson," the man elaborated. "Nice to meet you. Sorry about this, but it's like I said—"

"Actually, it's like *I* said," Rebecca interrupted. "I'm betting you don't have a clue what's happening here." She tugged her ID from her pocket and thrust it under his nose. "This is the twelfth case in the U.S. alone, *Doctor* Jackson. Then there's the six in Europe, one in Australia and three in New Zealand."

That popped his bubble of self-importance.

"And to answer that question you're just itching to ask, the only reason you haven't heard about those cases before now—" Rebecca snapped her ID wallet shut and gestured through the windows toward the television vans "—is because the finer details haven't been leaked to the likes of them."

Jackson's expression didn't change, but the tension level in the room instantly rocketed. Rebecca glanced around at his men. It was several degrees below freezing outside and not much warmer within, but beads of perspiration had broken out on the foreheads of two of them. Obviously they'd already gotten more than they'd bargained for. She had little sympathy. When it came to this case, *everyone* was getting more than they'd bargained for.

CHAPTER TWO

"**I**didn't say I was *complaining*."

"No need," commented Radek Zelenka as John Sheppard slid into the pilot's seat of the puddle jumper. "Rarely are your complaints so understated as to require identification."

"How droll," Rodney McKay snapped in reply. John glanced across at the copilot's seat to see Atlantis's chief scientist direct a withering glare over his shoulder at his colleague. "The intergalactic gate bridge was my design, if you'll recall, and I have no reservations about acknowledging its value. I'm simply pointing out the fact that there are advantages and disadvantages to having ready access to and from Earth. I'm very much in favor of the shortened turnaround time on our supply requests, but the tradeoff is being at the beck and call of any governmental bigwig who wants a report presented in person. They've already got Elizabeth under their thumb for a few days. Was it absolutely critical for them to drag us back as well?"

"Ah," Radek pointed out, "but is it not worth the trouble when you can bring back Colombian dark roast and Cadbury's chocolate each time Stargate Command asks you to drop in?"

"Elizabeth's visit was scheduled ages ago. You know how the IOA loves its biannual reports." John frowned as he ran an eye over the jumper's control panel. "Is it 'biannual' or 'biennial'? I never can keep those straight."

Rodney's wordless grumble could have been directed either at John's linguistic failings or at the practices of the International Oversight Advisory; it was impossible to say which. "That in no way explains General Landry's reasons for summoning *us*," Rodney said. "You could at least have waited until I'd had a mouthful of breakfast. My glucose levels were already severely diminished from pulling yet another all-nighter, and you know how that hampers my ability to function. The glucose, that is. All-nighters are a depressingly frequent occurrence."

John chose not to interrupt his teammate's griping. If he let the others in on his thoughts, he'd end up having to peel Rodney off the ceiling. No sense in getting the perennially excitable scientist any more spun up than he was already.

Of course, it didn't take a rocket scientist to recognize that any situation requiring Atlantis's entire senior staff to leave the city and report to Earth must be pretty damned important.

General Landry had also ordered the other half of his team to check out the planet designated as M1M-316, a place that had long since been flagged as inhospitable, for signs of an Ancient lab that Dr. Geisler believed to be there. When John had suggested that, given the slight problem they'd had previously with the prehistoric inhabitants of 316, he would lead the team when he got back from the SGC, Landry had made it abundantly clear that he—or, more alarmingly, the IOA—wasn't inclined to wait that long.

Glancing across the bay at Jumper Two, John saw Major Lorne settling into the pilot's seat, while Teyla and Ronon had just stepped on board with Geisler, who sported a bulky set of sample collection bags slung over his shoulders and a huge grin on his face.

Although John was fully confident in Lorne's ability to negotiate the jumper around a T. rex or two on 316, as well as in the rest of the Atlantis crew's ability to look after the city for a few hours, concern for Atlantis or his teammates wasn't what had his insides threatening to stage a revolt. It was the curtness of the communication from the General. Almost two decades in uniform had taught Lieutenant Colonel John Sheppard a few things about giving and receiving various types of orders. He'd known straight away that the clipped command to track down Rodney and Radek and report to

Earth ASAP foretold nothing good.

At least they wouldn't have to wait long to find out the details. Having acquired three ZPMs after they'd recaptured Atlantis from the Asurans, they could just as easily walk through the gate to the SGC as take a jumper. However, much to Rodney's disappointment, the additional ZPMs had been allocated to the *Odyssey* and the Antarctic base. In order to make the return trip, they needed a jumper to transfer between the Milky Way and Pegasus gate systems at the midway station.

While Jumper One was powering up under his mental command, John dug one hand into his jacket pocket and tossed Rodney a hoarded Snickers bar. He wasn't in the mood for it, and he could always buy more before the return trip.

The unprompted display of altruism seemed to make Rodney suspicious. His eyes narrowed even as he unwrapped the candy. "What's going on? You know why Landry called us, don't you? Spill it, Sheppard. At a minimum, just tell me that it has nothing to do with nuclear winter, mad cow disease, or an unexpected Canadian civil war."

John blinked. Sometimes the McKay mind was a very strange place. "I don't know what the hell Landry needs me for," he said. It was the truth; he was pretty sure he'd permanently crossed himself off Landry's Christmas card list when he'd hijacked the jumper to retake Atlantis not so long ago. The General was a pragmatist, but one with a very good memory. "You, on the other hand, he needs because Colonel Carter is tied up with some other big project."

"*Excuse* me? Oh, for— You made that up," Rodney accused, jabbing in his direction with the Snickers. "There is no field of study in this galaxy or any other in which I should be considered second fiddle to Samantha Carter. You're just trying to mess with me."

"No, that's just a perk." The jumper's systems were online and fully operational. John knew that, in part because of what the displays were telling him, and in part because the neural feedback he received from the Ancient operating systems of the jumper *felt* right in a way that he'd never been able to fully articulate.

With a fierce look, Rodney twisted in his seat to face Radek. "What about you?" he demanded around a mouthful. "How'd you get roped into this? Has the SGC taken an inordinate interest in any of your reports lately?"

"They may have requested additional data from one of my ongoing projects," Radek answered vaguely. "I would not want to speculate as to their reasons."

"Which project?"

"One in which you evidently had little interest, since you delegated it to me some time ago."

To John's ears, the normally even-tempered Czech sounded tense. Rodney, of course, was paying no attention to nuance. "Withholding information for petty amusement is beneath you," he snapped. "Was it the generator from P5F-216? If so, recall that I didn't actually claim it was worthless; I simply prioritized it below about sixteen legitimately vital—"

"I was continuing Carson's research," Radek cut him off with more bite than might have been necessary. "It was *his* work the SGC wanted. Are you satisfied?"

Out of the corner of his eye, John saw Rodney's supercilious expression freeze. How long would it be before they could talk about Carson and not feel every past tense verb like a sucker punch?

A while longer, at least.

"I see," Rodney replied, his voice half a step above inaudible.

Well, *this* was a fun-filled way to start the day.

"Jumper One, you are cleared for departure."

"Copy that," John acknowledged, maneuvering the craft down into Atlantis's gate room. The sooner they got to Earth, the sooner they could sort out all this secrecy and get back to coping with their typical, run of the mill hazards. "We'll try to be home before it gets dark. Jumper Two, try not to get eaten."

A hint of Lorne's dry humor accompanied the reply. "We'll do our best, sir. And good luck."

John appreciated the sentiment; he suspected he'd need more luck than Lorne.

The familiar liquid event horizon within the Stargate rippled gently as the jumper eased forward. Although John had long since become conditioned to flying through a gate on one planet and emerging seconds later on a different world, the fact that they could now traverse galaxies separated by three million light years with almost no effort was still a fairly novel experience.

The wormhole deposited them in the Stargate Command gate room smoothly. "Welcome home, Jumper One," greeted Chief Harriman, pokerfaced as ever behind his glasses, from the control room. "The General's waiting for you upstairs."

"Thanks, Chief. I assume our regular parking spot's available?"

"Yes, sir."

Guiding the jumper upward to the bay located above the gate room, John watched the stark concrete walls skim past the windscreen. The bland gray was broken by little more than a metal access ladder and collection of pipes and circuit boxes, reminding him yet again of the many reasons why he preferred Atlantis to the SGC as a duty station. There was a kind of majesty in the Ancient city's graceful lines and sky-lit spaces. The air smelled of clean saltwater instead of air conditioning; he could feel the wind and sun on his face anytime he liked, just by stepping out onto a balcony. Practical or not, the SGC's glorified underground bunker was no place for a pilot.

Parking between the jumper found by SG-1 a few years back and Jumper Three, which had brought the head of the Atlantis expedition to Earth, John was surprised to see Elizabeth standing with her arms crossed near the metal blast door. Alongside her were General Landry in short-sleeved blues and Richard Woolsey dressed in bureaucratic dullness, which prompted another gut clench. At least two of those three people were supposed to be in Washington reporting to the IOA, an organization that usually didn't tolerate absences or delays. The apprehension that seemed to be radiating from the trio likewise didn't offer John much in the way of reassurance.

As soon as Jumper One's hatch *clanged* onto the deck, Rodney was out of his seat and striding down the ramp. "We're here, our trip was fine, all's well on Atlantis. Can we move on to some actual explanations, preferably of the rapid and detailed variety?" He gulped down the last of the Snickers bar and looked around for someplace to deposit the wrapper.

"Always a pleasure, Dr. McKay." Landry gave him a tight, closed-mouthed smile and nodded once at John's 'better safe than sorry' attention posture. The General turned to the door and ran his card through the lock. Pushing the door open, he led them out. "If you'll all join me in the briefing room, we'll do just that."

The group started down the stairs, where John fell into step beside Elizabeth. "When did you get in from D.C.?" he asked, doing his best to ignore the dingy, featureless walls.

"Two hours ago," she answered quietly. "Shortest and therefore most pleasant IOA meeting I've ever attended—until they told me just what it was that took precedence over their vaunted biannual report."

There was only so much of this crap John could take, even if they were just minutes away from getting answers. With Woolsey walking just ahead of them, he lowered his voice. "Tell me this and put me out of my misery. Is one of us getting fired?"

Elizabeth's expression tightened, but it was still hard to decipher. "I almost wish."

Okay, that didn't bode well.

"I'll feel at least somewhat better when we get word from Atlantis that Major Lorne's mission has been successfully completed," she continued. "Preferably without any of the inhabitants from 316 accompanying the jumper back through the gate."

The fact that Elizabeth had even felt the need to mention that last part was an indication of the urgency of Jumper Two's assignment.

John feigned a cavalier shrug. "Good thing we sent Lorne. He's the best dodgeball player on the expedition."

In the briefing room, they found Dr. Daniel Jackson standing by the long rosewood conference table, one hand stuffed in his pocket and the other fiddling with a television remote control. Nothing on the table hinted at the nature of the briefing; no recently discovered Ancient artifacts or ominous-looking files with 'Top Secret' stamped across the front, the lack of which just contributed to John's increasing apprehension.

"Dr. Lam checked in a few minutes ago, General," SG-1's resident archeologist reported, offering a nod in greeting to the visitors. "She's just finishing up in the lab and says to start without her since she already knows the basics."

"I have a feeling no one here will object to that." From the head of the table, Landry waved the others into seats. "A rather unusual…situation cropped up a couple of days ago," he announced, making John wonder just what the Stargate program's criteria might be for labeling an issue 'unusual'. "In point of fact, it began a while back."

"That's one way of putting it," Jackson said, pulling out a chair and sitting down.

"Thanks to Mr. Woolsey here," the General continued, "we're learning some details that are, to put it bluntly, disturbing. Richard, why don't you get us started?"

The only person to stay on his feet, Woolsey stood unnervingly still, as if he expected some kind of shoot-the-messenger situation to arise at any moment. Either that, or he was genuinely troubled by what he was about to say.

"The recording you're going to see was taken by a sleep

disorder clinic," he began, indicating one of the room's wall-mounted screens. "The patient is my cousin, Mark Payton. He'd been suffering from chronic fatigue for some months and eventually became desperate enough to consult a well-regarded clinic in Virginia. Because the clinic was backed up with patients, the specialist elected to set up an observation camera in Mark's apartment rather than bring him to the sleep lab. One of the nightly recording sessions captured this."

At Woolsey's expectant gaze, Jackson took his cue and pressed a button on the remote. The screen came instantly to life.

Payton's bedroom was ordinary at best, although the green tint of the 'night vision' camera gave the whole setup a special ops look. For the first few seconds, John was just watching another man sleep, which was weird enough that he glanced away, only to have his focus snapped back by a movement in the corner of the screen.

"Someone is in the room with him?" Radek wondered quietly.

Woolsey's jaw twitched. "Mark lived alone."

John had the impression he wanted to add something to that but was intentionally presenting a minimalist case, presumably so that they could judge the situation without any kind of preconceptions.

As the recording continued, a shadowed figure moved across the camera's view. Too slender and lithe to be anything but female, she crawled onto the bed with the sleek movements of a cat and then stopped, poised above the still sleeping Payton. Long straight hair, pale in the unnatural light, hung down in a thick sheet, obscuring her face. A filmy skirt pooled around her legs while she slowly unbuttoned Payton's pajama shirt.

Before the obviously private moment could get any more uncomfortable for the briefing room audience, the woman placed her hand on Payton's chest and threw her head back—and a jolt of recognition pounded through John's veins.

Beside him, Radek muttered something, not one of the scientist's more familiar Czech curses.

For a fraction of a second John could feel the phantom pain of a clawed hand digging into his own chest. Quickly, though, he saw the differences between what he'd endured in Kolya's prison and what was happening on the tape. Payton cried out, his arms thrashing feebly, though he seemed otherwise fixed to the bed…but the expected transformation from middle-aged man to withered octogenarian never took place. The woman—she had to be human, not Wraith—almost appeared to treat him with care. When she'd finished…whatever she was doing, she brushed delicate fingers across his forehead and leaned down to place a gentle kiss on the place where her hand had rested.

Throughout the entire episode, which had lasted two minutes at most, Payton appeared not to have woken. He was still breathing and outwardly unhurt when the woman slipped off the bed and then out of the room.

The recording had ended by the time John noticed his runaway pulse and willed it back under control. That disquieting scene had come a bit too close to some not so well buried personal issues. A covert glance at his colleagues reassured him that Rodney, slack jawed and wide eyed, had missed his momentary freak-out, while Radek shared a distressed, knowing look with Elizabeth. John consciously squared his shoulders when her gaze slipped across to meet his. At the same time, he also felt a flash of suspicious uncertainty. Just who was and wasn't in the loop on this? And why had he and Rodney been shut out until now?

In the corner of the room, Woolsey was still staring at the now frozen image on the screen.

Carolyn Lam's arrival broke the surreal silence that had settled over the group. "I apologize for being late," said the SGC's chief of medicine, closing the door behind her. "Judging by the reactions I'm seeing, I'll presume I haven't missed much." She eased into the chair between the General and Jackson.

"Much?" Radek echoed, his voice a despondent murmur.

"That was no Wraith," John stated, maybe a tad too emphatically. "She didn't look like one, didn't act like one, and sure as hell didn't feed like one—okay, maybe she fed *like* one, but—"

"Let's not make any unsupported assumptions." Rodney's shell-shocked stare hadn't faded, but his mental gears obviously had started cranking. "It's not completely out of the question that a Wraith could manage to control the pace of its feeding well enough to stop before any observable aging occurred. And recall that some Pegasus cultures actually worship those monsters. How do we know the feeding process isn't…um, gentler when it's undertaken willingly on both sides?"

"Did that guy look willing to you?" retorted John. "Also, in case you missed it, we're not *in* Pegasus anymore, Toto."

"Fine, then how would *you* categorize what we just saw?" Rodney demanded with unrestrained tension.

The textbook definition of a nightmare, John was tempted to say. "It was like one of those…I don't know, seductive demon things. What's the name for it? A succubus?"

"A what?" Rodney's eyebrows shot up. "Do I have low-budget horror movies or videogames to blame for lodging that conceptual tidbit in your brain?"

Jackson was the one to finally break into their debate. "Actually, I believe Colonel Sheppard may be right." He angled the remote toward the television, and the image abruptly vanished.

That seemed to snap Woolsey out of his fixated daze, because he turned from the screen and, visibly taking control of himself, spoke up. "This tape was made four months ago. Less than a week later, Mark died in that apartment when the dry cleaning store downstairs went up in an electrical fire. I found the tape just recently among some boxes from Mark's office at the Pentagon. When I called the sleep clinic, the patient coordinator explained the reason for the recordings and shrugged off the 'anomalous' night as a prank. She very politely informed me what the fee would be for returning the camera late."

A sardonic smirk flicked across his features and quickly vanished as his gaze strayed to the wide windows overlooking the gate room. "After that, I made the call I should have made in the first place. We had Mark's body exhumed and flown here, where General Landry volunteered his medical staff for a full autopsy."

"The fire did mask the actual cause of death." Dr. Lam clasped her hands on top of a plastic file folder she'd placed on the table. "It couldn't mask the residual traces of the Wraith feeding enzyme."

John made an effort not to flinch. A Wraith on Earth. *Impossible*—yet, even before that thought had fully formed, he reminded himself that the word 'impossible' had disappeared from his vocabulary the day he'd flown General O'Neill to the Ancient outpost in Antarctica.

Woolsey might not have been one of John's favorite people, but the guy had lost family, and that entitled him to some consideration. Landry took over, subtly motioning Woolsey toward a seat. "It gets worse. Last night, one of our medical technicians, Logan Cabal, came home to find his wife, Jamie, murdered. He recognized signs of a Wraith attack and called for an SGC response team, but the smoke alarm had already activated and neighbors had called 911."

"Surely the military can play some type of national security trump card on the local cops when necessary," said Rodney, the end of his statement sounding more like a query.

"It's not quite that straightforward," Landry answered ruefully. "These killings are hardly typical, and they've attracted some attention."

"They? How would the actual circumstances of Payton's death be known?"

"Not Payton. Others."

John barely had time to process that startling new detail before Jackson reached over to slip the file out from under Lam's hands and rifle through it. Without looking up, he explained, "The FBI and local law enforcement are investigating Jamie Cabal's death as a bizarre ritual sacrifice. I spoke to the Bureau's profiler at the scene, and she informed me of a number of similar murders, including two prior incidents in Colorado Springs within the last month."

"Implying that some of the murders took place elsewhere." Elizabeth's poised demeanor showed signs of cracking at last.

Jackson nodded. "The first case was in L.A. in late 2001. Similar cases have been reported by Interpol, Australian Federal Police, and New Zealand Police. Unfortunately, because the fire is a central part of the M.O., we have no way of determining the actual number of victims."

Which meant that they probably were dealing with more than one Wraith. This day just kept getting better.

"In spite of what television has led most people to believe, a full autopsy isn't standard procedure," Lam pointed out, and for once even the cool, unflappable doctor seemed a mite edgy. "In fact it's a fairly rare occurrence. When a coroner sees significant burns—to the point where some victims were almost incinerated—it's not hard to misinterpret the deaths as being fire-related."

"If the tape of Payton is anything to go by, the victims may not always have been killed immediately," said Jackson. "For all we know, some might have had multiple encounters before the final act."

"Mark suffered from nightmares off and on for much of his life," Woolsey admitted. "He learned to live with them, but then he was diagnosed with chronic fatigue." A spasm of guilt crossed his face. "When we were teenagers I used to tease him because he always described the nightmare in the same way. A woman coming to him in the night, straddling his chest, touching him…" His eyes strayed back to the now-dark screen.

"It's a common enough dream, more so among pubescent boys, for obvious reasons," Lam reassured him. "You can't blame yourself for not recognizing it as something more significant."

John lifted his boot in anticipation of needing to shut Rodney up, but the scientist apparently had enough sense to keep any details of his own adolescent dreams to himself.

Finally locating the page he'd been searching for, Jackson tugged it from the file and set it down on the table's dark leather inlay. "This symbol has been a common factor in all the known crime scenes. The FBI's theory is that it's the emblem of a cult whose members kill with some form of yet-to-be identified toxin."

He pushed the photo across the table toward Rodney and John: one large aqua ring inside another, pierced by an elongated triangle. The drawing—or more precisely, spray-painting—was rough and simple, but John hazarded a guess. "A Stargate?"

"And a Wraith Dart," Rodney finished, slowly slumping forward until he could drop his head into his hands.

"We managed to get the authority to perform the Cabal autopsy here," said Lam, reclaiming her file from Jackson. "Waiting on the results is what kept me from getting to this meeting sooner. There were some minor variations in the chemical composition of the enzyme, which I'll be investigating further, but I can confirm that Jamie Cabal was indeed killed by a Wraith attack."

John had almost managed to forget that Radek was present until the scientist spoke up. "We may be able to account for the differences," he began. "Since the—"

"General?" The respectful yet firm hail drew everyone's attention to Chief Harriman, who had entered the briefing room via Landry's office. "Sir, sorry to interrupt. At least two news stations are reporting that a body was recovered from a fire in a local apartment complex last night. They've gotten word that the coroner's office is doing an autopsy."

Spinning his chair toward Lam, Rodney demanded, "Didn't you say the body from last night's attack is here? Are we now saying that there were *two* of these murders in one night?"

Harriman clasped his hands behind his back. "General, the reporters are speculating about a potential arsonist serial killer in Colorado Springs."

If anything could have darkened Landry's features further, that information had done the trick. "We were afraid something like this might occur," he said, half to himself. "Just not so soon."

Somewhere amid all this mess, beneath the obvious terror associated with the notion of Earth-based Wraith hiding under the proverbial bed, there had to be a 'how' and a 'why'. Although John didn't have the first clue where to look, he was starting to get the idea that finding those answers was about to become his primary goal in life. For that, he needed to get the rest of his team here—a thought that brought the M1M-316 mission back to center stage. Just what had Carson been working on?

"The Stargate program needs to assess and eliminate this threat. We can't rely on law enforcement."

Surprisingly, that assertion came from Woolsey. Whether it was due to his recent ordeal on Atlantis or Payton's murder, the IOA's lackey seemed to have grown a backbone, along with some common sense.

Woolsey's gaze moved over Elizabeth, John, Rodney, and Radek in turn. "You're here because you know more about the Wraith than anyone else on this planet. I suggest you get down to the county morgue and find out whatever you can, as quickly as you can."

While the task sounded like a good starting point on Earth, John didn't report to Woolsey. Furthermore, nothing in the discussion had yet told him how the Isla Nubla of the Pegasus

Galaxy figured into this. He cast a questioning look at the head of the table. "General? What about the rest of my team?"

Landry was looking at Lam, who was gathering up the contents of the file. "All in good time, Colonel. Carolyn?"

"We're ready," she said, pushing her chair back.

"Go," Landry ordered, standing up and signaling for Woolsey to join him in his office. "The FBI profiler appears to be the most knowledgeable person about the method of the killings. Get whatever you can from her without compromising classified information on our end."

"That'll be a challenge, won't it?" Rodney trailed the General as far as his office door. "Pumping her for information when we can't give her any in return? I would think an FBI agent would have an acceptable security clearance."

With one hand on the handle of his office door, Landry replied, "Not high enough for blanket access to the Stargate program. We'll reassess her need to know after you've spent some time with her." On this topic, the SGC commander was immovable. "Dr. Weir will brief you on the cover story on the drive there. Colonel—" his gaze met John's— "you'll accompany Dr. Lam and her team. I'll have the necessary paperwork in place by the time you get there."

"Yes, sir," John replied automatically, only to shake his head once they were outside the briefing room and the door was closed. "We can try to play cloak and dagger with this for a while, but it won't be easy," he told the remaining group. "We don't honestly expect to be able to withhold the truth from this profiler for very long when we've got Wraith coming out of the woodwork everywhere, do we?"

"That depends on what the truth actually is." Jackson exchanged a glance with Radek and Elizabeth, and John got the familiar sense that he was still behind the power curve.

CHAPTER THREE

A pair of huge, golden eyes peered up at Teyla. She froze, uncertain whether to withdraw her hand from the moss-encrusted remains of the wall or remain still—until a movement caught her attention. A second creature, this one with faceted eyes and four translucent insect wings each as long as her arm, flittered briefly around her head before settling on the broken wall. The lipless mouth of the first, golden-eyed creature opened wide, and a sticky pink tongue shot out at a blinding speed.

"Good God, did you see that?" Dr. Geisler asked for perhaps the fifth occasion since they had arrived on M1M-316.

The frog—Teyla classified the yellow and blue patterned creature as a frog, despite its size—snatched the unfortunate insect into its mouth. Gossamer wings dripping with moisture fluttered desperately for a moment before the victim was entirely consumed.

"I expected something bigger," Ronon said, joining them. "Didn't Sheppard say this place was full of animals called dinosaurs?" Water beaded his forehead and dripped from his nose, perspiration washed away by rain in the sticky, cloying heat. Blinking away a few more drops, he continued to sweep the nearby jungle with his gaze, alert for any dangers that had yet to make themselves known in this most unusual world.

Dr. Geisler turned to him with an indignant stare. "Young man, that amphibian was the size of a Labrador. In this lower than normal gravity, with such a high oxygen content in the air, be thankful that's all—"

"Get back here—*now*!" Major Lorne called aloud from the entrance of the nearby jumper, putting an end to the discussion. "Something's headed our way."

Although the pelting of the rain and low rumble of a nearby

waterfall served to mask the sounds of any large animals that might be approaching, Dr. Geisler did not argue with the Major's command. Indeed, despite his advanced years, the paleontologist turned and quickly made his way back across the remains of what once had been an Ancient structure.

"Perhaps we will have better luck at the next location," Teyla reassured him, thankful for the poncho that had kept her moderately dry—at least on the outside. Her shirt and pants were damp against her body, not from exertion but from the remarkable humidity. "Did you not say that the records pertaining to this world contained references to several different laboratories?"

"I'm not worried about finding something for McKay to go gaga over." Dr. Geisler grasped a twisted vine to steady himself and clambered over a rotting log speckled with a multitude of riotously colored fungi. Careful to avoid releasing any spores from the growths, which he had earlier warned them might contain poisons or hallucinogens, he added, "I'm just a tad perturbed by the familiarity of all this. The vegetation is *exactly* the sort of thing I'd have expected to see on Earth during the mid to late Cretaceous, right down to the masses of conifers, cycads and, most particularly, the huge number and variety of ginkgo trees. That rancid smell, by the way, is the butyric acid in the integument of the ginkgo seeds rotting all over the ground." With his other hand, he patted the plastic case he carried, already overflowing with samples. "Of course, I've yet to confirm my hypothesis, but I have a sneaking suspicion that much, if not all, of the vegetation on this world originated from Earth."

A curious frown accompanied his statement. Teyla was uncertain as to the reason why until the scientist, puffing slightly from his hurried effort, added, "Earth of sixty-seven to seventy million years ago. If I'm right, it means the Ancients were in the Pegasus Galaxy a long, long time before Atlantis left Earth."

"C'mon, we gotta get moving!" Major Lorne was still

standing at the jumper's hatch, gesturing for them to hurry.

That's when Teyla felt it: a rhythmic shuddering beneath her feet.

Seeing that the three of them were almost there, Lorne darted inside and flung himself into the pilot's chair. Dr. Geisler lost his footing and slid on a rain-slicked layer of leaves at the base of the ramp, dropping his bag as he fell heavily to the ground. Ronon quickly dragged him to his feet and inside, while Teyla recovered the bag. There was no mistaking it now. Something large enough to send shockwaves through the ground was heading in their direction—fast.

Ronon slapped his fist against the mechanism that raised the hatch just as a terrible roar shattered the air. Teyla caught a whiff of something even fouler than the pervasive odor that had met them on arrival, and then the hatch was locked.

"We're outta here," Lorne announced, powering up the jumper for departure.

Teyla stripped off her poncho and looked through the windscreen, but there was little to see. Even the Stargate, only a hundred feet away, was all but invisible in the dense mist. Just as the jumper lifted into the air, however, she could almost make out a shape in the darker shadows beyond. The shudders through the ground caused by whatever creatures were coming their way now sent ripples through the fog itself.

When Jumper Two lifted into the air, Lorne ineffectually brushed sweat from his forehead with his sleeve. "That was close."

"What was?" Ronon asked, moving into the cockpit and taking the front seat beside the Major.

Eyes bright with excitement, Dr. Geisler answered Ronon. "The dinosaurs you were so anxious to see."

Satisfied that the scientist's sample box was properly stowed, Teyla went forward with Dr. Geisler to the passenger seats. On the Head Up Display, the life signs indicator showed such an abundance of life that it was nearly impossible to distinguish individual readings. Becoming evident, however, were several dozen creatures moving swiftly across the ruins, through and around the Stargate, while two additional animals followed several jumper lengths behind, presumably in pursuit. There was no scale on the display to indicate the size of either hunters or prey. If the echoes she'd felt through the ground and the power of that roar were anything to go by, she was very glad to be airborne.

Dr. Geisler unzipped his jacket and removed it, then tugged with distaste at the saturated shirt clinging to his chest. Teyla removed her own jacket. It had indeed been excessively warm outside, and for once she was grateful for the artificially maintained temperature and humidity inside the jumper.

Pointing to the HUD, which displayed an increasingly detailed topographic map as they gained height, Dr. Geisler explained, "The Stargate is situated in a valley carved out by glaciers tens of thousands of years ago. The river, fed by the melt water from glaciers in the nearby mountains, must periodically flood and change course, which would explain those uprooted tropical hardwood trees we saw. Deluges of that magnitude would flatten the vegetation in great swaths, allowing passage through the forest to large land animals. The result has been to create those semi-open areas like the one around the Stargate."

"In this climate, I'm surprised the entire gate wasn't covered in jungle."

"Not jungle, Major," Dr. Geisler corrected, sitting forward to look outside. "Tropical rainforest."

"Got the rain part right." Ronon's hair was dripping, and he wiped his face with the sleeve of his discarded jacket.

"You can see, from the manner in which the vegetation surrounding the Stargate has been grazed at different heights, that a range of big herbivores live in this area. Those odd scrapes through the mosses and liverworts on the Ancient structures also indicate the presence of small, beaked dinosaurs. And where there are herbivores, there are also carnivores." At

Ronon's quizzical look, the scientist clarified, "Plant eaters and meat eaters."

"The natural history lesson is all very interesting, Doc." Lorne glanced back over his shoulder. "But General Landry wants us to locate those labs you found in the database. So far I've got no power readings anywhere in this area, aside from the trace activity of the DHD and gate."

"Which is no doubt why only ruins remain. The materials used by the Ancients in the construction of their cities aren't all that strong, relatively speaking. Without a force field for protection, it's a wonder there's anything left at all."

They abruptly emerged from the fog into brilliant blue sky. "Might I suggest that a way to narrow the search would be to scan for power sources that could indicate an active force field?" said Teyla.

"Doing just that," the Major replied.

The sky darkened as the jumper continued to climb into low orbit. The distant primary planet, a bluish gaseous world, briefly caught Teyla's eye, but then her attention was drawn back to the world below. It quickly became evident that M1M-316 was comprised of vast continents separated by equally vast oceans, speckled with many island chains that might have joined the land in times when the level of the ocean was lower. That observation came from the map on the HUD, however, because many of the landmasses and even the islands were covered in swirling clouds.

"It's the heat and atmospheric pressure," Dr. Geisler observed. "Probably rains most of the time on most days… just like home."

Smiling, Teyla asked him, "Where is home for you?"

"West coast of New Zealand's South Island. Annual precipitation on the coast itself is around three meters, but just a few kilometers inland on the Southern Alps it can be twelve meters—almost forty feet."

Even Ronon appeared impressed by that statement.

"The entire region has been sculpted by glaciers. We still

have two flowing through temperate rainforest—right down to the main highway. That's why I recognize the landforms here."

Within minutes the sensors had located all eight of the Ancient facilities presumed to exist on the planet. However, in all but one instance the power sources appeared to have either been depleted or removed, and the structures that remained were little more than rubble. Major Lorne adjusted the jumper's scan settings, and the image on the HUD altered, focusing on the remaining laboratory. "That's interesting," he noted.

Beyond recognizing that the stream of data as the component materials of the building, Teyla had no idea what it meant. "Major?" she inquired.

"I suspected as much—this confirms it!" She glanced across to see the aged scientist nodding in recognition. "The exterior of that lab is made from the same composite materials the Ancients used in the Milky Way Galaxy," he added.

"Are you sure?" Lorne asked, putting the jumper into a shallow descent over the landmass. "Maybe it's just—"

"Major, I've spent four of the last ten years on planets in the Milky Way Galaxy where Ancient structures have been found. I'm telling you, this predates anything we've seen so far in this galaxy—although 'we' might exclude you and Ronon," Dr. Geisler added with a deferential glance in Teyla's direction.

When a break in the cloud cover developed, Teyla was thankful, for the jumper descended between two majestic, snowcapped mountain chains and the view was breathtaking. Dozens of glaciers, glinting blue and white in the sun, threaded their way through the peaks. The true scale of the mighty frozen rivers could only be appreciated when Major Lorne brought the jumper down low. Jagged rents across their surface—crevasses, Geisler called them—were large enough to swallow the jumper whole. The scale was far greater than anything Teyla had previously beheld, and for a moment she felt the desire to stop and explore the crystalline caves.

"Look at that!" Dr. Geisler pointed ahead as the jumper followed one of the great ice tongues along the valley. "The glaciers extend far past the tree line, which means that any minute now we should see—"

The valley widened where a second glacier joined the first. Jumbled chunks of dirty white ice and black rocks the size of the *Daedalus* plowing into one another in spectacular, frozen fury, but along the cliffs on either side of the valley the snow had given way to verdant growth, as thick and luxuriant as the rainforest that surrounded the Stargate. Every few miles, waterfalls gushed out seemingly from nowhere, cascading down into the crumbled blocks below. Where the glacier came to an abrupt halt, a wide, milky river emerged and flowed through rubble covered with green growth.

The valley continued to widen and as it did so, much of the landscape changed to expanses of grassland. Dr. Geisler laughed with excitement. Years fell away from his lined face, to be replaced with the glee of childhood, for wandering along the grassy riverbanks were hordes of gargantuan, long-necked animals, the likes of which Teyla had seen only in Atlantis's collection of movies—except that these beasts were far more colorful and, if the tiny shadow of the jumper was any guide, considerably larger.

Slowing the jumper to offer a better view, Major Lorne glanced back over his shoulder, an indulgent grin on his face. "Well, Doc, guess you get to see your dinosaurs after all."

Unfamiliar and intricate words tumbled out of the doctor's mouth: names, Teyla assumed, of the many beasts that inhabited the valley. "Definitely late Cretaceous," he declared. "Before the decline, perhaps a million years prior to the K-T event. But the scale! It has to be the lower gravity. They're at least twenty percent larger than any fossil we've ever seen. And look at the colors on the head of that torosaurus—just magnificent!"

Preoccupied with the observing the hordes of great creatures, Teyla barely noticed several shadows overtaking them, until Major Lorne shouted, "Whoa!" He threw the jumper into a steep climb, but was not swift enough to avoid a collision with something unseen—something large enough to toss them tumbling through the air toward a narrow gorge and the foaming rapids beneath.

CHAPTER FOUR

One of the more pedestrian aspects of being stationed in another galaxy was the tendency to lose track of Earthside happenings, such as what season it was in Colorado. Since travel back and forth had become more frequent of late, many of the Atlantis expedition members had started keeping lockers at the SGC to decrease their chances of having to scramble for suitable civilian clothing. Unfortunately, Rodney had left his best cold weather gear, the coat that had seen him through multiple Siberian and Antarctic brushes with hypothermia, in Atlantis.

He cast a baleful gaze at the snowcapped mountains. Typical of the gleeful spite with which the universe seemed to be treating him these days. To compound the situation, a half dozen Marines assigned to accompany them were sporting fleece-lined jackets with 'CDC' logos on the front and back.

Valiantly suppressing a shiver, Rodney eyed the crusted rime of ice on the windscreen of the government-issue SUV provided to the rest of the team. "Does it have four-wheel drive?"

"We're going to the coroner's office, not up Pikes Peak," Sheppard replied. "It's not even snowing." He'd gotten the keys to both vehicles from the timid motor pool sergeant simply by virtue of being the only officer in the group, Rodney was sure. Wearing a uniform that looked stiff with disuse as well as starch, the Colonel climbed into a refrigerated biohazard truck also marked 'CDC' with an unconscious air of authority. Although Rodney knew the blue dress shirt under that leather aviator jacket wasn't made for warmth, the man didn't even look chilly, damn him.

"That's no predictor of whether or not it will *start* snowing. And try to remember that Chevrolets don't read your mind."

As if to further taunt him, Sheppard then tossed the SUV keys to Radek.

"Oh for pity's sake," Rodney objected. "At least let Dr. Jackson drive." He pivoted toward the archeologist. "Presumably *you've* been behind the wheel more recently than six months ago, and in this country?"

"I always enjoy exploring unfamiliar roads," Radek said pleasantly, tugging on a pair of warm-looking gloves; where he'd managed to find them Rodney would very much liked to have known.

As she so often did, Elizabeth put an end to the discussion. She held out a hand to Radek. "If it'll make you feel any better, Rodney, I'll drive." With a tolerant smile, she added, "You don't have any objections to that, do you?"

Taking some comfort from the fact that Elizabeth at least knew the Colorado Springs area, Rodney climbed into the front passenger seat and slammed the door behind him. Just as Elizabeth put the SUV in gear, he noticed Lam, also wearing one of the CDC jackets, climb into the truck beside Sheppard. Rodney supposed it made sense that they would have such vehicles on standby, given the nature of some of the life forms that had made their way through the gate and even, occasionally, escaped.

The thought crossed his mind that a Wraith must have somehow sneaked through the gate or stowed away aboard the *Daedalus*. It wasn't inconceivable. After all, a Goa'uld had hitched a ride to Pegasus inside Colonel Caldwell. However, that notion died almost before it was born, because if Jackson was correct and the various succubus myths were in fact based on Wraith attacks, it meant that the creatures had been on Earth for centuries, if not longer.

The four of them in the SUV weren't a terribly professional group in appearance; more like a bunch of ill-equipped tourists looking for a ski resort. Rodney wondered exactly what this cover story was supposed to entail. As Elizabeth pulled out of the parking lot, though, he ran out of trivialities to help cover his anxiety over everything they'd just learned. The lead weight that had settled in his stomach upon seeing that footage of Woolsey's cousin quickly made its presence known again.

Somebody had to start the unavoidable conversation, and so Rodney took it upon himself. "If there have been Wraith wandering around here years before we woke up their Pegasus compatriots, we need to seriously reevaluate what we know about their goals and methods."

"They are not Wraith," Radek stated from the seat behind him. "They are—"

"Oh, and you're basing that assessment on your extensive experience in a hive ship cocoon?" Rodney snapped his fingers. "Wait, no, I'm sorry—that was *me*."

"Gentlemen, are we really going to have *that* contest?" Their driver pointedly inclined her head toward the other vehicle in their small caravan.

Rodney conceded Elizabeth's point, albeit not out loud. When it came to Wraith encounters, nobody, not even Ronon, could claim to have had one quite like Sheppard's.

He moved on by twisting around in the seat to glare at Radek. "While we're on the subject of what each of us knows, at what point were you going to clue everyone in on your follow-up to Carson's project?"

"When you stopped grumbling long enough to let me. I am still waiting."

From the other back seat, Jackson leaned forward to address Elizabeth. "They always like this?"

She shrugged one shoulder. "More or less. Rodney's being particularly charming today."

"Your support is heartwarming," Rodney groused. "If I'd had something marginally more nourishing than a Snickers bar for breakfast—"

"Eighteen months ago," Radek said, interrupting, "Carson asked me to write a macro that would allow him to analyze his genetic data more comprehensively." He took off his glasses, which were starting to fog in the rapidly warming SUV. "Some of us are willing to contribute to interdisciplinary research. *Some* of us even view biological studies as something higher than voodoo."

Objecting almost on instinct, Rodney snapped, "I never called it 'voodoo'!"

"More than once," the Czech informed him, unruffled. "Also 'farm science' on one occasion."

Had he really dismissed Carson that harshly, and that regularly? Rodney covered a stab of remorse by pressing his offensive. "If I did, it was only because you were dedicating an unwarranted amount of your time to playing code monkey for a largely theoretical project when you could have been—"

"Working on your research instead? Were you really so lost without my help?"

"Radek." Elizabeth already sounded weary. In the rearview mirror, Rodney caught a glimpse of Jackson's rolled eyes. Maybe SG-1 wasn't into the sibling rivalry dynamic.

Coming back to the point, Radek said, "To be accurate, I should say that these attackers are not *precisely* Wraith."

"It's like I was saying in the briefing," Jackson supplied. "They're succubus, or incubus in the case of males."

Turning to face the road, Rodney tapped impatient fingers on his armrest and wished fervently that he'd gotten at least one more cup of coffee before starting out on this trip. "Aside from the medieval connotations, what exactly does that mean?"

"While Carson worked to isolate the ATA gene, he also found other genes worthy of note," Radek continued. "According to him, not long ago such genes would have been labeled junk DNA, considered useless to our understanding of the human genome. Carson, of course, knew better. The genes he identified—and he was the first to admit that there were many more besides—are actually viral DNA. Geneticists refer to them as endogenous retroviruses."

"Whoa, hold on a minute." That word set off a mental

warning bell for Rodney. "Generally speaking, I'm not a big proponent of anything retrovirus related, since that category includes the *iratus* virus."

"That is so," acknowledged Radek. "Most retroviruses of this type are inactive, however. The term 'endogenous' means that the viral DNA actually inserted itself, or was inserted deliberately, into human genetic code."

"Deliberately?" Rodney echoed. Feeling his earlier spike of panic intensify in amplitude, he barely noticed that the snow he'd earlier predicted had in fact started to fall.

"Carson cross-referenced many of his findings with the Mitochondrial Eve project, which traced the matrilineal heritage of all living humans back to a common female ancestor. He discovered that the first incidence of the ATA gene in humans occurred ten thousand years ago—"

"And that fact should come as a shock to precisely no one, since we already know that the Ancients arrived on Earth at that time." He shot a scathing look at Radek. "Can we possibly aim for speed over style in this explanation?"

"With fewer interruptions, perhaps so." Radek's unexpected glower nearly made Rodney wish once more for his winter coat. "The unique gene sequences Carson had found during his ATA research caught his attention again some time later, when he was developing the retrovirus for the Michael experiment."

Everyone in the vehicle, with the exception of Dr. Jackson, looked hardened by the reminder. Amid the incredible strides made as a result of the Atlantis expedition over the past three years, there had been episodes of which the expedition was less than proud. Ethical questions aside, the attempt to reengineer Wraith DNA into human hadn't resulted in the absolute worst catastrophe Rodney had ever witnessed, but it had been a very near thing.

It took a moment for that unpleasant memory to pass before he realized just what Radek had implied. "Wait—are you saying that Carson found a link between actual human

DNA and the *iratus* virus?"

Rodney hoped irrationally for a rapid denial, or at least an assurance that he was on the wrong track, as unlikely as that might be. Instead he got only a solemn, silent glance.

"Oh, God," he murmured, horrified. "That's it, isn't it? Humans have the virus. We've *always* had it. Oh, *God*."

"Rodney, calm down," Elizabeth advised, "and let Radek finish."

"Research shows that the virus was introduced to the human population at the same time and geographical location as the ATA gene," said Radek. "Not all humans possess it, of course—not even all humans with the ATA gene—but about half the population has fragments of the base code. Under certain conditions, gene therapy being one such condition, mutated versions of the *iratus* virus can become active."

"And something has suddenly triggered the virus in people here, like a kind of *iratus* time bomb?" Elizabeth started to twist around in the driver's seat.

"Eyes on the road!" Rodney barked, turning to face the front. Suddenly the cramped interior of the SUV was too warm, too constricting. He put his head down and tried to breathe deeply, but his lungs didn't seem interested in complying. *Wide open fields...clear blue skies...*

Rodney heard his name dimly, over the hammering of his heart, and couldn't have cared less. "Pull over," he panted. "Dammit, pull over!"

One of Elizabeth's many admirable traits was her willingness to act without hesitation when it mattered. No sooner had Rodney made his plea than the SUV made a swift right turn and came to a halt.

Barely lifting his head, Rodney shoved the door open and flung himself out of the vehicle. He sucked in a lungful of cold air and, ignoring the splashes of half-frozen mud, sat down hard on the rear bumper, trying to get himself back under control.

Other doors opened and closed, and before long he found

himself surrounded by his colleagues. He noticed that the faux CDC truck had pulled up behind them. A hand came down to rest on his shoulder. "Dr. Lam's gone to get you something to drink," Elizabeth said calmly, as if this sort of thing happened every day. "Just take it easy for a minute."

"Take it *easy*?" Rodney offered a harsh laugh, still bent low and examining the cracked pavement and dirty slush piled in the gutter. The bracing chill and random snowflakes barely registered when compared with the icy tendrils that gripped his stomach. "That gene therapy worked on me, remember? I probably have some variant of this damned bug. We created a whole group of *iratus* carriers ourselves, and any number of them must be hidden in the human population, just waiting to be switched on!"

Seeing Sheppard's polished shoes approach the huddle, he was about to add something further, but the Colonel, who must have received a similar briefing from Lam, got in first. "I need Ronon and Teyla here," he said, his tone matter of fact. "If there's some sort of clue on M1M-316 as to the Ancient who let this gene loose on Earth, then Rodney and Radek should have been the ones to go there with Lorne. Meanwhile, if we've got Wraith, or Wraith wannabes, on the loose on Earth, I can't track them down without Teyla and Ronon. No offense, Rodney. It's just that Teyla can sense them coming, and Ronon's been taking them on longer than anyone we've got."

"Oh, is that your grand strategy?" Rodney drew another frigid breath, quashing a vague twinge of guilt for not paying more attention to the activities of his other two teammates. "Do you really think you can contain this with a couple of hunting trips? You can't simply round up a few pasty-looking people and call it a day. The virus is in our DNA. It's *part* of us!"

When Elizabeth's fingers tightened, digging into his shoulder, Rodney glanced up and identified their stopping point as a gas station, complete with a line of snowboard-topped SUVs and various travelers. Several were looking in the direction of the 'CDC' van and the cluster of people hovering around him.

"Let's maybe talk about this somewhere less public, shall we?" Jackson suggested.

You're not dead yet, Rodney told himself. *And you're not a Wraith. Deal with everything else one step at a time.*

Lam held out a bottle of some kind of sports drink without comment. Rodney accepted it despite its strong resemblance to antifreeze. After a couple of swallows, he felt marginally human again—although apparently that was a relative concept now.

"Claustrophobia," he mumbled weakly. "Uh, please continue, Radek."

"I have told you all I know at this point," Radek replied, standing there with an infuriatingly masked expression.

Rearing up off the bumper, Rodney insisted, "That can't be *all*."

The other scientist unfolded his arms and, raising his gloved hands in surrender. "The research was, as you said, one of many projects, and not terribly high on the priority list."

"Not a priority? You went far enough to identify the problem and decided to take a lunch break before investigating a solution?"

"Rodney!" Elizabeth's admonishment was less effective than Sheppard's abrupt grip on his arm, hauling him upright and into the backseat of the SUV, then shutting the door behind him.

Once everyone had belted in, this time with Jackson in front, and they were in motion again, Elizabeth finally spoke. "Rodney, try to remember that not everyone in Colorado Springs has the same level of security as you. Carson notified me of his findings and submitted a report to the SGC last year. At that point we had no reason to think there was a problem. Until these killings, nothing had happened on Earth to suggest that any Wraith traits were present in humans. I did recognize some similarities to the succubus myths and possibly some old vampire tales, but that's all. To be honest, based on the manner in which many other myths have played out, including the existence of Merlin and even Atlantis itself, it seemed reasonable to assume that such legendary creatures existed only in the Pegasus Galaxy."

Rubbing his arm, which was certain to bruise, Rodney asked, "And what are those myths—besides the Hollywood version, I mean?"

Jackson turned around to face him. "Dr. Beckett's report traced the first occurrences of the *iratus* virus to the E'din Valley, between the Tigris and Euphrates Rivers in ancient Persia, the area fabled to be the location of the Garden of Eden—what's now Iraq."

"Still nothing I'd call surprising." Couldn't *anyone* process or disseminate information as quickly as Rodney? "We've already discussed the Ancients' evacuation to Earth ten millennia ago. They made that return through the Egyptian gate. *And?*"

As the SUV coasted to a stop at a traffic light, Jackson slouched back in his seat. "You can't imagine how I've missed working with you, McKay," he remarked under his breath, the words still perfectly audible. More loudly, he continued, "The Ancients' presence in that region explains the appearance of the ATA gene, but not the appearance of the *iratus* virus. Based on the mythology and what we saw on the tape Woolsey discovered, though, I think I have an idea what might have happened."

In the next car over, a mother leaned into the backseat to hand her young child a juice box. Rodney wondered if they carried the retrovirus and if their bright-faced ignorance would end up costing the entire planet dearly.

"Carson had a theory as well," Radek pointed out. "He believed the Ancients were pursuing a method of manipulating the *iratus* virus, either to disable it in the Wraith population or to make others immune to the feeding process."

"Like Ronon's immunity," Elizabeth said, accelerating when the light turned green.

"Or the Hoffan vaccine." One side of Radek's mouth curled upward in a wistful half smile. "It gave Carson a measure of peace to know that our failures were not unique to us."

Rodney took another sip of his drink, wishing they didn't have to face this issue with the ghost of his friend hovering over their shoulders.

"Dr. Geisler recently discovered records in the city database associated with one specific researcher named Lilith," Radek continued. "A number of planets were referenced in conjunction with the project files—possibly some testing was conducted on those worlds. One file in particular looked most promising, because it appeared to contain several references to Earth long before the Ancients left Antarctica for Lantea."

"Which is why General Landry ordered Major Lorne, Ronon and Teyla to check out M1M-316," explained Elizabeth. "We're hoping they'll locate Lilith's research laboratory."

The name set off a chime of familiarity in Rodney's memory, taking the edge off his terror and giving him something on which to focus. "Lilith is the researcher? That can hardly be coincidental."

The SUV swung into the parking lot of the county sheriff's office, which looked entirely too sedate and tranquil to contain a morgue. Jackson's head turned toward him. "Since when did you become a scholar of Talmudic texts, McKay?"

That threw him off. "What? I'm talking about the name—I've run across it in the Ancient database. What are *you* talking about?"

"I believe Lilith was also the name of Adam's first wife," Radek contributed, earning a surprised glance from both Jackson and Rodney.

"As in Adam and Eve?" Elizabeth parked the vehicle

and switched off the ignition. "There was a first wife?" She glanced over her shoulder.

"And you picked up that piece of trivia *where* exactly?" Rodney followed her gaze and watched as Sheppard's 'CDC' vehicle passed them, heading for the rear of the building.

Radek's response seemed to be directed at Jackson rather than Rodney. "Carson believed the Ancient Lilith continued her retrovirus research after relocating from 316 to Earth. Possibly the virus escaped, or else she intentionally released it into the population."

"I'm beginning to find myself agreeing with John's assessment of the Ancients," Elizabeth declared, sounding drained. "They created some staggering messes and made little or no attempt to clean them up."

Radek nodded his agreement. "Wraith, Asurans, succubus—"

"Succubi in the plural," said Jackson. "And we should include incubi, the male version, since, according to the profiler, a male was responsible for the Colorado Springs murders."

As if the FBI's profiler could have even the slightest clue what they were dealing with here. Rodney climbed out of the SUV and pulled his lightweight jacket tight around himself, uninterested in the details Elizabeth was providing on the profiler and the tall tale they'd be feeding her. He was focused on only one thing. "What do we know about this Lilith so far?"

He'd asked Radek, but it was Jackson who answered. *"Her gates are gates of death, and from the entrance of the house she sets out towards Sheol. None of those who enter there will ever return, and all who possess her will descend to the Pit."*

"Talmud?" Radek inquired.

The archeologist shook his head and started walking. "Dead Sea Scrolls."

Rodney stared at the neatly lettered sign near the front door of the building, helpfully directing coroner business to the lower level. The panic that had earlier threatened to overwhelm him now settled into a tight ball of nausea in the pit of his stomach. He doubted it would disappear any time soon.

CHAPTER FIVE

"*Quetzalcoatlus*," Geisler announced from where he'd fallen against the lower bulkhead inside the jumper. "An entire colony!" While all color had left his face, he seemed more excited than concerned.

Another of the enormous birds—or maybe they were bats—collided with the jumper, sending it careening into the side of the cliff. The shield and inertial dampeners protected them, but Ronon found the impact less disturbing than the fact that they were being attacked by animals the size of the airliners he'd seen on during his brief time on Earth. "I thought we were cloaked?"

"We are," Lorne replied shortly, struggling to bring the jumper under control. Below them, the river straightened out again as they emerged through the gorge and into another wide valley, misted by cascading water and remnants of the morning fog. According to the HUD, there were even more of the massive land animals here than they'd seen previously. The life signs indicator showed almost a continuous bright streak for mile after mile.

"You mean they can detect us through the cloak?" Teyla asked, glancing to the rear of the craft to make certain everything was still secure.

"I...don't think so." Once clear of the mist, Lorne angled the jumper to fly lower until he was nearly brushing across the tops of the strange trees, branches heavy with seeds, that Geisler had earlier called ginkgoes. "I think they just flew into us."

Ahead of them, four or five of the giant, long-beaked flying...things regrouped with the rest of their kind and kept right on flying, apparently uninterested in the jumper.

"See that?" With Ronon's help, Geisler picked himself up

off the deck and reclaimed his seat. "They fly in formation. Prezwilitz insisted that they were solitary predators, but look at that. He's wrong! And look at the size of them. It *has* to be a result of the lower gravity and denser atmosphere. They're half again as big as the *Quetzalcoatlus* of Earth."

How Geisler knew that, given that he'd just finished telling them that these same animals had become extinct on Earth millions of years ago, Ronon had no idea. Nor did he much care, because they weren't out of trouble yet. "Major!"

Lorne had already reacted, weaving the jumper through a cluster of giant serpents sticking up out of the trees. As they passed Ronon saw that the 'snakes' were in fact necks, attached to huge bodies ending in tails that appeared equally as long as the necks. He'd seen large animals before, but never anything on a scale even remotely resembling this.

"My God, did you see them? Titanosaurs!" Geisler was out of his seat and leaning forward over the center console, trying to get a better view.

"See them?" Lorne repeated, dodging another group of the yellow-necked beasts. "I'm trying to *avoid* them. This is nuts!"

"Look at those colors. They're magnificent. It couldn't possibly be restricted to a threat display mechanism because all of them have similar colorings!"

"Perhaps you should de-cloak us, Major," Teyla suggested.

Lorne shot her a look of disbelief.

"She's right," Ronon said, ignoring what sounded like a one-man argument from Geisler about names and colors. "Most animals I've encountered leave you alone unless they're hungry, scared, or have young." He pointed to another formation of flyers riding the thermals over the next gorge. "If those dinosaurs can see us, they'll probably avoid us."

"They're not dinosaurs." Geisler sounded mildly frustrated. "They're pterosaurs. You can't just blithely lump everything that roamed the Earth millions of years ago into the one category, which is why none of this makes any sense, because *that's* a diplodocus!" He pointed to a herd of green mottle-skinned giants, rows of sharp spines sticking up along their back all the way from their tiny heads to their whip-like tails. "They vanished eighty million years *before* the K-T extinction event, which pushes the time frame back to one hundred and forty-five million years!"

With an apprehensive shake of his head, Lorne uncloaked the jumper.

"Are we nearing the Ancient lab, Major?" Teyla asked, reminding them of their priority.

"Coming up ahead of us, about thirty miles," Lorne replied.

The next valley widened out to a coastal plain, and Ronon could see the ocean ahead of them. On the HUD, the signal describing an energy source appeared to be getting closer. Going by the map's topographic detail, the Ancient structure was about three hundred feet below them, sitting in the ocean between the mainland and a collection of wave-battered rocky islands just offshore.

"This is going to be a tight squeeze," Lorne warned, slowing the jumper and then bringing them in carefully over the cliff face.

Ronon heard Teyla pull in a sharp breath at the sight. He had to agree that it was impressive. The rugged coastline resembled a jumble of millions of tiles, crudely stacked atop one another and then carved into grotesque shapes by countless storms. Clusters of spiky leafed plants sprouted along the outcrops and clung to crevices.

"Just like Pancake Rocks," said Geisler. "It's karst—limestone, or dolomite more likely—which means there'll be sea caves and blowholes right along the coast. The Ancients probably built the lab inside one of the caverns when it was inland, and in the ensuing millennia the sea ate the land away."

A spray of foam shot out from a large hole in the misshapen rocks. Lorne eased the jumper lower, so that they skimmed just above the height of the waves coming in at a slight angle to the coastline. "There it is," he said, pointing to a shadow under a particularly large outcrop—which looked to Ronon like it was ready to crumble into the ocean at any minute.

The surf, filled with strands of thick black seaweed, pounded up against the rocks, then streamed back again, revealing a half-submerged sea cave. At the sight of the jumper, dozens of reptilian creatures gripping the battered outcrops dove into the water. Heads bobbed up here and there between the weeds, which swirled back and forth in the relentless movement of the ocean.

"Marine iguanas," Geisler said, gripping the back of Teyla's chair. "This is just incredible—some of them are the size of saltwater crocodiles!"

Ronon was more interested in the image on the HUD, which showed a force field of some sort protecting the Ancient structure about a hundred feet inside the cavern.

"According to this, it's intact," reported Lorne. He brought the jumper around to face the submerged entrance of the sea cave. "I'm just not sure how we're supposed to get in."

"Can you not produce a force field around the jumper to match that of the facility?" Teyla wondered.

"Dr. Zelenka could, probably, but I don't have any idea how to modify the jumper's force field. And trying to fly in through that narrow gap, even protected by a force field… with the way the ocean is surging, I don't know if we'd make it."

While Lorne examined the HUD for any potential alternatives, Ronon watched another wave slam up and over the cavern's entrance, sending a misty salt spray back across the jumper. "This world is a moon, right?"

"Of course!" Geisler favored him with an approving look. "The primary planet exerts a periodic gravitational force, which means that there will be tides—big tides, most likely." His eyes narrowed as he examined the rocks. "There's a definite high water mark—you see where those mussels and oysters have stopped growing? The bottom of that cave might very well be dry at low tide. If we check the position and phase of the primary planet—"

"It was fully visible," Teyla said. "And directly overhead as we left orbit."

"Well, then." Geisler folded his hands, pleased. "We're not likely to be too far off high tide, and it shouldn't take long to create a tide chart."

"According to the sensor readings," said Lorne, "it looks like there'll be room to land a jumper inside once we get past the force field. There also looks to be another entrance through the rock on top, but it's too narrow to get a jumper through."

He brought the craft up over the cliffs, but of the second entrance there was no sign, just an image on the HUD that indicated the rocks were absent. "Looks like it's also overgrown," said Lorne, accelerating and flying along the cliff tops for several miles.

The image on the HUD kept changing. Ronon didn't recognize its meaning until Lorne turned inland and added, "We got ourselves a big system of caves, here."

"That's to be expected." Geisler pointed to a series of deep ponds between large, sinewy trees. "Those are sinkholes. It's quite likely we'll find several entrances to where the lab is located. I'd imagine the network runs for dozens, most likely hundreds of kilometers underground. On Earth, spelunkers take years to chart such systems."

Lorne raised the jumper's nose. "Okay, well, that tells us all we need to know for the moment. Let's head to the gate."

"Wait!" Geisler nearly leapt out of his seat. "Aren't you going to go back along the valley? I simply have to see what other sorts of animals exist on this planet—there must be a reason why their size appears to be the only evolutionary change that's occurred since they were brought here."

Teyla turned to the scientist with an obliging smile. "I'm sure Dr. Weir would be most happy for you to return. For now, our mission is to report back that we have located an intact Ancient laboratory."

Tapping his fingers on his knees in frustration, Geisler nodded. "Yes, yes, of course, I understand. It's just...I'm a paleobiologist, you see, as well as an archeologist. This planet is like talking a journey back in time on my world. And it changes so much; really everything we know about when the Ancients came here."

"What makes you say that?" Lorne asked.

Outside, the sky darkened as the jumper climbed into the upper reaches of the atmosphere. Presumably the Major was trying to avoid any more flying creatures while they crossed the ocean to the continent where the gate was located.

"We know the Ancients came to the Milky Way from their home galaxy," Geisler explained. "Then later, after the plague, they re-created all life there, which of course means they predated the dinosaurs." The finger tapping stopped. "And it stands to reason that when the Ancients left Earth in Atlantis, they didn't just pull up stakes and head off into the unknown. They must have set things up in the Pegasus Galaxy millions of years earlier."

"Makes sense." Lorne kept his eyes on the HUD. "I mean, we've found cities like Atlantis on other planets, and a lot more outposts. For all we know there could be dozens of planets in this galaxy with Earth animals, all from different epochs, or eras, or whatever you call them."

"What an intriguing idea!" Geisler sat back in his chair. "If we found moas, we could reintroduce them back home."

Ronon began to lose interest in the discussion. Like Geisler, he wouldn't mind coming back to this world, but only to do some hunting of his own.

He'd had a long enough conversation with Radek to have some idea of why they'd been sent on this mission. Personally, he thought that breaking into an Ancient lab just to find out more about some Ancient named Lilith who'd played around with Wraith genes was a bad idea. The Wraith were predators, no more and no less. Trying to change them would be as useless as trying to reason with them. Nobody had listened when he'd said as much during the experiment with Michael. Even when they'd found the super-Wraith Michael had created, John had insisted that Ronon set his weapon to stun. After that incident Ronon hadn't bothered attempting to say anything further. One of these days, maybe the Atlantis expedition would finally shake off whatever strange sensitivities they'd learned on their home world and realize that around here shooting to kill was a much safer option than asking questions.

Tuning out Geisler's steady chatter about the animals he'd seen, all of which seemed to be called saurs of some kind, Ronon focused on the landscape that was coming into view as the jumper descended. The fog in the valley where the Stargate was located had burned off as the sun had risen. The animal paths that wound through the jungle—Geisler could call it rainforest if he wanted, but as far as Ronon was concerned, it was dense jungle—were only occasionally visible through the crowns of tall trees.

Major Lorne punched in Atlantis's address on the dialing console. The shape of the Ancient lab that had once housed the gate had been blurred by millennia of floods and overgrowth, and even the gate itself was difficult to make out until the familiar vortex erupted.

Teyla transmitted their IDC while Lorne brought the jumper in low. What happened next occurred so fast that Ronon barely had time to process what he saw. Something—a whole pack of somethings by the look of them—burst out of the jungle and skittered through the gate, just an instant ahead of a wall of speckled skin that belted the jumper aside with its shoulder and plowed in after them.

Barely keeping his seat, Lorne was the first to react. "Atlantis—raise the shield! I repeat, raise the—"

Something else slammed into the jumper, and shoved them into the wormhole.

CHAPTER SIX

When the hotel's automated wakeup call had drawn her out of bed at six that morning, Elizabeth had anticipated a contentious day in front of the International Oversight Advisory. She hadn't prepared at all for holding a negotiation in a morgue, with one side represented by SGC personnel and the other by a forensic psychologist who gave all indications of being at the end of her rope.

In one aspect, at least, the detour wasn't totally unwelcome. Elizabeth hadn't had the chance to explain to John or Rodney the main reason she'd been called to Washington in the first place, and she had no plans to bring it up now. They didn't need the distraction of worrying about Atlantis's future on top of everything else.

Although she knew better than to take lightly any threat to the expedition, she'd been down this road with the IOA before. Whenever one of the Advisory's member governments changed or reshuffled its bureaucracy, a new representative joined the committee and was promptly horrified to learn of secret intergalactic wars being fought on multiple fronts. Elizabeth couldn't blame any of them; she remembered her initial reaction to being told about the Goa'uld, who now seemed like trivial pests compared to the other dangers they'd discovered.

Not for the first time, the IOA's incoming members had examined the high cost, in both dollars and lives, of maintaining the Atlantis expedition. On this occasion, they'd actually voted to shut the expedition down. The Ori—or more accurately, their followers—were the immediate problem and focusing on them was a better use of resources. After all, the Wraith couldn't reach Earth.

Primed to defend Atlantis yet again, Elizabeth had found

an unlikely ally in Woolsey. The Payton video had, at first, added fuel to the committee's fire; a Wraith presence on Earth seemingly had to be a result of some action the expedition had taken. If nothing else, it demonstrated the risks of sustaining a link to the Pegasus Galaxy.

Then Elizabeth had played her ace, reminding the members of Carson Beckett's report on the retrovirus a full year earlier. She knew the field of international affairs, had learned her craft in many of the same places as these people, and she could see in their expressions that they knew they'd backed themselves into a corner. Some of them hadn't even read Carson's report the first time around. They read it this time, and they were forced to concede the truth, sealed by Lam's autopsy findings. The Wraith, such as they were, had been on Earth for a very, very long time. Like Jekyll's Hyde, the monster hid within. In this case, while the Atlantis expedition's exploration of Pegasus wasn't the cause of the problem, it might yet provide the solution.

If one existed.

Elizabeth refocused on the situation at hand. The county coroner, a soft-spoken man of about fifty, seemed accustomed to dealing with personnel from the handful of military bases within his jurisdiction. When a CDC 'containment team' had shown up on his doorstep, he probably had recognized the subterfuge for what it was, but he'd gone along without comment. The FBI profiler, on the other hand, was proving more difficult.

"This can't possibly be a public health risk," Dr. Rebecca Larance insisted, one hand resting in a fist on her hip. "The etiology—"

"The rate and method of transmission are still largely unknown," countered Daniel without missing a beat.

Across the room, Rodney hovered behind Lam and Radek, making no effort to conceal his discomfort. Three corpses lay side by side on tables: two sheltered inside body bags, the third exposed and charred almost to the point of losing any definition as a body, let alone a human one. While Radek handed Lam some type of magnifying lens, Rodney caught Elizabeth's eye and wordlessly urged her over to an alcove, away from both groups.

Joining him there, she asked, "Has Dr. Lam found something?"

"Nothing she hasn't found already on Payton and Cabal." Even as he spoke, Rodney's gaze inched over to where Larance stood. Elizabeth resisted the temptation to regain his attention with a sharp elbow. True, the FBI agent was rather striking, but it wouldn't help their cause if Rodney were to make some socially dubious remark to her. "Listen, who decided on this division of labor? Colonel Sheppard gets to play Fox Mulder with the profiler? Because it seems to me that I'd be more qualified, given that he has no investigative experience."

"And your own experience in that arena is so vast?" Elizabeth asked dryly.

"Research is investigation by another name." Rodney scanned the room with an incipient frown. "Where is he, anyway? Not only does he get the best role in this pointless farce, but he manages to avoid this dungeon."

The morgue was as open and modern as the rest of the sheriff's headquarters, but Elizabeth let the comment pass. "John's upstairs, taking care of the paperwork for the custody transfer so we can bring the bodies back to the Mountain."

"Which somehow requires the assistance of CDC 'specialists' who all appear to have the same stylish haircut and an impressive fitness regime. Elizabeth, what precisely is our plan here?"

She kept a firm hold on her patience. "How much of the cover story we discussed in the car did you miss during your panic attack?"

Rodney started to object to her appraisal and then apparently thought better of it. "Assume a substantial amount," he answered tightly.

Might as well start at the beginning. "If the victims' families, or especially the media, saw a team of soldiers barge in here and lock down everything associated with these cases, we'd attract far more attention than we're prepared to handle. Our explanation is that a joint military/civilian expedition to Antarctica discovered a 30,000-year-old virus in an ice core sample, and containment was breached upon their return. This virus appears to cause a form of rapid, acute progeria, hence the accelerated aging found in the victims."

Eyebrows climbing, Rodney admitted, "That's a remarkably good cover story."

Elizabeth smiled. "Thank Radek. The majority of it was his idea."

"And here's why it's transparently flawed." Rodney changed tack without so much as a blink. Amazing, she thought, the way he was able to do that. "The first thing the FBI will do to check our facts will be to consult the histories they've assembled for each of these people—victimologies, I believe they're called—and discover that none of the victims have any connection whatsoever to Antarctica. Also, a point that I'm confident this Dr. Larance won't miss: how are we going to explain the symbol of the gate and Dart found at all the scenes?"

"Listen and learn." Elizabeth led him over to join the contentious discussion between Daniel and Larance. When he neared the FBI agent's line of sight, Rodney subtly improved his posture.

The ends of Larance's dark blond hair brushed against her shoulders as she continued to shake her head. "I can accept the possibility of a virus in the progeria spectrum causing this type of damage. But the deterioration is the *only* factor it would explain." Her tone businesslike, she ticked off the details on her fingers. "Ritualized evisceration, the precise arrangement of the bodies, the missing hearts, not to mention the fires, which were unquestionably lit to obscure the cause of death—and may have succeeded in doing so in any number of unknown cases…" Pinning Daniel with a gaze that invited him to answer at his own risk, she challenged, "Does your virus draw patterns on floors, use a lighter, and make internal organs disappear into thin air?"

Perhaps more than anyone else in the Stargate program besides Elizabeth, Daniel was experienced in dealing with forceful people. It was never easy to accept an accusation of dishonesty, veiled or not, even when dishonesty was part of the plan. Daniel, though, displayed no reaction except to offer his most truthful statement so far that afternoon. "We're not concerned with the virus per se."

Rodney's brow wrinkled. "We're not?" When he received matching glares from Daniel and Elizabeth, he rapidly amended, "No—well, we *are*, of course, but it's more complicated than that." Looking contrite, he waved a hand at Daniel. "Please, go on."

Elizabeth closed her eyes. Maybe her instructions to Rodney should have been 'Listen and learn and, for the love of everything holy, don't *talk*.'

"We believe," Daniel continued, "that a cult devoted to the worship of Lilith stole the virus and has been using it as part of their rituals."

Some, but not all, of the suspicion cleared from Larance's face. Progress, maybe. Then her eyes shifted to something on the far side of the room, and Elizabeth turned to see John come through the doorway, his CDC Marines in tow.

This ought to be interesting.

John's pace slowed, and he and Larance sized each other up. Apparently Lam's en route briefing to him hadn't included the identity of the agent with whom he'd be working. Recognition appeared to dawn for both parties at approximately the same time, but neither betrayed much in the way of surprise. The profiler spoke first, cocking her head. "Major—Sheppard, right?"

"Lieutenant Colonel these days, believe it or not." John directed his 'team' to load the bodies for transport and crossed the room toward her. "Good to see you again, Dr. Larance."

He offered his hand and a friendly, low wattage smile. A smart move, Elizabeth thought, one possibly based on experience; she suspected that this woman would not be amused by a charm offensive. Nor was she likely to be very impressed by his immaculate blues or silver wings, although Elizabeth had to admit that John Sheppard wore them well.

Larance did seem to soften ever so slightly as she shook his hand. "Light bird," she commented, giving no indication that she knew full well how improbable attaining that rank had been for him. "Congratulations."

"Oh, naturally they know each other," Rodney muttered, not quite inaudibly. "The secret society of the attractive."

Elizabeth strongly considered doing him bodily harm. When the SGC had looked into Larance's records and discovered that she and John had crossed paths before, they'd banked on that small amount of familiarity working to their advantage. So, of course, Rodney just *had* to blithely trample on whatever goodwill they'd just established.

Judging by John's expression, he planned to make the scientist pay for the quip as soon as Larance's back was turned. "Did you get tired of us pole patrol folks, or are you moonlighting?" he asked her.

"Multitasking, not moonlighting." Larance faced Elizabeth and Daniel as she explained. "One of my duties is vetting personnel for winter postings at McMurdo. Not everyone is psychologically suited for an Antarctic tour, and the last thing anyone needs is a person with pathological tendencies stuck in an enclosed area with limited outlets for aggression. There's a very rigorous screening process. Colonel Sheppard passed my gauntlet some years ago." She studied the others, waiting.

Daniel answered the implied question. "There have been a handful of instances, on classified projects, where personnel have been vetted through different channels."

"In fact, I was stationed down there for months without

being subjected to any—" Belatedly, Rodney seemed to realize he'd just hung a metaphorical target on himself.

The profiler contemplated him, looking unmoved. "Just as well. I'm not sure I would've signed off on sending you to Antarctica even on a penguin-watching pleasure cruise."

Out of the corner of her eye, Elizabeth saw Radek fail miserably in his attempt to mask his amusement, while Rodney's eyes grew huge. Before his indignant sputtering could coalesce into actual words, Larance held up a hand. "Don't bother critiquing my bedside manner. They don't pay me to have one. I'm a forensic psychologist, not a therapist. My job is to climb inside the heads of humanity's honest to God monsters, not to hold people's hands and tell them that Mommy and Daddy are the source of all their problems."

Abruptly, Rodney closed his mouth. Elizabeth noticed John concealing a faint smile and wondered what he'd thought of Larance when they'd first met, whether or not he'd liked or respected her. Sometimes it was hard to tell with him. After all, she wouldn't have predicted that he and Rodney would get along.

"This cult of Lilith you mentioned," Larance said, glancing over at Lam and the team as they secured the first body inside a coffin-like container. "You're not actually suggesting that one or more of its members was on an Antarctic mission, are you? Cult members have distinct personality traits that even your 'different channels' of screening would have flagged."

Daniel delicately sidestepped the question. "How familiar are you with biologically related cult behavior?"

"If you mean the use of bioweapons by cult groups, very. Ever heard of the Rajneeshees?"

The name meant nothing to Elizabeth, nor did it seem to jog any memories for the others.

"They had issues with the court in Wasco County, Oregon, and tried to prevent residents from voting in the 1984 election by mass poisoning with *Salmonella typhimurium*. Over seven hundred people were sickened, none fatally. Provided some rich subject matter for my dissertation." Larance folded her arms in a thoughtful, rather than defensive, gesture. "Then there's Aleph—you may remember them as Aum Shinriko."

"Sarin gas on the Tokyo subway, right?" John recalled. "Sometime in the mid nineties?"

"Among other attacks. The group is less powerful in its current incarnation but still very much in existence. Before his arrest, the sect leader, a man named Asahara, had virtually unlimited funds and a self-proclaimed mandate to wipe out a significant percentage of the world's population."

Elizabeth had conditioned herself to accept, if not understand, horrors on a planetary scale, but it was still hard to imagine what could possess a person to attempt such unspeakable acts. Anubis had taken his shot at Earth, of course, and countless Pegasus civilizations had fallen prey to the insatiable Wraith—but she had never truly been able to comprehend the process by which human beings could become utterly convinced that their purpose was to destroy their own kind.

A psychologist had once assured her that that was largely because she wasn't a psychopathic mass murderer.

Still, she was beginning to get a glimpse of what made Rebecca Larance tick. The FBI agent's demeanor might be abrasive, but she at least had some insight into what drove such people, and she was willing to do whatever was needed to combat them. Elizabeth recognized and admired that kind of determination.

"After the subway attack," Larance was saying, "Congress broke down the FBI's door, wanting to know how Asahara had been able to assemble a worldwide network of operatives without drawing attention from Western law enforcement or intel agencies. My bosses at the Bureau had to explain that Aum Shinriko was a chartered religious organization, protected by civil rights legislation and constitutional limitations in both the U.S. and Japan. A frustratingly common roadblock to investigations of cult groups."

"A number of those rules changed after 9/11," Elizabeth pointed out.

"Which is why I'm willing to concede the possibility that you actually might have some evidence to support your virus theory." Her gaze moved over the SGC visitors, catching briefly on John, before she lifted an eyebrow at Rodney. From his abashed, slightly sullen look, he seemed to have realized she'd been baiting him earlier. Still, they evidently hadn't won her over.

"Sir?"

The CDC containers had been loaded onto wheeled carriers, and the team stood beside them, waiting on an order. John glanced at Larance, questioning.

"If you're determined to take them and have the ME's permission, I don't really have the authority to stop you, do I?" she said archly.

"Maybe not, but you could raise hell with either the county officials or the local television news, and I'm hoping you won't." John, as usual, was trying to be a straight shooter, even under the circumstances. Elizabeth figured it was as good a tactic as any. "Look," he continued, "we're on the same side here. We just want to figure this thing out and stop it from happening again. There's no reason for us to work against each other."

It was a clearly sincere sentiment, and it appeared to have the desired effect, more so after he weathered Larance's probing stare without a flinch. After a moment, she replied, "Let me tag along to whichever base you're calling home these days, to find out more about this ice core virus *theory* of yours, Colonel, and I might believe that."

"Done," said John, only darting a look at his companions in hindsight. Daniel nodded, and Elizabeth had to agree. They'd do the best they could to safeguard the Stargate program and the truth, but this woman had knowledge and experience they needed, and stonewalling her would get them nowhere.

"Then let's get going."

John gave a silent affirmative signal to the Marines and walked over to hold the door open for them to move the bodies out to their vehicle. If Larance noticed that they handled the containers with the precision of an honor guard, she didn't comment on it, picking up her coat from a nearby chair and following them out of the room. Elizabeth and the others trailed behind the procession as it headed for the building's outer doors.

A pair of coroner's assistants passed them in the corridor. As soon as they were out of earshot, Larance asked, point blank, "Are you really worried about contagion?"

With only a beat of hesitation, Daniel admitted, "Not terribly."

"Then why pack up the bodies?"

"There's every reason to exercise precautions against residual traces of the virus," said Lam, sticking doggedly to the cover story.

"So I'm supposed to tell anyone who asks that the Bureau is on the lookout for a cult responsible for several ritualistic killings through the use of a progeria-type virus. I assume the virus's point of origin is information not intended for public consumption?"

Almost before Daniel tendered the Antarctic cover story, Larance stopped walking and swiveled to face the group. "I want to be clear before we go any further. I don't entirely buy your explanation of what's going on here. Right now, I'm in 'go along to get along' mode, because this case is too big for one person and I'm not stupid enough to refuse help. Just be aware that if you try to play me, I'll be on the phone very fast and this will get *very* ugly." She looked at John again. "I'm putting some trust in an analysis I made four years ago. I hope it was accurate then and is still valid now."

John said nothing, but his gaze was as steady as hers. Out of the profiler's field of view, Elizabeth and Daniel exchanged a glance. Maybe the SGC's gamble had paid off after all.

A blast of winter air and flurry of snow chilled them when Lam opened the building doors. As the Marines began to carefully slide their cargo into the back of the waiting vehicle, Larance pulled on her coat and turned to Daniel. "Okay. You show me yours and I'll show you mine. Tell me what Adam's first wife has to do with all this."

CHAPTER SEVEN

Daniel swiped his ID card through the reader attached to the elevator that would take them down to the lowest level of the Cheyenne Mountain complex. Behind him, McKay was describing to Rebecca Larance in minute detail what would have happened to him if the air freshener he'd found in the SUV had in fact contained twenty percent real lemon juice as advertised.

The elevator doors opened, and McKay, oblivious to Dr. Larance's pained expression, kept up his running commentary of symptoms as he stepped in.

Catching Elizabeth Weir's eye, Daniel said, "Talking is pretty much his default state, isn't it?"

"That is so," mumbled Radek Zelenka, stepping in behind them and turning to face the front. "The total time would be greatly reduced if he would stop while eating."

"Do you think I can't hear that?" Forced to choose a single target for his glare, McKay selected Daniel. "Do you have any idea what it's like to live with the sort of allergies that—"

"Yes, now that you mention it," Daniel interrupted, pressing the button.

"Really?" McKay regarded him with a look that suggested he'd found some common ground on which they could bond. Terrific.

While allergies were no longer a problem for Daniel, he wasn't in the mood to remind McKay of the reason. As soon as the non-cleared member of their little gang was out of hearing range, the scientist would no doubt want to regale him with tales of his own recent brush with Ascension. Well, 'close' only counted in horseshoes and hand grenades, as Jack would say.

Thankfully, the elevator doors opened before long, and

Zelenka stepped out. Larance, giving McKay as wide a berth as possible, followed and fell into step beside Elizabeth. "I have to ask," she said, studying the utilitarian tunnels with intense curiosity, "what roles could an expert in international relations and an archeologist play within the U.S. Air Force?"

McKay only got as far as opening his mouth before Elizabeth beat him to the punch. "That's a question best answered during the briefing." She offered Larance a smile, as if to reassure her that they weren't being deliberately evasive. It didn't convince Daniel much more than it appeared to convince the FBI agent.

No one involved in this situation lacked for questions at the moment, to be sure. Daniel wasn't completely certain even he had all the available facts, limited though they were, just yet. He'd been playing catch-up on most of the events of the past few months when Carolyn Lam, who'd been keeping an eye on Carson Beckett's research, had dropped this bombshell with her usual no-nonsense approach. As unsettling as he'd found the prospect of humans carrying fragments of the *iratus* gene, Carolyn had explained that it was no different from having fragments of the ATA gene or, for that matter, the DNA for any one of six thousand currently known genetic disorders, ranging from cystic fibrosis to sickle cell anemia. Possessing a flawed gene didn't automatically cause a disease to manifest; that took a rare confluence of events, such as a series of environmental triggers, or a child inheriting two copies of the gene.

Given that detail, McKay's anxiety attack on the road had seemed over the top, until the scientist had reminded them that he'd received therapy to trigger the ATA gene. So far, however, they'd lucked out on that score. Both Beckett and Carolyn had searched long and hard for a link between the ATA and *iratus* genes and found none, aside from the fact that they'd been introduced into the human population simultaneously. There was no reason to expect Wraithlike attributes to start appearing within the gene-activated Atlantis expedition.

But *something* had to be triggering this outbreak on Earth. Daniel didn't know whether they'd find the answers they needed in molecular biology or in the exasperatingly cryptic lessons left by the Ancients. Either way, for now, nearly everything remained a question.

Lengthening his stride to match their visitor's brisk pace, McKay asked, with awkward civility, "So…what kinds of cults do you specialize in studying?"

Larance barely glanced over at him. "Violent ones."

"Ah. I suppose that makes sense." McKay let himself fall a half step behind again. Whether he had some interest in her or had been trying in his own way to uncover more information, Daniel couldn't tell, but it was always entertaining to watch him fumble.

Elizabeth led them into the briefing room, which felt smaller with the blast doors closed over the gate room windows. The monitors that usually displayed the status of the gate and offworld teams had been switched off, and on the table beneath them, a carafe of water and pot of bubbling coffee stood beside a stack of cups and a plate of cookies. Bland and unremarkable, the room could have belonged to any company or hotel conference room in the world, complete with a potted plant in one corner.

As McKay made a beeline for the food, Sheppard and Carolyn arrived, presumably having taken the bodies to the SGC's morgue. While Carolyn admitted that she trusted the county ME, she'd also stated that she'd be scrutinizing his autopsy notes thoroughly. She also had a few additional tests to perform—primarily a check for the Wraith enzyme.

There was barely enough time for everyone to grab coffee before Landry strode in. Civilian or not, Larance straightened noticeably at his arrival. Daniel couldn't blame her; most people didn't bump into two-star generals every day.

"Agent Larance, welcome." Landry briskly pumped her hand twice. "Hank Landry. I'm the commander of this facility. We're grateful for any insight you can provide into the situation."

"Thank you, sir. I assure you the sentiment goes both ways." Larance's tone still held a sizable amount of caution. Daniel couldn't blame her for that, either.

While they shuffled around enough to get everyone a seat at the conference table, McKay darted a glance toward Sheppard, who frowned at him.

"What?"

"Nothing. It's…" McKay waved a hand inarticulately in the Colonel's direction, perhaps indicating his uniform shirt. "That combination, the tie and the hair—I'm just saying, it's incongruous."

Sheppard's answering look bordered on insolence. "Live with it."

"Our earlier briefing on this subject was cut short," Landry said, "so if Dr. Jackson is prepared to pick up where we left off…"

"Of course." Daniel moved over to the computer positioned against the wall and called up his files on one of the room's main monitors. The leads he'd had to follow so far were flimsy and vague enough that it wouldn't take much more than a short description of the mythological context to get the others up to speed. There were numerous aspects of the Lilith story that he was eager to pursue further, as soon as possible. The urgency of the current situation aside, it had been some time since he'd had the opportunity to do the type of pure research that had first drawn him to this field, and after everything that had happened recently he could admit to feeling the need to reconnect with his roots.

"Lilith," he began, "as Drs. Larance and Zelenka pointed out, is identified by some Talmudic texts as the first wife of Adam."

"I may not have been paying attention, but I think my Sunday school class skipped over that," commented Sheppard.

"Very likely, since she doesn't rate a mention in the Bible. Having said that, Lilith does make an appearance on the roof of the Sistine Chapel in Rome, in Michelangelo's *Temptation and Fall*." Daniel brought up an image on the monitor. In the painting, a half-serpent/half-woman creature wound itself around a tree. "Essentially, Lilith represents a compilation of fabled demons found in the Kabbalah and Babylonian mythology. One interpretation suggests that Adam and Lilith were created simultaneously and given joint dominion over the Garden of Eden. However, Lilith refused to lay beneath Adam."

Quickly swallowing a sip of coffee, McKay raised a tentative hand. "And by 'lay beneath,' you mean—"

"Yes, Rodney," Elizabeth answered briskly. "Daniel, you were saying?"

Clicking the computer mouse to display the next image, a map of ancient Persia, Daniel walked over to the screen and indicated the region between the Tigris and Euphrates Rivers. "Anyway, refusing to adopt a subservient role, Lilith invoked the name of God, an act that in many cultures is considered sacred and powerful in its own right. She then took to the air and left the Garden of Eden." He traced a line from Iraq to Egypt. "And settled on the coast of the Red Sea, where she became the consort of Samael and bore him countless *lilin*—offspring."

"And Samael is…?" Landry asked.

"Satan." Daniel pushed ahead. "According to Talmudic mythology, at Adam's request, God sent to Lilith three angels—Senoy, Sansenoy, and Semangelof—who ordered her to return to Adam. If she refused, the angels would kill one hundred of her demonic children for each day she stayed away. Lilith countered that she and her *lilin* would prey eternally upon the sons of Adam, namely humans. The Talmud further states that such children could only be saved by invoking the names of the three angels."

"Which is why," Larance broke in, "Hebrew tradition dictates that an amulet inscribed with those three names is placed around the neck of each newborn boy, to protect him from Lilith."

Her unexpected contribution took Daniel by surprise. From the curious expressions of the others, it was clear he wasn't alone.

"I didn't wander into my line of work yesterday, Dr. Jackson. If this mythology primer is all you've got, we're wasting everyone's time." The profiler started to rise from the table.

"Sit down, Doctor." Landry's voice resonated with all the authority of his rank. "Before you arrived, I had a phone conversation with your Director. He assured me that we'd have the full cooperation of the Bureau in this investigation, starting with you."

After a tense moment, Larance managed to check her obvious resentment at being overruled, and settled back into her chair. "No disrespect intended, General," she replied with cool civility. "Let me simply say that I've done the same homework as your people. Lilith appears in Roman mythology as a night demon called a strix, who stole children. The strix was a nocturnal flying creature, similar to a vampire in the way it fed on human flesh and blood, with the ability to transform into a wild animal such as a lycaon."

"Lycaon," echoed McKay, the word slightly garbled as he finished chewing a bite of cookie. "Lycanthropy—isn't that…" He swallowed quickly. "Werewolves?"

"Does this mean we have to start taking the *Underworld* movies seriously? Because that might be kind of tough." Sheppard plucked the cookie out of Rodney's hand and set it down on the table. "Two hours of Kate Beckinsale kicking ass," he muttered to his teammate, "and what you remember is the mythological *name*?"

"Therianthropy is the correct term," Daniel said. "The metamorphosis of humans into wild animals of all types—even chimeras, or creatures made up from the parts of multiple animals. They're also interpreted by some as night monsters, succubi, and vampires. Keep in mind that all these creatures are considered to be the demonic offspring or, less literally, the creations of Lilith, not Lilith herself."

"Not to mention the fact that there are known genetic disorders that can account for the existence of many of these supposed monstrosities," Larance countered, her impatience clearly returning. "Hypertrichosis can cause the excessive body hair identified with werewolves; porphyria has been explored as a potential explanation for some of the traits associated with vampires. It's the age-old story of people fearing and marginalizing things they don't understand. Based on the physical descriptions of suspects in these murders, the Bureau has already investigated Marfan's syndrome and cystathioninuria, an enzyme deficiency disease, as possible factors, with a view to tracing perpetrators through a national database of registered recipients of the prescribed medication for such disorders. None of this is news, Dr. Jackson."

"And yet," Zelenka remarked quietly, "despite this knowledge, the FBI has not managed to identify the…perpetrators, yes?"

Larance's expression conceded her frustration, either—or perhaps both—with them or with the case.

A file folder sat on the table in front of Landry, and he slid it down to the agent. "That's a nondisclosure agreement," he stated. "Your security clearance is valid, and no doubt you're familiar with the penalties for disseminating classified information. Yes, we know more than we've told you. If you want the rest, you'll have to sign that document."

Without responding aloud, Larance opened the folder and scanned the two-page agreement inside. Lifting her head, she looked in turn at each person present. Daniel, accustomed to being evaluated by more intimidating beings than her, stared back when her gaze reached him. She moved on to McKay, who attempted a smile and then uncomfortably averted his eyes—most likely the precise reaction she'd wanted. Finally her appraising look settled on Sheppard.

The klaxons chose that moment to start wailing.

"Unscheduled offworld activation," announced Walter from the speakers.

Landry and Sheppard were out of their chairs before the warning had finished. Throwing open the door, the General fell in behind the security squad double-timing down the corridor.

"Unscheduled *what*?" Larance shot to her feet, taken aback by the sudden activity. "Why in God's name are there Marines tearing around a secure facility with weapons like *those*?"

"Sign that piece of paper and you're about to find out." Elizabeth crossed the room to the windows, still blocked by the blast doors. Her brief stint in command of the SGC evidently hadn't been forgotten. "Otherwise, security will be happy to escort you to the surface."

As the alarms continued to bleat, Larance took out a pen and scribbled a hasty signature on the nondisclosure agreement. Watching her, Elizabeth brought a hand to her ear and spoke in a low voice. Daniel wasn't wearing his radio, but he assumed that she'd given an instruction to the control room, because soon the blast doors pulled back to reveal the gate room, the iris locked in place over the Stargate, while watery hues reflected off the rear wall.

The klaxons fell silent. Zelenka stepped over to the nearest monitor and activated it, displaying a video uplink from Atlantis. Elizabeth turned toward the screen, Sheppard moving to stand at her shoulder.

Seemingly without being aware of her own motion, Rebecca Larance had been drawn to the windows and now stared openly at the gate below. With the iris closed, the sight wasn't as impressive as it could have been. Still, Daniel watched their visitor and remembered the awe that had accompanied his first view of the gate, over a decade ago. Granted, for him the experience had been first and foremost a vindication of his strongly held belief in the origin of the

Egyptian pyramids. He could only imagine what must be going through Larance's mind, seeing the huge ring flanked by a pair of massive weapons. For the first time since they'd met, though, some of the jaded skepticism she wore began to slip, giving way to a look of pure amazement.

"You're kidding!" Elizabeth's exclamation grabbed Daniel's attention. "No, of course you're not. When this mission was authorized, I was assured that under no circumstances would one of those creatures be allowed through the gate." She shot a glance at Sheppard, who affected an air of contrived innocence.

On the screen, Teyla Emmagan was looking mildly chagrined. Larance's expression didn't change as she turned from the window to the screen and studied the exotic location. "Where is that place?" she asked Daniel.

"Atlantis." He didn't try to suppress his smile.

Her head whipped toward him, disbelief finally taking up residence alongside the wonder in her expression. "Not the resort, I'm guessing."

"Somewhat further away than that," confirmed Colonel Sheppard.

"And no longer lost, as you can see." McKay appeared to be bouncing smugly on the balls of his feet. "We found it a few years ago."

"We?" Zelenka echoed pointedly.

"If you want to split hairs, it was Dr. Jackson who—"

"Where?" Larance took a step toward the monitor. "Crete?" Hesitating, she glanced at Sheppard. "Antarctica?"

"Pegasus, actually," Daniel offered, distracted by Elizabeth's pinched look. "It's a galaxy approximately three million light years from here."

"Well, good work in locating the Ancient laboratory," Elizabeth was saying. "We can only hope it will offer some insight into Lilith's work. Meanwhile, just tell me that Ronon and the Marine team will take care of all the animals that managed to escape past the gate room. We can't have anything like that loose in the city."

Nodding her assurances, Teyla moved to one side. Daniel could see over her shoulder into Atlantis's gate room, where a large body lay motionless on the floor. *I'll be damned.* He'd assumed the previous mission reports had been oversimplified, but the thing *did* look like a T. rex...which opened up an alarming array of possibilities about how it had ended up in the Pegasus Galaxy.

Cocking his head, Sheppard studied the animal critically. "I think that might be the same one that almost had us for lunch a couple of years ago."

"How could you possibly distinguish one from another?" McKay demanded.

"I tend to be pretty observant when something's trying to eat me."

"Very helpful. Elizabeth, tell them not to destroy the carcass. I'd like to take a look at it when we get back."

Zelenka raised a cynical eyebrow. "Now you develop a sudden interest in biology?"

"There is nothing sudden about it! Just because you lack insight into some areas of my research..."

Everyone but Daniel appeared to have forgotten their visitor. As Larance stood there, still staring at the screen and seemingly trying to convince her mouth to close, he moved in beside her and said, "That's ours. Now, you show us yours."

CHAPTER EIGHT

"Three teams of four each," directed Lorne, fastening his tac vest. "Leads are me, Ronon, and Teyla. One gene carrier per team to operate the life sign detectors. All teams should be equipped with stunners and P-90s. Use either or both as required."

A chorus of "aye, sir" issued from the squad of Marines scattered around the armory. Ronon gave his pistol a cursory inspection and checked the locations of his blades. Chasing a pack of two-legged wild animals through the halls of Atlantis wasn't how he'd planned to satisfy his itch to hunt, but it would suffice.

"That's not necessary." Geisler hovered in a corner, visibly out of his element among the racks of weaponry. "Microceratops are herbivores—they won't hurt anyone."

"Maybe not intentionally, Doc, but you saw what they did to the gate room." The Major clipped his P-90 automatic to his vest. "They could do a lot more damage in the city than we're prepared to fix, and I for one don't want to have to explain that to Dr. Weir. Besides, you said the Earth species was only the size of a rabbit. These guys are five feet tall. How do we really know what they like to eat?"

"Because everything about them, right down to the shape of their jaws, tells me these are microceratops. Their size is purely a function of the lighter gravity on 316, I'm certain. And they're not likely to be the least bit aggressive. Just very frightened." He took a step forward, his hands imploring. "In fact, I suspect those bright red crests are an indication of terror, not anger. You also have Atlantis's higher gravity and slightly lower atmospheric oxygen content working in your favor. They're likely to tire quite quickly."

When Lorne didn't back down, Geisler fell unhappily

silent, his hands going slack at his sides and his shoulders slumping in defeat.

"We will stun them if at all possible," Teyla reassured him with a quick smile.

Ronon doubted a stun bolt would penetrate the creatures' thick-looking hide. Since he knew the Marines would be thinking along the same lines, he didn't bother to mention it.

Lorne tapped his earpiece. "Control room, you got the Operations tower locked down?"

"Done, Major," replied a technician. "All access points have been closed off, and the transporter system has been taken offline."

As soon as the animals had fled the gate room, everyone in the Operations tower had been told to remain in their offices or labs and lock the doors. The hunt, then, ought to be confined to the corridors and open spaces—although their quarry was obviously experienced in avoiding predators and might have a few tricks to play, including the ability to conceal themselves through what Geisler had earlier described as chameleon skin. Apparently the name came from another lizard thing on Earth that could change the color of its hide, an attribute Ronon had witnessed in life forms on other worlds. Despite their size, there were plenty of places in which, individually, the 'ceratops could hole up.

"All right," ordered Lorne, his eyes conveying his readiness. "Let's move out."

Leading his team down the hall, his weapon a reassuring weight in his hand, Ronon rolled his head in an attempt to shake loose the lingering stiffness in his neck. He'd struck the jumper's bulkhead a couple of times during their return from M1M-316. First time had been on the planet, when the larger animal—a T. rex, he'd been told—had knocked the craft aside. The next had been when the jumper had careened—or more probably been shoved by a second T. rex—through the gate at an odd angle, scraping against the rim of the Stargate as it went.

The control room technician, shocked into immobility by the sight of the arriving monster, had failed to respond to Lorne's command to raise the iris. For once, panic had worked in their favor, because the jumper hadn't been disintegrated when they'd reached the Atlantis end of the wormhole. Fortunately, the technician had closed the iris directly after the jumper had arrived; otherwise Ronon suspected they'd have been contending with another of the beasts in the already overcrowded room.

While the smaller 'ceratops had been running around so fast that the security team couldn't safely get a bead on them, the confused T. rex had proved fairly simple to overcome, more or less. Startled by the jumper slamming into its butt, the creature had been distracted long enough for the Marines to fire a storm of bullets. That had not proven very effective until the furious animal had swung around and attacked the jumper with an impressive set of teeth. Frustrated by its inability to find purchase on the craft with jaws that were just slightly too small to swallow it whole, the creature had reared back, promptly exposing its underbelly to a volley of concentrated fire. When the T. rex had finally crashed to the floor, the vibration had briefly fooled a monitor in the control room into emitting a quake warning.

Tossed around in the jumper's cabin, Ronon had only seen bits and pieces of the takedown, but those technicians in the control room who hadn't needed to find a change of pants had given his team a rapid if disjointed account, laced with a bunch of unnecessary descriptive words. Ronon could only conclude they'd been taking vocabulary lessons from McKay.

The enclosed space had taken some of the sport out of it, but after seeing the things up close, Ronon now relished the idea of hunting one of the T. rexes in its natural environment. Aside from a fish his team had once encountered in the Lantean ocean, he'd never before seen so many jagged fangs in one mouth.

Now, though, the problem wasn't the T. rex, but the smaller two-legged 'ceratops the meat eater had been chasing. In the short time the sandy colored animals had spent tearing around the gate room, they'd proven to be more of a threat to equipment than to people, gravity differences notwithstanding. As Geisler had said, they were obviously terrified. Scampering back and forth on powerful hind legs in search of an exit, equally powerful tails whipping around, smashing into whatever was nearby, they'd made a mess of the place before finding their way out. If they got into any of the labs—or, worse, the infirmary—the results would be ugly, especially if they started using their beaked jaws to chew on things.

"Biometric sensors have accounted for all expedition personnel in lockdown locations. It's showing a total of eight dinosaurs roaming the halls," reported the control room tech through Ronon's radio. "They've split into two groups, both on Level Seven. Looks like they've calmed down some and are just exploring."

Sergeant Hawthorne held up his life sign detector to show Ronon the positions of the teams and the dinosaurs. One team, probably Teyla's, had moved fastest and was nearing the east group of three animals from an area Ronon knew to be a skywalk one level above. The other teams were closer to the west group of five, approaching the animals from opposite sides.

"We've got five poking around the open storage area in the center of this level," said Lorne. "Teyla, can you handle the group below you?"

"We do not yet have a good line of sight." From the low timbre of Teyla's voice, Ronon knew she must be near enough to fear spooking the creatures. "They may have heard us coming, for they have hidden in the alcoves along this corridor. We will take the stairs to their level."

Rounding a corner, Ronon and his team got a better view of their playing field. The storage area was easily three stories tall with an entrance on either side. The floor was stacked with large, variously shaped containers of both Earth and Lantean origin. Mostly it held the empty packing cases for the computers and equipment used by the science division, so little would be damaged if the animals made a mess of the area. Even so, the piles of boxes and low light created a lot of hiding places. The animals' chameleon skin would work just as well here as on their planet. This would be a close quarters fight.

Through a gap between rows of metal-ribbed containers, Ronon could see Lorne arrive from the other corridor and hold up a fist to halt the team behind him. Catching Ronon's eye, the Major pointed to himself, then down one aisle, silently announcing his intentions. Ronon nodded once and signaled his plan to cover the opposite side. Also without words, he directed one of his Marines to guard the entrance. They'd try to stun the creatures if possible, but nothing could be allowed to escape back into the halls.

"I can see one of the animals' heads," Teyla said quietly, still three corridors over. "It appears to be watching its companions. The color of its crest has faded considerably. They seem more fearful, and perhaps somewhat curious, rather than aggressive."

A dull sound, like a limb or tail hitting heavy plastic, brought Ronon's gun up. P-90 in one hand, life sign detector in the other, Hawthorne silently took off toward the back corner.

A stun blast and a curse came from somewhere on the other side of the room. Ronon heard scrabbling noises off to the left and pivoted in time to catch a glimpse of hide, now the color of packing cases, disappear behind another container. Giving chase, he soon had the dinosaur trapped between two large cylindrical boxes and a wall. As he aimed his pistol, the animal raised its sloped head. The crest abruptly changed from a bland nothing color to a deep purple, and the animal looked directly at him—

—and Ronon was suddenly struck by a powerful wave of something he almost didn't recognize: compassion. Leaning slightly forward to balance itself, the dinosaur was the size of a teenaged child, with eyes set wide but forward looking, like a human's, and short front limbs like arms held close to its body. A sense of fear and loss, and a terror Ronon hadn't felt since his first days on the run from the Wraith, now hit him with a force that was almost palpable.

"Don't shoot them!" he called out on impulse, lowering his gun. As if understanding his action, the animal visibly calmed. A moment later he realized that, despite the chaos that had previously gripped the room, only one weapon had been discharged. Were the others sensing the same strange connection that he had?

Lorne's voice, heard from behind a row of boxes a few yards away, gave him his answer. "Anybody else getting a strong 'please don't hurt me' vibe from these guys?"

"This is just plain *weird*," muttered Hawthorne.

Ronon wasn't so certain; he'd had plenty of experience with the sorts of illusionary tricks the Wraith could project. While this was different, perhaps even a trick to lull them into complacency, he still had the option of shooting them. Although the compulsion he felt was strong, it wasn't strong enough to stop him from acting if he thought it necessary. As much as it went against everything he knew, this was one time when pausing to ask questions seemed like a good idea.

"All teams stand down." Teyla's urgent instruction rang in Ronon's earpiece. "These animals are docile. They have come out of hiding and are not threatening us."

Ronon stepped back, allowing the dinosaur freedom to move. Slowly, it crept toward the center of the room, where its friends were gathering. That first stun bolt must have either missed or had no effect, because all five animals now clustered together, unharmed.

"Same here," reported Lorne. "Is it possible we might be able to herd 'em back to the gate room?"

"I believe so," Teyla said. "They seem aware of our intent and our reluctance to harm them. As long as we do not frighten them further, I sense they will follow where we lead."

Ronon wouldn't have believed it, but she was right. The Marines covertly blocked all corridors except the desired path, and the five animals from the storage area willingly joined Teyla's group of three down the hall. A surreal silence reigned as the Athosian guided the small pack through the Operations tower, finally reaching the gate room.

Waiting in the control room, Geisler sprang to his feet and hurried down the steps, relief written openly on his worn features. "I *knew* they'd come peacefully. They're not built for attack."

"Damnedest thing I ever saw, Doc. Teyla the Pied Piper." With that strange comment, Lorne gestured to the gate tech. "Dial it up."

"But—"

The Major put out a hand to stop the paleontologist from approaching one of the animals. "Not here. You'll get your chance. Let's send these critters home."

Teyla stepped back to join Ronon as the activation lights began to circle the Stargate. "You look troubled," she said, making the statement sound like a question.

"I thought they might taste good," he admitted. "I was about to shoot one. I still don't know why I stopped."

Teyla nodded in a way that told him she had no answers for him. "Right now there is much we do not know."

The little dinosaurs didn't appear in the least bit startled by the vortex, and without even a glance back, they scampered through.

CHAPTER NINE

"**Y**ou know what would improve this place immeasurably? A duty-free store."

Radek opened a cabinet, stuck his arm in up to the shoulder, and came up with a handful of oatmeal cream pies. "Atlantis does not charge an import tax, but your point is well taken. I, too, was hoping for a shopping opportunity."

"I sent one of the more eager airmen off to the nearest Starbucks to stock up for us." Rodney perched on a stepstool to inventory the contents of the highest shelf.

"Most likely he will not make it back in time," Radek warned, catching the pack of pudding cups Rodney tossed down to him. "We are set to leave in less than half an hour."

"If that's the case, he can put it in my locker for our next visit. Given the size and scope of the current crisis, the odds are exceedingly good that we'll be on M1M-316 for about two minutes before being summarily ordered right back here." A large coffee can sat on the counter. Rodney examined the generic label and blew out an aggrieved sigh. "If we need to muddle through with this slag for a while, I suppose it's a sacrifice we'll have to make."

"Martyrs, all," Radek agreed dryly, sliding the can across to join the collection of snacks accumulating on the counter.

The door of the SGC mess hall's stockroom swung open. "We have authorization to do this!" Rodney called defensively, tensing on instinct.

"No, you don't." Sheppard strolled in and started perusing the shelves. "And neither do I, so how about keeping this just between us pals?"

"A reasonable arrangement. In case you wondered, the popcorn is in the third cabinet from the right." Radek tipped his head to indicate the correct location.

Breaking into a sly grin, the Colonel headed in that direction.

"So what did your FBI acquaintance have to say about our unlocked secrets of the universe once she picked her exceptionally well-formed jaw up off the floor?" asked Rodney.

"She's still getting the Stargate 101 crash course from Elizabeth and Dr. Jackson. All I've heard out of her since she first saw the gate room was a mumble along the lines of 'They're trying to reach the Stargate.'"

"'They' being the Wraith-succubus-whatever?"

"I guess. Seems like kind of a big leap to me, but then I'm not an FBI profiler who's been on the trail of these things for years."

"Years?" Rodney paused and glanced down at him. Now that he fully grasped the situation, it seemed conceivable that deaths of a similar nature might have been exasperating authorities for generations. "Hmm. I suppose that tracks, given the context."

A stack of microwave popcorn packets tucked into the crook of his arm, Sheppard eyed the large can in the scientists' pile of loot. "Don't we have plenty of coffee on Atlantis?"

"In the mess hall, yes. The inventory control officer, however, tends to get very unpleasant when anyone borrows from the citywide supply. You never should have given that job to a Marine. Have you *seen* her biceps? Anyway, we keep a separate stash and a coffeemaker in the labs. It's inefficient to keep going to the mess for refills."

Rodney climbed down from the stepstool and surveyed their take. "This will have to do. As much as I appreciate the opportunity to replenish some of our most critical stores, this visit has been little more than a waste of time and effort. We've accomplished nothing other than acting as bit players to your obligatory weekly Kirk moment. You were correct in your assessment that Radek and I, not Ronon and Teyla, should have been sent to 316 at the outset, but hey, as long as those in charge can make themselves feel better by yanking us around..."

"At the risk of sounding like an apologist for the brass," Sheppard said, leaning against the counter, "the IOA reacted to this threat pretty much the way you did. They hit the panic button."

Wasn't that just typical? "I did not *panic*," Rodney explained with far more patience than his teammate deserved. "You know I don't function well in enclosed spaces. Add that to the lemon scented booby trap planted in the SUV, which was just asinine—please tell me the base motor pool isn't in charge of pre-flighting our ride home. It would complete my day to discover that some enthusiastic airman decided to polish Jumper One's windshield with lemon Windex."

"Like I said," Sheppard continued evenly, helping Radek load their supplies into a cardboard box appropriated from a neglected corner. "They panicked, and they told all of us supposed Wraith experts to hike our asses back to Earth and do something about it. The mission to 316 was set up as standard recon because the only thing we could be sure of finding there was a really big carnivore. It's an understandable response, knee-jerk or not." He shook his head as he hefted the box up from the floor. "That said, our friends in the IOA need to wake up and recognize that Teyla and Ronon are two of our very best people for the job back here. Being an Earth native shouldn't be an exclusive requirement."

"As long as we're on the subject of bestowing enlightenment on the IOA, it would be nice if they would spring you loose to come back with us. I'm surprised Elizabeth agreed to let them borrow you." When Sheppard didn't respond right away, Rodney glanced over at him. "Did she have a choice?"

"Tough to say." The sudden tightness in the Colonel's features was a clear signal to drop the subject.

Deciding he might as well lead, Rodney started toward the door. He paused only briefly to grab one last item, a small package of cookies that had fallen behind a row of cans on a shelf. "Oh, *jackpot*." He ripped the foil open. "Ancients and Ori be damned. Divine light surely shone upon whoever invented Oreos."

"Preach it," Sheppard agreed, relaxing a little. "Save one for me."

After that crack about panicking? Not likely. Rather than reply, Rodney crammed a cookie into his mouth and stepped out into the corridor, the others trailing behind.

Stargate Command was an odd facility, in his view, and not merely by virtue of its mission. Its layout, with numerous levels and narrow tunnels leading every which way, might give an observer the impression that it was short staffed. Only in cases of emergency—granted, around here 'emergency' was a common condition—were more than a few personnel ever seen in one place. In fact, the SGC boasted a sizable research staff, but it was dispersed among many separate labs and offices, each enclosed by concrete. Quite a test for a dedicated claustrophobic, though that wasn't Rodney's primary worry. As competent an organization as it was, there were times when he wasn't fully convinced that the program's right hand knew what its left was doing. Since his life frequently depended on the knowledge and proficiency of the people in this building, he found distractions like the IOA to be irritating at best, dangerous at worst.

"Dr. Lam has only just confirmed that the enzyme found in both of last night's victims is a variant of the Wraith enzyme." Radek seemed to be addressing Sheppard. "Additionally, evidence supports Carson's theory that a variant of the *iratus* gene exists in humans and may be triggered through as yet to be determined circumstances. If that is so, its presence could be subtler than Teyla's ability could detect. Tracking a pureblood Wraith on a sparsely populated planet is one thing. This…is something else."

"In which case I don't see why Jackson can't link up his investigation into Lilith's history on Earth with whatever leads the FBI agent has been tracking." Rodney swallowed the last of his cookie and picked up his pace. There was a rustling sound as the Colonel adjusted his grip on the box. "There's no need for you stay here and play Fox Mulder with them."

"Wasn't I Kirk just a second ago?"

"When M1M-316 was last discussed, I believe you made it clear that you would under no circumstances explore any world populated by, and I quote, 'school bus sized carnivores.'" Radek had adopted an overly patient tone that set Rodney's teeth on edge. "There may have been mention of a traumatic childhood experience in a museum."

That tore it. Rodney spun around, nearly knocking the box out of Sheppard's arms in the process, and jabbed a finger at Radek. "You know what? I've had it with you lording all your inside information over me. Atlantis has an organizational chain, and one person in that chain who should *never* be bypassed when dealing with issues of scientific merit and risk is the head of science! *Why* was I kept out of the loop on this virus?"

Radek glanced at the other member of their trio, no doubt expecting backup. Sheppard didn't oblige, however. "Sorry, Radek. Same question from the military side."

"No information was withheld. I assure you, Colonel." Before Rodney could protest the fact that Radek appeared less interested in convincing him than in convincing Sheppard, the conversation moved on. "This is the nature of research in a new galaxy. Every day we are making new discoveries. Some lead to results of obvious significance; others are more difficult to categorize. While Dr. Weir reads a summary of each report before forwarding it to the SGC, no one person could possibly keep abreast of all our fields of study."

"If you believe that, you've underestimated my commitment and certainly my capabilities." Rodney had always tried to give his subordinates space to work. Evidently he'd allowed too far much latitude if things like this were getting missed. "From now on, I want weekly updates on all ongoing projects, starting with yours."

"You'll be committed then, that's for sure," Sheppard muttered.

So much for solidarity. Rodney ignored him, walking past him to the elevator and swiping his security card.

Shaking his head, Radek said, "If you wish to increase your tyranny and eliminate sleep from your schedule, be my guest. Micromanagement will not prevent situations such as the one we now face. None of us could have anticipated this—not even you."

And that was the crux of the problem, wasn't it? There was a reasonable chance that Radek was right, that Rodney learning of the virus earlier would have changed nothing. But they'd never *know*, and Rodney despised the unknown.

The elevator doors opened, and he did his best to shift his focus back to the here and now. Sheppard stepped inside first, and Radek reached in front of him to press the button for the jumper bay.

"For the time being, what matters is getting back to Atlantis." Rodney watched the lights for each floor blink sequentially, not fast enough for his liking. "Also, Dr. Lam will reduce my stress levels considerably when she examines the DNA records from all of our people—" *chiefly, me,* he chose not to say aloud—"and confirms that the expedition is free of the virus."

Radek offered a wholly unnecessary clarification. "Fragments of the virus, you mean."

"Of course I meant fragments. I hardly think any of us has been harboring the complete unadulterated virus…" A restrained cough from Radek triggered awareness. Wincing, Rodney turned toward his team leader. "Sorry. In retrospect, that shouldn't have been quite so flippant a response."

"No sweat." Sheppard gave a taut smile but kept his gaze forward. "Glad someone could forget." Just before the doors slid open, he deposited their box of provisions in Rodney's hands. Great. Well, it wasn't as if they had to pass through any kind of security screening to take this flight.

Elizabeth was waiting in the jumper bay, talking with the

lieutenant who'd chauffeured her to the SGC days earlier. Upon noticing the arrival of the rest of the group, the lieutenant quickly moved to Jumper Three's pilot seat and began working through the preflight checklist.

A brief, cool glance passed between Atlantis's leader and her military commander. Elizabeth quickly shifted her gaze to Rodney, studying his cargo with amused tolerance. "Critical supplies, gentlemen?"

"You'd better believe it." Rodney lugged the box over to Jumper Three and dumped it just inside the hatch. In his peripheral vision he noticed Landry approaching the group with long strides. "Although I can't say I'm entirely thrilled with the notion of being sent to M1M-316, a place where the average resident has teeth the size of my arm, without my team leader."

"Relax, Rodney. Lorne knows better than to let anything snack on you." Sheppard's guardedly wry tone was less than convincing.

"Be that as it may…" Rodney lingered on the ramp of Jumper Three, wanting to push further but not sure what he was up against. He had the distinct impression that there was more behind the decision to keep Sheppard on Earth than the mere fact that he happened to be vaguely acquainted with the FBI agent. The closed expression now worn by both the Colonel and the General served to confirm it.

For his friend's ears only, Rodney said, "This isn't the way it's supposed to work."

"Yeah, well, mine is not to reason why, and all that jazz." Matching his low volume, Sheppard responded to Rodney's intent as much as his statement. "Thank you. Now drop it. And put that popcorn in my quarters, or I'll kick your ass and then tattle to Teyla."

Reluctantly Rodney gave in and closed his mouth. They all could take care of themselves for a while, Sheppard included.

"Mr. Woolsey will be anxiously awaiting your report from M1M-316," Landry told Rodney and Radek tersely before turning to Sheppard. "Colonel, we have a slight change of plans. I need you and Agent Larance to accompany Dr. Jackson. He believes he knows where to find records of what this Lilith might have done after she evacuated to Earth."

"I thought he already knew." Radek's brow furrowed.

Rodney was only marginally gratified by that reaction. It appeared Radek was not entirely conversant with every aspect of this situation, either.

"In general terms. Given the information just recently provided by Agent Larance, it's beginning to look as though the details are a bit more complicated." Landry rolled his eyes. "Imagine my surprise. The original plan was for Colonel Sheppard to assist Agent Larance in continuing her investigation. Now that the good doctor has been briefed on the Stargate and in turn provided us with some very specific details that may be of some use, the IOA has asked her and the Colonel to go along with Dr. Jackson."

And the IOA always got what it asked for, didn't it?

Landry called into Jumper Three's cockpit. "Lieutenant, you have a go. Dr. Weir, we'll bump up the check-in schedule to once every twelve hours. Good luck."

"Safe trip," added Sheppard, hands clasped behind his back in a very military and uncharacteristic manner.

"You, too," Elizabeth echoed quietly.

Somewhat mollified, if not entirely certain he had grasped the entire picture, Rodney settled on a jerky wave as he activated the control to raise the jumper's hatch.

Over the hum of the mechanism, her heard Sheppard ask the General, "Sir, where exactly would a member of SG-1 and an FBI agent need to be accompanied by another field trained officer?"

Rodney had wondered that same thing. The hatch sealed, obscuring Landry's reply. Radek, though, had kept a more careful watch through the narrowing gap, and now he drew back with a wary expression.

"Did he just say *Baghdad?*"

CHAPTER TEN

John entered the briefing room in time to watch Jumper Three descend into launch position in front of the open gate. He didn't try too hard to quash the resentment that flared at the sight. Temporary assignment or not, he was being left behind, the rest of his team carrying out a separate mission three million light years away.

No matter what Landry said, John knew there was more than one reason for keeping him here. Radek's explanation notwithstanding, being kept out of the loop was an indication that you were about to find yourself demoted.

Honesty was something he'd come to expect from Elizabeth. The evasive look she'd given him in the jumper bay frankly worried the hell out of him. Of course, he was the only person around who'd had the pleasure of hosting the *iratus* virus. Dr. Lam was expecting him in the infirmary in a few minutes, so he had an evening of blood tests and cell samples to look forward to. He wasn't convinced there would be anything there for her to find, especially since he'd never produced the feeding enzyme even while he'd been infected—thankfully. *That* would have been a whole new level of wrongness. In any case, he'd made it his policy not to argue with people who wielded big needles, so he'd play pincushion like a good boy. Right now, any act, no matter how small, to persuade his superiors that he *wasn't* a hotheaded maverick who leapt at any chance to blow off an order seemed like a smart move.

John had been around this block before. He recognized the signs. While his defiance during the Asuran invasion of Atlantis hadn't gotten him exiled to Antarctica again, it hadn't been forgotten, either. Four of them had borrowed that jumper, but of those four only John had been military, assigned to the SGC, and given a direct order to turn back. The fact that they'd saved the city, not to mention General O'Neill and the IOA's pet mouthpiece, was a secondary consideration to some. Hell, there were days when he still found himself surprised that Woolsey and O'Neill's support had been enough to keep him in his post.

Since he was on a short leash with Landry and most of the IOA, maybe being confined to Earth for a while would give him an opportunity to demonstrate his value and dependability. If so, he'd take it. He'd do whatever was necessary to stay on the Atlantis expedition, because the alternatives didn't bear thinking about.

He had to smirk. *Confined to Earth, huh?* He wasn't sure when Atlantis had become such a fundamental part of his identity, but it had happened all the same.

Stepping fully into the briefing room, he raised his voice to address the only other occupant. "Kind of overwhelming, huh?"

From her place at the window, Rebecca Larance glanced over at him. Almost immediately her gaze was drawn back to the gate, now partway through the dialing sequence. When the final chevron locked and the wormhole exploded into being, she sucked in a startled breath, taking an involuntary step back. "My God," she gasped.

"I know the feeling. I got dragged into all this just by sitting in a damn chair." John joined her at the window and did his best not to clench his jaw when Jumper Three disappeared into the event horizon. The rippling blue disk disintegrated, revealing nothing but a blank gray wall behind it.

The FBI agent slowly shook her head, captivated. "It really exists," she murmured, staring out at the now quiet gate. "The portal to another world." A curl of vapor rose from the coffee cup in her hand, the contents apparently forgotten as reality provided a more immediate stimulant.

"Another galaxy, in this case." Seeing that she looked troubled, he offered a smile. "I'll admit it takes some getting used to, but it's not all bad."

She snorted softly. "I don't even know how to react to that, Maj—pardon me, Colonel."

"Try 'John' instead," he suggested on impulse. "Since at one time you were in possession of more personal information about me than just about anyone I know."

For a moment, she regarded him in silence, as if sizing up his motives. He must have passed the test, because some of the hard lines set into her features eased. "Rebecca, then," she said finally. "Since the doctor/patient dynamic is no longer applicable. John, I've spent the lion's share of my career explaining away UFO cults as a coping strategy to reconcile the ontological gap between mainstream religions and modern science. In the last couple of hours I've been given a Who's Who of known gods—or, more accurately, known false gods and energy beings. Your little operation here efficiently demonstrated to me that my profession, which dismisses such beliefs as based entirely on flawed reasoning and weak rhetoric, is itself misguided."

John had never pinned much of his worldview to any particular set of religious beliefs, or even to an absence of belief. Nevertheless, he could understand why Dr. Larance—Rebecca—might find the gate's very existence disturbing.

Possibly mistaking his lack of response for a lack of comprehension, she scrubbed at tired eyes with the side of her hand. "I'm sorry. What I got right and wrong before, and why, isn't important. What matters is *that*." She laid her index finger against the glass, indicating the gate below. "This Stargate; it's real, and in light of that fact, many things I previously labeled as mythology—indeed, all so-called mythologies—now merit serious consideration."

Her hand fell away from the window, and for a moment John caught a glimpse of something familiar in her bearing: a combination of resignation tinged with despair. He'd seen it plenty of times from military comrades, maybe even worn it himself, when setting out on a mission that carried an inescapably tragic consequence as part of its unwritten rules of engagement.

The moment passed swiftly, illusive to the point where he began to suspect it was a reflection of his concern for his teammates more than anything else. Given that Rebecca had been on this case for several years, she'd no doubt witnessed her own personal set of tragic consequences.

"Up until now," she said, "the Bureau had theorized that our suspects—the group's followers call themselves cambion, by the way, and their priests are known as Watchers—were searching for a metaphorical gateway to a place in the heavens where they believed themselves to have originated."

"That was the name of a cult, wasn't it?" He recalled the news stories, maybe ten years back. "Heaven's Gate? They committed mass suicide in order to hitch a ride on a comet."

"A spaceship hidden in the tail of the comet, but close enough. They weren't unique, aside from their matching sneakers. Dozens of cults, even a popular religion making the rounds of Hollywood, preach variations on the same UFO theme." With a sardonic smile, she added, "Dr. Jackson just enlightened me as to why I'd never been able to access any substantive information on the Seth cult from a few years ago. Turns out the leader really was a reptilian alien who'd turned his followers into zombies. Go figure."

Leaning his shoulder against the window, John consciously warned himself to disregard the fact that Rebecca was a beautiful woman and focus on her role, no matter how temporary, as a professional colleague. "So what led you to believe that this Lilith cult is trying to get to the Stargate? Leaving aside the fact that there's no way they could succeed, since the security around here is tighter than Fort Knox and Bill Gates's house combined."

The corner of Rebecca's mouth turned up. "All belief structures—religions, cults, call them what you will—share certain underlying premises that fulfill the needs of their followers: namely, the concept that the world was created by superior beings or forces, as well as the recognition of mortality and the desire to transcend it—before or after death."

"By separating the consciousness, or soul, or whatever, from the mortal body." As she'd said, a common theme. "Around here we call it Ascension. There are even some folks in the program who've dipped their toes in that pool once or twice. Thing is, that doesn't really answer my question."

She lifted her eyebrows, and he wondered if she recognized the parallel to their first encounter, when she'd been the one calling him out on his various avoidance tactics. Surely she did; it was her job, after all. "I'm still working on that answer myself," she said, glancing at the cup in her hand as if surprised to find it there. "If you're asking me how to find these…Wraithlike people, until I'm able to put this new information into the proper context, all I can tell you is the chain of events up to this point."

"I'll take what I can get," John said.

"Generous of you." Turning away from the gate room at last, Rebecca placed her neglected coffee on the side table and laid out the case in standard law enforcement style. "As far as we've been able to ascertain, the first victim was a television network executive associated with the production of a low budget sci-fi series. The Los Angeles D.A.'s office assumed that an irate, unstable fan had carried out one of the death threats leveled against the network for canceling the show."

John grimaced. "You're talking about *Wormhole X-treme*." He'd only heard about the series when some of Atlantis's more warped minds had campaigned to have it added to the city's DVD library. He still had trouble believing that anyone had actually thought it might serve as a cover story for the real Stargate program. After seeing the pilot episode, he hadn't been sure whether to laugh his ass off or sandblast the experience out of his brain.

"I understand the character of Dr. Levant was modeled

on Dr. Jackson." Rebecca's gaze shifted, like she might be comparing John against what she knew of the show, and he promptly raised his hands in surrender.

"Don't look at me. I was still in the operational Air Force when they dreamed up that fine example of quality broadcasting."

Her faint smile let him know that he'd been had. "In any event, I can take you through the details later, but for the moment I'll cut to the chase. Based on the pattern and victimologies of subsequent murders spread out over the last six years, it's become evident that this cult has identified Cheyenne Mountain as their Mecca. Apparently they were right."

Before John could ask how they might have found their way to that conclusion, Daniel Jackson appeared in the doorway, a stack of dusty books under his arm. "Good. You're both here." Without another word, he turned and continued down the hall.

By now John was accustomed to dealing with scientist quirks of all stripes. He waited patiently, giving Rebecca a shrug when she cast him a questioning glance.

Sure enough, Jackson was back in the doorway six seconds later. "Why is it that nobody ever follows me when I ask them to?"

"You forgot to have that part of the conversation out loud," John informed him helpfully.

"Ah." Jackson didn't seem bothered. "Come with me, please?"

"Sure thing." Pushing off from the window, John held out a hand toward Rebecca in an 'after you' gesture. Looking once again like she'd fallen down the proverbial rabbit hole, the agent obliged.

During his brief tour of duty at the SGC, John had stuck his head into most of the facilities in the Mountain, but Jackson's office was one of the places he'd never had cause to visit. Probably for the best, he decided as he viewed the room now—he might have destabilized something just by stepping inside. Egyptian artifacts and Ancient technology were jumbled together on every horizontal surface in the room, a few larger pieces of each shoved into corners. A dry erase board leaned against one wall, covered with smudged hieroglyphs, gate symbols, and sharp, dense Ancient lettering in various colors. On its face, the collection looked incongruous, but of course the archeologist had spent years connecting the dots between those fragile pieces of papyrus and the graceful Ancient devices that lay alongside.

Jackson deposited the books in his arms into a padded duffel bag perched on a chair. "General Landry's finishing up a call," he began, rifling through a stack of papers, which appeared to consist mostly of overdue notices from half a dozen libraries. "He—"

A cell phone chirped. Startled out of her incredulous exploration of the office, Rebecca reached into her pocket. "Got your own cell tower down here?" she muttered.

"Something like that," said Jackson, obviously not surprised by the disruption. He set down the papers, tugged another heavy volume off a nearby bookshelf, and laid it in the bag.

Rebecca read the number of the incoming call off her phone's display and frowned before putting it to her ear. "Larance."

Trying to find a place to stand where he couldn't possibly knock into anything in the cluttered room, John almost missed her quiet, shocked, "Sir!"

He glanced up to see her spine stiffen and her mouth open and close twice without sound. It wasn't tough to guess that Landry had gone over her head.

Her side of the conversation was limited to a few periodic interruptions. "Yes, sir…yes, I understand that, but…of course, sir."

Had it not been for Landry's arrival John would have smiled. Instead, he straightened as well. "What's our mode of transport over to the desert, General?"

"C-20's waiting at Peterson," Landry replied, taking only one step inside the office doorway. Maybe all the piles of random stuff intimidated him as well. "You'll have to refuel but it's the best we can do."

A subsonic Gulfstream jet was the best they could do? John hesitated. "Sir, due respect, but don't we have a couple of jumpers available to us?"

"Not for this. I don't know what would be worse—an Ancient spacecraft showing up on radar and triggering a defensive response, or an Ancient spacecraft *not* showing up on radar and causing a midair collision. Given Major Lorne's recent encounter with the inhabitants of M1M-316, we have to consider the latter a serious possibility. And I don't even want to think about trying to hide the damned thing on base at Balad." As if anticipating John's next question, Landry continued, "The *Odyssey*'s too far out of range, and her current mission's too important for her to return to beam you over. Also, all your movements while in country will have to be coordinated through Central Command, and you'd better believe they'd notice if you just appeared without having been on a recognized transport. They've got more important things to do over there than deal with our smoke and mirrors."

So they'd be on an aircraft—a cushy VIP aircraft, but still—for most of a day instead of making the trip almost instantaneously. "Understood, sir."

Rebecca put away her phone then, still looking rocked. "Can I assume that was our boss?" the General asked her pleasantly.

When she responded with a wordless nod, he smiled. "The IOA may have jurisdiction over the Stargate, but when it comes to federal employees such as yourself, the President still calls the shots. Before he rang your phone, he spoke to the Director of the FBI. Responsibility for the investigation into this cult has been transferred to the Air Force under section 11C9 of the National Security Act. As such, Agent

Larance, you have been temporarily assigned to the Stargate program."

"Welcome to the family," John couldn't resist telling her. "We've got matching outfits and everything."

The profiler fired off a disbelieving glare in his direction and quickly banished it again before turning back to Landry. "General, if I'm going overseas with your people, I'll at least need to stop by my home in D.C. for my passport."

"Not an issue," the SGC's commander assured her. "You'll be traveling on military orders; Balad Air Base doesn't have a customs checkpoint. Your Bureau ID will do fine. Someone's gone to your hotel to pick up your luggage, so it will be waiting for you on the plane."

Offering a cautious smile, she said, "I'm guessing those matching outfits won't be black suits and sunglasses. Do I at least get one of those handheld flashy things to wipe bystanders' memories?"

John had to give Rebecca Larance credit. In the span of a few hours her view of the world and her life's work had been run through a blender. Not many people could accept that so quickly. Yet here she was, trying her damnedest to roll with the punches.

"Only people with naquadah traces in their blood can operate hand devices," Jackson replied absently, opening and closing desk drawers in search of something unknown to the rest of them.

Rebecca stared at him for a long moment, apparently trying to evaluate whether or not to take the comment seriously. Shaking her head, she asked Landry, "Why Iraq? None of the murders have taken place there."

"We have reason to think otherwise." The General stepped out into the hall. "Dr. Jackson will explain on the way. A car's waiting for the three of you topside to take you over to Peterson. Wheels up in two hours."

"Yes, sir," John said, just for good measure. Landry was already halfway down the corridor.

When John glanced back, he found Rebecca giving him a piercing look, arms folded across her chest. Her foot wasn't exactly tapping, but the demand for an explanation was broadcast loud and clear. "Hey, I just work here," he claimed, backing out of the office himself. "And I'm supposed to go give Dr. Lam some blood samples before we take off, so I need to stop by the infirmary. I'll meet you guys topside."

Her voice followed him down the hall. "Still a firm believer in avoidance, John?"

He winced. Trapped on an airplane with a shrink who knew his file. They'd better have plenty of mission-related topics to discuss, or this had the potential to be a very long trip.

CHAPTER ELEVEN

"So," Elizabeth said. "Safety assessment?"

"We can make it work, ma'am." Major Lorne delivered the textbook definition of a military response.

Rodney suspected the officer would have given the same decisive answer if asked to scale the city's central tower using dental floss and a soupspoon. Across the table, Teyla and Ronon were nodding. Naturally.

"The animals won't be able to bother us inside the Ancient lab if we can stay shielded, which Dr. Zelenka says is no problem," Lorne finished.

"In order to gain access we will match the force field frequency of the jumper to that of the laboratory," Radek put in. "No different from shield modulations we have achieved in the past."

Rodney was anxious to move on. "I'll accept your word on the accessibility of the structure, against my better judgment. More important, in my opinion, is a protocol to prevent any more of those reptiles—"

"They're not reptiles," Geisler put in.

Whatever. "Those fleet-footed menaces from coming back through the gate with us. *Every* gate activation from M1M-316 needs to be preceded by a life signs sweep with a radius of at least two hundred yards."

"Five hundred," Ronon countered. "They may have gone home willingly last time, but those guys were smart *and* fast."

Hearing the Satedan err on the side of caution was unusual. Disconcerting, too. "Five, then." Rodney looked to the expedition's leader for approval.

"Agreed. Let's consider adding that protocol to our standard procedure for travel to worlds of this type. And yes, I realize that the 'standard procedure' lists keep getting longer and longer." Elizabeth rested her elbow on the table and pinched the bridge of her nose. "Are we ever going to reach a point where all our guidelines and safeguards actually become sufficient to protect us?"

"When we have learned all there is to learn about this galaxy," Radek answered. "At which point there will be nothing more that can surprise us—and nothing more to discover."

Cheery thought. "Once we arrive on the planet, we'll need to secure the gate area there as well," Rodney stated. "Not to put too fine a point on this, but I prefer to minimize my risk of being mauled by a dinosaur while coming or going."

"Bailey's team is up on the rotation," said Lorne. "Two of his guys are qualified on the AT4."

And the fact that Rodney recognized 'AT4' as the designation for a rocket launcher was a testament to how wildly his life had detoured since his first doctorate.

"Three jumpers, then." Elizabeth inclined her head in agreement. "Major, you and Rodney can split a security team between you and fly the first two jumpers to the Ancient facility. The third will stay with Lieutenant Bailey's team near the gate."

Rodney hadn't failed to notice Geisler's eager expression. Apparently neither had Elizabeth, because she next turned to him. "You should go as well, Doctor. With the activities of the cult on Earth escalating, the IOA has identified the investigation of Lilith's research as our top priority. We need as much expertise as possible on this mission."

So Rodney would get to play chauffeur this time. That always went swimmingly. Although he sincerely doubted that any research on Geisler's beloved lizards could help illuminate Lilith's work, he didn't particularly care who tagged along to M1M-316. Of course it would have been nice to have Colonel Lite-Brite around to activate any recalcitrant Ancient tech that refused to recognize Rodney's artificially triggered gene, but someone seemed to think Sheppard was needed more on Earth. In Iraq, of all places. *That* certainly sounded like an inspired distribution of resources. He also felt certain the decision had not been entirely based upon the Colonel's prior experience in the Middle East, nor on the presence of the attractive and somewhat disturbing FBI agent.

It would be painfully ironic if the Colonel were to survive innumerable confrontations in the Pegasus Galaxy only to run into a roadside bomb on his own planet. No, not painfully ironic—just flat-out painful. A man could only lose so many friends to explosively violent deaths.

Abruptly, Rodney stood. "If there's nothing else, I have equipment to pack."

Allowing him some latitude, Elizabeth dismissed the meeting. "Be ready to depart in an hour. Good luck."

Under less urgent circumstances, M1M-316 might have been an interesting place to explore—from the climate controlled comfort of the jumper, of course. The valley in which the gate was located had a certain aesthetic quality when viewed from the air. Having left the Marine team to set up a defensive perimeter around the gate, Rodney glanced out at the vista below as he eased his jumper into a trailing formation behind Lorne's.

They climbed to some fifty thousand feet, which, Geisler had assured them from his seat behind, would be sufficient to avoid the pterosaurs encountered on their initial sortie. What little Rodney saw of the land they passed over hinted at massive, striking features. Approaching what the HUD indicated was the coast, the mist thinned sufficiently to reveal steep ravines overgrown with tree ferns the size of redwoods and impossibly dramatic waterfalls. It left him with the impression of a primordial landscape, one that had been shaped but never cowed by the passing of eons. Once over the shoreline, he used the zoom function on the HUD to focus on what Geisler said were gigantic crocodilians, wading contentedly in the shallows, and plesiosaurs in a narrow channel between several barrier islands. It was evident that the plesiosaurs were hitching a ride on the tremendous current set up by an outgoing tide and funneling through the narrow shallows. Whether it was for the purpose of catching fish or for the sheer pleasure of it, like dolphins and whales surfing offshore breaks, Rodney had no idea. He enjoyed an unexpected flicker of amusement at the sight until he realized that what fascinated him was the resemblance of the beasts to the supposed Loch Ness Monster.

"What is it?"

He turned partway in his seat to find Teyla studying him. "What is what?"

"Just for a moment, you smiled," she said quietly. "It has been some time since I've seen you do so. Why did you stop?"

There was no use offering flimsy excuses. Teyla's earnest, probing stare was a more effective interrogation technique than many methods banned by the Geneva Convention. "For the same reason I started." Rodney directed his gaze forward again, noting with vague indifference that the variegated patterns beneath the surface of the ocean indicated a long stretch of tropical reef. "Those animals down there, the long-necked ones, reminded me of a mythical creature from Carson's homeland. I just…"

"He would have liked to see them." Comprehending, she laid a gentle hand on Rodney's arm. "Perhaps he sees them now. I for one would not be surprised."

The sentiment was nice, but it left Rodney cold. They'd all kept moving, kept working, in the aftermath of Carson's death, having no other choice. Those people comfortable enough to mention him in conversation seemed to manage the task without any overt emotional displays, which only reinforced Rodney's sense of isolation.

Geisler was saying something to Radek about the presence of magnesium in the caves they were approaching being indicative of other heavy metals. Shutting out the chatter,

Rodney focused on the distant horizon. Categorizing relationships had never been easy for him. Although he considered his teammates to be friends, in many ways a surrogate family even, he was the odd man out among them, the only one who hadn't come into this with some type of warrior background. Each time they went through the gate he had to prove to them, whether they realized it or not, that he could handle himself in the field. To his scientists—Radek included—he had to prove that he was worthy of being their superior. With Carson, there had been nothing to prove, and Rodney missed the simplicity of that friendship more than he would have imagined.

Sometime later, Radek's voice over the radio cut short Rodney's musings. "Starting descent and life signs sweep."

The coastline of the next continent was coming up fast. Unfortunately, just as Lorne had advised, the life signs indicator was crowded almost to the point of forming a continuous blob across the entire screen. This ocean was teeming with life, even more so than the waters surrounding Atlantis.

Rodney knew to expect unusual crenulations in the coast; nevertheless the bizarre shapes that came into sight drew a brief grunt of surprise from him. Following Lorne's lead, he leveled off about fifty feet above the crests of the surging waves. It was then that he saw the narrow cuttings and sea caves in the patterned cliffs that made up the shoreline.

Ahead, Lorne slowed his jumper and flew parallel to the coast until reaching a rather unsteady looking outcrop, beneath which was a massive arch. The roof of the arch was about twenty feet above the waterline, although that varied somewhat as foaming surf surged back and forth through the gap. Teyla's sharp intake of breath was followed by a sound of satisfaction. "The outgoing tide has indeed allowed us access."

Rodney followed Lorne's jumper through and was gratified to note that the waves only reached a few yards inside. The arch—or perhaps tunnel was a more accurate term, because it was almost forty feet long and angled sharply up—was pockmarked by miserly shafts of sunlight through a multitude of holes and long cracks. The entire formation looked entirely too unstable to Rodney's way of thinking, so he focused on the ground, much of which was covered in tangled skeins of kelp and various other items discarded by the retreating tide. The tunnel also appeared to serve as a refuge for several dozen large lizards, which fortunately scuttled away at the sight of the slowly moving craft.

Ahead of them, it broadened out into a cavern, although strictly speaking it wasn't a cavern, since much of the roof had long since collapsed and been washed away. Somewhat smaller than the diameter of the jumper, and therefore not a viable option for access, the opening was cluttered with verdant growth that almost entirely blocked the view of the sky. Rodney's incipient claustrophobia was alleviated only by a few gauzy curtains of filtered sunlight trickling through the overhead greenery.

Once past the light's soft glare, he saw that the entrance of an Ancient building was contained within quite a stunning example of dolomite flowstone. Millions of years of magnesium-rich calcium, liquefied by weakly acidic groundwater and trickling through countless small cracks, had created a roseate wonderland. Glistening pastel stalactites and stalagmites were dotted here and there with rich veins of glossy blue-black manganese oxides. Encasing entire sections of the Ancient outpost, the living rock protected it from the ravages of time even as it slowly entombed it.

"Oh…my!" Geisler declared. "Extraordinary."

"It is quite beautiful," Teyla agreed, while one of the Marines in the rear of the jumper let out a low whistle of approval. "I have seen such things in caverns elsewhere, but nothing so extensive."

Looking beyond the formations, a barely visible bubble offered a different mode of protection for what was evidently the entrance to a more recently constructed Ancient lab. Presumably the sea level had been somewhat lower when the

Ancients had abandoned the planet, making access to the lab far less dependent on the cyclic movement of the ocean.

Geisler confirmed this hypothesis with his observation. "Eons ago this entire region was underwater. That's how dolomite forms, you see: the result of coral reef building and then tectonic forces thrusting up the land. The process must be ongoing, or the mountains would have long since been eroded by the high rainfall. This tunnel was once part of a system of underground rivers exposed to the surface here and there by way of sinkholes."

"I'm filtering the life signs indicator to detect only larger animals," reported Lorne.

Rodney did the same, and the riot of color, which had previously indicated dozens of iguanas and assorted marine life in intertidal rock pools, vanished. "Small favors," he muttered.

"The iguanas are not likely to have any interest in the lab." Geisler leaned forward in his seat to offer unsolicited reassurance. "In any case, the force field will keep them at bay."

"Assuming there are no fluctuations in the power levels or the coverage," Rodney said, glancing over his shoulder. "Jurassic Park was safe, too, until the power went out."

The paleontologist's normally ruddy complexion turned a deep red. "Don't talk to me about that worthless piece of celluloid. The gross misconceptions it perpetuated in the name of entertainment…"

Glimpsing Teyla's attempt to mask a smile, Rodney was forced to recall his own vocal objections to *Back to the Future*. Of course, *his* points of contention had been rooted in hard science, as opposed to a few prehistoric bones and a lot of conjecture surrounding a few pieces of amber and some mosquitoes.

"I liked that movie," Ronon contributed from Jumper Two.

"The raptors kicked ass," added one of the Marines.

"Rodney, I am transmitting the frequency modulation

algorithm to you now," said Radek over Geisler's continued grumbling.

"Receiving." Rodney activated Jumper Three's shield and began making the necessary adjustments to allow it to merge with the lab's force field.

"...every one of you is so bloody convinced that they're *reptiles* when in fact—hello, what's this?" His rant forgotten, Geisler peered out through the windshield and up at the greenery piercing the sunlight. "My word, that's amazing. They shouldn't be able to survive in the harsh saltwater conditions this close to the coast."

Trying to follow his gaze, Teyla asked, "Are you speaking of the plants, Doctor?"

"I am indeed." Geisler got to his feet and leaned over the center cockpit console for a closer look. "The flax and other succulents that we saw outside are understandable, but those tree ferns growing over there—this is all very indicative of a constant stream of freshwater through the cavern."

Which surely would be a fascinating find if the *trees* were in any way related to their mission objective, Rodney thought, until Geisler added, "It suggests this area is still connected to the underground river that services the sinkholes we saw on our first visit. I suspect it's subject to partial flooding on a regular basis."

In which case Rodney's priority upon entering the facility would be to determine whether the frequency of the force field expelled water. In the meantime, he focused on the HUD's readings of the lab building itself. "The component materials not encased in rock appear to be a combination of standard Ancient materials and something considerably older."

"As I noted on our earlier visit, the architectural form of some of the ruins is remarkably similar to the Ancient structures we've found in the Milky Way Galaxy." Geisler was practically vibrating with impatient enthusiasm. "The Ancients must have had a rationale for choosing to come to

Pegasus when they left Earth. It stands to reason that they had other cities here—cities in excess of one hundred and forty-five million years old."

An intriguing thought, certainly, but it didn't quite add up. "If the dinosaurs had been here *that* long," Rodney pointed out, "it stands to reason that they would have evolved, at least enough that we wouldn't recognize them so easily."

"Not necessarily," Geisler argued. "Evolution isn't spontaneous or automatic; it's driven by the survival needs of a species. These animals existed for an extremely long time on Earth, even through various ice ages and continental drift. There's no evidence to suggest they would have naturally become extinct had it not been for the catastrophic K-T event. It's entirely plausible that they've maintained a stable, healthy population here without outside intervention."

"What is a K-T event?" Teyla asked.

Yet another case of a misleading acronym. While Geisler explained what was in fact the Cretaceous Paleogene event—a massive comet that impacted the Yucatan peninsula and wiped out a large chunk of life on Earth sixty-five million years ago—Rodney edged Jumper Three through the frequency-matched force field without so much as a bump.

"Don't mean to be ignorant, Docs." One of the Marines spoke up from the back. "But what do the dinosaurs have to do with this Ancient lady, Lilith? I mean, what was she doing here?"

"That's what we're here to find out." There was only one area under the force field that was large enough to accommodate both jumpers, so by default it became their landing zone. Rodney guided the craft in to settle on a largely barren rock surface inside the smaller cavern that acted as a sort of vestibule. While it also featured a collapsed section exposed to the surface, minimal sunlight penetrated a veritable screen of mosses and delicate maidenhair ferns. Shutting down the jumper's shield, he signaled to the sergeant nearest the hatch controls. "Go ahead and open it up."

Almost immediately, a sharp odor found its way into the cabin. Rancid butter, Rodney's brain labeled it, although if questioned he'd deny having any prior experience with which to make that determination. Teyla's nose wrinkled. "It is similar to the aroma we encountered at the Stargate."

"The force field repels solid objects. Air, as you've noticed, gets through just fine." He climbed to his feet and grabbed his pack as he headed for the hatch.

As the Marines fanned out around them in the twilight, Rodney joined Radek at the outer wall of what Rodney had mentally labeled the 'modern' facility. The foliage inside the force field had thrived just as well as its counterparts on the outside, a mass of ferns vying for space along those sections of the wall in receipt of the scant sunlight. This indicated that water vapor and plant spores had also found a way in, and it made him wonder exactly what the force field was repelling. "There is an entrance here," said Radek, stepping close to an unobtrusive doorway. Experimentally, he tapped a few keys on the control panel mounted beside it. "It does not appear to respond to inputs."

"To a lesser man, that might present an obstacle." The force field served as proof that the laboratory had power, and Rodney had dealt with enough of these types of controls to know which conduit directed the failsafe. He pulled a screwdriver out of his pack. Ignoring Radek's admonishment that he might trip some sort of defensive response, he worked the tool's head into the seam between the panel and the wall and slid it down the narrow gap until it caught. "Bingo." He levered the handle up and felt the conduit give way. The doors snapped open exactly as he'd expected, while behind them a brief shimmer indicated the force field had dropped.

"It seems you have missed your calling as an Ancient cat burglar." Radek aimed his flashlight into the dim space.

"I doubt the owners will press charges." Nevertheless, Rodney waited for Ronon and Teyla, weapons ready, to enter first. The life sign detector showed nothing of interest, but they'd learned long ago not to rely on 'warm fuzzies,' as Sheppard and Lorne called such dubious indicators of security.

The lab's interior, lit by a dull ambient glow, appeared to be divided into sections. The area they'd entered featured a row of darkened computer terminals against the far wall and not much else. Rodney and Radek traded a glance and each headed for a terminal. Despite Radek's attempts to activate it, his screen remained stubbornly silent. When Rodney put his hand down on a console, however, the entire row came to life.

"Go ahead. Be smug about your acquired gene." Radek's grumble had little bite. "Is this a database?"

"In the three seconds since it powered up, I'm supposed to have catalogued its contents?" Trying very hard to forget the fact that he might also have acquired unwanted Wraith genes, Rodney reached out to press another key—but was interrupted by a static-laced call.

"Major," reported Lieutenant Bailey. "Got…situation here."

Standing in the open doorway, Lorne tapped his radio. "Wildlife starting to worry you, Lieutenant?"

"Not that kind…situation, sir. Some kind of force field just popped…around …Stargate."

Rodney jerked his hand back from the console even before Radek's head swung toward him. *Off*, he thought hurriedly.

The terminals stayed active.

Well, crap.

CHAPTER TWELVE

Cheyenne Mountain, while an ideal location for a top-secret military program, lacked a couple of things most people would consider key features of an Air Force installation: aircraft and a runway. John had always done his best to not hold that against the place. Tonight, it meant that they'd needed to take a ride across town to Peterson Air Force Base in order to catch their flight.

Stepping out of the car next to the base's Operations building, he felt the evening mountain wind slice through his clothes. The snow flurries were also coming down with more vigor than before. Desert camouflage BDUs, unsurprisingly, weren't the warmest gear around, but he'd gotten used to a little cold in Antarctica. In front of him, Rebecca had put on her wool coat over the BDUs she'd gotten on loan from a member of SG-7. Five yards ahead of both of them, Jackson walked briskly toward the waiting plane, oblivious to the white flakes settling in his hair.

Rebecca waited and fell into step with John. "Sounds like there may be some related cases in Iraq after all."

"I'm sure the coalition leadership would like to see us prove that those civilian deaths were due to something other than white phosphorus." They'd been briefed in the car about their cover story for the visit, which wasn't really a cover at all. On and off for the past couple of years, there had been allegations that the coalition had killed Iraqi civilians through the use of white phosphorus weapons against insurgents. The U.S. Army maintained that the incendiary WP had been used primarily for illumination, not as an antipersonnel weapon; still, the burned bodies offered damning evidence, despite the fact that most of them had been found inside undamaged buildings with no trace of burning anywhere nearby. Since the condition of those bodies closely resembled that of the purported cult victims in Colorado Springs and elsewhere, they had good reason to investigate them. If that gave Jackson an opportunity to hunt down whatever information he needed in Baghdad, well, that was just convenient.

"Of course, if we can prove that some kind of alien influence caused those deaths, the white phosphorus explanation actually might be more palatable to all concerned," Rebecca pointed out.

"That's above our pay grade." John lengthened his stride to catch up with the archeologist. "So. What's in Baghdad?"

"More than you can imagine." Jackson started to climb the stairs that led onto the aircraft. "Before I was approached to join the Stargate program, I spent a considerable amount of my postdoctoral fellowship at the Iraq National Museum. They have—or had, prior to the lootings in 2003—the single finest collection of Mesopotamian historical documents in the world."

Following him up, John stepped onto the C-20. All of his previous MILAIR flights had involved a webbed foldout seat in the aft section of a noisy, frigid transport, so he could see why these jets were used for 'distinguished visitors.' The cabin layout made the most of its space, the plush seats oriented to allow passengers to face each other. "And we need something out of Mesopotamian history?"

Jackson nodded, selecting a seat on the left side of the cabin as if it were his accustomed spot—which, John mused, it might well be. "The first recorded reference to Lilith, also known as Lilitu or Ninlil, appears in *Gilgamesh*."

A shuffling *thud* behind John caused him to turn around in the aisle. Rebecca had stumbled over the raised threshold of the aircraft door and caught herself on the bulkhead. Flushing slightly, she raised her head and covered her misstep by joining the conversation. "I've read *Gilgamesh*, more than once. It's the cornerstone of most UFO cults. They view it, along with Genesis 6, as a literal history of warring alien gods coming to Earth and creating mankind…" Chewing her lower lip, she offered them a weak shrug. "At least put my mind at ease and tell me Elvis isn't really alive and well and on another planet."

"No, he's not," Jackson replied. "Alec Colson is, though."

Her grin vanished when Jackson continued without missing a beat, "The *Gilgamesh is* a literal history; just one that was interpreted by writers of that period in the best way they could comprehend."

While John stowed his duffel and claimed a seat across the aisle, Jackson gave their FBI colleague an understanding smile. "That's all anyone, in any era, can hope to accomplish."

"I suppose." Rebecca slid into the rear-facing seat across from John.

"*Gilgamesh* documents the Ancients' arrival on Earth, among other things," Jackson continued. "Based on what Vala and I learned from Morgan le Fay—"

"Morgan le Fay," repeated Rebecca, looking as though she didn't have enough energy left to react with surprise one more time. "As in Merlin's nemesis?"

"That's the one, although it turns out she was actually protecting Merlin. That's neither here nor there at the moment. The epic of Gilgamesh appears to explain the fate of several Ancients, both in Atlantis and on Earth. Specifically, Gilgamesh built a sanctuary for Ninlil, as Lilith was called in the Babylonian text, in the city of Uruk after she was banished 'from the heavens'. Which presumably refers to her escape through the Stargate from Atlantis."

Since Jackson seemed oblivious to the fact that he'd figuratively left his audience in the dust, John spoke up. "Not to call attention to my ignorance or anything, but can someone tell me who this Gilgamesh was?"

The aircrew secured the cabin door, and before long the whine of an idling turbofan engine could be heard. "A Sumerian king," Jackson answered. "Sumer was in the southern region of Mesopotamia, now Iraq. Uruk is known today as Warka."

"There can't be much left of the original city after ten thousand years."

"I don't expect so, especially since Lilith must have left or been run out by the other Lanteans." Jackson clicked his seatbelt into place, prompting the others to do likewise. "Based on later texts, it appears she fled to Egypt, where she continued her genetic experiments. In fact, that might explain some of the chimeras that Ra had in his service, at least for a time."

As the aircraft taxied into position on the runway, John reached into his pocket and withdrew a package of cookies. At Rebecca's raised eyebrow, he held it out to her, but she shook her head.

"Hey, half my blood's back in the SGC infirmary," he defended. He was pretty sure Lam could test him for every known ailment under several systems' suns with the number of samples she'd taken. Besides, he'd never gotten his share of the Oreos Rodney had scavenged out of the storeroom, and he suspected it hadn't been an oversight on his friend's part. Just for that, he'd asked for lemonade when the medical techs had offered him something to drink. Sure, it was winter, but he liked lemonade, and for once Rodney wasn't around to screech about its toxic qualities.

The acceleration of the jet pushed John back into the well-padded seat, and he watched as the lights of the Peterson flight line whizzed past before shrinking below them. When his cookie was gone, he turned his head toward Jackson. "I understand that the investigation into the potential victims in Iraq gives us an opening to do some poking around over there, but couldn't you get everything you need out of this book about Gilgamesh without wandering into a war zone?"

"Not everything. Translations often lack nuances of context. The modern version of the book is an English interpretation of a set of broken tablets, inscribed in one of the world's oldest written languages. These tablets were stored—"

"At the Iraq National Museum," John finished. "Didn't someone ever take pictures of them?"

"Of course, but the tablets are only a secondary aspect of the story. When I was undertaking research at the Museum, I came across several unusual scrolls in the archives that had never been translated. At the time, I was focused on Egyptian history, so I mostly noted the style of the text and moved on." Jackson leaned on his armrest and faced them. "It wasn't until much later that I learned to recognize lettering of that type as Ancient."

"Still sounds like a long shot," Rebecca said, making an obvious effort to bring herself back to the conversation. "For all we know it could be a laundry list."

When John snorted softly, Jackson said, "Actually, she's right. The only reason we have such an incredible picture of ancient Sumer and Babylon was because of their meticulous detailing of the utterly banal—like laundry and shopping lists." Gaze shifting to Rebecca, he added, "Which is why we're hoping McKay and his people can trace Lilith's last movements in the Pegasus Galaxy. Between that and whatever we can find in Baghdad, we should get a better idea of just what we're dealing with."

John looked at Rebecca and saw that her expression illustrated his own thoughts. Neither of them felt fully prepared to take on a plot that spanned ten thousand years and two galaxies. Even so, she was a professional investigator, and he had three years of experience with assorted Ancient ventures. By teaming up they'd be able to unravel this.

It wasn't as if they had many other options.

"You'll have to forgive me for being less than confident in Dr. McKay's investigative abilities." Rebecca leaned back against her seat.

Again, John had the vague sense that she was just making conversation while her mind was focused on something else. He reminded himself that she was a profiler; she saw the world with a completely different set of eyes than most people, and through the dark-side version of rose-tinted glasses.

"Don't let his shaky social graces fool you. He's the smartest person I've ever met, and we have a lot of very smart people on Atlantis." John idly rolled the loose end of the seatbelt between his fingers. "Give him a puzzle to solve and he'll get it done, no matter what. He's just twitchy about the possibility of having Wraith genes. Biology's not his favorite field, and the thought of something being able to take over his mind—"

"Excuse me?" Rebecca paled. "What makes you think *that* could happen?"

"A member of my team has Wraith DNA. Probably not the same as the occurrences here on Earth, though, since her people are native to Pegasus and were subjected to Wraith experimentation."

Her lips tightened fractionally. "Experimentation?"

"To make them taste better, as it turned out. The Ancients experimented on making people *less* appetizing, but Lilith's recipes here on Earth seem to have featured more than a pinch of Wraith." And if the profiler hadn't been freaked out before, this would definitely do the trick. "The upshot of it all is that Teyla sometimes can make telepathic contact with the Wraith. Not too long ago a very powerful hive queen took complete control of her mind and body. It didn't last long, but add that to everything else that's been happening lately and you've got a prime Rodney McKay anxiety issue."

Rebecca didn't seem as worried as he might have expected. Or maybe she was hiding her concern by studying him. "What about you?" she said.

"You mean, am I okay with the possibility that I might have Wraith DNA?" John wasn't in the mood to tell her about his 'bug for a day' episode, which had ensured that he unquestionably carried *iratus* DNA. Wraith DNA was a few generations removed.

He hoped.

"I can't blame Rodney for getting worked up," he continued. "I'm not crazy about the idea, either. At least Teyla's abilities should give us some help. And, for what it's worth, the SGC medical staff has started checking the genetic profiles of everyone in the Stargate program for any fragments of the virus."

"You're telling me you have everyone's DNA on file?"

For some reason, full security clearance or not, he wasn't sure she really needed to know the details of Carson's ATA gene therapy or the disaster formerly known as the Michael Project. He had no reason to distrust her, but while he could categorize her as a colleague, she wasn't exactly one of the team. "Let's just say that there are certain occupational hazards that even dog tags don't survive."

Changing the subject, he said, "What I don't understand is this whole ritual killing thing. If they're trying to get information, what's with the symbols? And the actions of that succubus woman on the video…she almost seemed compassionate."

Rebecca pushed a weary hand through her hair. "Even with everything I've learned today, I've got at least as many questions as I did before. Several aspects of this case still don't add up." She stifled a yawn and glanced toward the rear of the cabin. "Is there anything resembling a bed back there?"

"Should be a couple of couches in the aft compartment," Jackson replied absently. John wondered when he'd had an opportunity to travel in such style in the past. "Probably a good idea for all of us to get some sleep."

"For me it's approaching the point of necessity. I haven't seen the inside of my eyelids for a couple of continents and I have no idea how many days." The aircraft had leveled off, so Rebecca unbuckled her seat belt and stood. "Give me a few hours to clear my mind. Then I'll be ready to reexamine all the victimologies in light of this new…" She shook her head. "I don't think 'evidence' covers it. Let's go with 'paradigm shift.'"

She walked to the back of the plane. Jackson turned on the

light over his seat and pulled out one of the bulky texts he'd brought along.

John glanced over at him. "Sleep, huh?"

The other man replied without looking up. "In a while."

If that was how he wanted to spend his time, that was his prerogative, but it was late and John believed in gate lag, so a nap sounded pretty good. Since his time in the military had taught him how to fall asleep just about anywhere, he let Rebecca have the aft compartment to herself and stretched out in his seat.

The moment he closed his eyes, though, his mind turned to his teammates. Jumper Three had probably been on M1M-316 for a couple of hours already. Rodney would be ordering Radek around whatever Ancient lab they'd found, while back on Atlantis Elizabeth would be working through the day's schedule. The business of the city always went on, of course. No doubt it would survive without its military commander for a while longer.

Damn it, that was a road he really didn't want to go down right now.

John pulled his BDU cap out of his pants pocket and set it over his eyes. Rebecca's need for sleep and Jackson's penchant for dusty books meant that he'd dodged the standard conversational intimacy that tended to develop on long flights, so all he had to do was focus on preparing himself for Iraq. And the only way to do that was to catch at least a little sleep.

CHAPTER THIRTEEN

"Okay, let's approach this logically." Rodney took three steps back toward the Ancient facility's entrance, then slowed and veered off in another direction. "Only the gate is shielded, Lieutenant? Your team's on the outside?"

"Yes, and so's…DHD," Bailey replied.

"Try dialing out," instructed Rodney.

"Copy that." There was a pause, and then a muffled curse. "Nothing doing, Doc."

"What about the jumper's dialer?" suggested Lorne.

Rodney shook his head. "The DHD isn't the problem. The signal's obviously not getting through."

Although he said nothing further, Teyla recognized the gate shield to be a very large obstacle. If they couldn't dial at all, there was no way to get even a message back to Atlantis. They would have to figure this one out on their own.

"Can you disable the force field?" she asked.

From her place near the computer terminals, she saw Radek direct a look at Rodney that was undeniably accusatory.

"Oh, so you automatically assume that me opening the door had something to do with triggering a force field on another continent," Rodney snapped. "There's nothing to indicate the two events were in any way connected."

Radek's expression remained unchanged. Ignoring it, Rodney addressed Teyla. "Just give me a few minutes to get into the systems here and I'll have it sorted out in no time."

"I hope so," Radek said. "Travel time to the nearest planet with another usable Stargate is in excess of one hundred and fifty light years."

"It has to be a safety protocol, that's all," Rodney told him shortly. "No reason to panic."

"When have some of us ever needed a reason?"

With a glare at his colleague, Rodney continued to speak as he paced the room. "I concede that the force field around the gate *might* have been triggered when we disabled the shield here, in order to prevent any accidental wildlife incursions of the type we experienced on Atlantis."

"Might?" Radek regarded him with mild disbelief. "For what other purpose would the shield have suddenly appeared?"

Rolling his eyes, Rodney said, "Can't you think outside the box just once? I'm not in any way disagreeing with the purpose of a force field blocking access to the gate. I'm simply exploring the manner in which it activated. For all we know a clumsy Marine triggered it by stepping on some hidden switch."

Major Lorne's raised eyebrow suggested otherwise, but he wisely refrained from comment.

"Most likely the gate shield will deactivate as soon as we reactivate the lab force field," Rodney added. "Which we'll need to do anyway once I've established that it does in fact repel water."

"Water?" Only now did one of the Marines appear to consider that factor. Looking worried, he added, "You mean, like high tide?"

Rodney flicked his hand, dismissive. "The sea isn't going to reach anywhere near this far, as evidenced by this growth." His face twisted in annoyance as he batted aside several fronds laced with delicate orchids. "But as was pointed out earlier, if you'd been paying attention, it's obvious that fresh water flows through here on a regular basis. Additionally, I'd like to ensure those lizards can't stage an invasion."

It did not escape Teyla's notice that he'd used 'we' when identifying problems—real or perceived—and 'I' when outlining the solution. She made no remark about the disparity; she valued Rodney for the whole of his character, self-importance included…though he often tested her resolve on that point.

"While you work on that and investigate whatever data is stored in this place, I'd like to explore the area outside," Dr. Geisler said, peering out through the doorway. "These caves are absolutely fascinating, and—"

"Fine, go." Rodney had already turned back to the row of consoles, once again oblivious to anything outside his immediate frame of reference.

Major Lorne held up a cautioning hand. "Only if somebody goes along for backup. Last thing we need is for anyone to get caught out by themselves when one of those T. rexes is walking by."

"I will accompany you," Teyla told Dr. Geisler.

Leaning on a counter affixed to the wall, Ronon glanced up with a spark of renewed interest. "Me too."

"Check in on a half-hour schedule," advised Lorne, walking outside with them. "And don't hang out too long. Meanwhile, we'll set up ladders and park the jumpers up there—" he turned his gaze to the hole in the ceiling of the cave— "so access to the lab won't be dependent on the tides."

It was not necessary to exit the cave system by the archway through which the jumpers had traveled, for large cracks in the rocks allowed them passage down to the steep, shingled beach just outside. The pounding of the ocean vibrated beneath Teyla's feet as they made their way with care along the sharp outcrops, which added to her fascination with the unusual landscape. Lantea's mainland, which provided the bulk of her experience with coastal areas, had no such formations that she had seen.

When they had descended to the black sands of the beach, a visibly thrilled Dr. Geisler darted back and forth across the narrow shore, taking photographs of animals that scurried past and gathering samples of tissue or bones from the various carcasses littering the damp ground. More than a few creatures, it seemed, had been caught unawares by the recent tide. Or at least that's what Teyla had presumed until Dr. Geisler explained that such animals lived in the ocean and, upon dying, were carried ashore by the waves. The scientist showed more interest in these than in the living specimens he described as crustaceans and mollusks living in the many rock pools.

Unsurprisingly, it wasn't long before Ronon's initial curiosity dimmed. "I don't see what's useful about looking at dead things," he said, carving an arc in a patch of broken seashells with the toe of his boot. "Especially things that have been dead on your world for millions of years."

Dr. Geisler didn't appear to take offense at the implied criticism. "The Ancients brought the prehistoric animals of Earth here for a reason. What we find on this world may shed light on the nature of Lilith's DNA manipulations on Earth. Back on Atlantis, the biology division is analyzing the remains of the juvenile T. rex from the gate room. I do wish we'd gotten a better sample from the microceratops when they, ah, dropped in to visit. I'm very curious as to why they were in the gate valley, since they preferred a diet of ferns and cycads to the flowering plants that we saw there."

Stooping to examine a three-foot long carcass he had previously identified as a marine iguana, Dr. Geisler shooed away several hard-shelled creatures with long eyestalks and thin legs. The animals—crabs, Teyla was certain they were called—scuttled off with a peculiar sideways gate and clattering of bright orange claws.

"Dr. Brown's team is working on the vegetation specimens," Dr. Geisler added, scooping the remains of the iguana into a sample bag. "She sounded quite overwhelmed by the possibilities."

"Probably wondering if McKay's allergic to any of it," Ronon said, bending to pick through the remains of the opened, palm-sized shells.

"They are an unusual pair, aren't they? You have to wonder if she ever gets a word in edgewise on their dates." Eyes twinkling in the bright sunlight, Dr. Geisler stepped up to the mouth of a cave, the rock edges worn smooth by countless tides, but with many more of the butterfly-shaped shells lying just inside.

"These look like they would be good to eat," Ronon said, collecting one. Black and covered with soft growth on the outside, it was pale inside and, when held in a certain way, reflected multihued light.

"Mussels," Dr. Geisler informed them. "And yes, they are. In fact…" His voice trailed off as he examined the pile that Ronon had been sorting through.

"What is it, Doctor?" Teyla asked.

With a puzzled smile, he shook his head. "Something has certainly been feasting on them. Possibly a large octopus, except…" He turned his attention to the interior of the small sea cave. "There appears to be a blowhole or two in the ceiling. Think we could go in for a bit without getting turned around?"

From where Teyla stood, it appeared to extend inshore a considerable distance, curving in the direction of the Ancient facility. Based on their first visit in the jumper, it was not inconceivable that the caves were linked. She exchanged a glance with Ronon, only to confirm what she knew his answer would be. His sense of direction surpassed hers, and that was not an easy task. The Satedan slipped his weapon out of its holster and held it loosely at his side. "Why not?"

The three of them started inland. "Doctor, you mentioned that the animals that escaped in the city—the microceratops—ate certain types of plants," Teyla began. "How do you know this if they no longer exist on your world?" Though more tolerant of the Earth team's scientific pursuits than Ronon, she was willing to admit that she didn't grasp the significance of the numerous tests they had planned.

"It's all about comparisons," replied the older man.

The shells covering the steep gradient of the cave floor quickly came to an end, and a series of natural steps, where sections of rock had given way, led them well above the high tide mark. Mossy growth padded the cave's floor as they moved further along. There was no need for her flashlight, for daylight continued to find its way through several cracks overhead, and a large pool of filtered sunlight illuminated a section of the cave some distance ahead of them, promising an opening to the outside.

"In my work," Geisler continued, moving cautiously forward up the incline, "we study the fossilized remains of long-dead animals in order to find anatomical similarities to species that are still living. Through analogy, we can make informed guesses about what the extinct animals looked like, how they walked, and so on. Teeth indicate diet, for instance. All these factors contribute to a general picture of their behavior."

"So?" Ronon wanted to know. "What's the point of learning about something that can't hurt you anymore?"

Although Geisler's sigh was soft, it echoed off the surrounding rock. "Many pursuits on Earth don't revolve around countering threats, son. I suppose that might be tough to understand out here."

"Not as difficult as you might think," Teyla felt compelled to respond. Her singing, indeed the creative endeavors of many of her people's artisans, had never been undertaken to 'counter threats'. "Fearsome though the Wraith are, we would have nothing worthy to defend if we allowed them to dominate every facet of life."

In the dim light, she saw Geisler's nod of acknowledgement before he replied to Ronon. "On our world, most weapons evolved from tools, which were products of necessity, and those in turn gave us time to explore our creativity and curiosity, two of the defining characteristics of the human race. Something of great interest kept the Ancients returning here for millions of years. We know that they chose this planet to protect a biosystem now extinct on Earth, and we know that a product of the research on this planet was introduced into Earth's human population with potentially disastrous results. Exploring those links may give us a defense, or even a weapon, to use against the Wraith—if not all Wraith everywhere, then at least in the form Lilith gave them on Earth." He offered Ronon a quick smile. "To vanquish an enemy you must understand it well enough to exploit its weaknesses. Species do not spring into existence fully formed. Each has a history, and knowing the history of the Wraith may provide us with the key to their weakness."

Any response Teyla might have given was pushed out of her thoughts, for they had emerged into a sunken glade inside the cavern. She could almost imagine it to be the bottom of an enormous, shallow well, the rim just out of reach.

"Another old sinkhole," Geisler declared.

Sunrays spilled through branches weighted down with clusters of seeds and the peculiar spade-shaped leaves that seemed to dominate much of this world's landscape. The scene was tinted a dozen shades of green by the vegetation thriving on every available surface. Richly colored blossoms wove in and out of thick vines that trailed down to the floor, from which a few slender saplings reached up, angling for position under the best light. It was a breathtaking sight, a pocket of beauty springing out of nowhere. "How can such things grow in this place?" she asked, reaching out to stroke the petals of a deep violet flower with an enticing scent. Several tiny bees flitted between the blossoms.

"It has all the requirements," Geisler said, sounding less surprised than her but every bit as captivated. "We're well above the high tide mark. There's light, freshwater from rain, and compost from the unfortunate animals that have fallen in." He bent low over a rotting carcass.

On an issue that had been occupying Teyla's thoughts for some time, she said, "Doctor, can you explain the sense of empathy we experienced with the microceratops on Atlantis? I have never encountered such a connection to an animal before."

"Extraordinary, wasn't it?" Geisler held an ineffectual

hand over his nose as he prodded the remains of what looked to have been a four-legged animal. "Most mainstream scientists have discounted the notion of genetic memory ever rising above the most basic, instinctual level. I was one of them until I learned of the Goa'uld." He withdrew a measuring instrument from his overloaded pack. "And, as you well know, the Wraith exhibit telepathy. It's entirely conceivable that intelligence and communication developed on this world with or without genetic manipulation. Of course, such abilities wouldn't have evolved in isolation."

Ronon was standing on his toes, attempting to get a better view of the forest outside but finding the walls too high. "What do you mean by isolation?"

"Nothing evolves without reason."

Teyla noticed that Geisler was frowning as he talked. Perhaps he was intent on extracting samples from the carcass, but she sensed in him a growing disquiet.

"It's more of an ecological arms race." He ceased in his movements and slowly stood. "To catch sufficient food, meat eaters became faster and more powerful, so plant eaters developed agility or heavy armor to defend themselves. The meat eaters grew even larger in response. In this case, the emotional influence wielded by the microceratops affected us, but it didn't seem to slow the T. rex that was chasing them, so…"

The lack of any sort of conclusion to his statement, and the look of apprehensive realization dawning on his face, set Teyla on edge. Obviously Ronon was of like mind, because he demanded, "What?"

Geisler stared distantly at the rough wall, the smell and the humid air forgotten. The slight ruddiness usually present in his features abruptly vanished. "That projection ability could only work on a being capable of feeling compassion. It apparently doesn't exist to combat T. rexes, which means that something considerably more intelligent resides on this planet—something large enough to hunt microceratops."

He didn't voice the obvious conclusion: *something that*

may or may not be friendly to us. Teyla wasted no time in activating her radio. "Rodney, this is Teyla. If you have not yet reactivated the force field around the laboratory, do not wait for us before doing so. We may have more reason to be concerned with speed than we once thought."

She waited for a sharp-tongued response that never came. "Rodney, are you receiving?"

"The mussel shells!" Geisler whispered. "God, I should have recognized the evidence straight away. They weren't cracked open. Something pried them apart—something with dexterous hands!"

Still nothing, not even the hiss of static that often plagued transmissions sent through rock. "Major Lorne? Lieutenant Bailey?" Teyla's fingers tightened around the stock of her P-90. "Any team member receiving this message, please acknowledge."

No reply.

Before she could direct them back to the cave's entrance, the scientist inhaled a startled breath, wide eyes fixed on something over her shoulder. The instrument and sample kit tumbled from his hands as he took a fearful, faltering step backward. When he at last managed to force his voice to obey, he could articulate his terror only in a fractured whisper.

"*Raptors.*"

Teyla turned very slowly in place and felt a cool, tingling dread settle over her. A pack of reptilians, two-legged and mottle skinned, had somehow approached in absolute silence—incredible—and now blocked their path. This time, there was no projection of empathy.

Perhaps not all the unfortunate animals in this cave had been merely victims of a fall.

His weapon already drawn, Ronon shocked her with his sudden grunt of pain. As she stood frozen, he clutched at his head, giving a harsh, wordless cry, and collapsed to the ground, crushing the flowers beneath him.

CHAPTER FOURTEEN

When Daniel had last traveled to Iraq, the ink had barely been dry on his PhD, and he'd spent much of his stay in abject awe. Consumed by the depth of history all around him, the modern state of affairs at that time had only registered as an afterthought. In the years since then, he'd learned, sometimes the hard way, that there was no set point at which the past could be distinguished from the present. Yesterday or five hundred years ago—both were linked to today, and often both were equally relevant.

On this visit, of course, recent events were undeniable. From the air, Baghdad hadn't looked markedly different to him, until he'd sought out a few specific landmarks and found them crumbled or missing. It wasn't until they were on the ground that he'd really begun to wonder if this was the same country he'd known.

Landing at Balad Air Base, one of the nerve centers of the coalition forces, Colonel Sheppard had done the talking for their unusual trio. Although Daniel could communicate in twenty-three Earth languages, he'd never truly adapted to military speak, so he was comfortable with letting Sheppard arrange a convoy for him. The SGC had always been officer-heavy; out here a lieutenant colonel was a pretty high rank. Possibly as a consequence, Sheppard seemed more reserved than usual, more…well, more like a lieutenant colonel. In any event, he'd gotten Daniel's ride arranged in record time, and he'd been the only person not visibly surprised to see an archeologist ace the annoying yet compulsory qualification to carry a nine millimeter sidearm.

Now, as the armored vehicle passed through scarred streets, where passersby moved quickly past shattered storefronts and ducked their heads away from the military presence, there could be no doubt that this was a war zone. On Daniel's first visit, the people had been ruled by fear; this time the fear had been replaced by chaos. Which was worse, if there was such a thing as 'worse,' wasn't for him to say. Wars had defined this society's existence since the dawn of civilization—and there was an oxymoron if ever he'd encountered one. Nothing, certainly not civilization, evolved without struggle, which in a perverse way explained why the culture here was so rich, so vibrant. Throughout the millennia of one ruler after another tearing the region apart, society—and the everyday men, women and children who made up that society—struggled to cling to some semblance of a normal life.

Daniel looked out the vehicle's small, reinforced windows and wondered just how worried he should be for his safety. The squad of soldiers accompanying him had modified a routine security patrol in order to deliver him to his appointment at the museum. While the soldiers would stay with him for the duration of his time away from the base, he was nonetheless on his own. He had no need for a translator, and Sheppard and Larance were heading for the coalition's pathology lab to examine the evidence gathered on the burned bodies.

They'd agreed for the sake of convenience to call the focus of their mission 'the Lilith cult,' even if the moniker didn't perfectly describe what they'd agreed was some sort of organized group of succubi and incubi. Since nobody on Earth outside of the Stargate program was familiar with the history of the Ancients—and absolutely no one on the planet knew their language as well as Daniel—the idea of such a group finding its way to Iraq concerned him more than the threat of an insurgent attack. While these people might not be Wraith, the pattern of their murders indicated that they were endowed with the Wraithlike ability to draw information as well as life from their prey, a vital clue that had given Rebecca Larance the critical link she'd been looking for.

On the flight, she'd detailed the pattern of victims in the U.S. that had led to Colorado Springs and, presumably, the

Stargate. Daniel agreed with her assessment that the postmortem display—the gate icon and the removal of the victims' hearts—was symbolic rather than functional, although it was likely that the cult members were unaware of that fact. Plenty of religions, particularly those who worshipped supposed gods such as the Goa'uld and Ori misrepresented themselves to be, continued to engage in rituals whose meaning had been all but lost to time. This 'Lilith' group had had a full ten millennia of secretive existence in which to evolve its rites and customs.

Unfortunately, that didn't provide any insight into the bizarre pseudo-feeding behavior they'd seen on Woolsey's tape, nor did it explain why victims had also been found in Germany, Australia, or New Zealand.

Or Baghdad.

Agent Larance had confirmed McKay's fears: something she referred to as the 'Awakening' in the Lilith doctrine appeared to be a direct reference to activating the genes responsible for the retrovirus in the population at large. Still, that couldn't have taken place just yet, or they'd be seeing victims without the ritualized behavior and attempted cover-up. More likely, now that Daniel thought about it, the cult was searching for something in addition to the Stargate—and he had a sneaking suspicion he knew what it was.

Finding the Stargate was only half the battle. Finding the right address was a very different proposition.

The trio of vehicles drew to a halt outside the angular, turreted building that had once opened Daniel's eyes on so many subjects. He waited for the sergeant in charge of the convoy to perform a quick visual sweep of the area before waving Daniel outside the vehicle. Four soldiers formed a knot around him and hustled him into the Iraq National Museum.

Since the Museum was again closed to the public, the emptiness of the main hall and the echo of their boots across its tiled floors evoked memories of after-hours research, many nights that had vanished out from under him while he'd pored over a revealing text. The illusion vanished when Daniel turned a corner and found most of the hallways sealed shut with concrete, an attempt to protect the priceless treasures within from further looting. It was those ugly gray barricades more than anything else that signaled to Daniel the walls that now separated the people of Iraq, and all of mankind, from their cultural heritage.

Tariq Zahwas's office was right where he remembered it, though apparently that was also soon to change. Unaware of the visitors, the gray-haired museum director flitted back and forth across the cramped space, gathering personal possessions. When Daniel got his attention with a knock on the doorframe, Tariq dropped the books in his arms into a box. "Daniel Jackson, is it you?" He hurried to clasp his guest's hands with the same effusive hospitality Daniel recalled from their first meeting. "You look so very different. The hair…" His wide, honest smile dissolved as he took in Daniel's desert fatigues, matching the uniforms of the soldiers flanking him.

"I'm not with them," Daniel told him, only to wince inwardly. "Well, of course I *am* with them, but what I mean is that I'm not in the military. These men are here to keep me out of any local trouble."

"Of that you will find no shortage." Tariq studied him, still looking anxious and uncertain. "While I am pleased to see you again, my friend, why have you come?"

Daniel frowned and repositioned his glasses, already coated in dust from the short walk between the vehicle and the Museum's entrance. "You didn't get my message?"

A shadow crossed the older man's deeply set eyes, and his features darkened. "I received no word of your visit, which is not unexpected. Communications to my office are now—how shall I say—*vetted* by my new superiors in the Ministry of Antiquities." He laid another book in the box with perhaps a little too much force, and Daniel realized he wasn't packing to move to a larger office.

Dr. Tariq Zahwas had long been one of the most charismatic and passionate champions of his country's legacy as the birthplace of human civilization. In the weeks before the Gulf War, he'd convinced the Ba'ath leadership to have the bulk of the Museum's collection moved to secret underground bunkers. During the next nine years, while the Museum had remained closed to visitors, Tariq had continued cataloguing thousands of irreplaceable artifacts, including the parchments and clay tablets that had brought Daniel to see him today.

Tariq's dedication to the Museum had made him an institution in his own right. The idea that he would even consider leaving was incomprehensible. "I'm sorry, Tariq," Daniel said. "I don't understand."

Under his thick gray mustache, Tariq's smile was tinged with resignation. His hand closed around Daniel's shoulder. "Come. We have time for a coffee. You can tell me all about what has happened in your life over these many years. Mine…" He made a listless gesture. "You know what there is to know."

"Apparently not all of it," Daniel answered quietly, tipping his head toward the open box.

They were rescued from the awkward silence by the sergeant standing behind him. "Sir, our orders were to bring you here and then back to base. I can't allow you to go out on the streets."

"That was not my intention," Tariq assured the Marine, his gaze sharpening. "I am well aware that lingering on Haifa Street is not safe for anyone, let alone an American."

The sergeant accepted the mild rebuke without comment. Daniel followed the Museum director down the hall, the soldiers trailing them by a few steps, to a communal staff area. A half-dozen employees seated at a table pointedly cut short their animated conversation. Daniel assumed they were reacting to the sudden military presence, but their gazes as they rose to leave the room were directed instead at Tariq.

When the archeologists were alone—or as alone as they ever would be with a quartet of well-armed men keeping a respectful distance—Tariq moved to the coffee pot on the counter and poured two cups. "Five years ago, some months before the current conflict began, I once again had the majority of the Museum's most valuable pieces moved to the vaults under the western side of the city. As soon as it became clear that war was inevitable, I then had thousands of additional artifacts moved to secret bunkers elsewhere in the country. My entire staff swore on the Quran that they would never reveal the location of those bunkers." He handed a cup to Daniel. "Your government kept its word that the Museum would not be targeted, even though the Republican Guard engaged your forces from within these walls. Of course, the lootings were almost as bad as a bomb would have been. Every office and safe was ransacked; fires were lit throughout the building."

"I know you've worked incredibly hard to assist Interpol and our FBI in locating many of the stolen items."

Tariq nodded. "Forty thousand manuscripts and several thousand artifacts have been recovered. The pieces hidden earlier remain so, protected by devoted servants of history. We dare not return them to the Museum because of the ongoing danger."

Most of this wasn't news to Daniel, but the man deserved better than impatience. "If you'll forgive me for being blunt, Tariq, that doesn't tell me why you're leaving."

With a heavy sigh, Tariq rubbed thick fingers, calloused from hundreds of hours spent in Iraq's innumerable archeological sites, against his mustache. "I am…unpopular with the current regime, for several reasons," he said finally. "I was a member of the Ba'ath Party. While I am hardly alone among former government officials in that regard, I also have the less common distinction of being a Christian. The people who have been appointed to the new Ministry of Antiquities have no understanding of archeology. Being devout Muslims, they wish to focus our limited resources on the country's Islamic heritage."

Suddenly, Daniel understood Tariq's quiet outrage, and quickly suppressed a surge of anger welling in his own gut. Iraq's history encompassed six thousand years—longer, in fact, for it truly was the cradle of civilization and thus contained the heritage of all mankind—not only the thirteen hundred years since the time of Mohammed.

After he took a sip from his mug, Tariq continued, "I also worry for the safety of my family. In the past month, many of my staff have been killed, some apparently with burning chemical weapons."

Daniel had spent years cultivating a pokerfaced expression, but it was of little use when swallowing overly strong coffee. A painful gulp resulted. Fortunately, Tariq seemed not to notice. "People are blaming the American military," he said. "I believe otherwise. My staff swore to keep secret the whereabouts of our hidden artifacts, and yet we revealed the sites to U.S. authorities. I fear that fundamentalists are using a covert store of chemical weapons to seek revenge for our perceived treason." He shook his head. "Whatever the motive may be, I have been threatened quite enough for one lifetime. I have accepted a position in Rome and will take my family there as soon as possible."

"I can't blame you," Daniel said honestly. "I must ask you for something before you go, though. There's a set of tablets—it's very important that I find them. I'm hoping they're in one of your secret storage locations, and because time's a factor I'm also hoping you can point me right to them."

"Of course I will do my best to assist." Tariq set down his cup, clasped his hands together on the table and examined him with interest. "What is it that you seek?"

"The original Sumerian King List and the *Gilgamesh*. They were initially found with manuscripts whose dates never made sense."

"I recall cataloguing those items for storage. The fact that no one has ever been able to translate the unique writing on the manuscripts seemed significant." Tariq's expression suggested that a good news, bad news scenario was coming. "A facility in Ramadi holds these pieces. I can show you how to find them. How you reach Ramadi…in that, I cannot help you."

Dredging up a mental map, Daniel felt an immediate tug of war between anxiety and frustration. The capital of Al Anbar province, Ramadi was about ninety miles from Baghdad. Ramadi itself was hardly considered safe—and to get there they'd have to go through Fallujah, widely recognized as one of the most dangerous cities in the most incendiary region on Earth.

Piece of cake, right? As much as he understood the rationale, he was starting to resent General Landry's reluctance in allowing them to use a jumper.

Tariq led Daniel back to his office. He printed out a map and scrawled a series of letters and digits in the corner. "There are over two hundred containers in that location. This is the catalog number of the one you need."

"Sirs, we're running behind," the sergeant broke in. "Procedure dictates that our convoys not stay too long in any one place."

Of course. Daniel exhaled a forceful breath. He wanted to be able to tell his old friend and mentor just how critical this information was, to explain that someone *had* in fact translated the Ancient language and that those tablets might hold the key to saving innumerable lives, possibly on several planets, if they contained useful notes on Lilith's work. Since he could say none of those things, he simply offered a weak smile. "Thank you, Tariq. You have no idea how much you've helped."

Thankfully, Tariq didn't push. "Some day you will visit Rome and tell me," he said simply. "It has done me good to see you, Daniel. People who truly understand what it is we do…they are becoming harder and harder to find in a world that seems to have forgotten that our future is firmly rooted in our past."

The Museum director walked with his guest down the front steps of the building. The soldiers mounted their vehicles while he shook Daniel's hand again.

"Give my best to your family," Daniel told him sincerely, then climbed into the rear seat of the first vehicle.

As the convoy pulled away from the curb, he spared a moment to consider the future of the Museum now that it had lost its primary advocate. The end of an era—

An explosion rocked the vehicle, lifting the back end and slamming Daniel's head into the seat in front of him.

"Shit—IED!" bellowed the sergeant. "Go, go, go!"

Improvised explosive device, Daniel's scrambled brain provided. The driver jammed on the accelerator, only to brake again when a truck blocked the road ahead. Vision swimming, Daniel tried to turn around to see what had happened. All he could make out through the choking black smoke was a severed leg and a charred, unidentifiable heap on the steps where Tariq had stood.

Daniel had only a split second to wonder who had been the target of the ambush before a second impact threw him out of his seat and awareness was ripped away.

CHAPTER FIFTEEN

It had been a while since John had spent any time in a traditional military unit, and he'd never before worn a lieutenant colonel's oak leaves around this many young enlisted. His arm was starting to get tired from returning salutes. Ironic, really, since he was little more than hired help when compared to the two people he'd accompanied to Iraq.

Rebecca Larance seemed to be in her element in the coalition's pathology lab and morgue, moving from table to table with a brisk professionalism that implied she knew exactly what she was looking at. Peering through a microscope at a tissue sample, she asked her fellow FBI agent, "This was one of your contacts?"

The agent, a redheaded, freckled guy whose name John had already forgotten but who apparently had worked with Rebecca before, gave her a nod from his place against the back wall. "We were working with her on the ongoing efforts to recover the Museum's looted antiquities. Locals claim her home was hit with Willy Pete, but there was no evidence of that in the building. Then there were those weird symbols I showed you. The rings and triangle thing."

"There's also no chemical residue present in this or the other bodies you've shown me to suggest white phosphorus." Rebecca straightened up from the microscope. "These victims show the advanced decrepitude common to my other cases. It's safe to say they're linked."

"Same M.O. on the other side of the planet?"

John waited to see how Rebecca would deflect her colleague's curiosity. "It's a small world after all," she deadpanned. Her phone chirped, and she unclipped it from her belt to read a message off its screen. "Bingo. We've got what we need, Colonel." She looked up and offered him a cryptic smile. "Shall we head back?"

'Back' in this case meant the Air Expeditionary Wing headquarters, where they'd been given space to bunk and talk tactics. John raised his eyebrows at her. "You work fast."

"She's just that good." The other agent grinned and, pushing himself off the wall, walked over to join them. "You'll write up your findings for the local division and for Washington?" he asked Rebecca.

"I'll send you a copy," she promised him, offering him a smile as she packed up her notebook and laptop. She seemed a hell of a lot more relaxed after getting some sleep on the flight. "For the moment, you can at least reassure a few Army colonels that their guys are off the hook for these deaths." Her fingers reached unerringly for the pair of sunglasses that had been propping her hair off her face, and she slipped them on.

Assuming she'd relay the contents of the text message when they'd ditched her Bureau cohort, John didn't push. Instead, once they were outside the autopsy bay, he hailed the motor pool corporal to find them a ride back across to the Air Force side of the base.

Before long he was behind the wheel of a Humvee, rounding the end of the flight line. The bright sun and warm, arid landscape made for a hell of a contrast against the frigid grays they'd left in Colorado.

Rebecca spoke first, beating him to the punch. "I suppose this must look a lot like Bagram." She gestured to the activity surrounding the rows of helicopters, many receiving maintenance and being loaded with cargo or weapons.

Uh-uh. We're not going there. "I wouldn't know, these days," he said. If his tone was a little abrupt, well, he'd live with that. "Afghanistan was a long time ago for me. What was the message you got back in the lab?"

She cast a quick glance over at him, otherwise not reacting to the brush-off. "Details," she answered levelly. "Based on that and what we just saw from the bodies here, I think I have a more comprehensive profile of the…cult."

"We still sticking to that term?" They weren't Wraith and they weren't entirely human, but he supposed they couldn't go around calling them incubi and succubi, and somehow ''buses' didn't cut it.

"Admittedly it doesn't fit the Bureau's definition. The Lilith worshippers don't actively seek membership or solicit money."

John took the corner at a higher speed than might have been advisable; he didn't get many opportunities to drive a Humvee. "On the other hand, they do literally suck the life out of people, so…"

"So they're distinctly abnormal." Holding onto the door-frame, Rebecca didn't comment on her chauffeur's skills. "Given that their members carry a specific set of genes, it raises an extremely difficult ethical question I suspect we may have to face at some point. What does it mean to be human?"

To his ears, she sounded uncomfortable with that prospect. He found the entire issue pretty disturbing himself, especially since he'd had to deal with it from a very intimate perspective. Sometimes he found himself wishing he could see things with Ronon's single-minded clarity.

Sidestepping the issue, she added, "Outside a purely legal framework, the term 'cult' is still applicable. While their genetic makeup may drive them to behave as they do, as a group they're acting on a mythology, a belief structure. One based on fact, to be sure, but still largely ritualized—other-wise we wouldn't be seeing behavior like the removal and souveniring of organs, or the positioning of bodies within those symbols."

As she stared through the windshield, John had the impression she was focused on something other than the squat, non-descript buildings and 'severe clear' sky.

"In any case, the term 'cult' is applicable in a psychological context," she continued. "They've existed since Babylonian times, so there's nothing unusual about it from that point of view. The group never made it onto our radar until recently because as far as we know—or knew—its members had never engaged in any overtly illegal activities. It's just the alien bent that's eye-catching. But even that's common. Despite Freud's claim that religion is a neurosis, Karl Marx recognized its usefulness as a socializing tool. Bottom line is that people need some form of spiritual guidance, something beyond themselves, and they look for it in all sorts of places. Some find comfort through the worship of one ancient god or another; others see the image of the Virgin Mary in a grilled cheese sandwich or a fence post."

"I once convinced Rodney that his Jell-O was trying to show him how to optimize Atlantis's power grid." John shrugged. "In both my defense and his, we all were pretty sleep deprived at the time. Anyway, the Lilith cult got the FBI's—or at least your—attention not too long ago. You were saying?"

In his peripheral vision, he caught the ghost of a smile. "The followers saw their Gate of Heaven on television in *Wormhole X-treme*. They labeled it, as did a few other paranoid and generally delusional personality types, as a government-sponsored attempt at a disinformation campaign."

"Aside from the sponsorship thing, that's more or less true."

Wincing, Rebecca shook her head. "As I've noticed. Still, the facts notwithstanding, there are some pretty wild notions out there. Hell, one group of…'fans' is convinced we waged war on Iraq to acquire Saddam's Stargate. The profile I'm working on, the one I'll be writing up tonight, goes something like this: The Lilith cultists differ from the textbook conspiracy theorists in that they saw the show as a sign, one heralded in their texts. The gate is their version of the Holy Grail, or maybe a better analogy would be the Ark of the Covenant, because to them it's a literal doorway to their origins in the heavens—another galaxy. One of them fed on the network executive and in so doing gained information leading to D.C. Further attacks thereafter provided pointers to Colorado

Springs."

Her head turned to follow the sudden rumble of a helicopter starting up—John identified it by the engine sound as
one of the Hawk variants. Continuing, she said, "The cultists
were smart in a couple of ways. They concealed their activities by burning the buildings where their victims bodies'
were left, and until now they'd managed to avoid drawing
attention from the only people who might recognize their aim:
the SGC. They haven't killed anyone directly involved with
the Stargate program, because they knew they had plenty of
time—eleven years—to fulfill what they see is their destiny."

John frowned, wondering if he'd missed something.
"Where'd you come up with a specific timeframe?"

"It's in their set of doctrines." Rebecca threw him a self-
deprecating smile. "It's my job to know as much about them
as they do themselves. In their scriptures it's written that,
eleven years after the 'revelation of the truth hidden in plain
sight,' the misuse of the Gate of Heaven will allow the forces
of evil—meaning aliens with godlike powers—to prey on
Earth." Her gaze returned to the front windshield. "Either the
creation of the television show or the SGC's standard operation of the gate could be interpreted as misuse, and one of
those at least is in plain sight."

"What, you think we never should have used the gate?"
John retorted, immediately getting defensive. He hadn't been
a part of that decision years ago, but he sure as hell considered
himself a part of the program now. "Should've just locked it
up in some vault? You have no idea what we've discovered
out there—"

"Easy, Colonel." Rebecca lifted her hands in surrender.
"Whatever else you might say about the Stargate program, it
did expose humanity to predation. I'm not in a position to pass
judgment; I'm just showing you the situation from the viewpoint of the cult. Their doctrine tells them that these metaphysical alien gods need human souls to give them power, in

order to finally subdue and destroy the forces of good. God and Satan battling over immortal souls—it's the same dualistic 'good versus evil' premise employed by virtually all religions."

"Not to mention plenty of comic books."

Rebecca glanced over at him with mild amusement. "Where do you think they get their ideas from? Books, movies, games—the most successful stories are all based on mythology, even if they create their own. Anyway, fast-forward eleven years from the premiere of *Wormhole X-treme* and we end up with 2012. A dozen cultures and countless New Age cults, citing the Mayan calendar and others as guides, have marked that same year as the arrival of Armageddon, the Apocalypse, whatever you want to call it. That coincidence is a powerful reinforcement to the Lilith cult's convictions. 2012 will mark eleven years after the gate was first seen to be the 'revelation of the truth hidden in plain sight.'"

"Which proves right off the bat that they've got a couple of screws loose," John said, pulling the Humvee up to the Headquarters building. "*Wormhole X-treme* may have first started airing in 2001, but the gate was first used long before then."

"Regularly?"

He stopped in the middle of opening his door, unsure. "Depends on your definition of 'regularly.' Not counting any Goa'uld stunts back in the bad old days, the gate was first used in 1945, then again in 1969 and 1994, but the program didn't really get going until 1996."

"In that case, if the Lilith worshippers are right, the final war is already underway." Rebecca swung her door open and climbed out of the vehicle, then turned and tossed him a considered look. When he didn't immediately reply, she moved to go inside.

There was something spooky about all of this, John had to admit. Looking around to make sure no one was within earshot, he lengthened his stride to catch up to her. "The Ori have attacked Earth a few times," he admitted. "That epidemic we had a couple of years back, for starters. The SGC thinks they've finally managed to take all of 'em out, but the 'true believer' nut jobs don't seem to have gotten the memo that their gods are dead. Assuming they *are* dead."

At that, Rebecca seemed to pick up her pace, spine rigid. John hurried up the steps of the building and reached for her arm. "Hey, what'd I say?"

She paused on the top step and faced him. "Mock their beliefs all you want," she said coolly. "The difference between a cult and a religion is often just a legal distinction, one that varies from country to country. We have 'alien god' religions in the US that the UK and Germany have outlawed. It doesn't matter how baseless you might think their faith is. Bottom line, Colonel: whether their beliefs are founded on fact or fallacy is not the point. *They* believe it, and they're willing to kill for it, so we need to take that devotion seriously."

"I do take it seriously," he said, surprised at her vehemence. "I don't think murder's a joke under any circumstances. Being a smartass…it's just what I do."

Rebecca acknowledged the subtly offered truce with a nod. "In any case, what we're seeing here is symptomatic of two sects within an overarching framework, one more violently inclined than the other."

"Maybe it's related to the number of *iratus* genes a person has. The more Wraithlike you are, the more you believe."

Shaking her head, she said, "Think about it. Cults attract more believers, not less, when their leaders demonstrate manifest abilities. I realize charisma is ninety-nine percent of the attraction, rather than any actual ability to perform sleight of hand, but being able to suck the life out of someone is awfully damned manifest. I can't see how such an obvious demonstration of power would cause a rift unless they all believe with equal fervor but have fundamentally opposing epistemologies." She paused, biting her lip. "It's possible that they've split into two entirely different factions, each claiming to follow the one true 'Lilith'."

Recalling the bitter divide between the peoples of the country in which they currently stood, John could understand how easily such a situation might arise.

Pushing open the door, Rebecca took off her sunglasses. "That conclusion fits with the evidence I've personally accumulated. It's also the only explanation I have for the videotape that uptight paper-pusher showed me—"

"Oh, so you're open-minded about cultists, but not bureaucrats." John couldn't pass up that opportunity, even if Woolsey got on his nerves.

"Everybody's free to believe what they choose. Personally, I believe that God created a different heaven for bureaucrats, lawyers, and accountants."

Only the slightest glimmer of humor was visible in her eyes, and John had the distinct impression that she was holding something back.

"Dr. Jackson pointed out earlier that succubi and incubi are fabled to take a liking to certain individuals," she continued, "sometimes plaguing them all of their lives. That looks to be the case with Mr. Payton. There are even accounts of succubi becoming so protective of their 'pets' that they'll kill to protect them, restoring them to life under certain circumstances."

And there it was again: that phantom hand clawing against his chest.

When John's pace slowed, Rebecca glanced back at him. "Please don't say you're remembering that episode of *The X Files*," she warned.

"Actually, I've got a real life experience to draw on this time." No need to be too specific. "I've seen a Wraith restore life to someone on whom they've previously fed. I know it's possible."

She seemed briefly jarred by that news, but covered the

reaction by starting up the stairs toward their assigned office, propping her sunglasses on her head as she went. A moment later, she said, "That adds substance to the profile suggesting we have two sects with conflicting epistemologies—no, I need to stop using that word. It's not an epistemology, since we know the Stargate and Ascended beings really exist. These two factions have different goals, different motives. According to what we've seen, and based on what you've just told me, one is deliberately poaching the other's pet victims." A frown settled on her face. "Dr. Jackson mentioned Lilith's Babylonian name, Ninlil. I briefly…encountered a couple of followers of Ninlil several years ago. They're so far below the radar they're flat-lined, but…"

When she trailed off, John again got the impression she was wrestling with something. "But?"

She pulled in a deep breath and, pausing midway up the steps, turned to look at him. Her expression had closed off, and any trace of uncertainty had vanished, replaced by a mask of focused professionalism. "They fit the profile of the more pacifist sect of the Lilith cult like a glove. The sect doing the killing is the more fundamentalist of the two. Having found the location of the gate, they're also searching for something more."

"So we need to figure out what that 'something more' is." John had accompanied Rodney on plenty of similar treasure hunts in the Pegasus Galaxy. Most of them tended to start with a stroll through Atlantis's Ancient database. The local equivalent of that would be… "What else is in the cult's scriptures?" He removed his own sunglasses and tucked them into his pocket.

Ahead of him on the stairs, Rebecca tossed an approving look over her shoulder. "You're not bad at this investigative stuff," she said lightly. "The symbology provides the best clue."

"Okay. Should I be reading Dan Brown?"

Her lips twitched. "Maybe you can pitch the Jell-O theory

to him for his next book. Symbols are representations, generally designed to provide meaning on more than one level. For the Lilith cult, the circles and geometric shapes represent the Stargate, which is both a metaphorical and in fact a functional 'gate' to the 'heavens'—celestial bodies in the sky, other worlds. There's a second component overlaying that: the isosceles triangle."

"Rodney's Wraith Dart." He nodded. "I have to admit there's a close resemblance, especially those markings indicating the cockpit."

"If you're right, then that's the physical representation, but what's its function in terms of its symbolism? There's an important detail to this that no one's mentioned yet. No matter where in the world these symbols are located, the tip of the triangle always points due south. You found a Stargate and evidence of Atlantis in Antarctica, so I asked General Landry to have someone check the list of victims for any known link to your not-quite-normal-channels Antarctic expedition. Relatives, close friends, professional colleagues—anything." She detached her cell phone from her belt again and held it up for John to read the text message she'd received back in the lab.

DR L: YOU WERE RIGHT. LANDRY.

John had to grin. Just like the General to get straight to the point. "Then there *is* a connection between all of the victims."

"All except the ones here." Rebecca pushed open the stairwell door to the second floor. "I'm betting the Iraqi victims had something to do with whatever it is that Dr. Jackson is after, and that it links back to Lilith."

No sooner had they taken three steps toward the office than a lieutenant came speeding down the hallway. "Colonel Sheppard!" The young man skidded to a stop in front of them. "Sir, been looking for you. Joint Operations Center reported that a convoy was attacked outside the Iraq National Museum. The area's been secured, but there were a number of casualties."

John's gaze flicked to Rebecca, who went pale. "Any word on Dr. Jackson?" he asked, half certain he already knew the answer.

From the grim hardness of the kid's expression, it looked like he was almost as experienced at delivering bad news as John was at receiving it. "He's missing, sir. Most likely he was identified as a civilian and abducted for possible ransom."

Damn it. John closed his eyes, all too aware that ransom was the one of the *better* options they could hope for. There were plenty that were much, much worse.

CHAPTER SIXTEEN

Since the very beginning of his association with the Stargate program, Rodney had prided himself on his ability to function at peak performance under extreme stress. It was a talent not many people possessed, certainly not at his level. At the moment, however, that capacity seemed to have deserted him. He couldn't move, couldn't speak, couldn't even force himself to swallow to alleviate his abruptly parched throat. The pounding of his heart assured him that at the very least his autonomic muscles were functioning. Of course, being frozen with terror hadn't done anything to prevent a rush of adrenaline, urging him to put as much distance as possible between him and the creatures that had seemingly appeared out of nowhere. Regardless, the analytical part of his brain informed him that he was currently incapable of any voluntary movements whatsoever.

The dinosaurs—the dozen or so bipedal animals now slinking into the lab had to be dinosaurs, right? Although the things looked more like two and a half meter tall escapees from a tolerable old television series called *V*, Geisler would no doubt bite Rodney's head off for even suggesting that they were reptiles. Then again, at this point, head biting was a far more significant concern in the literal sense than the figurative.

Seated in front of an Ancient computer connected to his laptop, his fingers frozen mid-stoke on the keys, he had barely enough control over his eyeballs to watch what was bound to be his final minutes of life.

Honestly, what was the point of bringing the Marines along if they couldn't handle the simple task of watching…?

Rodney ended that train of thought as soon as he realized he could now move his head sufficiently to see beyond the lab's entrance. The entire area was crawling with the two-legged dinosaurs, including, he could tell by peering through the windscreens, a bunch making themselves at home inside the jumpers. That was less worrying than the fact that several of the reptiles were carrying limp, uniform-clad bodies in their grips.

Through the floor, Rodney could still feel the rhythmic pulse of the ocean as the surf pounded up against the beach outside. For the first time, it occurred to him that the sound of seabirds was one sensation that was absent from this place. On Earth, gulls would descend on a low tide area in droves, dive-bombing and snatching up anything edible that had been stranded by the receding water. Some small recess of his mind tried to imagine what animal filled that ecological niche here. Another part wondered what had possessed him to waste his last thoughts before becoming a dino snack on the contemplation of the planet's *ecology*.

Seconds now, that's all that were left to him until he was eaten alive. God, of all the deaths he might have imagined—and he'd imagined quite a few even before coming to Atlantis—the only time he'd seriously acknowledged the possibility of being consumed was when he'd been contemplating his role as this galaxy's version of Jonah. But that experience at least had come with the consolation of knowing the water pressure would crush him to death prior to his consumption. And while death by Wraith was unquestionably horrific, nothing, absolutely nothing, beat the thought of having parts of him being ripped out and chewed upon while he just sat there helplessly, screaming inside his mind.

From vast experience with such matters, Rodney was fully aware that even he could only maintain an elevated level of dread for a certain length of time. When one of the creatures brushed past him without so much as a sniff, he got a wholly unwanted closer look at its smooth skin, patterned like a carpet shark, no doubt for camouflage. But he also got a sense that this entire situation might not end as badly as he had first assumed. This despite the fact that they definitely were cousins to the velociraptors made infamous by *Jurassic Park*, right down to the tails and the massive feet complete with a deadly upright killing claw on the third toe. The only real difference he could discern, given his limited range of movement, was that the cranial section of their skulls seemed significantly enlarged.

They were totally silent in their movements. No groans or grunts, and barely a crunch underfoot despite the litter that had been left behind by the obviously hasty departure of the lab's prior residents. More importantly, they didn't move with the sense of malevolent purpose usually present in hunters. Instead, intelligent eyes took in their surroundings in a manner that was oddly reminiscent of the way he and Radek had explored the space only an hour earlier.

Speaking of Radek... Rodney tried to turn his head to find his colleague. As he did so, he suddenly found himself freed of the inexplicable grip that had held him paralyzed since the raptors had arrived. His initial impulse to yell at the top of his lungs had also passed.

So it hadn't been simply fear after all. Of course it hadn't. He'd faced down Wraith before; he couldn't be scared into catatonia by a few overgrown—

One of the creatures aimed a hooded, ochre-eyed gaze at him, and he mentally backpedaled from that assertion. He was quite prepared to be scared into any state whatsoever if it would render him unappetizing.

"I think they will not hurt us." Radek's low voice was irritatingly calm.

"Oh, that's what you think, is it?" Before Rodney could argue the point out of reflex, the dinosaurs carrying what Rodney could now see was Lorne and the Marines stepped through the lab's entrance. Although there was no particular sense of care attached to the manner in which they placed the men on the floor, neither was it reckless or haphazard. 'Indifferent' was the best description Rodney could summon.

"Ah…hi," he began with a weak smile, and then stopped. He recalled reading somewhere—or maybe it was something that Geisler had been babbling about once—that a smile was some sort of bizarre evolutionary outfall from the bearing of fangs during displays of aggression. So, no smile. He was about to raise one hand in his best universally accepted greeting when his radio crackled to life.

"Rodney, Radek, Major Lorne, if you can hear me, do not make any sudden movements. We will be there very shortly."

That reassurance from Teyla ushered in an overpowering sense of relief. Right on its heels, however, was frustration; even though Rodney finally could move enough to toggle his radio and bombard her with questions, such an action would have fallen fairly decisively under the heading of sudden movements.

"Their hands," Radek breathed. When Rodney glanced over at him, he pushed his glasses further up on his nose. "Look at their hands."

Primed to point out to Radek that adjusting his glasses definitely constituted a sudden movement and that, generally speaking, flesh eating giant chickens from hell didn't have hands, Rodney was startled to see that the raptors' powerful forearms in fact ended in long fingers with curved claws and…could that be an opposable *thumb*?

Teyla arrived then, stepping through the entrance just ahead of Geisler, who was beaming like he'd just won a Nobel. His excitement seemed glaringly inappropriate, given that the creature following him had Ronon's body clutched in its forearms. Was it the damned opposable thumbs that had him all worked up? Rodney could admit that the discovery was staggering, but even his scientific curiosity had limits. After all, monkeys had opposable thumbs, and monkeys were some of the nastiest creatures in existence.

His expression must have reflected his distaste, because Teyla reassured him, "It's all right. I have been able to make contact with these…" Turning, she met the gaze of one of the dinosaurs, slightly larger and more muscled than the others. "The beings who inhabit this world."

Beings? She was calling them *beings*? The dinosaur carrying Ronon deposited him on the floor next to the sprawled Marines, who seemed to be slowly starting to wake. At that point, Rodney realized—a bit late, possibly, but under the circumstances the delay seemed justifiable—that there was no evidence of blood anywhere. None of the men had been injured; at least, not visibly.

When Lorne pushed himself upright enough to reach for his weapon, though, his motion was halted almost as soon as it began. Immobilized, he fairly radiated tension and frustration. Rodney recognized the same circumstances in which he'd been caught earlier. Good God! That meant these creatures were actually capable of—

"Be at peace, as difficult as that may be for you," Teyla warned the group. "Although I sense from them only curiosity, not malice, they are meat eaters and very protective of their own kind. If they consider us to be a genuine threat, they will have no compunctions about killing us merely by wishing our hearts to cease beating."

If this really was what it appeared to be, namely ESP—telepathy as well as some form of telekinesis on an unprecedented scale, and Rodney saw no evidence that it could be anything else—the implications were staggering. The existence of these dinosaurs confirmed that the Ancients had been experimenting with entirely different forms of intelligence evolving on Earth.

After a moment's hesitation, Lorne gave a small nod. It wasn't apparent whether the rest of the Major's body was still immobilized or whether he didn't want to inflame the situation by moving, but Rodney was convinced the Marines would have shifted from their clearly uncomfortable positions on the ground if they'd had the option. Maybe they were having trouble thinking happy thoughts. Tough to blame them, although they needed to shape up rapidly for everyone's sakes. Ronon, lucky him—and quite possibly lucky for all of them—still appeared to be out cold.

"I am able to share mental images with this one," Teyla said, still facing the larger raptor, likely the leader if size and exceptional coloration mattered. Maybe all that meditation nonsense was good for something besides Ascension after all. "It is...complex—a vastly different way of perceiving the world, and us, than anything I have ever encountered." She smiled and her entire bearing relaxed as the two of them seemed to settle into an unspoken tête-à-tête.

The whole situation ranked up there with the most bizarre meetings Rodney had ever witnessed. It was like something he might have envisaged in the way of first contact with a truly alien life form, an area in which the SGC had had only limited experience. The rest of the—whatever they were; he settled on raptors for the moment—continued their prowl around the laboratory, sniffing experimentally at objects. To their credit, they had the good grace not to actually touch anything or, more unnervingly, drool on anything. Particularly him.

Unable to curb his impatience for some form of information from Teyla, he was about to demand a description of the images she'd mentioned, but she nodded slowly and spoke before he could begin. "They comprehend that we communicate using sounds, for there are other animals on this world who also still vocalize, but they regard this as a...primitive attribute, something for which they have little need."

"Of course!" Geisler put in, practically bouncing with enthusiasm. "That would explain the enlarged craniums in counterpoint to their jaws remaining essentially identical to their ancestors on Earth. They don't need the mechanical structures to support speech."

Comparative anatomy lessons? Did no one have a sense of priorities around here? "Fascinating, and yet not helpful in the slightest," Rodney snapped. "Teyla, ask them what they *want*. Also, if you can do it without making them angry, ask them why—"

Teyla shushed him with a quick shake of her head. She seemed to be concentrating rather hard, her eyes closed and her graceful features creased in a frown. "Their world is so vibrant, so rich in sensory perceptions. They see the pulse and flow of life between all things. Through this, they share with one another an awareness far beyond themselves."

"Okay, that's definitely an Ascended trait."

"They are gathered around the computers," remarked Radek, causing Rodney to turn. Sure enough, several of the dinosaurs were focused on the information scrolling across the Ancient screens. They couldn't possibly comprehend what they were seeing, could they? It was most likely the equivalent of a dog watching television. Wasn't it?

"Teyla?" Rodney said again, this time more quietly.

"My contact with them is tenuous," she replied without opening her eyes. "This is unlike anything I have ever encountered. It is not a hive mind, as the Wraith have, for they are very much individuals. Rather, it is a completely different way of comprehending their world and their place in it. While I cannot explain it, it is clear that they are extremely intelligent—possibly more so than we are, in some respects."

As if the rest of this mission wasn't difficult enough to believe already. "We wouldn't know it from the way they've been behaving like animals," Rodney objected.

"How can you define their actions as 'animal'?" Geisler demanded.

Oh, here we go. "If they're so intelligent, where's their civilization? Buildings, clothes, books, art?"

"Where is the Ascended's civilization? What of their works of art?" Geisler retorted.

"These beings," Teyla said, "exist in a richly woven tapestry of life. That is more manifest to them than anything taken from the living world and fashioned into dead things. That is why they find the jumpers so curious, for they sense no connection to the life force that embraces them."

"Yes, fine, the noble savage and all that," Rodney said. "Until, of course, a T. rex comes along and they have to defend themselves. I'm assuming they use that mind-freeze trick, but what I'd really like to know is whether they evolved that ability naturally or the Ancients had a hand in it. And if so, how?"

Ignoring him, Teyla continued, speaking in what even Rodney recognized as unbridled wonder. "I have always thought of my people as deeply spiritual, but compared to these... We have faith in something greater. They *understand* it."

"And so do I, having recently had a near miss with Ascension." As much as Rodney wanted to be patient with his Athosian teammate, they really didn't have time for the Hare Krishna thing.

Teyla shook her head. "This is unrelated to Ascension. It is..." For a moment, she had to search for words. "The empathy we felt from the microceratops on Atlantis was barely a glimpse. They are capable of control over so much." Locked in a surreal staring contest with the raptor leader, apparently conversing with it—Him? Her?—she only continued after a protracted pause. "Beyond a vague genetic memory of the Ancients, they have no concept of what a human is. Even so, they comprehend our basic emotions. They are aware that some of us regard them and their world with respect and fascination, but they are also well aware of our...savagery."

Rodney wanted to burst out laughing at that, given the video footage he'd seen of the T. rex, but then he recalled that humans were nothing more than a branch from the same evolutionary tree that had produced monkeys. He glanced at Radek, who had pursed his lips in a guilty-as-charged look, and right at that moment Rodney had the distinct impression that something was lightly rummaging through his mind. He tried to shake it off, but his eyes were drawn across to where two of the raptors were staring at him, unblinking. *Calm*

*places, wide-open fields, communing with nature...prefer-
ably pollen-free...certainly not thinking about any expertise
in blowing up things...especially not entire planets.*

Breaking her long gaze, Teyla glanced over at the Marines,
who finally were showing some ability to move. "They will
show us no mercy if we take any action to threaten the balance of their world. We cannot and will never be able to find a
place here, and so they do not wish us to remain. I believe we
should leave as soon as possible."

Feeling distinctly queasy, Rodney wasn't inclined to argue
for a change. He saw no good reason to antagonize question-
ably intelligent but evidently well-armed beings zealously
maintaining some kind of primeval utopia. "Fine. I've down-
loaded plenty of information from the database here. I'll be
able to examine it more carefully back on Atlantis, but it's safe
to say I have the gist of what Lilith and her compatriots did
here. Let's head out."

"I do not wish to burst any bubbles, but it will not be quite
that simple." Radek rubbed his chin. "So far we have been
unable to shut down the force field around the Stargate. It may
take several more hours to accomplish this, if it is even possible, and we will have no way of knowing whether or not we
have succeeded because we cannot contact the security team
at the gate."

"I will try to convey our concerns." Teyla faced the head
raptor again and closed her eyes.

Doing his best to project a sense of serenity, Rodney edged
around a couple of the animals as he gathered up his data
devices. Lorne climbed slowly to his feet and instructed the
Marines in a low voice to carry Ronon out to one of the jumpers.

It occurred to Rodney that his teammate's condition might
be cause for some concern. "Uh, Teyla? Not to interrupt, but
do you have any idea why Ronon is still out?"

Her task—or at least her attempt—presumably finished,
Teyla answered, "I believe his initial reaction to the crea-

tures was stronger than the others. They have assured me that he will wake in a short time. We must proceed to the gate—now."

Well, if a giant lizard said it, it had to be true. More importantly, Teyla's expression bore a distinct *don't argue* air.

Although Rodney wasn't certain just what he was meant to do with the force field at the gate when all the applicable equipment was *inside* said force field, he followed the Marines out of the lab for lack of any better ideas. The raptors trailed along behind, two of them flanking an embarrassingly euphoric Geisler, who kept reaching out to touch their forearms and backs. Surprisingly, they didn't seem the least bit bothered by his pestering, but Rodney didn't trust them to stay that way if it continued. "Would you knock it off?" he muttered. Either Geisler didn't hear, or he pretended not to.

"He does not threaten them," Teyla said. "They sense his genuine delight and wonder, and that inspires in them a measure of regard for him."

At the very least, it was still discomforting. Rodney chose to ignore the man in favor of stepping aboard Jumper Three and focusing on the preflight procedure. Settling into the pilot's seat, he powered up the craft and turned to ask Teyla to offer their goodbyes to the raptors—only to find two of the beasts stooped over in the rear cabin, gazing unblinkingly at him.

"Holy—" When his suddenly racing heartbeat returned to something close to normal, Rodney glared past them at his teammate. "At the risk of sounding entirely too much like Sheppard, what the *hell*, Teyla?"

"They insist on accompanying us to the gate," she replied, a layer of steel behind her placid expression. "Would you prefer to risk angering them with a refusal to cooperate?"

"When you put it that way…" Rodney forced a smile, trying desperately to think inoffensive thoughts. *Don't think of an elephant…* "Ah, welcome aboard."

Radek came forward to sit in the copilot's seat, while Teyla and Geisler crouched beside the two raptors, the paleontologist still grinning like an idiot. The rest of the Marines piled into Jumper Two with Lorne, which certainly looked like the wisest choice for all concerned. Sighing, Rodney closed the hatch and eased Jumper Three off the ground.

The Atlantean puddle jumper, in all other respects a nearly ideal vehicle, obviously had not been designed for dinosaur use. The two raptors, including the one Rodney thought of as the boss, took up most of the cabin all by themselves, and their rather pungent scent gave the air scrubbers a considerable test. Rodney was sure he could feel their breath on the back of his neck as he guided the jumper toward the continent that hosted the Stargate.

As the two jumpers rose out of the grotto, Lorne spoke up over the radio. "I don't know if this should matter to us, but how are your passengers going to make the return trip? If we let them off at the gate, they'll be thousands of miles and an ocean away from home."

If the raptors were let off at the gate? They weren't planning on hitchhiking all the way to Atlantis, were they? Flushed with renewed panic, Rodney twisted in his seat to face Teyla.

The Athosian shook her head. "We need not concern ourselves with their journey, nor with the force fields. I am certain that all we must do is return to the gate."

High overhead, dozens, maybe hundreds of pterosaurs circled. A few darted down to snatch bits of food from among the rocks, thus answering his earlier musings, but the majority of the winged animals seemed to be...waiting.

"Whoa," said Lorne at the exact moment Rodney noticed a new signal illuminated on the jumper's instrument panel. "The force field around the lab—"

"—just reactivated," Rodney cut him off. "What did you do?"

"Me? What do you think I could do that might result in *that*, McKay?"

"Our new acquaintances are responsible for restoring the force field," said Teyla.

Oh, really? Rodney glanced back at the boss raptor, whose head and shoulders now poked between the front seats as he looked out through the windshield. Apparently the jumpers had picked up an escort: the group of pterosaurs had closed in to fly alongside the craft. One animal came in for a near pass and peered in at Jumper Three's occupants, eliciting a soft laugh from Teyla.

"Major," she called, "I believe we have found the flyer who collided with us early in our first visit. He seems to be conveying his apologies."

"Well, uh, tell him not to worry about it. No harm done." Lorne's disbelief was clearly audible. "And tell them we appreciate the company, but we're going orbital for the rest of this hop."

The avian dinosaurs—okay, *ptero*saurs—must have understood the basics, because they peeled off before the air could get too thin. Even though the boss raptor didn't look perturbed by the jumper's climb toward the stars, Rodney knew it had to be a distinctly new experience. New experiences, more often than not, made for tense situations, and this situation was plenty tense enough already. "Teyla, what's on his mind?"

Teyla paused a moment and then smiled. "Mostly he is thinking of his young. I still cannot grasp more than basic concepts, but I sense a kind of satisfaction—something related to an old mystery regarding the Ancient lab."

The suborbital flight path made the trip fairly brief. Lorne brought his jumper down next to Jumper Four, parked just outside a shimmering blue energy field that surrounded the Stargate. Reducing power to do likewise, Rodney was baffled by the presence of hundreds of ridiculously oversized animals gathering around the shield and, like the pterosaurs above the lab, waiting.

"Torosaurus," Geisler murmured behind him, sounding

overwhelmed. "Look at that bright red cranial plating. My God, it's nearly glowing—and the iguanodons…"

More critical to their current status and thus more interesting to Rodney was the force field, which lowered as the jumpers settled onto the jungle floor beside the third craft. He didn't bother questioning Jumper Two this time; he was satisfied that neither Lorne nor Radek had triggered the action.

Teyla moved to the back of the jumper and lowered the hatch. When their stowaways padded down the ramp, Rodney exhaled a relieved breath. As much as he trusted his teammate's intuition, he hadn't fully trusted the raptors not to change their minds about what was planned for the evening's menu.

"The force field will be raised again once we are gone," Teyla said. "Permanently this time, I believe. It will leave an area just large enough around the gate for any later visitors to dial out and depart."

While Rodney was still wrapping his head around the idea that the animals had such fine mental control of Ancient technology, another thought came to him in parallel. "If they want to be left alone, why couldn't they have put up the force field before? Surely we're not the only people to use the gate in the past ten thousand years."

Standing at the hatch, Teyla bowed her head to the departing raptors and turned toward him. "We are not. We are, however, the only ones who did not fall prey to the T. rexes living in this valley."

A muted groan over the radio signaled Ronon's return to consciousness in the other jumper. "We'll fill you in later, buddy," Rodney heard Lorne say. "Jumper Two is dialing the gate."

They'd achieved their objective, more or less. That said, Rodney felt a bit like he'd been hit by a bus. Several dozen questions vied for attention, most of which stemmed from the issue of Lilith's work on the planet. She and the other Ancients could not possibly have created this bizarre form of intelligence, because the inhabitants had obviously been seeded here millions of years earlier. Had they merely been observing its progress? Or were they looking for something that might be used against the Wraith? Or to enable Ascension?

As Teyla raised the hatch, the event horizon rushed into being. Geisler's choked laugh captured everyone's attention. Rodney followed the other scientist's outstretched finger. Beyond the windshield, the raptors who had accompanied them now climbed onto the backs of two huge creatures the paleontologist identified as *Quetzalcoatlus*. As Jumper Three rose from the ground, the winged animals did the same.

"Perhaps they should have inherited Earth after all." Geisler's eyes were unashamedly bright. "They've been far better custodians of this planet than we have of ours."

Feeling somewhat charitable by virtue of not having been eaten alive, Rodney allowed Geisler the last word and guided the jumper into the wormhole.

CHAPTER SEVENTEEN

Daniel came to with indistinct memories of a fireball and a jolt of searing pain anchored in his mind. That alone was enough to be troubling, but he already could tell that he wasn't badly injured. Hushed murmurs came from somewhere above him: Arabic, he identified, reminding him where he was…or at least where he'd been at the start of all this.

Dragging his eyes open, he struggled to adjust to the low light and found three—no, four—men standing around him. There was no immediate evidence of weapons, although he knew better than to make any presumptions along those lines. Still, he wasn't tied up or gagged, which was a good sign. It beat the alternatives, at least.

A dull throb on one side of his head made itself known, and he reached up to brush his fingers over a light bandage just behind his right ear. Since he had a better than passing familiarity with concussions, he was confident that this didn't qualify. The material draped along his arm also alerted him to the fact that he was no longer dressed in desert camouflage but instead in traditional robes. Another good sign.

His hosts watched him, their facial hair and the uneven lamplight colluding to make their expressions unreadable. Wondering what had happened, Daniel tested his voice and found it scratchy but serviceable. *"Aih elly hassal?"*

All four men showed the same amount of surprise—namely, no surprise at all. Stepping closer to him, one of them answered, "Your group was attacked. Insurgents, you would call them. We were nearby and pulled you from your vehicle before they could capture you."

"Shukran—thank you."

"Mafi mushkillah—no problem. It is our way of taking some small measure of control back from the many factions

in this country that claim to act on our behalf."

It was a reasonable response, but Daniel took it with a grain of salt all the same. Cautiously, he pushed himself into a sitting position and looked around. His pallet rested on the stone floor of a cellar-like room, lit only with lamps and a couple of flashlights and smelling vaguely of goats and other animals. In the corner unmatched chairs surrounded a worn wooden table cluttered with several pots and plates, a small bowl of fruit, and what looked to be homemade candles. There were no windows; he could tell it was night only because one wall was damaged and offered a porthole view of the darkened street outside.

Glancing up at the man who'd spoken, he said, "Are we still in Baghdad?"

"Not quite."

Lack of power notwithstanding, a steaming cup of black tea was offered, and Daniel sat fully upright and accepted it with gratitude. As soon as the sweetened drink touched his tongue, he recalled the coffee he'd had just before— "Tariq!" he said sharply, almost sloshing the tea over his hand. "He was there when the attack started."

The reply was laden with the burden of loss. "I regret to say that there was little left of him to be found."

And Tariq had been so close to getting out. Would his family still try to leave for Rome now? Would there even be a place for them there, with so many trying to escape the nightmare that now defined Iraq? Offering a silent, utterly inadequate apology to his lost friend, Daniel realized a beat late that if these guys recognized Tariq's name, they'd been near the Museum for a reason.

He wasn't sure if that was a good thing or not. "What do you plan to do with me?"

"That is your choice."

Someone made a quiet comment about standing watch—and just then Daniel realized that, without thinking, he'd spoken in the language the men had been using:

Egyptian Arabic.

Three of them left through a splintered doorframe. The speaker stayed behind, gesturing toward the chairs across the room. "Please."

Daniel got stiffly to his feet, glad he was still wearing his boots, and carried his tea over to the table, taking in his surroundings as he walked. The walls, he could tell, had once held shelves and been carefully painted. Now they were pitted with bullet marks and shrapnel, the latter most likely from whatever had created the hole. Even in the flickering candlelight, he recognized the pattern of stains and blotches against what few patches of plaster remained. There was nothing to identify the room as part of a home where children might have laughed and friends dropped by to share a coffee. "Not to sound unappreciative, because I really am glad to be alive, but who are you?"

"My name is Baqir Abdel Harim."

"Servant of the wise," Daniel translated, starting to get a familiar vibe from the man. Though he hadn't a clue where they might have previously met, Baqir's pharyngealized consonants identified him as a native of the region around Cairo.

Giving a nod, Baqir took a seat as well. The chair creaked softly against the silence of the night, and Daniel realized that wherever they were, it was far from the bustle of the city.

"This has always been a dangerous area," Baqir said, producing Daniel's sidearm from a bundle of cloth piled on the chair beside him. He handed the weapon to Daniel. "Although the streets are quiet now, militia activity has been increasing. As to Tariq, we had been keeping watch over the Museum in an attempt to guard against events occurring under what your countrymen call the fog of war. Be assured, Dr. Jackson, that we feel Tariq's loss far more keenly than even you can imagine. Although he was a Christian, he dedicated his life to guarding a heritage that will one day save us all from a far greater evil than that which now besets this country."

Now Daniel was well and truly wary. Setting down his tea,

he spoke as evenly as possible. "Would you mind telling me how you know my name?"

"I followed much of your early work, as far back as fifteen years ago." Baqir fingered his teacup and smiled. "I attended several of your lectures. I seem to recall one in particular where the entire audience walked out." His smile turned apologetic. "I confess that I left as well, at the urging of my colleagues at the museum, but not before I saw that one person had remained behind. Watching you from the door was an older European woman with a pendant bearing the Eye of Ra."

What were the odds that Baqir had decided by chance to mention that day, the day Catherine Langford had handed Daniel an airline ticket and an offer that would vindicate his work in ways he could never have imagined? Although his host's face revealed nothing, his eyes were knowing. For the moment, Daniel was inclined to keep playing close to the vest.

"You vanished soon after," Baqir added. "Not even a paper to your name. I had often wondered if you had found the proof that you sought. Then some years later I learned that you had chosen to lead a somewhat reclusive existence far from your life's work, in Colorado Springs."

So far, nothing that couldn't have been learned from sixty seconds on the Internet. Daniel chose not to answer directly. "What is it you need from me?"

"I believe this is more a matter of us being able to help each other."

Baqir lifted the urn and poured himself a second cup. Daniel also accepted a refill, not merely to be polite, but because he was incredibly thirsty.

"Four years ago," Baqir continued, "certain artifacts from the Museum were entrusted to my companions and me for protection. Among those artifacts was the original Sumerian King List, along with a set of vellum scrolls that have yet to be officially translated—scrolls written in the original language of the Annunaki, the sky gods who came to Earth through the Gate of Heaven."

With that, what was left of Daniel's belief in coincidences vanished. The King List that he had identified to Tariq had inscribed the names of one hundred and thirty four kings who'd ruled the eleven cities of Mesopotamia. One of the most intriguing aspects of the list was its scope: it recorded over two-hundred and twenty *thousand* years of leadership and drew no line of demarcation between rulers of fact and rulers of legend—assuming such a line even existed, Daniel reminded himself. The first kings were said to have been the direct descendants of the sky gods and 'gatekeepers' known as the Annunaki—or Nifilim, as they were called in Genesis—and each purportedly had ruled for tens of thousands of years. During the period covered by the list, the capital of Mesopotamia had rotated between cities, primarily Kish, Uruk, and Ur—which, Daniel had theorized during the search for Atlantis, had originally been names of Pegasus cities, given namesakes on Earth by the Ancients who'd evacuated here and remained in the region that would become known as the Middle East.

Did Baqir's group subscribe to a faith similar to that of the Lilith cult? Or was his interest merely scholarly? Daniel did his best to maintain his claim of ignorance. "That's nice to know, but what makes you think those items would be of interest to me?"

"Since the time of the Annunaki, we have been charged to hold the secret fast until the Final Days were upon us."

Daniel met Baqir's eyes over the rim of the cup, making an effort to conceal his reaction to that statement. He had absolutely no doubt that the Annunaki were the Ancients, but the chances of any one group of people tracing its lineage back ten thousand years…even in Iraq, that was a stretch.

Before he could point out that his question hadn't been answered, Baqir continued. "Generations of my…family have passed down the secret that, eleven years after the

Gate of Heaven was secretly revealed to the world, one of the Annunaki would reveal himself, having come from the heavens to take human form. This one would stand beside mankind and direct him in the Final Battle." The man's gaze focused more intensely on Daniel, who recognized in it a level of respect he hadn't noticed earlier.

"Now that these things are coming to pass, your protection will be our worthy task as well. We understand that adopting human form has made you vulnerable."

Apparently taking a break from the tea had been a smart move. If Daniel had been drinking during that last statement, the resultant spit-take would have been spectacular. "You think *I'm* one of the Annunaki?" Granted, the idea wasn't as farfetched as it could have been, particularly given his role in orchestrating the destruction of the Ori via the supergate. In fact, Baqir's explanation had come alarmingly close to the overall intergalactic picture. It was probably useless by this point, but Daniel made a last vague attempt to play dumb. "I'm sorry. I think you've got the wrong guy. I only came to Iraq to do some research on the Babylonian goddess, Ninlil."

An indulgent smile made it clear that Baqir wasn't fooled. "There is no need for deception, Dr. Jackson. Although you do not carry the blood of the Annunaki, what in your language you call the Ancients, you nevertheless carry the aura of one who has abandoned his mortal body and then returned. I can sense this trait. The ability was given to us by Ninlil when she charged us with our sacred duty."

Okay, then. Regardless of Daniel's actual Ascension status, maybe this wasn't a completely disastrous turn of events. "I see," he offered lamely, trying to give himself a moment to think. If these people really did form some secret group or sect and saw themselves as carrying out the instructions of Ninlil...

Baqir's eyes shifted to a point somewhere across the room. Daniel turned in his chair. Emerging from the shadows was a woman wearing a dark chador. Her eyes were hard to make out in the flickering light, but his first instinct, to stand, was rewarded with a raised hand. Still searching for her eyes within the shadows cast by the scarf, he failed to notice her exceptionally long, spidery fingers until she swept the garment back off her head. She was already directly in front of him before he had fully taken in her long burgundy hair and delicate, pallid features.

With a sudden jolt of recognition, he leaped back. "Whoa, wait—" All his instincts primed him to flee, but he succeeded only in knocking over his chair before her other hand reached out and latched onto his chest.

CHAPTER EIGHTEEN

It was difficult to tell exactly when the debriefing had run off the rails. Negotiating was Elizabeth's bailiwick; nevertheless, she didn't enjoy playing referee between two of her own people. The intent of the meeting had been for Rodney, Radek, and Dr. Geisler to present their M1M-316 findings to the group of scientists that had been assembled to support the investigation. Instead, not long after Geisler had begun his account, Rodney had started a running commentary of his own, and it was clear his assessment of the mission was markedly different from his colleague's. More important, however, was the brutally judgmental attitude with which he delivered it. It was true that Rodney had never suffered fools politely, but Geisler was nobody's fool.

While Elizabeth didn't want to rake her chief scientist over the coals in front of his staff, her tolerance had limits. "Rodney, you'll have to forgive me for not being as familiar with dinosaur physiology as you are. If you don't mind, I'd like to hear what Dr. Geisler—"

"Elizabeth, the man is romanticizing them past the point of all reason. First and foremost, the dinosaurs' intelligence—although classifying their unique skill set as 'intelligence' is debatable—was obviously augmented by the Ancients."

Geisler bristled. "Such a callous and, frankly, ignorant dismissal of a remarkable evolutionary—"

"Did you just call me ignorant? Are you delusional or just oblivious?"

"Rodney!" Elizabeth shoved her chair back. "Everyone, please excuse us for a moment. Rodney, with me." She strode toward one of the louvered doors without waiting to see if he would follow.

Fortunately, he did. Once they were out of the briefing room and inside her office, she shut the door and rounded on him. "Did Geisler wrong you in some monumental way to deserve that? Those people aren't graduate students for you to terrorize. What the hell were you trying to prove in there?"

"People are being killed on Earth," Rodney fired back, unrepentant. "We don't have time to wax poetic about lost worlds."

"I agree that time is an issue." She folded her arms. "Stay here. I'll continue the meeting and call you when your input is needed."

"Excuse me?" He jumped on the perceived slight, though not in quite the way she'd anticipated. "Oh, I see. This is the new norm. I was excluded from the initial briefing with Carson about the *iratus* gene prevalence in humans, and now it continues."

"Is that what all this has been about? You're taking that omission as a personal affront?" Elizabeth pinched the bridge of her nose, feeling the first twinges of a tension headache. She'd probably have to go through this scene with John, too. Assigning him to work with Agent Larance rather than join his team on M1M-316 hadn't been her idea, but her dealings with the IOA had armed her with enough situational awareness to know that this was not a decision she could safely protest. Nonetheless, when Elizabeth hadn't instantly leapt to John's defense in the SGC jumper bay, the fleeting glance he'd given her had said plenty. As inscrutable as he often was, she recognized wounded pride when she saw it.

She could appreciate both men's feelings on the matter, up to a point. However…

Elizabeth stepped nose-to-nose with Rodney. "You need to accept the fact that not everything on this expedition can revolve around you," she said, her tone blunt. "There simply aren't enough hours in the day for you to be the chief scientist of this expedition, a full-time researcher running your own lab, and a full-time member of a gate team. Therefore, occasionally things take place on this expedition without your supervision or approval. Somewhere along the line you have to delegate and trust that your people know their jobs. At the moment, I personally would like to understand what happened on 316 from all perspectives, not just that of the person who speaks the loudest. So what will it be? Can you find it within yourself to give your fellow scientists and teammates the respect they deserve, or do you need to stay here and sulk for a while, thereby missing yet *more* pertinent information that you can use to support an argument bordering on paranoia?"

She'd never seen Rodney honestly furious with her on a personal level, and she half expected to get her first demonstration of it right now. When he instead remained focused on the original offense, she realized she couldn't have been more wrong.

"There's no reason why Carson shouldn't have informed me," he insisted. "Officially or otherwise. It's not as if he never had an opportunity. How many times did we have lunch together?"

The supposed protest continued, but Elizabeth barely heard it, preoccupied with a dawning realization of just what all this was truly about. The relentless pace of the expedition was an inescapable reality. When they suffered a loss, there was never enough time to mourn properly, to come to grips with it on their own terms. They were simply thrown headfirst into the next crisis. At one time or another, the strain took its toll on all of them.

More than anyone else, Rodney had had a true peer in Carson. In addition to the sense of isolation he likely felt now, the *iratus* research must be reminding him on a regular basis that his friend hadn't confided in him about absolutely everything.

"...all it would have taken is an off-duty moment—"

"Rodney, you're never off duty," Elizabeth said, softening her tone.

As much as she sympathized with him, she couldn't be his armchair therapist. Not while her own conscience was weighed down with the task of telling her people that some of their friends or family might be among those who had been cruelly murdered on Earth. There were a number of Lilith cult victims who didn't fit the pattern that began at *Wormhole X-treme*, and Agent Larance had speculated that the Stargate program itself had been the link. Rather than spend a substantial amount of time on background checks, it had made more sense to question the Antarctic and Atlantis expeditions about the list of known victims.

Therefore, later today Elizabeth would have the unenviable job of distributing that list to the department heads, well aware of the strong odds that more than one city resident would read it and gasp in horrified recognition.

Absorbed in his own conflict, Rodney only blinked at her. They were rescued from the difficult silence by a rap on the glass door, where Katie Brown stood, looking somehow hesitant and excited at the same time.

Elizabeth forced a more pleasant expression and opened the door. "Dr. Brown, good afternoon."

"I'm sorry to be late for the meeting." The botanist twirled a data storage device between anxious fingers. "So many of the samples from 316 merit further study, and I only have two hands. That being said, I think I've already found something very interesting."

It was her presence rather than her promise of information that seemed to lift Rodney out of his fixation. As a rule, Elizabeth tended to be wary of intradepartmental relationships, but Katie seldom had to report directly to Rodney, and no one could find fault with the calming influence she often appeared to have on him.

Maybe this disaster of a meeting could be salvaged after all. "Why don't we join the others?" Elizabeth suggested, raising her eyebrows at Rodney in a pointed query. "All of us."

Slowly, as if realizing he'd just been pardoned, he nodded. The three of them headed for the briefing room in single file. Elizabeth heard the last vestiges of a shared laugh fade as she walked in with Rodney following. The expected awkwardness never gained traction, thanks to Katie's arrival; apparently others were aware of her effect on their chief scientist.

Acknowledging nothing and no one, Rodney reclaimed his seat. "Please continue," Elizabeth told Geisler, settling into her chair.

With a faint chill lingering in the air, Geisler cast a brief look of assessment at Rodney before beginning again. "I was telling the group that the evolutionary differences between Earth dinosaurs and the beings we encountered on 316 are too complex to have occurred over a period of only ten thousand years. DNA manipulation is certainly a possible cause, but that alone couldn't account for the magnitude of the changes we're seeing. These changes are evident in the genetic assays we've performed on several samples, including Dr. Brown's detailed botanical analysis."

At his wordless nod, Katie spoke up. "The vegetation samples are remarkably close to the modern equivalents of birch, elm, a few variants of orchid, and cycad." In marked contrast to Rodney, she glanced over at Geisler as if uncertain about overstepping her bounds.

"In my view," the older scientist said, "it seems probable that the Ancients saw something of value in the biota of the middle to late Cretaceous and chose to preserve it in the Pegasus Galaxy. Since this must have occurred long before the Wraith became a threat, I can only assume the Ancients were studying some aspect of the ecology that they thought might lead them to Ascension." He gave a small shrug. "It could be that their focus was not the raptors we met, but instead some other species that has since Ascended from the planet."

Clearly itching to jump in, Rodney managed to exercise some restraint. Elizabeth raised the issue that had to be on his mind. "That doesn't explain the more recent Ancient activity on 316. Your research in the city database showed that Lilith ran experiments there just prior to the Lanteans' abandoning the Pegasus Galaxy. Were you able to find any details about the nature of those experiments?"

Geisler shook his head. "Nothing beyond her name and a general reference to testing, both executed and planned. We can only speculate about the Ancients' motivations; all I know for certain is that they were forced to leave in a hurry and that Lilith intended to return."

"A sudden departure seems quite likely," Radek agreed. "The condition of the lab we explored—it was not the controlled shutdown state we found upon first arriving in Atlantis. No steps had been taken to cover or otherwise preserve equipment." He absently disassembled and reassembled a pen. "Not exactly a *Marie Celeste*, but very close."

Elizabeth decided to reward Rodney's forbearance and swiveled her chair in his direction. "What did you find in the lab's records?"

"I've only had time to skim the files so far," he said promptly. "There's no doubt that the Ancients transplanted a large representation of Earth's biota some millions of years ago, which would explain the existence of the extremely old Ancient structures. Lilith and other more recent Ancients were in fact working on the 'empathic' gene, so to speak. It looks like they hoped to make humans immune from Wraith attacks by inducing a kind of dynamic emotive feedback. Essentially, any attempt to feed on a human would result in the Wraith experiencing the same terror, agony and, ultimately, death."

It was a fascinating idea, but was it practical? Had the Ancients who'd originally stocked the planet abandoned their efforts because of a lack of progress or because they'd opted to let natural evolution to take its course? In either case, why had Lilith revisited the experiment?

"A considerable number of the lab records are focused on

botany," added Radek. While Rodney's gaze blanked, Katie's lit up, although she didn't voice her eagerness. She reminded Elizabeth of a young student who knew the answer to the teacher's question but was too shy to call it out.

"Dr. Brown, you said earlier that you'd found something of interest?" Elizabeth prodded.

Katie returned her smile. "Everything Dr. Geisler brought back from 316 is of interest. In particular, I think there's a lot to be learned from the ginkgoopsida."

Well, that wasn't a word that often came up in conversation. "I'm sorry?"

"A class of plants commonly known as ginkgoes," Katie clarified.

Rodney frowned. "Those rancid-smelling pods that were all over the ground?"

She nodded brightly. "Ginkgoes originated on Earth nearly three hundred million years ago. However, only one species survived the K-T extinction event. In fact, until a few years ago, only a single population of trees, located on Tian Mu Mountain in China, was known to exist. Instead of seeding, however, they spread from a type of basal root. On 316, the ginkgoes would seem to be mostly seeding."

What that meant in regard to their objective, Elizabeth hadn't a clue, but she trusted the botanist to come to the point soon. "Isn't ginkgo biloba one of those herbal supplements people take to enhance memory?"

"That's right. It's also used to relieve the symptoms of many types of brain dysfunction. I've been testing the active ingredients from the 316 ginkgoes—they're drastically more concentrated than their Earth counterparts. Up to ten thousand times stronger, in some cases. They also contain several dozen more active ingredients, most of which I haven't been able to identify yet, although I did recognize a few as being used in the treatment of genetic disorders." Completely in her element, Katie was almost beaming. "These plants have incredible potential for medical applications."

Her last comment seemed to go unnoticed by Rodney as he zeroed in on the one that had preceded it. "Genetic disorders?"

"Those trees were abundant in every area we visited on the planet," Geisler said. "Whatever properties they contain would have completely saturated the food chain."

"Did you say *genetic* disorders?" Rodney demanded. "How?"

Katie appeared more than willing to explain. "Well, some of these components can be used to trigger dormant genes. We often think of retroviruses in a negative context, but not all of them are bad. Take the ATA gene, for instance. The gene therapy Dr. Beckett developed is a retroviral trigger. The ginkgoes on 316 may contain ingredients that trigger any number of useful retroviruses."

Although the expedition would soon learn about the recent developments on Earth when the victim list began to circulate, only a few members had been fully briefed so far. Katie hadn't been included in that group, so it wasn't surprising that she'd taken a rather optimistic view of the possibilities. Elizabeth, by contrast, felt an uneasy sense of recognition begin to coil in her stomach.

Seeing that Rodney suddenly looked ill as well, Katie's oblivious enthusiasm faltered. "Did I say something wrong?"

"Useful retroviruses," repeated Rodney, making a visible effort to stay calm. "As opposed to, say, Wraith retroviruses?"

"Let's not jump to conclusions," Elizabeth warned, scanning the faces of the other scientists at the table. "Can I infer that you have several worthwhile lines of study to pursue at the moment?" Heads nodded. "Then I won't keep you any longer."

One of the traits she most appreciated in Atlantis's science team was its collective willingness to dive into any topic, no matter how arcane or fantastical, without hesitation. When she dismissed the meeting, the participants gathered their notes and began to scatter, leaving the room in huddled pairs and trios to discuss options. Rodney followed, cautioning them all in a raised voice to take adequate protective measures when handling any and all samples from M1M-316.

Geisler trailed behind, moving as though his aging joints had had enough excitement for a while. Seeing an opportunity, Elizabeth called after him. "Dr. Geisler, may I have a moment?"

He paused, fixing her with a rueful, knowing smile. "If you're feeling the need to apologize for Dr. McKay, it isn't necessary. You're not responsible for his behavior, and he's hardly the first forceful personality I've come across in my career."

"I appreciate that. Unfortunately, this is a different and more serious matter." Elizabeth slid a printout of the victim list out of a folder on the table. "The group Colonel Sheppard and the SGC are investigating on Earth appears to carry out its killings according to a specific ritual. They also seem to be focusing on family, friends, and acquaintances of Stargate program personnel. The reason I'm telling you this before I announce it to the expedition at large is that there have been some deaths reported in New Zealand and Australia that fit the pattern."

A look of alarmed comprehension sprang into Geisler's eyes. Elizabeth pushed ahead. "I'm very sorry to have to ask you to do this. I need to know if you recognize any of the names on this list."

Summoning a reserve of composure, Geisler reached for the printout. While he read it, Elizabeth found another file to occupy herself, not wanting to intrude on his awful assignment.

After a minute or so, he exhaled on a sigh. "None of my family, thank God," he said at last. "Three of these poor souls, though—I knew them through my research. I wouldn't have called them friends, but they were decent people and good at their jobs."

Elizabeth offered him a pen. Still shaking off the shock, he circled a name. "This one worked at the U.S. Antarctic Division supply depot in Christchurch. She could be quite the battering ram when it came to our equipment requisitions." He made another mark. "This one was a crewman on the *Aurora Australis*, a ship that transported researchers and cargo from Hobart down to the Antarctic base. I barely ever heard him speak, but he was a fine sailor. This last one…" The pen hovered over a third name. "I can't imagine how he fits into this. He helped me many years ago with an unrelated project and had nothing to do with the Antarctic program."

"How did you know him?" Elizabeth asked.

"He worked for the Tasmanian Parks and Wildlife Service as a guide in the Newdegate Cave. It's near Hastings, about two hours south of Hobart."

The bottom of the world, or at least about as close as one could get while remaining in a recognized country. Elizabeth remembered Tasmania as the starting point of her own Antarctic journey. Why, though, would a wildlife official have been targeted alongside so many others with links—direct or otherwise—to the Stargate program?

"It's interesting," Geisler said, his thoughts clearly elsewhere. "The Newdegate Cave bears a striking resemblance to the caves we found on M1M-316."

CHAPTER NINETEEN

John cinched up the chinstrap on his helmet before stepping out of the Humvee. The faint rays of sunlight on the horizon were no longer strong enough to punch through the haze that still hovered over the street. He inhaled slowly, recognizing the pervasive, acrid smell of cordite and dried blood. The Museum building itself hadn't been damaged in the ambush, but the front steps were a mess of crumbled concrete and shell casings.

It had taken a maddeningly long time to get here. The Army had had its hands full, trying to secure five different sites throughout Baghdad where explosions had occurred almost simultaneously. As critical as John and Rebecca's mission was, it didn't trump ongoing urban warfare. They'd been stuck on base at Balad, the outlook for Jackson getting bleaker by the minute, until word finally had come down that the Museum area was under control—at least for the moment.

Climbing down from the Humvee, Rebecca adjusted her Kevlar vest and studied the other vehicles on the street, many of them scarred, inoperable hunks of twisted metal. "Good God," she said quietly. "If Dr. Jackson was in one of those—"

"Let's not go off half-cocked on that just yet." John scanned the helmets of the assorted soldiers patrolling the block, checking their rank insignia. There was a lieutenant standing next to a damaged personnel carrier, supervising the repairs being attempted by two of his maintenance troops. Bingo.

"What do we know, Lieutenant?"

The young man straightened at John's approach. "Sir, this was a three-vehicle convoy. We believe it took the first hit of a coordinated citywide assault. Four of the ten soldiers in the convoy were killed by the blast, along with a local; med-evac took five more to Balad. The last one—"

"—was a civilian and is missing. I know. He's the reason we're here." John glanced at the Museum steps again, averting his gaze when he noticed the dark, drying stains on the shattered stone. "Any leads on what might have happened to him?"

The lieutenant shook his head. "Everyone who survived was wounded badly enough to lose consciousness at one point or another. None of them even remembered Dr. Jackson's name, let alone where he'd been when all hell broke loose."

"But you didn't find a body." Rebecca joined the conversation. "No unidentified limbs, no uniform scraps."

"No, ma'am. We've gone door to door on the surrounding blocks. If the locals know anything, they sure aren't talking."

John had expected as much, but it still irritated him no end. He'd called back to Colorado Springs from one of Balad's secure phone lines, hoping that the SGC might be able to track Jackson's locator beacon even without the *Daedalus* or *Odyssey* around. Maybe they could use a satellite, or something—the workings of those beacons were pretty fuzzy to him. Just another example of how much he didn't know about homeworld defense.

In any case, he'd come up empty so far. At this point, the chances of finding Jackson before either his inevitable injuries or someone unfriendly caught up to him were remote at best. The security squad now cleaning up the site would most likely wrap up their efforts soon so they could leave the area before darkness settled in completely and masked any nearby threats.

All that advanced technology back on Atlantis, and John couldn't find one man on his own damned planet. He nodded to the lieutenant and walked a few paces away, trying to come up with some kind of plan and keep a lid on his frustration at the same time.

Rebecca matched him step for step. "Getting worked up

won't help Dr. Jackson or anyone else," she said, keeping her voice low.

Apparently he hadn't done very well at that second task. "Easy for you to say. The stuff that guy's done over the past ten years... If he's really dead this time, I have to wonder if we have any shot at all of figuring this out."

It was a sign of her growing familiarity with their situation that the phrase 'really dead this time' didn't seem to faze her. "Then we'd better find him alive." She bent to examine a series of scorch marks in the road. "Battlefields make for lousy crime scenes. It's next to impossible to weed out the relevant evidence from all the extraneous chaos. If I knew which vehicle he was in, that might be a start."

"Probably the middle one. That'd be procedure, since he didn't have an assigned role in protecting the convoy."

They walked over to the wrecked Humvee. As the profiler eyed one of its unhinged doors, a shriek of static issued from John's radio, followed by a startling voice. "This is Daniel Jackson calling any coalition forces who can hear me, particularly Colonel Sh—"

John yanked the radio off his belt. "Jackson, it's Sheppard. Switch to channel Delta."

"Copy." There was a pause as both made the change in order to free up the common frequency. "I'm with you on Delta. Glad to know today's frequency protocols haven't expired yet."

The sheer relief of hearing Jackson's voice just about knocked John over. "Are you okay? Where the hell are you?"

"Ramadi, and I'm okay. I had some, ah, help getting out of the combat zone."

Rebecca's grin morphed into a puzzled frown, and she mouthed *Ramadi?*

John shook his head, already feeling the beginnings of an adrenaline nosedive. "Don't take this wrong, because it's really great to know you're still in one piece, but is there some reason you couldn't have clued us in on that fact a couple of hours ago?"

"There is, actually." Jackson sounded pretty calm for someone who'd practically been blown sky high not too long ago. "My new acquaintances and I had some trust issues to work out. It took us a while to get this radio working as well. The important thing is that I know a lot more about what we came here to investigate. The people who rescued me are worshippers of Lilith—or, more accurately, Ninlil."

A sharp gasp from Rebecca was hurriedly suppressed.

"Say what?" Although John knew better than to press for details on an open frequency, that statement was more than a little worrying.

"I'll explain later. Right now I need a ride back to the base. Think you can come pick me up?"

"We'll make it work. Keep monitoring this channel. Sheppard out." John tried to dredge up a mental map of the country and failed. He went back to the lieutenant, whose group had gotten the personnel carrier's engine running and was preparing to head out. "Lieutenant, what's the best option for getting to Ramadi?"

"Best option is to stay home, sir," the soldier told him without a trace of humor. "Going through Fallujah's a crapshoot even in daylight, and it doesn't get much better from there. If you really have to make the trip, see if you can take a chopper. Might have to wait a while for an aircrew to become available, though. They're stretched pretty thin these days."

If that was the biggest obstacle of the moment, things were looking up. John decided he didn't want to know how Jackson's helpers had sneaked him through the gauntlet by ground. "Assuming there's a Hawk free, finding a pilot won't be a problem."

John hadn't come to Iraq with any intention of returning to old habits, but the well-practiced rhythms of powering up an HH-60 Pave Hawk were distinct and comfortable in his memory. He glanced behind him at Rebecca, securing her seat restraint. "All set?"

"Sure." She hadn't even blinked at the idea of flying through the helicopter equivalent of shark-infested waters. She'd just accepted the proffered helmet and climbed aboard. He had to give her credit for that. "I take it you kept your flight qualifications current while you were on special assignment?"

Under the guise of turning to face front, John checked his assigned copilot for a reaction to the 'special assignment' remark. Captain Baker merely continued uploading their mission profile to the navigation computer, her downcast eyes obscured by the night-vision goggles perched on top of her helmet.

"Remember how I told you about that six-week vacation I had a few months ago?" John answered Rebecca. "I re-qualified during my downtime."

"That's encouraging." Over the helmet intercom, a hint of a smile was audible in her voice. He was glad to hear it, if a little wary. Although she hadn't lost her cool for long, her earlier shock upon hearing Jackson's explanation of his situation had been plain to see. John was getting an increasingly strong sense that Rebecca Larance wasn't being completely forthcoming, and he was starting to wonder just how she'd managed to pick up some of the information she had on the Lilith-Ninlil scriptures.

He closed his hands around the collective and throttle and eased the chopper into the air, recalling yet again how very different it was from his usual ride these days. The intuitive controls of a puddle jumper were indescribably cool, but the jumpers' power was understated, the accelerations muted. Here, he felt the helicopter's strength thrumming through every surface.

Although this hop would be relatively short, he couldn't afford to treat it like a stroll down memory lane—not at night over unfamiliar terrain that likely held a few would-be shooters. Once he'd left the floodlights of the Balad flight line behind, he pulled his goggles into place and scanned the barely visible horizon.

Rebecca's voice filtered through his headset again. "Is there an established coalition base in Ramadi?"

"The Army and the Marines have been trading shifts there," replied Baker. "They've got a decent landing zone, which is all I ever— Incoming!"

Even as she called out the warning, John saw the brilliant flash from the ground below, whiting out his goggles for an instant. He banked the chopper sharply to the left and climbed, hoping the projectile had been a mortar and not something that could track his engine's heat signature. "Hang on!"

An explosion rattled the craft, stealing its lift and forcing John to battle the cyclic for a moment. Thrown forward against his harness, he quickly reestablished control. "Damage?"

"Don't think so," Baker reported. "Looks like we were far enough above it when it blew, whatever it was."

"All aircraft, be advised," came a controller's voice over the radio. "Reports of ground fire in sector Kilo."

"You don't say," John muttered. More points of light flickered below—muzzle flashes. The bullets wouldn't reach them at this altitude, though that wouldn't stop the insurgents from trying, because sooner or later the helicopter had to land.

John checked his green-tinted view against the nav computer. Within the cluster of buildings at his ten-o'clock was the courtyard that would serve as his landing zone. "Find me a descent path that won't put us in the middle of that fireworks show," he told Baker.

"Can do. Turn right to zero-two-zero, hold course for ninety seconds, then back left to two-nine-zero."

She talked him down to an altitude of five hundred feet, and he pulled out the evasive-approach tricks he'd honed in Khabour. Only a few bullets sang past the windscreen as he swung down between two buildings, which then blocked the shooters' aim while the chopper descended through the remaining seventy feet to settle on the ground.

"Well, that could've been worse," Baker commented as the rotors slowed to a halt in the high-walled courtyard. "Nice job, Colonel."

"Team effort. Go report our arrival to the area commander, would you? I'll handle the post-flight." John tugged his goggles and helmet off while she left to obey. Without his headset he could hear the clash beyond the wall for the first time. By the time he finished his post-flight checklist, the gunfire had faded out. "Guess we provided the excitement for the evening," he said over his shoulder to Rebecca.

When she didn't reply, he turned around in his seat. "Hey, if that whole thing freaked you out, I'm sorry."

"It did, a bit." But she looked more interested than concerned as she moved forward to take the seat vacated by Baker. "Getting shot at didn't seem to bother either of you too much."

He shrugged and powered down the avionics. "It's a fairly standard occurrence in our line of work, on Earth or elsewhere."

Rebecca's scrutiny didn't let up. "Do you miss this?" she asked suddenly. "Not the part about taking fire. All this—it's the life you had up until I met you in that conference room back at Hurlburt Field."

In John's mind, nothing good ever came from dwelling on roads not taken, so he'd been avoiding thoughts of that nature for a while. When he met her gaze, however, there was genuine care behind it, not just professional curiosity. For that reason, he decided to give her a real answer. "When I was in high school, a guidance counselor told me I could be pretty much whatever I wanted if I'd just straighten the hell up. I did, and I chose this. Yeah, I miss it." He stowed the checklist and climbed out of the cockpit. "Doesn't mean I'd change where

I ended up."

"I guess I'm relieved to hear that." Rebecca accepted the helping hand he offered as she jumped down to the concrete. "I cleared you for the Antarctica assignment, after all. Obviously I didn't know it would lead you to another galaxy. Still, I'd hate to think I was indirectly accountable for wrecking up your life."

"Gracious of you, but nobody dragged me through the Stargate. I'm okay with taking responsibility for my own choices."

"Except you're responsible for a lot more than that, aren't you?" She watched him with an expression he couldn't decipher. "You've been in command of a major forward-deployed unit for going on three years."

What was she getting at? Had someone told her about Sumner—or did she know more than she'd let on about his prospects for getting back to Atlantis? Or was she tossing chaff to deflect attention from some personal issues of her own? "It's a lot more paperwork than power trip," he said, a defensive edge creeping into his voice.

"Actually, I was going to say that it sounded kind of isolating. And not just geographically."

That threw John for a loop. "I don't really think about it that way. Like I said, it's the choice I made, and I haven't looked back."

"I can sympathize. I've got a botched marriage under my belt, too, courtesy of a focus on my work to the exclusion of everything else." She glanced at her bare ring finger. "It's kind of like a merit badge in the Bureau."

And there it was. Maybe it was a product of too much tension and not enough sleep, but he saw something familiar in the rueful smile she threw him—something that suggested she really might understand—and it made the whole situation marginally more tolerable. He wasn't the type to bare his soul; usually, when things were rough, all he needed to hear from a friend was 'I get it,' and that would see him through.

Receiving that from her was an unexpected gift.

Offering a quick smile of his own, he nodded toward the nearby building. "We'd better go find ourselves a vehicle and give Jackson a call."

As it turned out, getting directions to Jackson's location wasn't difficult. Getting the local militiamen to let more Americans into the bunker where he was holed up, on the other hand, was more of a challenge—as was convincing their Marine chauffeurs to stay outside with their vehicle.

Inside, dressed in robes and speaking in what sounded like an Arabic dialect, Jackson stood up from a wooden table lit by candles. The guards reluctantly stepped aside to clear the doorway.

The archeologist switched to English. "Good to see you guys." Surrounded by chipped clay tablets, with a number of scrolls strewn across the table, he looked none the worse for wear aside from a damp patch of blood on his arm—in approximately the place where the SGC usually implanted its locator beacons.

"Same here," John said warily, trying to put two and two together and coming up with thirteen. "Were you even in that ambush at the Museum? Everyone else in the convoy got the crap kicked out of them."

"No, I was there, and I probably got it as badly as the rest of them. That radio I used to call you was the only thing of mine that survived anywhere close to intact. Hence these clothes." Jackson awkwardly scrubbed a hand through his hair. "I'm told my heart stopped at one point."

There weren't too many possible ways to make such a rapid transition between half-dead and perfectly healthy. Since Ascension probably hadn't been involved for a change, John had a sneaking suspicion he was going to be disturbed by what was coming.

Rebecca pushed back the scarf of the chador she'd donned for the drive and took a step forward, looking like she didn't quite dare to believe what she saw. "So it's true," she said softly. "There are succubi that restore life instead of taking it."

Jackson nodded. "There are definitely two separate sects. As a group, they're considerably more widespread than we first thought, and it's divided for reasons that, believe it or not, are centered on which faction carries the 'true' blood-line of Lilith—or more accurately, Ninlil's—creations. The woman we saw in the video of Woolsey's cousin was trying to help him; he has—or had—an associated genetic disorder that should have killed him in childhood. Anyway, he carried traces of what they believed to be the 'correct' bloodline."

"What makes you so sure?" John asked.

"Because she's the same woman who healed me and saved my life. Her name is Hanan." The corner of Jackson's mouth quirked wryly. "It means 'mercy' in Egyptian Arabic."

John figured he'd better get ready to accept a pretty bizarre tale. "She pulled you out of the convoy?"

"No, that was a cambion named Baqir. He left with Hanan a while ago." Jackson shook his head. "It took me a while to place his name—I'm blaming that lapse on a skull fracture from the attack—but eventually I remembered reading about Baqir Abdel-Harim in Catherine Langford's notes on the recovery of the Stargate. I assumed this Baqir to be his grand-son until he told me that *he* had made certain that a pendant of Ra made its way into the hands of a young girl at the Giza excavation in 1928. He was pleased to learn that Catherine had continued to wear it all these years."

Jackson's wistful smile vanished as he continued. "We were wrong about their motivations. Neither group was ever interested in locating the gate; they know *exactly* where it is. This entire time they've only been concerned with either protecting or eliminating this bloodline. The Ninlil succubi and incubi make certain the carriers survive childhood ill-nesses and adult diseases, while their cambion take care of the details, like hiding them and running biomedical research wrong, if for no other reason than they would serve to empower the Ori. She'd brought along the Wraith genetic material from the experiments on M1M-316 she'd been forced to abandon, which would allow her to reproduce laboratory clones."

"Whoa, hang on." Even though John often mocked Rodney for his paranoia, sometimes a reasonable amount of alarm was justified. "Are you saying she actually created Wraith on Earth?"

"Not Wraith per se." He paused and pursed his lips before glancing through the narrow doorway. "That's as far as I've managed to get. Trouble is, the people who guard these artifacts take their job very seriously. Removing the scrolls or tablets from the building is out of the question. All they'll let me take is this." He withdrew a small rectangular device from beneath a sheet and held it up. John tried to contain his surprise when he saw that it was an Ancient data recorder. "They found it in among some outdated computer parts left in storage since the Gulf War."

The sound of semi-automatic gunfire in the near distance immediately drew everyone's attention. Muffled shouts outside were swallowed up by the sound of a small explosion that John estimated to be just a few blocks away. Time to get the hell out of Dodge.

"We can come back later if we have to follow any leads further." Jackson strode toward the door, paying no mind to the growing commotion outside.

"Come *back*?" Rebecca gave a short, disbelieving laugh. "We'll just drop by Iraq sometime on the way home from the grocery store? We almost got shot up, and you almost got blown up—actually, there's no 'almost' about that one. And apparently it's not over yet. You really want to repeat this grand adventure?"

John was all set to agree with her until Jackson paused, caught his eye, and surreptitiously rubbed the bloodied patch on his sleeve. Following his gaze, John identified the miss-

facilities that fund their activities."

Suppressing the urge to repeat his *Underworld* allusion, John focused on the unfamiliar word. "Cambion?"

"The half-human offspring of demonic *lilin*," Rebecca replied absently. John got the impression that the prospect unnerved her as much as it did him, which was saying something.

"Made famous by Shakespeare as Caliban in *The Tempest*," added Jackson. "In this context, they're the half-human offspring of succubi or incubi, which can't produce viable children between them."

John looked around the room again and saw no one except the guards at the door. "Where did this Hanan and Baqir run off to?"

"Hanan…needed rest."

The hesitation in Jackson's response was a belated wake-up call. If he'd been critically injured, healing him had to have taken a lot out of the succubus. The odds were good that she'd have to replenish that life by getting it from someone else.

Some hint of John's revulsion must have been visible on his face, because Jackson was quick to explain. "She's the ideological equivalent of a Tok'ra. When necessary, she'll take a few years off the lives of her cambion and replace it whenever she can. Around here these days, though, she's able to get all the nourishment she needs from giving mercy to the mortally wounded. That's where she's gone now."

In the abstract, it sounded almost reasonable—but this was far from abstract. There was a woman out on the streets looking for a shooting or bomb victim to drain of life. How was John supposed to rationalize that?

"I can't say I'm wild about the idea, either," admitted Jackson. "Even if it's the reason I'm standing here. Having said that, I believed Hanan when she swore that she only takes the remaining life from people who are in great pain and have no hope of surviving. Aside from informing me of the existence of the two opposing groups, she wasn't too forthcoming with details. Baqir gave me access to this place and promised it would give me answers."

"And has it?" Rebecca asked.

"Oh, you could say that." Jackson returned to the table overflowing with artifacts. "From what I've gathered, the bloodlines are only the beginning. The two sects have very different agendas."

So Rebecca had been right on target with her profile. John glanced over at her and tilted his head in acknowledgement.

"For the sake of clarity, the easiest way to distinguish between the two is to call the predatory group Lilith, which keeps itself in business by running various shipping, airline and travel companies, and the one that wants to protect humans, Ninlil." Rifling through the array of scrolls and tablets, Jackson selected a surprisingly well-preserved parchment. "I haven't yet figured out how the rift occurred or where it fits in with these divergent bloodlines in the general human population, but we'll get to that later. I started out by rereading the intact tablets of Gilgamesh and found that much of the text, including the references to sky gods, had been copied from this earlier set of documents."

He opened the scroll casually, not bothering to handle it with the care often shown to such relics. Before John could question him, Jackson lifted the manuscript for inspection. "This isn't parchment or vellum. It's almost like plastic, except even more durable. And then there's what happens to be written on it."

While John was by no means a language expert, he recognized Ancient when he saw it. "Guess that confirms once and for all just who got this party started."

"We need to read it in the context of what we know now." Jackson closed the scroll again. "When Merlin and his group of refugee Lanteans returned to Earth ten thousand years ago, they realized they hadn't come through the Antarctic gate like they'd expected. The continents had drifted, and Antarctica was under a massive layer of ice."

"You'd think they would have planned out where they end up before making the trip." John glanced at the building's entrance and wondered how much time they had before their security escort told them it was time to leave.

"Maybe." Jackson rolled up the scroll. "It's going to take me a long time to examine all the texts, but what I've read so far suggests that Atlantis may not have been the only Ancient city in Antarctica. We've wondered for a while why we found an older Stargate and a weapons chair there, since Atlantis has its own chair and gate, and Morgan Le Fay did tell us that some Lanteans made their way to the gate at the southern pole. What if there's a lot more than one outpost buried beneath all that ice?"

John wasn't sure what to make of that idea. "If so, shouldn't we have detected it by now?"

"We went years without detecting the chair," Jackson countered, packing the scrolls in an open crate as he spoke. "Antarctica is almost half again as big as the continental U.S., and the ice that covers it is several miles thick in some places. My point is that the Lanteans left the Pegasus Galaxy for Earth expecting to have access to the same level of facilities that they'd left behind, and instead they encountered a primitive world. They learned from the humans they met that a Goa'uld, Ra, was running the galaxy, and the last thing they wanted was another war with a malevolent alien species. The Lanteans agreed they had to leave the immediate region where the Stargate was located—Egypt—most of them with just one thing in mind."

"Ascension."

Jackson nodded. "They viewed themselves as literally the last of their kind and believed that their only options were Ascension or extinction. Some sought to Ascend through reclusive meditation, but Lilith and others strenuously opposed them, arguing that Ascension through nonscientific means had led to the existence of the Ori. Lilith further believed that leaving the humans of the galaxy behind was ing locator beacon, affixed to one of the crates containing the tablets. Smart move; if they needed this stuff later, they could beam it out as soon as the *Odyssey* or *Daedalus* was back in range. Besides, an Ancient recorder held a lot more information than crumbling blocks of clay.

A second explosion, nearer this time, shook the bunker and sent a puff of dust wafting through the entrance. Two Marines and one of the militiamen followed, shouting similar orders. They had to get out of here—now.

"It'll be all right," he told Rebecca simply.

She shot him a doubtful look but pulled her chador back into place. Then she ran ahead of him out onto a street lit by balls of flame and punctuated by streaks of tracer fire.

CHAPTER TWENTY

After the sandblasted atmosphere of central Iraq, the interior of the C-20 felt humid by comparison. John had barely found a seat before the crew closed the hatch and started the engine run-up. He settled back, relieved they'd made it here in one piece and grateful to have a few hours with no immediate duties, even if he had to spend them in the cabin of an aircraft he wasn't flying.

Once they'd dodged the minor flare-up outside the bunker, getting out of Ramadi had turned out to be easier than getting in. The potshots taken at their helicopter on the arriving flight had been the prelude to an attack that had moved rapidly toward the heart of the city. Larger but still uncoordinated, the assault hadn't put much of a crimp in flight ops at the small airfield on the outskirts of town. "Just the nightly fireworks show," Captain Baker had called it. As a result, John had been able to get the HH-60 up and out with little difficulty.

Jackson, who hadn't been fazed by any of the pyrotechnics, seemed to have no plans to take a break even on the long return flight to Colorado. Focused on setting up his laptop, he dug the Ancient datapad out of his pocket and held it out across the aisle. "Initialize this for me, would you?"

Slouched in the corner formed by the seat and the bulkhead, John had to stretch to reach the device. Rebecca, sitting opposite Jackson, took it and started to hand it over, only to jerk back in shock when the screen came to life.

John sat up straighter. "Welcome to the ATA club," he commented. "We don't have a secret handshake or anything, but it's a good bet you'll get a ceremonial bloodletting from Dr. Lam when we get back to the SGC."

In response, Rebecca tossed the datapad to him. Although she quickly pasted on a calm expression, he still got the feeling she could have done without any more surprises today. He of the Alterans' old neighborhood, he wasn't sure 'passive' was the best description.

Multitasking, Jackson continued to speed-read the contents of the datapad while continuing with his short history of the universe. "Several million years ago, a plague similar to the pandemic that afflicted Earth a couple of years back wiped out all life in this galaxy. Our best guess is that the Ori found a way to Ascend and released the plague to finish off their ideological enemies. We believe that many Alterans escaped by Ascending, while others left the Milky Way—though presumably not before using their technology to recreate life here." He frowned thoughtfully and glanced through the window. "Of course, it's possible as well that they waited until the plague had burned itself out before returning and recreating life. The details of that are sketchy. Anyway, they must have encoded their own DNA into the baseline, because the same human form once again evolved on Earth."

"This sounds remarkably like the Babylonian mythology of the Annunaki." Looking unsure what to do with her newly discovered magic touch, Rebecca folded her hands in her lap.

A small smile crossed Jackson's face. "Funny you should mention that. Baqir referred to them as the Annunaki. It seems the Epic of Gilgamesh was considerably more literal than scholars imagined—Sitchin was right."

"So both sides carried their disagreement into the afterlife."

"And then some. In their home galaxy, the Ascended Ori figured out that they could gain even greater power through a type of psychic feeding from their worshippers on the mortal plane. I know it sounds like New Age mystic nonsense, but these advanced life forms embody energy—"

"Let's leave the physics to the scientists," Rebecca broke in. "I get the basic picture. More followers mean more power for the Ori, so they came up with this dogmatic proselytizing religion of theirs. What I don't see is how any of it relates to did his best to sound reassuring. "It's no big deal. At least you didn't get a holographic map of the universe buzzing around your head."

Jackson looked up at her, seemingly unaffected by the new development. "There's some additional background you should know about the Ancients, especially in light of this news about your heredity."

Rebecca hesitated for a moment and then surrendered, giving him her full attention. "You can start by telling me who these Ori are that you mentioned back in Ramadi."

As the C-20 began its takeoff roll, John gave the datapad back to Jackson.

"Thanks. Okay, backing up to catch a couple of details we didn't explain earlier: the Ancients were once called Alterans, and they and the Ori were once a single race living in a distant galaxy. While the Ori took a spiritual approach to achieving Ascension, the Alterans went for a scientific path. At first the Ori route seemed more reasonable, because the Alterans had locked themselves into a rigid set of rules centered on a policy of non-interference with younger races in their galaxy."

Rebecca lifted an eyebrow. "Sort of like a Prime Directive." When John glanced at her, bemused, she opened her mouth to explain and then changed her mind, flicking her hand. "Inside joke from when I was a kid. Never mind."

"That's one way to put it." The aircraft rose smoothly into the air. Tapping a button on the side of the datapad, Jackson went on. "According to Merlin, the Ori started with good intentions of helping people Ascend. Ultimately, though, their philosophical differences with the Alterans led to a kind of religious crusade. Persecuted and unwilling to engage in a war, the Alterans left their galaxy. After a thousand years of wandering, they ended up here in the Milky Way, where they built an empire while maintaining a passive link to their home galaxy."

From what John had heard of the incident where Jackson and Vala had been body-snatched and dumped into residents

CHAPTER TWENTY

After the sandblasted atmosphere of central Iraq, the interior of the C-20 felt humid by comparison. John had barely found a seat before the crew closed the hatch and started the engine run-up. He settled back, relieved they'd made it here in one piece and grateful to have a few hours with no immediate duties, even if he had to spend them in the cabin of an aircraft he wasn't flying.

Once they'd dodged the minor flare-up outside the bunker, getting out of Ramadi had turned out to be easier than getting in. The potshots taken at their helicopter on the arriving flight had been the prelude to an attack that had moved rapidly toward the heart of the city. Larger but still uncoordinated, the assault hadn't put much of a crimp in flight ops at the small airfield on the outskirts of town. "Just the nightly fireworks show," Captain Baker had called it. As a result, John had been able to get the HH-60 up and out with little difficulty.

Jackson, who hadn't been fazed by any of the pyrotechnics, seemed to have no plans to take a break even on the long return flight to Colorado. Focused on setting up his laptop, he dug the Ancient datapad out of his pocket and held it out across the aisle. "Initialize this for me, would you?"

Slouched in the corner formed by the seat and the bulkhead, John had to stretch to reach the device. Rebecca, sitting opposite Jackson, took it and started to hand it over, only to jerk back in shock when the screen came to life.

John sat up straighter. "Welcome to the ATA club," he commented. "We don't have a secret handshake or anything, but it's a good bet you'll get a ceremonial bloodletting from Dr. Lam when we get back to the SGC."

In response, Rebecca tossed the datapad to him. Although she quickly pasted on a calm expression, he still got the feeling she could have done without any more surprises today. He ing locator beacon, affixed to one of the crates containing the tablets. Smart move; if they needed this stuff later, they could beam it out as soon as the *Odyssey* or *Daedalus* was back in range. Besides, an Ancient recorder held a lot more information than crumbling blocks of clay.

A second explosion, nearer this time, shook the bunker and sent a puff of dust wafting through the entrance. Two Marines and one of the militiamen followed, shouting similar orders. They had to get out of here—now.

"It'll be all right," he told Rebecca simply.

She shot him a doubtful look but pulled her chador back into place. Then she ran ahead of him out onto a street lit by balls of flame and punctuated by streaks of tracer fire.

with details. Baqir gave me access to this place and promised it would give me answers."

"And has it?" Rebecca asked.

"Oh, you could say that." Jackson returned to the table overflowing with artifacts. "From what I've gathered, the bloodlines are only the beginning. The two sects have very different agendas."

So Rebecca had been right on target with her profile. John glanced over at her and tilted his head in acknowledgement.

"For the sake of clarity, the easiest way to distinguish between the two is to call the predatory group Lilith, which keeps itself in business by running various shipping, airline and travel companies, and the one that wants to protect humans, Ninlil." Rifling through the array of scrolls and tablets, Jackson selected a surprisingly well-preserved parchment. "I haven't yet figured out how the rift occurred or where it fits in with these divergent bloodlines in the general human population, but we'll get to that later. I started out by rereading the intact tablets of Gilgamesh and found that much of the text, including the references to sky gods, had been copied from this earlier set of documents."

He opened the scroll casually, not bothering to handle it with the care often shown to such relics. Before John could question him, Jackson lifted the manuscript for inspection. "This isn't parchment or vellum. It's almost like plastic, except even more durable. And then there's what happens to be written on it."

While John was by no means a language expert, he recognized Ancient when he saw it. "Guess that confirms once and for all just who got this party started."

"We need to read it in the context of what we know now." Jackson closed the scroll again. "When Merlin and his group of refugee Lanteans returned to Earth ten thousand years ago, they realized they hadn't come through the Antarctic gate like they'd expected. The continents had drifted, and Antarctica was under a massive layer of ice."

facilities that fund their activities."

Suppressing the urge to repeat his *Underworld* allusion, John focused on the unfamiliar word. "Cambion?"

"The half-human offspring of demonic *lilin*," Rebecca replied absently. John got the impression that the prospect unnerved her as much as it did him, which was saying something.

"Made famous by Shakespeare as Caliban in *The Tempest*," added Jackson. "In this context, they're the half-human offspring of succubi or incubi, which can't produce viable children between them."

John looked around the room again and saw no one except the guards at the door. "Where did this Hanan and Baqir run off to?"

"Hanan...needed rest."

The hesitation in Jackson's response was a belated wake-up call. If he'd been critically injured, healing him had to have taken a lot out of the succubus. The odds were good that she'd have to replenish that life by getting it from someone else.

Some hint of John's revulsion must have been visible on his face, because Jackson was quick to explain. "She's the ideological equivalent of a Tok'ra. When necessary, she'll take a few years off the lives of her cambion and replace it whenever she can. Around here these days, though, she's able to get all the nourishment she needs from giving mercy to the mortally wounded. That's where she's gone now."

In the abstract, it sounded almost reasonable—but this was far from abstract. There was a woman out on the streets looking for a shooting or bomb victim to drain of life. How was John supposed to rationalize that?

"I can't say I'm wild about the idea, either," admitted Jackson. "Even if it's the reason I'm standing here. Having said that, I believed Hanan when she swore that she only takes the remaining life from people who are in great pain and have hope of surviving. Aside from informing me of the exis-
the two opposing groups, she wasn't too forthcoming

"You'd think they would have planned out where they'd end up before making the trip." John glanced at the building's entrance and wondered how much time they had before their security escort told them it was time to leave.

"Maybe." Jackson rolled up the scroll. "It's going to take me a long time to examine all the texts, but what I've read so far suggests that Atlantis may not have been the only Ancient city in Antarctica. We've wondered for a while why we found an older Stargate and a weapons chair there, since Atlantis has its own chair and gate, and Morgan Le Fay did tell us that some Lanteans made their way to the gate at the southern pole. What if there's a lot more than one outpost buried beneath all that ice?"

John wasn't sure what to make of that idea. "If so, shouldn't we have detected it by now?"

"We went years without detecting the chair," Jackson countered, packing the scrolls in an open crate as he spoke. "Antarctica is almost half again as big as the continental U.S., and the ice that covers it is several miles thick in some places. My point is that the Lanteans left the Pegasus Galaxy for Earth expecting to have access to the same level of facilities that they'd left behind, and instead they encountered a primitive world. They learned from the humans they met that a Goa'uld, Ra, was running the galaxy, and the last thing they wanted was another war with a malevolent alien species. The Lanteans agreed they had to leave the immediate region where the Stargate was located—Egypt—most of them with just one thing in mind."

"Ascension."

Jackson nodded. "They viewed themselves as literally the last of their kind and believed that their only options were Ascension or extinction. Some sought to Ascend through reclusive meditation, but Lilith and others strenuously opposed them, arguing that Ascension through nonscientific means had led to the existence of the Ori. Lilith further believed that leaving the humans of the galaxy behind was wrong, if for no other reason than they would serve to empower the Ori. She'd brought along the Wraith genetic material from the experiments on M1M-316 she'd been forced to abandon, which would allow her to reproduce laboratory clones."

"Whoa, hang on." Even though John often mocked Rodney for his paranoia, sometimes a reasonable amount of alarm was justified. "Are you saying she actually created Wraith on Earth?"

"Not Wraith per se." He paused and pursed his lips before glancing through the narrow doorway. "That's as far as I've managed to get. Trouble is, the people who guard these artifacts take their job very seriously. Removing the scrolls or tablets from the building is out of the question. All they'll let me take is this." He withdrew a small rectangular device from beneath a sheet and held it up. John tried to contain his surprise when he saw that it was an Ancient data recorder. "They found it in among some outdated computer parts left in storage since the Gulf War."

The sound of semi-automatic gunfire in the near distance immediately drew everyone's attention. Muffled shouts outside were swallowed up by the sound of a small explosion that John estimated to be just a few blocks away. Time to get the hell out of Dodge.

"We can come back later if we have to follow any leads further." Jackson strode toward the door, paying no mind to the growing commotion outside.

"Come *back*?" Rebecca gave a short, disbelieving laugh. "We'll just drop by Iraq sometime on the way home from the grocery store? We almost got shot up, and you almost got blown up—actually, there's no 'almost' about that one. And apparently it's not over yet. You really want to repeat this grand adventure?"

John was all set to agree with her until Jackson paused, caught his eye, and surreptitiously rubbed the bloodied patch on his sleeve. Following his gaze, John identified the miss-the Ancient Lilith or the Wraith."

Regarding her over the top of the datapad, Jackson silently acknowledged the implied request to move the story along. "The Ascended Alterans, by contrast, are so adamantly opposed to any kind of interference that they banish any member of their collective who breaks the rules. According to Merlin—and the scrolls I read confirmed this—the unascended Ancients in the Pegasus Galaxy realized that, if left unchecked, the Ori would become dominant enough to defeat the Ascended Alterans and subsume their energy. Naturally, that would completely undermine the vaunted goal of Ascension. Being on the higher plane actually put the Alterans at a disadvantage."

"Because their rules prevented them from helping mortals, which the Ori were psychically enslaving," Rebecca finished.

"But Lilith wasn't Ascended," said John. "The rules didn't apply to her."

"Exactly," replied Jackson, glancing at him. "Lilith revisited an experiment that had been abandoned several million years earlier. A group of Ancients had been working with the gene for empathy in lower-order animals with the goal of evolving it to telepathy in higher orders. Since the Ascended share a form of group mind, a 'oneness with the universe,' so to speak, the theory was that the empathy/telepathy genes might provide a mechanism for Ascension—excorporeal excursions being another aspect of telepathy."

"M1M-316," said John. "Those dinosaurs that Ronon and Teyla rounded up were empathic."

"Hopefully McKay and Zelenka will be able to fill in the blanks from that end." Jackson jerked his chin toward the datapad. "Give me some time to go through this and maybe I can learn the details of what Lilith did once she got to Earth."

To John, that sounded like a cue. Since the aircraft had leveled out, he unbuckled his seatbelt and stood. "Bet there's some food in the back," he suggested to Rebecca.

The worry that had taken up residence when she'd activated the Ancient device began to clear from her features. "Think the Air Force stocks anything chocolate in its galleys? A Milky Way Dark bar would go a really long way toward restoring my overall outlook."

John smirked, wondering how she'd react if she knew how much she'd sounded like Rodney just then. "Jackson, you had anything to eat lately?"

His gaze never leaving the screen in front of him, the archeologist gave a quick, dismissive headshake. "Thanks—I'm fine. I think Hanan may have left me in better shape than before the attack."

Which was yet one more of the growing number of topics that John didn't want to dwell on. He headed aft to investigate a column of stainless steel storage cabinets.

The bottom one was refrigerated and held bottled water and cans of Coke, along with a few plastic-wrapped sandwiches. He crouched down and retrieved two sandwiches. "Coke or water?" he asked Rebecca as she came up beside him.

"Water, thanks. Don't stand up." She opened an upper drawer above his head. "Oh, *score*. Want a brownie or a cinnamon bun?"

"Brownie, definitely." And no Rodney to pilfer it. Double score.

They each claimed one of the couches that lined the bulkheads at the very aft of the aircraft and tore into the food with something less than perfect decorum.

"So these Ancients," Rebecca began after swallowing the last bite of her sandwich. "Despite the name, some of them still exist? Unascended, I mean?"

"We've run into a few," John replied. "Either unascended or deascended, if that's even a word. Most of them seem to have…issues. The first one I met had been kicked off the higher plane for protecting her home planet from the Wraith. She was exiled to continue defending that planet for the rest of eternity."

"I'll bet meeting you was the excitement of the millennium for her."

"Why's that? It's not like she'd never seen anyone with the gene before. I was just…" And then John realized he'd protested too soon. Rebecca had meant the collective 'you,' not him in particular. He took a drink of his Coke while trying to figure out how to get out of the hole he'd just dug himself. Not likely; being perceptive was in her job description.

As expected, Rebecca cocked an eyebrow. "Why, John Sheppard, did you have a romantic encounter with an alien goddess?"

Great. He didn't bother trying to deny it. "Even the shrink thinks I'm Captain freaking Kirk," he muttered, reaching for his brownie.

"I didn't say that. You're not the swaggering, melodramatic type, and so far on this trip you've managed to keep your shirt in one piece." Amusement glimmered in her eyes, but she soon damped it. "Based on what I've observed and what I remember of your profile, I'd expect you to connect best with strong women. That's all."

All right, this line of discussion was a disaster waiting to happen. "New topic," he said, not bothering to attempt any kind of graceful transition. "Are you doing all right with your whole new worldview? I know you're used to dealing with a lot of weird stuff, but by any measure this is a lot to take in over a span of just a couple days."

She considered the question for a while, taking a bite of her brownie in the meantime. "Facing the unknown is something that bothers almost everyone," she answered at last. "There's a lot we don't know about the situation we're in at the moment. What keeps me from panicking, at least for now, is the fact that we seem to be making progress. I'm not offering any guarantees about how I'll fare when all this is over."

"Yeah, I think all of us will need some time to have our own private meltdowns if and when we get the chance later."

He looked at her steadily, wanting her to really *get* the fact that she wasn't alone in this. "I said earlier that I wouldn't change where I am and what I do even if I could. That doesn't mean I don't wish certain aspects were different. After some of the things that have happened out there…let's just say I can admit to having a bad day now and then, even the occasional nightmare."

"I'm no stranger to those. Like *I* said earlier, there's a reason I'm no longer married." Rebecca crumpled up her food wrappers and lobbed them into a wastebasket attached to the bulkhead.

Although John didn't want to look too far down the road just yet, it seemed like the SGC could benefit from making Rebecca a permanent addition. She had the gene and the clearance, two things that didn't coincide too often, and she didn't panic when things got a little hot. "You have much family? Any kids?"

"With my job? I'm not that crazy." She finished her water. "As for family, not really. Only child, raised by my aunt, who was more Catholic than the Pope. You wouldn't have believed the whipping I got for accidentally eating a hamburger on a Friday during Lent. Funny how that method didn't exactly sell me on religion."

"You ought to meet Cam Mitchell when we get back to the SGC. Your aunt makes his grandmother sound lenient." John flashed a grin. "I can't see you being quite as bad as me as a kid, but you must have given out some gray hairs yourself."

"I—don't spend time on memory lane. Not much really stands out, so there isn't any point in it." Rebecca swiftly turned the focus back to him, a tactic he probably should have expected, but also an indication that she too had a few topics she'd prefer not to dwell on. "We talked about family during your McMurdo interview, I remember. You of all people understand that not everyone gets a stereotypical Norman Rockwell childhood."

John was starting to get the feeling that, if anyone was

going to squirm in this conversation, she was going to make sure it wasn't her. He was rescued from having to evade the subject by a voice from the main cabin. "Guys, I think we may have a problem."

Naturally…because God knew they didn't have any *other* problems at the moment.

Abandoning their drinks, John and Rebecca strode into the cabin to see Jackson standing with the datapad in hand and a deep frown etched on his face. The archeologist, radiating a fair amount of nervous tension, handed John the datapad.

With Rebecca standing at his shoulder, John peered at the screen in disbelief. Lined up and neatly categorized were images of dozens of fantastical creations. Minotaurs, harpies, vampires, satyrs, centaurs—hell, even mermaids. John whistled low and long, not trusting himself to come up with a more insightful response.

"Lilith left Morgan Le Fay in the dust," said Jackson, pulling off his glasses and rubbing his eyes. There was no doubt that he was considerably more disturbed by this new wrinkle than he'd been at any point during their getaway from Ramadi. "They're all in there. Every mythological chimera you can imagine. They existed—and may still exist."

CHAPTER TWENTY-ONE

The cracks in the ancient stonework dripped rank fluid, nourishing the slimy growth covering most of the roof and walls. He loathed coming to the Sanctum through this ancient *qanat*. He could have cared less that the superbly engineered hydraulic structures had been designed thousands of years earlier by his forefathers to carry life-giving water to the lands west of E'Din, to Syria and Israel, Jordan and Egypt. Nor did he have the slightest interest in how the technology to build the subterranean irrigation system had spread east to China along the Silk Road, and north into Bavaria, where he had entered this secret passage from the modern-day sewers of Blaubueren. It only mattered that the original builders had counted among their number other cambion like himself, those who carried the blood legacy bequeathed to them by Lilith, the Creator. As a cambion, the son of the succubus Desiderata, he had always known of this long-abandoned 'back door' into the vast network of limestone caverns.

"Misbegotten spelunkers," he muttered as he wormed his way through a partially collapsed section of stonework. Thanks to a group of damned curious cavers from Munich, the pit of discarded human husks had been discovered. The entrance to the caverns that he normally used was currently crawling with Blaubueren police. Additional squads were on their way from Ulm, one of the villagers had informed him when he'd stopped at a café on the pretense of buying coffee. There was some talk that the American military had also been dispatched, all of which had raised the gossip level in the café to fever pitch.

The proprietor, a wizened woman who had recognized him as a regular visitor to the town, had confided in him that, although killing people in such a bizarre manner was not *Her* style, *She* must be responsible. It was a sign, said the old woman, that very soon the *Blautopf*—the sinkhole aptly named the Blue Pot—would soon boil over with *Her* anger, just as it had in the old days.

He didn't have to ask for details. Local folklore had it that *Die Schoene Lau,* the Beautiful Lady, a mermaid, had been banished into the *Blautopf* by the mer-king of the Black Sea. The sinkhole, with its remarkably clear turquoise waters, did indeed provide an entrance into the cave system, and the waters had certainly been home to several of Lilith's creations for centuries. However, unable to procreate, they had long since died out.

Nursing their coffees in the front seat of the truck, he and the driver had chewed over the problem for several minutes. There were already too many police for the two of them to consider a frontal assault, and that situation would not change during the night. By morning the entire place would be teeming with people. They might have been able to use fake IDs to get past, but it still would have been a risk. That had left them with only one option.

Some moron had illegally built a garden shed directly over the sewer access grate. He'd allowed his driver to feed off the homeowner, extracting from the woman the location of the shed's key. Dragging aside rows of hydroponic vegetables, they'd uncovered the rusted grate and levered it out with a crowbar. While the driver had waited inside the house for the rest of the family to come home, he'd climbed down into the sewers. The first thing he'd done after entering the wretched place was to relieve himself of the dozen coffees he'd downed that afternoon. Then it was merely a matter of finding the entrance to the *qanat*, something that had resulted in a painful encounter with a rat. No matter. The creature could do him no harm and the wound on his hand had already healed. It just irritated him in principle.

As the offspring of a succubus, his genetic memories were more lucid than those born to incubi, like the driver of the truck. Nevertheless, his 'memory' of the entrance was two hundred and fifty years old, from the time when his mother, one step ahead of a peasant mob, had returned this way to the Sanctum to give birth to him and sleep off fifty years of feeding.

The fetid smell of the sewer at last behind him, the crumbling walls of the *qanat* now also gave way to living limestone. Beads of calcium-bearing water clung to the ends of hanging clusters of stalactites. The formations, broken in several places by the passage of Lilith's creations, had developed about an inch of growth on their fractured tips, signaling that he was indeed the first to come this way since 1758 AD.

He was in no great hurry. Neither the police nor the military would find the Sanctum tonight, or likely ever, no matter how far into the cave system they searched. Access was keyed only to those who bore the bloodline of Lilith. While many among the general populace unwittingly carried that bloodline, it had yet to be activated.

Nonetheless, the entire situation was a gigantic annoyance, because it meant that the Awakening of the last chamber would be fraught with a different kind of danger. After sleeping for two and a half centuries, the potent hunger of succubi and incubi made them damned near impossible to control. Awakening to a cavern full of fresh meat—the homeless and easily bribed youth of Ulm and Munich that he and the other cambion had rounded up and trucked to the caves these last few weeks—had taken the edge off the appetites of those in the first two chambers long enough for them to regain their sensibilities. But this last chamber…

Damn it. He squeezed his belly, the result of an easy life these last sixty years since that stupid bloody war, between two tall columns and smashed a collection of delicate helictites with a thoughtless brandishing of his flashlight. It wasn't unheard of for the succubi and incubi, driven by an insatiable, blinding hunger, to turn on their own children, the half-blood cambion, and feed until nothing but withered husks remained.

He turned off his flashlight and waited for his eyes to

adjust. As with all the sleeping chambers, the anteroom was suffused with a soft amber glow. The light was powered by an unseen force that Lilith herself had bequeathed them five thousand years earlier, when she had led her surviving creations here after the great Deluge.

Taking a moment to scrape the crusted grime from his boots, he then removed his ski jacket, worn in anticipation of an evening snowfall. "Stupid, shortsighted humans, abusing the planet," he muttered. Outside, the seasons were a mess, but the temperature inside, like in all caves, was a constant nine degrees Celsius. He was now perspiring freely.

After two further passages through the ornate formations, he at last emerged into the antechamber, lined with a filamentous membrane, soft and yielding to the touch. He ran his hands along the taut, sinewy flesh that held the membranes in place and smiled in fond memory of his childhood here, basking in the mental companionship of his older half sisters, the cambion who had cared for him from birth. The warmth faded when he recalled how many of them had been burned as witches in the year 1782—except, of course, for beautiful Anna Goeldi, whom the Swiss had hung instead ten years later. He and the other cambion had wanted to save her, the oldest cambion of them all, but Anna had insisted that her martyrdom would assure the protection of the others until the time of the final Awakening.

And so it had, for no more of their number had since been butchered—except when they'd encountered the bastard heretics and their misbegotten creations.

A few steps beyond lay the last of the vaulted sleeping chambers. His smile widened and he glanced up at the hexagonal patchwork of webbing stretched across the roof, his eyes drawn to the third cell from the left, where Desiderata lay sleeping. For seven years after his birth he had been held in the cooling embrace of her membranes, sharing her memories of a time when Lilith had walked among them, learning of his rightful place in the universe and their sacred duty to the Annunaki—what the ones who had stolen the Gate called Ancients or Alterans.

To an extent he could understand why those cambion fathered by incubi failed to comprehend their birthright. Born to human mothers, they were raised as human. It was only in adolescence that, compelled by a fitful longing, many sought out their true heritage. And yet, just as many denied their blood ties and the calling that sang from within their veins. They lived and died as mortal humans without ever knowing the richness and power of what it was to feed.

What he truly couldn't fathom, though, was the choice made by some to follow the heretics. The traitorous bitch Hanan and her cohort had *deliberately* helped the humans discover the Gate back in 1928, for pity's sake! Still, he conceded, it had eventually resulted in the humans drawing the attention of the Ori, and since that had been prophesied, he supposed he should concede the point that Lilith did, indeed, work in mysterious ways.

Even those who remained oblivious to their birthright had inadvertently fulfilled their obligation to Lilith by passing their blood heritage on to sons and daughters. Although thousands of their number had succumbed to the Inquisition, the seeds had been well planted across the planet among the burgeoning human population. Once this final Awakening was complete, the heretics and the abominations they had bred would be defeated, the unsullied bloodline that tied the offspring together could be Awakened, and the last Great Battle would commence.

The mind of the Watcher who remained in the Sanctum touched his, and he bowed down before her as she swept into the chamber. *All is well*, he declared wordlessly. *They have safely arrived in their new home.*

His assurance was unnecessary, for the Watcher maintained a powerful mind link to the first groups to have Awakened, but because he had come into the Sanctum without food he'd felt compelled to offer some form of platitude.

Where is the sustenance? she demanded.

Explaining to her the spelunkers' discovery of the human husks, he added that he anticipated the arrival of more police sometime during the night and the military at dawn. At his obvious irritation, she smiled and smoothed away his anger and his fears. *It is another sign—a good sign.*

The truth suddenly dawned on him. Since 2001 and the appearance of the Gate, 'hidden in plain sight' as predicted, the cambion and other Watchers had taken great care in searching out the bloodlines of the abominations and eliminating them. It came as no surprise that many who carried both pure and corrupted bloodlines had instinctually been drawn to the Stargate program. Two of the corrupted carriers living in Colorado Springs had been pregnant with fully realized abominations who, if allowed to live, might have passed their bastardized retrovirus on to countless others. Aside from the absolute necessity of killing them and their mothers before that could be allowed to happen, the Watchers had been careful to eliminate only lower-ranked members of the military and those peripherally related to the Stargate program—too many high-ranking carriers of this misbegotten bloodline existed to safely eradicate them all at this stage. The cambion had carefully covered their tracks by burning the remains.

For the American military to take such an interest in a group of bodies found in a barely known set of German caves was a clear indication that they considered the Colorado deaths to be connected. More significantly, it meant that they had recognized the nature of the deaths.

He allowed joy to suffuse him. *Then it is true. They have indeed encountered our forefathers in the Pegasus Galaxy—who have fed upon their kind!*

The Watcher inclined her head in agreement. *The Great Battle is almost upon us. When it is done, we will be rewarded. The abominations will be forever purged from the bloodline, while the sons and daughters of Adam learn their true destiny.*

CHAPTER TWENTY-TWO

"Have a seat up here. This won't take long." The nurse patted the bed and handed Rebecca a Q-tip. "Just run this along the inside of your cheek, and then we'll do the blood draw."

Rebecca didn't bother telling him that she knew the procedure as well as he did. She'd ordered the test on others more times than she could count. Not because she'd needed the results to determine guilt or innocence—at least not of the crime under investigation—but because judges and juries needed physical evidence, something they could understand with the recognized five senses.

Pulling the stick from her mouth, she watched the young lieutenant, built like a linebacker but with a cherubic face made for Hollywood, drop the evidence that would incriminate her into a tube. He offered her a brief but genuine smile and took the tube away to someplace presumably less austere than the SGC's examination room.

The results were foregone; of that Rebecca had no doubt. She carried within her considerably more than the ATA gene. It was probably too much to hope that the escalating situation at hand would be resolved before Dr. Lam's biomedical staff ran the genetic assay. Of course, they'd more than likely end up running it twice, since the first result would prompt a double-take worthy of the Three Stooges.

The lieutenant returned carrying the collection of instruments he needed to take a standard blood sample—or maybe six standard blood samples. He set the tray down and placed a squeeze ball in her hand. "Regular blood donor, I take it?" he asked politely, tapping the veins in the crook of her elbow.

The tiny puncture scars were a dead giveaway. "Yeah." Which triggered a gut-wrenching thought. Was the Wraith retrovirus only transmittable through the generations? Or was it, like HIV and other retroviruses, stealthily capable of infecting a new host who'd been unfortunate enough to need a blood transfusion? All these years she'd thought she was doing a good deed...

No doubt that was one of the many leads the medical staff was already investigating. She put it out of her mind and let her thoughts turn, as they so often had these past few days, to the past.

It had been easy enough to dismiss her childhood memories as ninety percent suggestion blended with years of work on one cult-oriented investigation after another. Certainly the FBI had never found any reason to suspect Rebecca's parents of having been part of Ninlil's loyal cadre of cambion. For one thing, the Bureau had been unaware of the Ninlil 'cult's' existence until Rebecca herself had dug up a few references and written a report so spartan that it barely ranked as a memo. And the Bureau's meticulous background checks generally didn't flag a person as suspect simply because they'd been orphaned under circumstances that the county coroner had ruled 'accidental.'

Rebecca had been only five years old when she'd gone to live with—or, more accurately, Social Services had dumped her on the front doorstep of—her only living relative, a widowed great-aunt related in some tenuous way by marriage. The Bible-thumping old biddy had promptly declared Rebecca demon spawn, because her parents had healed others by the laying on of hands, which her aunt had labeled as a way to steal their souls. That conviction had been augmented by daily lashings with a barber's strap, hours of Old Testament readings, and weekly dousings in holy water. By the age of ten, Rebecca had performed so many prostrations before the altar, begging for absolution for her wickedness, that she'd become personally acquainted with every threadbare stitch in the local church's miserable carpet.

The situation had only worsened when Rebecca had begun

to give voice to her observations of the people around her. It had never occurred to her that her gift for identifying what motivated people, what secrets they hid, what pain they suppressed or diverted into their own pathological behavior, might be considered unusual. A few fights at school and even more trips to the principal's office for what her teachers had described as 'spying' on their personal lives, plus the additional Sunday evening prostrations, had eventually taught her to hide her insights.

That was, until her old aunt, having scrimped every nickel and dime to send Rebecca to college, had died satisfied that she'd saved her niece from the fires of damnation. By then Rebecca had categorized her 'talent' as just a knack, a lucky attribute of birth, like an artist's skill or musical genius. Her ability to climb inside the minds of others and understand what made them tick could serve her well in life.

A sharp prick drew her attention to her arm and resulted in a mumbled apology from the lieutenant, who genuinely disliked inflicting pain, even if only minor. She smiled her reassurance at him and watched the first vial fill. It was a familiar process, one she'd begun in college. Donating blood was such a small and simple way to contribute to society, something her parents had instilled in her: *People will need your help, Rebecca.* It was the clearest lesson she could remember receiving from them.

College had exposed her to a wider world, a place where she'd begun to understand that her skills could help people and that others like her existed. Profilers, they were called and, far from being evil, they quietly went about protecting those who could not protect themselves from human monsters.

Rebecca had been a superlative student, her achievements noticed by peers and professors alike, and she'd published several papers on serial killers and cults long before graduating. Working with the FBI had given her a world where she'd been respected rather than vilified for her talents, and so she'd found a home at last. Her aunt would have been pleased to see her take on such a righteous cause, a latter-day crusade against Satan's minions.

In truth, the old lady could never have comprehended that Rebecca's initial research into cults had begun as a need to piece together some of the fragments of her lost childhood. Contrary to her aunt's lectures, Rebecca's memories assured her that her parents had not been demonic monsters who'd brought a fiery death upon themselves by practicing their 'witchcraft', but rather genuinely compassionate people who'd treated her and all those around them with love and kindness. During those first bleak weeks after their funeral, Rebecca had held a tight grip on those memories and on her mother's promise that she would grow up to be someone very special, someone who would one day not merely help people but 'save the whole world.'

Maturity and a few undergrad courses in psychology had eroded those fragile recollections until Rebecca came to regard them as no more significant than any mother's hopes and dreams. The warmth of the memory, though, had never faded.

A siren blared in the corridor outside. "That's a regularly scheduled gate departure," the lieutenant assured her, the needle steady in his hand. "Happens several times a day around here."

Sure. Just your average commuter trip to the next star system.

The mere existence of the Stargate had exploded all the walls of logic she'd carefully constructed, all the academic safeguards she'd instilled in her thinking. It was only through her childhood defenses, the abilities she'd developed to hide her reactions to the bizarre and unthinkable that lurked in people's thoughts, that she'd been able to contain an almost primal need to scream. Nothing she'd ever witnessed—no gruesome crime scene, no rummaging around in the mind of a madman—had ever left her so traumatized that she'd locked up inside and been unable to speak…until the next shocking realization that Atlantis and indeed the entire Pegasus Galaxy were not metaphysical constructs of some cultists' minds, but real, tangible places.

But the bombshells hadn't ended there. While John Sheppard, whom she'd tagged as ridiculously well-grounded for someone whose formative years hadn't been any picnic either, had sat in the Gulfstream munching on an Oreo, the truth had come crashing down on her. A long-buried suspicion had suddenly resurfaced and demanded immediate attention: her parents' deaths, in the fire that had consumed their house while Rebecca had been playing at a neighbor's, had been no accident.

Sleep, when it had come as the aircraft carried them to Iraq, had been at once haunted and restless and cathartic. The scattered shards of her life story had been bonded together with peculiar and unpalatable truths. Upon waking, more disturbed and yet more refreshed than she'd felt since she could remember, she'd managed to construct a mask of rigid professionalism and focus on the job at hand. Despite any genetic connection she might have to Ninlil—Lilith being a term she could no longer bring herself to use—Rebecca now knew without question that the two opposing groups intended two very different outcomes for humanity, regardless of the war with the Ori. She also understood that she had indeed been raised by her parents to help mankind, and whether she was truly human or something else entirely was not relevant to that fact.

The inevitable questions couldn't be ignored forever, though. What she'd said to John still stood. What did it mean to be human? He carried the Ancient gene, and he'd been fed upon—and restored—by a Wraith; she was certain of that, despite his transparent claim that he'd merely 'witnessed' the act. One of his team members, a woman who would soon be arriving from the Pegasus Galaxy, had Wraith genes, while another was immune to Wraith feeding. And they were human—weren't they?

She'd never considered the very definition of being human to be up for debate before. Now she desperately missed the innocence she'd worn until this week.

The vials now filled with blood, the lieutenant apologized again and withdrew the needle. He deftly placed a cotton swab over the tiny puncture and taped it in place. Rebecca rolled down her sleeve and watched him label each vial. All in the name of science and defense. Ninlil might have lost her grip on reality, but her original goal had been to protect Ancients and humans from the Ori, and so she had created a form of human with the best possible combination of Ancient, Wraith and human genes. Did that make those, like Rebecca, who carried such genes, less than human…or more?

"Agent Larance, please report to the briefing room," came a disembodied voice that she identified as belonging to Chief Harriman.

As was often the case in her line of work, the facts didn't matter. It was what people *believed* that drove them to act in ways that her textbooks and a hundred gruesome crime scenes had defined as less than human. What would the people of Earth believe if and when this truth was brought to light? When the current crisis ended, where would it leave her and those like her?

With a nod from the nurse to confirm that she was free to go, she eased off the bed just as Daniel Jackson strode in, a grim expression on his face. "We've just gotten confirmation from Dr. Lam in Germany," he informed her without preamble, shoving his hands into his pockets. "You were right. Using the enzyme test she's devised, Carolyn checked the bodies you were sent to investigate last week, the ones from the Munich sewers. They were victims of a succubus feeding—presumably a succubus, since the victims were all male."

He spoke so fast that Rebecca had to watch his lips to keep pace. No doubt he'd cultivated the trait in an environment where details were considered less critical than actions. She was about to tell him to slow down, but his next declaration struck with a force that robbed her of breath.

"Carolyn also confirmed that the same enzyme is present in a random sample of what they now estimate to be around two hundred bodies found a few hours ago in the Blaubeuren caves. The corpses they've pulled out so far all have had their hearts and livers removed."

Oh, hell. Until that moment she'd been operating under the theory that the term 'Awakening' in the doctrine of the Lilith cult had been a reference to those who carried the bloodline, not something more literal. She swore softly, fighting the urge to throttle something—preferably herself. How had she let herself be so badly blindsided? Focused on her own starring and as-yet-to-be-disclosed role in this, she'd made the most fundamental of errors: an *assumption.* "Crap."

"Yeah. The authorities also have confirmed that a large icon, two concentric circles bisected by an isosceles triangle, has been carved into the limestone structure of the cavern. Given what we know of Wraith hive behavior, this 'Awakening' may be applicable to both the first generation of incubi and succubi as well as the bloodlines hidden in the human population." He gestured for her to precede him into the gray-walled maze, then turn right outside the doorway.

"I can't believe I didn't see that sooner." Rebecca ran a tired hand through her hair as she walked.

"Don't beat yourself up over it. I should have thought of it too. While you may be more familiar with the 'cult,' the genuine alien context is still pretty new to you."

She glanced over at him as he fell into step beside her. "Charitable of you, Dr. Jackson, but that's no excuse. In my line of work you hit the ground running, no matter the circumstances. If you don't, more people die."

Pulling his hands from his pockets, he offered her a pensive smile. "I'm not a psychiatrist, but we hit the ground running over a decade ago and we haven't stopped since. Even so, good people, human and otherwise, still die. No one person can or should assume the blame for that. While we never forget our failures—and trust me, we've had some real show-stoppers—we're still here, and we'll keep going."

If they can do it, so can you. Get a grip, and get past it—now. She took a deep breath. "Okay, how old are the bodies?"

Passing a sergeant who carried an exceptionally large wrench, Jackson turned toward the stairs. "They can't be completely sure until they bring in a team that can reach the bottom of the cave where the rest of the bodies were tossed. From what they've been able to ascertain so far, there are two groups of victims. One has been deceased about two weeks and the other around four weeks, although it's difficult to be exact given the desiccation. It'll be a while, if ever, before they can ID all of them, but local authorities believe most came from Munich and Ulm. Based on a quick glance at dental work and other factors, the forensics team unofficially theorized that the majority were transients originally from East Germany or Russia."

More victims of economic and political fallout. "It tracks. Even now the Lilith are trying to keep a low profile."

"Were, you mean." Jackson shook his head. "Around 0300 local time, Blaubeuren villagers heard gunshots and cries from the area. Several local men went to investigate and found—well, they described it as a massacre." Reaching the top of the stairs, he paused and looked back at her expectantly.

As she took a moment to process that information, she realized something else, just as interesting: she was having difficulty assessing Daniel Jackson. Before now she hadn't really tried, but even a concerted effort got her nowhere. He seemed to carry an aura that rendered his mind impermeable. As if...

It hit her. Taking the offensive, she said, "You were Ascended, weren't you?"

His expression flickered briefly but settled on cool curiosity. "What makes you think that?"

"John mentioned a couple of the SGC personnel had 'dipped their toes in that pool.' You seem to be the most likely candidate. So…?"

He shrugged with practiced nonchalance and kept walking. "Once or twice. Didn't really take to it."

"No, that's not it at all." It was a stab in the dark, but one based more on good old-fashioned psychology than any natural insight she might have. "You couldn't turn your back on humanity."

And suddenly, she felt her burden lessen ever so slightly. If there existed a definition of what it was to be human, that was it.

Jackson appeared taken aback by her remark until she continued, "You've very neatly defined the difference between the Lilith and the Ninlil. The ritualized removal of organs by the Lilith has been bugging me, but I think it's further proof that they're on the wrong track—that they've entirely misinterpreted the intent of the Ancient who created them and have instead evolved a set of behaviors peculiar to them. Once again, it doesn't matter what's real and what isn't; they're acting on what they choose to believe."

"I thought we'd already established that." He continued to look at her in a way that made her wonder if all her thoughts were on display for him to see. It was something she was accustomed to doing to other people; she'd never been on the other side of it before. To say it was disconcerting would have been a grave understatement.

She shook it off as they entered the briefing room. "You formulated a solid theory, Dr. Jackson, one I happen to agree with. This facet of their behavior provides proof." Catching a glimpse of the wormhole shutting down, she walked across to the window, speaking as she went. "The Watchers are the equivalent of high priests, and the first generation cambion must act similarly to those John described as hive keepers."

The gate immediately began to dial again.

"That's what we think, too."

Rebecca turned to see General Landry, wearing a genial expression that told her more about the faith he had in his people than the man himself.

"We've just had further word from Germany," he added, coming up beside her to watch the chevrons lock into place. "The Army's Fifth Corps just arrived to secure the caves. They passed what they estimated to be about forty desiccated bodies in a group by the road, including the eight policemen who'd been patrolling the cave entrance. No symbols and no organs removed this time. I think it's obvious that we're no longer dealing with a handful of zealots."

Rebecca felt a new level of tension coil around her spine. "Abandoning their rituals is a signal that they believe such rituals are no longer necessary."

Daniel also moved to stand next to her at the window. "Which means they've found what they've been looking for."

"I think you're right, Dr. Jackson. This is the beginning of an outright war—one they're determined to wage whether the Ori are dead or not, because they want what was promised to them."

"And what would that be?" Landry asked.

The now familiar boiling cauldron shot out from the gate and settled with disarming speed into a rippling tranquil pool. On the other side, Rebecca knew, was the Pegasus Galaxy, teasing her with its proximity, urging her to run down to the wormhole and make her way home. She blinked away that distraction and replied, "Dominion over the human race."

CHAPTER TWENTY-THREE

"**O**w! Damn it, Ronon, this kind of activity offers what we Earth natives call a 'hostile work environment.' Back home it's illegal to intentionally put coworkers into hazardous situations."

Ronon kept his face completely impassive, knowing it would aggravate Rodney all the more. "So?"

"So I—" Rodney's complaint ended sharply as he scuttled forward to avoid the wave that slapped against the pier behind him. As soon as he came within range, Ronon reached out and easily knocked the practice weapon out of his hand. "Ow! For the love of— Is this really necessary?"

"I didn't drag you out here." Ronon retrieved the wooden staff and handed it back.

"Yes, but neither did you mention the downpour or the fact that the pier gets extremely slippery when wet." Rodney wiped a sleeve across his face to clear the rain from his eyes. From the looks of it, the action made no difference.

'Downpour' was an obvious exaggeration. A light shower was falling on Atlantis, offering pleasantly cool conditions in trade for a slicker surface underfoot. The added challenge was good; it would keep their wits about them.

Ronon had chosen the location, and not by accident. This section of the lower pier was just wide enough for a hand-to-hand match. If Rodney backed up too far, he'd end up in the water—again. It wasn't a mistake the scientist was likely to make twice, considering how much he'd squawked when Ronon had to haul him out the first time they'd sparred. The man's later attempt to fight while wearing a floatation jacket had been a useless, ridiculous exercise, so there was now a life preserver and towline hanging from a nearby railing. A hundred yards away, two Marine squads were training with rappelling harnesses on the northeast tower, prepared to practice their water rescue skills on Rodney if needed.

"This is reality," Ronon told him, tying back his damp hair. "When you meet an adversary on a mission, it won't always be on a sunny day."

"When I meet an adversary on a mission, I'll either dazzle him with my grasp of Laplace transform functions or shoot him. Hitting him with a stick is a distant Plan C." Despite his grousing, Rodney didn't move to end the lesson. Instead he clutched the staff in both hands and bent his knees in a reasonable imitation of a fighting stance.

Ronon said nothing as he assumed an offensive position. He'd understood some time ago that his silence was the main reason Rodney was here.

"Supposedly I need an outlet, Heightmeyer said," the scientist continued, awkwardly blocking the basic attacks Ronon slowly delivered. "A certified psychiatrist, and all she can come up with is 'Get a hobby.' Actually, meditation was her first suggestion, and when I shot that down out of hand she came back with the workout idea. According to her, many physical activities have elements in common with meditation."

"She's right."

"She's *not* right, but I'll let it go because it's a waste of energy to argue with her. *Damn* it!" Rodney hurried to reclaim his staff after Ronon sent it skittering across the pier. "And she must be tag-teaming with Elizabeth, because I've essentially been ordered not to supervise any of Katie's or Geisler's current projects. Did you know I could be kicked out of my own lab? It was certainly news to me. Elizabeth restricted me from doing anything resembling useful work for twelve hours. Sleep was strongly recommended, but I never sleep for more than six hours at a time even on the rare occasions when imminent doom isn't on the agenda." He dodged Ronon's swing and nearly lost his footing. "And since Sheppard's not around to amuse me with his *creative* chess strategies, that leaves…whatever it is we're doing right now."

With a quick feint and a sweep of his leg, Ronon buckled Rodney's knees and forced him to sit down hard. "You're talking. I'm entertaining myself until you start paying attention long enough to learn something."

Sputtering a little as a nearby wave coated him in a fine mist of saltwater, Rodney glared up from the deck. "Fine."

Ronon grasped his hand and pulled him to his feet. "Remember what I told you the first time. Watch my eyes."

"I vaguely recall something of that nature. Why your eyes?"

"I can always tell which way you're going to go because your eyes get there first." He wondered how many lessons it would take for Rodney to start remembering that.

"No telegraphing moves. Got it." But Rodney's gaze kept straying to one side or the other, checking his proximity to the pier's edge. "Regulated downtime is a farce," he said under his breath. "All it does is make us complacent. The worst thing to happen to this city in months happened on a downtime weekend."

And that was the real reason Rodney had come out here, Ronon was sure. Not long ago they'd all been caught unawares, believing they were safe within Atlantis's walls, and five people, including Carson Beckett, had died. Maybe Rodney had agreed to spar because he needed to feel more prepared for every contingency, or maybe he just wanted to vent his anger or pain. Ronon wouldn't presume to know his teammate's motivations, but in either case he was willing to help.

That didn't mean he had to let Rodney run things, control issues or not. "You're tensing up your arm. Keep your shoulder down."

Rodney lifted his chin defiantly. "I can't swing if—"

"You can't swing if an off-angle impact breaks your arm, either."

After that, Rodney closed his mouth. For a while they circled each other with only the accompaniment of the steady raindrops, the periodic waves, and the occasional good-natured shouts between the Marines in the background.

The threat of another type of injury seemed to have sharpened Rodney's concentration, because he stopped making the beginner's mistake of over-committing to a motion. Eventually, if he worked at it every day for a year or two, he might be able to develop his focus and ability to learn into an effective defense. Ronon was well aware that Rodney had no intention of putting forth that level of effort. Still, they were making some progress.

When the scientist's gaze wandered again, this time to a specific point over his adversary's shoulder, Ronon turned halfway to see Lorne jogging toward them.

"Dr. Weir's trying to get a hold of you two on the city-wide," the Major informed them, raising his voice to be heard over the thrum of the water.

"Thanks," Ronon called back, watching Rodney's reaction. Gripping his staff tightly enough to whiten his knuckles, Rodney looked determined to hold his stance, yet it was obvious he was battling the temptation to lunge for his radio earpiece, sitting in a small waterproof case on the nearby steps.

Testing him, Ronon kept eye contact as he retrieved his own earpiece, lying alongside the other without any protective covering—they were supposed to be durable in any weather, after all.

"Dr. Weir?"

"Ronon, there you are," she responded at once. "Is Rodney with you?"

Since Rodney could only hear half the conversation, Ronon purposely kept his response vague and his staff at the ready. "Yeah."

"Good. Can you ask him to report to the jumper bay in half an hour?"

"Sure." He watched Rodney struggle to control his impatience.

"Thank you." Elizabeth hesitated for a beat. "He'll be traveling to Earth, and I'd appreciate it if you'd consider going with him. You're certainly not obligated in any way to help there, but John's asked for you, and the IOA agrees that we can use all the help we can get. If this effort fails, it's almost a certainty that the expedition will be recalled permanently… and this time I think any future contact with Pegasus, authorized or otherwise, will be halted."

Was the situation that dire? Motion off to the side caught Ronon's eye: the Marines were hauling all their gear down from the tower and packing with brisk efficiency. The electricity in the air had nothing to do with the clouds overhead. Something big was happening on Earth.

If Ronon's team leader wanted him there, that was good enough for him. He was willing to fight the Wraith wherever he found them—and these were still Wraith, no matter what they looked like or what they were called.

Aware of Rodney's heavy gaze on him, all he said aloud was "Okay."

"Thank you." Elizabeth sounded relieved as well as grateful. "Teyla's also agreed to go. We're sending as many people with Wraith combat experience as we can spare. See you in a few minutes." She ended the transmission.

Having shown more restraint than Ronon had expected, Rodney practically vibrated with tension. "Well? Did Elizabeth want us for something?"

Ronon still didn't break his stance or his stare. Patience was a vital part of battle, an attribute Rodney needed to master above all others. Besides, they had some time yet.

At last, Rodney's need for information overwhelmed his concern that his instructor might hit him if he let his guard down. "That's it!" he snapped, jabbing his staff in the direction of the departing Marines. "If *they* know what's going on, *I* need to know. Start talking, Captain Laconic!"

Well, it was a start. "We're going to Earth," Ronon answered.

"When?"

Although John had requisitioned him a watch, Ronon hadn't gotten into the habit of wearing it. Once his years as a runner had ended, it had taken a while to get used to the idea that time mattered again. "Almost half an hour."

"Excuse me?" Rodney's eyes went huge, and he thrust his staff at Ronon. "You didn't think that was worthy of an immediate mention?" He scrambled to gather his earpiece and water bottle from the deck. "Honestly, some days…"

When he started toward the door at top speed, Ronon called, "Hey, Rodney."

The scientist glanced over his shoulder, obviously reluctant to lose any more time. "What?"

With no better way to make his point, Ronon gestured with the staffs, indicating the whole of their training area. "This was good."

Rodney huffed a short, derisive laugh. "I can feel six distinct bruises forming, to say nothing of the onset of pneumonia. Your definition of 'good' lacks a certain resemblance to reality." But when he resumed walking, it was with a different kind of confidence than his usual, one that suggested he knew what his teammate had meant.

Shaking his head, Ronon headed inside to dry off and then stop by the armory. He had no reservations about leaving the galaxy to follow this fight. Even if he didn't owe it to the people of Earth as a civilization, he did owe it to the small number of them who had helped him reclaim his life.

He'd traveled to the planet briefly to bring Carson home some weeks ago. Though he hadn't had a chance to explore much, he'd been awed to see such a thriving culture, a haven as yet unstained by the Wraith. The absence of resignation and constant fear made Earth unique among all worlds he had ever visited, and he wanted to keep it that way.

Maybe, now that those who knew about the threat could no longer pretend Earth was safe, they might finally abandon their maddening viewpoint that the Wraith were somehow misunderstood, either ill or disabled, entitled to a degree of compassion. Maybe the danger was near enough this time that they would recognize the only option for lasting peace: the annihilation of every last Wraith in this galaxy and all others.

CHAPTER TWENTY-FOUR

Looking up from the screen, Elizabeth saw Teyla arrive in the control room and motioned her over to join their inter-galactic conference call.

"There's nothing inherently fantastical about chimeras," Agent Larance was saying from the SGC briefing room. "Russian virologists successfully engineered an Ebola-small-pox hybrid more than fifteen years ago. You don't want to know what kinds of genetic Tinkertoys some of our so-called allies have been brewing up since." Her expression quickly became contrite. "I apologize, Dr. Weir. You're probably the last person who'd need that explained."

Elizabeth couldn't tell whether the profiler was referring to her onetime role as a diplomat on Earth, negotiating intricate and treacherous political landscapes, or the failed experiment to 'cure' the Wraith of the *iratus* virus. Then again, she wasn't entirely certain Agent Larance had been fully briefed on all aspects of the Atlantis program, good and bad, so she chose to acknowledge the apology with nothing more than a rueful smile.

General Landry, who had been called away from the meeting a few minutes earlier, now reappeared on the screen, grim-faced and thin-lipped. "I'm afraid the IOA is in something of an uproar," he reported. "The international media is buzzing with the rumor that a deadly 'progeria virus' first identified in the U.S. has infected hundreds of Germans."

Already? "How did anyone make the connection so fast?"

The General shook his head resignedly. "YouTube. One of the Blaubueren villagers recorded the crime scene on his cell phone. It won't be long before word gets out that we may have another pandemic on our hands. The CDC and the Pasteur Institute are preparing a joint statement right now to reassure the public that the 'virus' is not contagious and infection is only via direct blood-to-blood contact. Trouble is, not nearly enough people are going to understand the distinction, mainly because an increasing number of reported cases are coming from several other locations in Europe, Canada and, of all places, Tasmania, Australia. How long before your team gets here?"

Digesting that information, Elizabeth said, "Fifteen minutes, General."

"Good." Landry glanced at something off-screen. "I'm told my red phone is ringing, Doctor. We'll talk again soon."

He disappeared from the camera's view and was quickly replaced by Daniel Jackson. "Thank you for the comprehensive reports on M1M-316," he greeted her. "They very nicely filled in a lot of the gaps in Lilith's project notes."

"We aim to please," Elizabeth replied. "Is there anything else you can tell us at this point? We could use some help to prioritize the multiple lines of research we're pursuing."

"Open up the file I just sent in the data burst. It contains in-depth information on the genetic products of Lilith's research."

On Elizabeth's nod, Radek leaned over a console and brought the file up on a side screen. Soon the attention of the control room personnel had been captured by the fascinating images scrolling past, displaying one being after another that had long since been relegated to mythological status on Earth.

Daniel continued. "In her journal, Lilith alludes to the telepathic gene discovered in certain ancient Earth animals; presumably that would be the dinosaurs on M1M-316, because she also mentions having to abandon promising research when the advancing Wraith chased her back to Atlantis. On that subject, she also expresses regret that earlier experiments in the Pegasus Galaxy resulted in the evolution of the Wraith."

Startled by that candid detail, Elizabeth asked, "Lilith

admitted that the Wraith were a genetic accident?"

"Not in so many words. Bear in mind that this journal—" he held up what Elizabeth recognized as an Ancient datapad— "spans a period of almost six thousand years. Her entries are surprisingly disjointed, often contradictory. It's more of an emotional record than a scientific one. It'll take months, if not years, to go through all of her notes, but the earliest passages reflect her perception of herself as one of the elite Ancients who wrote off the Wraith and humanity in the Pegasus Galaxy as a failed experiment."

As he went on, Elizabeth cast a sidelong glance at Teyla. The Athosian seemed to have accepted Daniel's statement with characteristic equanimity. Elizabeth wasn't sure she could be quite as gracious. This was an entire *galaxy* full of human lives they were talking about. Those people—Teyla and Ronon's forefathers—shouldn't have been so easy to cast aside.

Certainly some Ancients had acted selflessly, often at great expense to their own lives, but the vast majority appeared to have borne little consideration for 'lesser beings' in their single-minded pursuit of Ascension.

"Lilith repeatedly used the same inverted, sometimes…" Daniel turned slightly to the side, moving enough to allow the camera a view of Agent Larance talking to Dr. Lam in the background. "…what Agent Larance described as sometimes psychotic reasoning to justify her subsequent actions on Earth. In some sections, however, she seems perfectly lucid, discussing her view of the Lanteans' return to Earth as a temporary measure to buy them time. Yet several passages refer to Earth as nothing more than a glorified laboratory, where mistakes carried no consequences."

This time it was Teyla who darted a glance at Elizabeth, offering a solemn yet sardonic expression that said the equivalent of *welcome to the club*.

Oblivious to their silent exchange, Daniel went on. "Only one element remains constant throughout Lilith's writings:

her fixation on defeating or at least holding the Ori in check before she Ascended. She used her own DNA to enhance her experimental subjects. Although it's still possible that the ATA gene was also introduced naturally, by a few Ancients interbreeding with the human population ten thousand years ago, this data certainly indicates that the gene was deliberately spliced into human DNA."

"As were Wraith genes," Elizabeth said.

Daniel nodded. "And, as Agent Larance explained, animals as well. Most of Lilith's creations weren't viable, and very few were capable of reproduction, although some were considerably long-lived; hence the existence of 'monsters' and mythological creatures embedded in every culture across the planet. Eventually she hit on what she believed to be the 'best' combination."

"Succubi and incubi." Elizabeth sensed someone hovering in her peripheral vision and turned to see a tech waiting patiently by the dialing console. Accepting the clipboard he held out to her, she scanned the form: a repair order for the windows shattered by their dinosaur visitors. Some of the more mundane aspects of the expedition persevered through just about any crisis, it seemed. Once she'd signed the form and returned her attention to the screen, she saw that Daniel had moved aside to allow Agent Larance to join him in the frame.

"They weren't entirely viable insofar as they couldn't reproduce with each other, but they passed for humans in all other ways," Daniel continued. "They could produce cambion offspring with other humans and were able to spread that bloodline through the generations. They also have a standard lifespan—except when they feed on humans, in which case they can regenerate and live pretty much indefinitely. And some apparently have done just that."

"How does that offer them, or anyone in their bloodline, any real protection against the Ori?"

"I'm not sure that it does, though it's doubtful Lilith ever realized how far off-track she'd drifted. She became so obsessed that she ultimately started behaving like the Ori."

When he didn't elaborate on that comment right away, Elizabeth prompted, "Dr. Jackson?"

"We'll be beaming the original Gilgamesh tablets out in a few hours," he said. "Once I read those, I should be able to home in on what we need to know to deal with the current situation."

Agent Larance answered Elizabeth more directly. "What Dr. Jackson is saying is that Lilith's original motivations matter less right now than what her creations believe."

"Lilith instilled in them a kind of religion," Daniel explained. "When the other Ancients discovered her work, they ordered her to destroy the 'abominations.' By refusing to submit to their judgment, she positioned herself as a martyr. Also, when the climate changed about five thousand years ago, the increased rainfall and melting glaciers caused sea levels to rise, flooding E'din, or Eden, the region between the Tigris and Euphrates Rivers where Lilith's extensive laboratory was located." He shrugged. "It ties in to the flood myth, particularly in Babylonian and Biblical mythology."

"The animals that didn't make it into Noah's Ark," Elizabeth suggested.

"Something like that. Most of the chimeras died out, and Lilith lost pretty much all of her equipment. Gilgamesh built her a sanctuary in Uruk. However, Lilith vanished soon thereafter, most likely to Egypt—which tracks with Talmudic mythology—but not before indoctrinating the viable chimeras with the belief that they were descendants of the Wraith in the Pegasus Galaxy and that they had a sacred duty to protect 'them' from the Ori."

Across the control room, Radek held up a data storage device and gestured toward the door, seeking permission with raised eyebrows. Confident that the scientists' time would be well spent delving into the information Daniel had sent, Elizabeth made a shooing motion, out of camera range.

"'Them' being the Ancients?"

A shadow seemed to cross Agent Larance's face. "That's one interpretation." Before Elizabeth could ask for clarification, she explained, "One sect worships the Ancient using her Babylonian name, Ninlil. Its members believe that they have an obligation to protect *all* sentient beings from the Ori."

"I think it's safe to say they're on our side," Daniel added. "They're the group I met in Iraq."

Elizabeth nodded. "And those responsible for the murders?"

"They consider the Pegasus Galaxy their spiritual home. They want to return there, presumably with the goal of bringing the Wraith here to help defeat the Ori."

A chilling idea, and, as far as Elizabeth could tell, completely unfeasible. "How do they intend to achieve that without access to the Stargate?"

"I don't know," admitted Daniel. "We think it has something to do with Antarctica. Given the way the body count is climbing, I think we're about to find out."

CHAPTER TWENTY-FIVE

Because Teyla had been among the first notified of their impending mission, she had been fully prepared for departure with ten minutes to spare. She'd joined Elizabeth in the control room in time to hear Dr. Jackson and Agent Larance reveal the nature of the beings that endangered Earth.

Elizabeth stood near the front of the room, the light of the active gate casting her in a wavering blue glow. "You mentioned earlier that this Awakening could be a two-pronged event," she said into the camera. "That would suggest the cambion are also looking for a way of triggering the Wraith genes in the human population at large. We may have a clue in that direction, or at least a partial explanation of how the Wraith communicate with each other."

As she detailed the science team's preliminary findings on the M1M-316 ginkgo, Teyla tried to brush aside a sense of unease. She could not yet rid herself of the lingering visceral terror of the *iratus* insect crawling up her body, poised to feed on her in order to become the vicious new species developed by Michael. This situation stirred many of the same conflicts in her mind.

In spite of the horrors Michael had perpetrated on the blameless Taranans—in spite of his actions against the Atlantis expedition in general and against her in particular—she could not find it in herself to completely vilify him, for she understood what motivated him. Intelligent, resourceful, accepted by neither Wraith nor human because of events over which he had had no say, he now sought what any being sought: a place for himself in the universe. Ancients, humans, Wraith, and the amalgamation of all three species, succubus and cambion—each struggled in their own way to define their existence and to seek meaning in their lives.

And yet the memory of the countless people Michael had discarded still lingered. While she could comprehend what drove him, neither could she forgive him for his terrible deeds.

"McKay to Control," Rodney's edgy voice came over the radio. Teyla smiled. She was aware that Ronon had taken him outside for a sparring session. "I was given a barely reasonable time limit with which to prep for this trip, and yet here I am at the appointed place exactly on schedule. Anyone else planning to join me?"

"We're on our way," Elizabeth told him, sharing a look of amusement with Teyla. They took the stairs to the jumper bay, where Major Lorne was dividing a group of about twenty Marines between three jumpers. The amount of personnel and armament being readied underscored the importance of this mission; Teyla had not seen such a high level of combat readiness in the city since the long-ago siege. A few seconds later, Ronon appeared in the bay wearing the long coat he favored, the one that concealed more weapons than any two Marines could carry.

"It's critical that you follow through on Katie's ginkgo research." Acknowledging the arrivals with barely a glance, Rodney was lecturing Radek from the ramp of Jumper Two. "Make sure her sub-literate lackeys run a biochemical analysis to determine the effects of various doses of ginkgo on the Wraith gene fragments found in human DNA. The experiments can be run as simulations based on—"

"These tests are in progress," Radek assured him, tucking his clipboard under his arm and helping one of the Marines load a large container into the jumper. "Dr. Brown and her staff have deferred much of their other work for this. They are using the program Carson and I developed for his initial experiments with the Wraith gene."

Making no attempt to assist with the loading, Rodney's only response to Radek was to charge ahead with additional instructions. "And then I want you to test them on actual bio-logical material. Get volunteers if necessary, but the tests need to include the sample I left behind." A pointed look, one Teyla interpreted to mean that the samples included Rodney's blood and DNA, passed between the two scientists. "Get the results to me immediately. No more of this circumventing the chain of…" Stepping out of the way of two Marines carrying the last of the equipment, Rodney glanced over at Elizabeth.

Atlantis's leader, handing instructions to a technician, raised her eyebrows at Rodney. Perhaps she allowed his implication because she recognized his anxiety; he clearly feared what might become of him should the ginkgo indeed activate Wraith genes. In any case, she dismissed the techni-cian and, striding to the rear of the jumper, said only, "We can take care of things on this end, Rodney. I promise you'll get a full report the moment we know anything."

"All right. We'll, uh, be in touch." Looking faintly appeased, Rodney turned and stepped into the jumper. The Marines had already stowed their equipment in the other three jumpers and were closing the hatches.

Teyla finished fastening a cargo net, then followed Ronon into the cockpit and took her customary seat while Rodney completed the preflight checklist with methodical efficiency. She knew the people of Earth were unaware that life existed on other worlds, and the tight grip with which they still held on to their naïveté continued to surprise her. It was not her place to question the wisdom of hiding the truth, though. From the outset, Teyla had understood that Earth was unlike any world she had encountered on her many travels. Its popu-lation was enormous and segmented, societies often warring with one another over differences that seemed trivial in com-parison to the constant struggle just to survive in the Pegasus Galaxy. How would the dynamics of their closely packed society change if they were to learn just how different 'dif-ferent' could be? While she knew Colonel Carter had recently visited a parallel Earth world where just such a scenario had occurred, Teyla suspected the poor outcome there had resulted for reasons beyond merely the knowledge that the people of Earth were not alone in the universe. The reasons likely were more complex, resting with the fact that such knowledge might challenge the customary beliefs of many inhabitants.

While the jumpers descended, one by one, into launch position in the gate room, Teyla gazed out at the patterned glass of the far wall and recalled the histories of her fore-fathers, when some among them had been taken and then returned by the Wraith. What her people had at first seen as a blessed gift had all too quickly been branded as an abomination. It was disheartening to her that bigotry could arise so swiftly and bring with it such tragic results, opening a dark place that seemed to reside in all of humanity, regardless of what galaxy they inhabited. Even here on Atlantis it had been evident from the first awareness of her heritage that some members of the expedition did not trust her.

But not many, she reminded herself. For the most part, expedition members regarded her as a friend and viewed her skills as useful attributes in their mutual struggle against the Wraith. Still, fear of the unknown was a powerful emotion, and no one was entirely immune from the terror that they might harbor something within them that could transform them into a Wraith. Rodney was on edge, others seemed distracted, and Teyla's own recollection of the *iratus* insect lurked at the edges of her consciousness. Perhaps it was for the best that the people of Earth did not know that some among them likely carried the genes of a ruthless, insatiable species, for they would surely turn on one another.

Jumper Two was the last of the four craft to enter the wormhole. Once it did so, Teyla had just enough time to wonder if she would like this world, the birthplace of her cherished friends, before she was propelled through the gate and into an austere gray room fronted by a huge glass window.

The images she had seen on Atlantis's monitor when speaking to the SGC had not misled her; the gate room was every bit as confined as it had appeared. Where Atlantis's architecture melded practicality with grace, this facility had been designed strictly for utility. Indeed, the very room they had entered had once housed a nuclear weapon John had described as a Titan missile. Her eyes went to the first level visible through the windows, and she smiled as she caught sight of John, standing behind a seated man who she knew from previous communications was Chief Harriman.

John's lips moved, and his voice came over the radio. "All four jumpers accounted for, Atlantis. Shut down at your discretion. Good to see you guys," he added, looking in through Jumper Two's windshield, and even from a distance Teyla could see in his expression how sincere a statement it was. "Welcome to Earth, Teyla. It gets a lot prettier than this, I promise."

"I have no doubt of that, Colonel. Thank you."

"Go ahead and park in the bay, Rodney, and stick around up there. We're going to head out as soon as possible. You'll get most of the briefing on the way."

"This is what I get for traveling with the Marines," Rodney muttered, complying with John's request and lifting the jumper toward what Teyla soon saw was a chamber above the gate room. "Supposedly they're always 'first to go, last to know.'"

In the bay, which also felt stark next to its Atlantis counterpart, technicians had quickly swarmed in to install additional equipment on the other jumpers. Jumper One, which John had brought to Earth some time ago, had already been outfitted with the new devices. A spectacled, balding man with a beard, whom Teyla did not recognize, was supervising their work, and the Marines had gathered in an empty corner of the room to await further orders. Before long, the bay doors opened to admit General Landry, followed by Dr. Jackson, Agent Larance, and John.

"Thank you for coming." The SGC commander addressed Teyla and Ronon directly. "I know this isn't your fight."

"I do not believe responsibility for this fight can be cleanly divided, General," Teyla replied. "We are the same people, created by the same beings, and we face the same destiny."

Acknowledging her viewpoint with an approving nod, Landry turned to the assembled Marines. "There will be some major unknowns in this situation. First and foremost, we have no way at this point to distinguish succubus from cambion, Lilith from Ninlil—or any other human for that matter."

Rodney broke in, sounding dubious. "You're calling them the Lilith and Ninlil?"

"The Lilith worshippers are the ones we're after," said John. "The guys subscribing to Ninlil's philosophy supposedly are on our side, although it's hard to say what their motivations are." He glanced at Agent Larance, whose expression was unreadable to Teyla.

"Lilith and Ninlil." Rodney shook his head. "Military originality strikes again. With ten seconds of thought you might have been able to come up with marginally less ridiculous names."

"Well, we could have gone with 'dark side succubi and incubi' versus '*maybe* good side succubi and incubi,'" Dr. Jackson pointed out, "but these names have ten thousand years of history to them. Changing them now just to accommodate your idea of coolness, McKay, seems a bit tacky."

Landry's frosty look silenced the group. "There's a good chance some of you will be going into a cave system that I'm told is anything but simple," he continued, "so be prepared for close-quarters combat. Maneuverability will be very limited and, while the outer galleries have staircases and good lighting, the inner areas are not as user friendly, so staying oriented will be critical. Remain in radio contact at all times."

This time Rodney raised his hand tentatively before speaking. "If that's the case, is it absolutely necessary for me to go along? There are plenty of people better suited to climbing around in enclosed spaces—not that I'm complaining," he hastened to add. "I'm a professional and an offworld team member, and I'm perfectly willing to—"

"We need you to work with Dr. Lee on something else." Daniel Jackson tipped his head toward the man supervising the jumper modifications. "He and Agent Larance have a theory about using harmonics to repel or even disable the succubi and incubi."

"We've tried that before," Rodney said dismissively.

"Only on Wraith," countered Agent Larance. "These are hybrids. We believe there's a reason why mythology texts suggest invoking the names of the angels Senoy, Sansenoy, and Semangelof as protection against an attack by Lilith's children—or what we now know are her creations using her DNA. The vocalization of those words sets up an unusual harmonic wave."

Rodney looked as though he wanted to scoff at the idea, but he restrained himself. "So, Germany?"

"Nope. Tasmania." John crossed the bay, heading for the hatch of Jumper One. "Like I said, I'll fill you in on the details in the air."

General Landry dismissed the Marines to their jumpers with a curt "Good luck." Teyla went with Ronon, Agent Larance, and Dr. Jackson to join John in Jumper One's cabin while Major Lorne, Rodney and Dr. Lee took Jumper Two. A squad of Marines dispersed between the two craft and boarded as well.

As Teyla slid into the right cockpit seat, John's fingers skipped over the instrument panel with practiced ease. "Tasmania is off the southern coast of Australia, not too far from Antarctica," he told Teyla and Ronon, activating his radio link to the other jumpers. "While Jackson was getting you guys and Elizabeth up to speed, I was listening in on a phone call between Woolsey and the Australian government. Both national and international law enforcement agencies have had their sights on a particular shipping company for some time. The company, Goeldi Limited, is suspected of transporting illegal goods—drugs, guns, people, all the usual under-the-radar stuff that makes big money and would give the Lilith access to worldwide transport. The Australians have offered us their full support."

Jumper One rose from the floor as John went on. "German authorities spotted a group of climate-controlled container trucks, the kind that are often used to transport live animals, parked at the entrance to the Blaubueren caves twice in the past couple of months. They were back this week, on the night the police were killed. Anyone want to guess who owns the trucks?"

"Goeldi," Rodney responded from Jumper Two. "Quite the coincidence. What are we going to tell the Australians when we get there?"

"Their government is aware of the actual situation, since they're signatories to the Antarctic treaty. They're also concerned that over the past few weeks a number of hikers have failed to show up as planned at the southern end of the Overland Trail, a well known walk. Tasmania doesn't have large carnivores, and aside from a few bush fires the only natural hazards are rapidly changing weather conditions.

"The cover story for the military and the general public stays the same. We're there to contain a virus discovered by an Antarctic expedition and which may have fallen into the hands of a fundamentalist terrorist organization." John's mouth curved into a smirk. "You really need to give Radek more credit for his good ideas."

Teyla heard Rodney's grumble of acknowledgement only peripherally as she turned her attention to the view through the windshield. The smooth, stone-like walls seemed to stretch upward for miles. "Jumpers, engage cloak," ordered John. "We're cleared for a rapid climb to low orbit."

When they at last reached the surface, Teyla realized for the first time that it was night. She would have liked to get a better view of this world, to observe for herself what she had seen in so many pictures and movies, but she soon found that nighttime offered its own spectacular sights. As they climbed, the lights on the ground shrank to pinpricks, quickly joined by hundreds upon thousands more, brighter and denser than a star field.

"We couldn't take a jumper to Iraq because of airspace concerns," John said. "Luckily for us, the air traffic around Tasmania is just about nonexistent, so it'll be easy to avoid scheduled commercial flights. It's a pretty sparsely populated region by Earth standards. The only access to the cave system comes from logging roads controlled by the Forestry Commission, and those are being closed off for us as we speak. There are several large forest fires in the region, so the general public has been alerted to keep clear."

As if a line had been drawn below them, the lights abruptly ended, indicating that they were now crossing one of Earth's vast oceans. Then a sliver of sunlight burst across the thin atmosphere blanketing the curved horizon. Teyla found herself captivated by the sunrise illuminating her first view of Australia.

"Anyway, based on all the information we have so far, we think the Lilith are holed up in a cave system south of the capital city, Hobart," John concluded.

"How'd they get there?" Lorne asked. "Smuggled in on cargo ships?"

"Goeldi owns some aircraft as well as an international tour company," said John. "Two tour groups of almost a hundred people each arrived on separate flights within the past month. One group is supposedly traveling around mainland Australia after finishing up a three-week wilderness trek in Tasmania. Although their plane did leave the island, supposedly with the correct number of passengers, there's no guarantee any of them were on board, because the first stop was an uncontrolled airstrip in the South Australian outback. The other group's still wandering around out in the wilderness. The Southwest National Park, where the caves are, is a popular destination for European tourists, mostly wilderness hikers, so there was no reason for anyone to be suspicious about this earlier. Now, though, the Tasmanian state government's trying to get a fix on their location."

"It's summer down here," Dr. Jackson said, "and at this time of year Hobart is one of the ports from which ships leave for Antarctica. A lot of Atlantis's scientists traveled through there during the planning stages of the expedition."

"They're trying to get to Antarctica. I'm sure of that." Agent Larance's voice was quiet, and she did not expand on her assertion before Dr. Jackson responded.

"What we need to keep in mind, though, is the fact that Tasmania was actually part of Antarctica while the Ancients were still on Earth. They could be searching for something that's now located in the extensive limestone system."

"How much distance are we going to have to cover inside these caves?" asked Lorne. "Miles?"

Jumper One descended over mountain peaks and lush forests bisected by tracts of cleared land—farms, Teyla guessed. She pulled her gaze away from the windshield in time to see Jackson wince. "That's one of those unknowns General Landry mentioned. A few caverns have been mapped and are, as Colonel Sheppard pointed out, popular tourist haunts, but no one really knows the extent of the system. It's called the Tasmanian Wilderness World Heritage Area for good reason. The Lilith could vanish in there and never be heard from again."

"They have to eat," Ronon said simply, causing Teyla to wonder whether these beings were living more like humans or Wraith. In either case, she doubted they would find sustenance in a cave.

"Between that and the lack of easy transport to Australia until the last two hundred years or so, we think Europe must have looked like a better place for them to hang out until this recent Awakening." John brought the jumper around in a wide arc as the treetops drew closer. In the near distance, the forest was blanketed by a thick ashen haze. "There's also a third group of travelers—the ones responsible for the German policemen's deaths—somewhere in transit. More unknown factors."

Dr. Jackson nodded grimly. "They've been preparing for this event for thousands of years. It's virtually guaranteed that they have numerous alternate routes through the caves. Our plan at the moment is to stake out the known entrances and hope we catch them either coming or going."

Ronon voiced Teyla's immediate thought. "Not much of a plan."

"That's just our end of it," Dr. Jackson reassured him. "All airports and shipping ports have been alerted. The Australians are well prepared for this kind of thing; terrorism lockdowns are a fact of life these days. We just have to hope that no additional complications sneak up on us."

If hope was an integral part of their strategy, Teyla could not consider herself confident in their chances for success—particularly when she caught sight of the forest fires.

CHAPTER TWENTY-SIX

"**O**h, this looks promising," McKay grumbled over the radio, pulling Rebecca's attention away from the dirty, umber-colored sky. "Colonel, was it your idea of a joke to have me plunk my jumper in the middle of a blackberry thicket? I recall from previous experiences that these jackets offer only minimal protection from brambles."

During the pre-flight briefing, Rebecca had learned that the jumpers would be dispatched to cover the major entrances to the caves. That still left dozens of minor access points, which the Australian Army was moving quickly to secure.

John settled Jumper One gently onto the ground in a glade of tree ferns. "The idea is for you and Dr. Lee to stay in the jumper and work on the frequency modulation system while the Marines secure the area. If you decide to wander outside and go sightseeing, it's up to Lorne as to whether or not he feels like rescuing you from the killer blackberry patch."

"Tough call, sir," replied the Major, a smirk in his voice. "Don't know if I'd want to risk it."

Ronon opened the jumper's hatch, and immediately Rebecca could feel the traces of smoke in the air tickling the back of her throat. The threatening fires were going to be a factor here no matter what. She stepped down from the craft and walked a half-dozen paces to the right, taking in the nearby parking lot—empty except for a vacant Land Cruiser bearing a National Parks emblem on the door—and the walkway toward a small shelter. This had to be the main entrance to the caves. She turned back to ask John a question and was caught off-guard to see him step out of thin air.

He flashed a grin at her obvious surprise. "Just in case somebody we don't know happens to pass by."

The cloaking device. She'd been told about it, but this was

the first time she'd witnessed it in action. After the steep learning curve of the past few days, it seemed there were still some things to which she hadn't acclimated just yet.

Rebecca heard a murmur behind her and spun around. Only a tree stood there. She shook her head, trying vainly to chase out a creeping sense of fatigue. She hadn't had nearly enough sleep lately to deal with this, but they didn't exactly have time to take a break.

"Com check," John said into his radio. "All scout teams report in."

Marine voices sounded off in rapid succession.

"Alpha here." "Bravo." "Charlie."

"Alpha and Bravo, head out to your assigned areas," John directed. "Any indication of recent activity, let us know ASAP. Charlie, gear up for cave entry. Remember that you're going to have to wade through some water to get where you're going."

"Aye, sir."

John twisted a dial on his handheld radio. "This is Lieutenant Colonel Sheppard, U.S. Air Force, calling local Army command post. Please respond."

"Army here," came the prompt, accented reply. "Captain Rhodes speaking. I take it you're on the ground, then, Colonel?"

"Just landed. Have you been briefed on the situation?"

"Yes, sir. We've secured the main highway twenty kilometers from your position. Haven't yet dispersed patrol teams."

"Hold off on that for the moment," said John. "Our teams have been inoculated against the virus, so we'll take point."

"Understood, sir. Standing by."

"We'll be in touch. USAF out." John glanced up at the sky. "Huh. Wasn't expecting that."

Rebecca blinked, realizing belatedly that a light snow had begun to fall. "I thought it was summer here."

"Tasmania's weather systems are notoriously fickle," said Dr. Jackson, zipping his jacket. "It's the first stop for wind systems coming straight off Antarctica."

"We probably only have about an hour of sunlight left." John clipped a P-90 to his vest and pressed a button on some kind of remote control to close the jumper's hatch. "Let's get moving."

As they headed down the walkway through a glen of trees neatly labeled to educate tourists, Rebecca got a fleeting look at a rather intimidating gun concealed in a holster under Ronon's coat. These aliens, apparently, didn't mess around.

The entrance's waiting area, where helpful signs detailed the history and geology of the karst area, was empty. His weapon ready, John clicked his radio with one hand. "Rhodes, Sheppard. We were supposed to meet a pair of guides at the cave entrance. Do you know if they were delayed?"

"They passed our checkpoint an hour ago, Colonel. Look for a Toyota Land Cruiser with a National Parks logo on the door."

John cursed under his breath. "Thanks." Cautiously, he approached the metal door that blocked the entrance itself. "Lock's broken."

"As is this one." Teyla stood by a smaller door within the shelter, shining the light affixed to her weapon inside. "There is a radio on the floor in pieces."

Distantly, it occurred to Rebecca that she had a sidearm and that procedure would suggest she ought to have it unholstered. She wasn't sure why she hadn't done so earlier, but she made no move to correct the oversight.

"So much for my very faint hope that this might be simple." John exited the shelter and strode back along the path. "Fall back to the jumper."

Once the group was inside the Ancient ship again and the hatch had closed, cleaner, smoke-free air began to circulate. Rebecca drank it in, hoping it might clear her head. She wasn't sure what was wrong with her, why she felt so…disoriented. John was already relaying what they'd found at the cave entrance via satellite phone to General Landry, who was in continuous contact with the Australian authorities. The pilot's steady voice faded into the background as Rebecca hunted around in the jumper's supply locker, looking for something to eat. If she could just find a snack, get some energy back...

A handful of power bars was the best she could do. Sitting down, she tore into one of them and finished it in three bites. It did nothing to help.

The sun might still be above the horizon, but down here in the glade it was already dark, leaving the jumper's interior lights to take over. John stowed the sat-phone and took a seat next to Rebecca on the long bench. She could feel the heat of his irritation. "It's going to be two hours until we can get another guide out here," he reported. "Landry's orders are to wait. The other teams are in place, but we're just going to have to sit tight."

Teyla stood near the closed hatch, a strange expression on her face. "May I go outside?" she asked abruptly. "I will not go far. I merely want to confirm a perception."

John frowned, obviously recognizing her intent. "Something pinging on your radar?"

The alien woman gave a single nod. "Not in the way a Wraith would, but...I cannot place it."

Tensing almost imperceptibly, John said, "It's starting to sound like we're in the right place. Go ahead. Stay in visual range." He cast a glance at Ronon, who rose to follow Teyla without a word, and activated his radio. "All teams, be on alert. Teyla might have something. Remember, no one is to enter the caves until you hear my order. And stay in pairs or threes at all times. Don't forget what happened to those cops in Germany."

The hatch opened, and Rebecca could see snow beginning to accumulate on the ground outside, marred by scattered gray flecks of ash from the nearby fires. The fire...

"It was a fire, Becca. It happened so fast—your mom and dad couldn't get out."

For years her memory of that awful night had centered on nothing more than those words, or words similar to them, but now she recalled the events much more clearly. She hadn't been sleeping over at a friend's house; her parents had brought her to *their* friends, to people like them, for her protection, because they had sensed what was coming.

"Can you help me put some pieces together?" John's voice brought her back to the present. "Why is it that you're so sure the Lilith followers want to enslave everyone? Is it in their doctrine somewhere?"

She didn't have an answer for him. She'd barely understood the questions through a dull, constant ringing in her ears, like the background noise of a room full of people. It was a struggle just to concentrate. Jackson was giving some kind of response to John, but instead she heard her parents' voices, suddenly crystal-clear after decades of obscurity.

"They know about her. They know she is the one to free us of our inhuman burden."

The Lilith followers had discovered young Rebecca's existence; they wanted her dead, as they wanted all heretics dead, but her in particular because…because she was *the one*. Her parents had cultivated those false memories for her and had given them also to the Watchers who had fed on them and then set fire to the house to cover their actions.

Wait. I'm almost there.

Rebecca stiffened. That voice hadn't been a memory. It had been as real and lucid as the conversation between Dr. Jackson and John.

A burning need, almost like hunger but more compelling, began to overtake her.

She knew things now, so many things about her destiny. After the fire she'd been taken from her hometown and helped to vanish into a new life, with a new name—had her aunt even been a real aunt? Her parents' friends had realized they could not protect her, had deliberately refused to find out where she'd been taken—because if even one of them had known the secret and been fed upon by a Lilith, the truth of her existence would have been exposed.

The sense of purpose that now drove her was almost blinding, as was the hunger…it *was* hunger, a consuming need to feed that could not be satiated by any number of power bars.

Resist, Rebecca. We're on the way; we'll help you find what you need.

She understood that need, the desperate hunger that drove men and women to commit unspeakable acts of cruelty that branded them monsters. She'd spent years getting into their heads, tasting their desires. Never until now had she truly comprehended what it was to crave something so powerfully that the pain of denial was enough to make her want to weep. Reason and logic were hindrances as flimsy and transparent as wet tissue.

And yet she clung to them while John and Dr. Jackson talked: about the Ori, about Atlantis, about so many things… None of it mattered, because nothing was as important as the need to *feed*.

Dimly she heard one of them tuning in to a radio broadcast. "…authorities report that a terrorist organization has gained access to the bioweapons. The White House has refused to comment on leaked reports suggesting that the virus did not originate in Antarctica, as first reported, but in Iraq. Nevertheless…"

Someone touched her shoulder. "You okay?"

Tall and strong and reeking of life that was oh, so sweet—if she could just reach out her hand and take what she desperately needed from him—

"Don't touch me!" she hissed, jerking back. Without conscious thought she was running down the ramp, past Teyla, and out into the forest. The path was clear, clearer in her mind than it had ever been before. The smell of life surrounded her, but she had to get away, away from the Marines, people—humans, because she wasn't entirely human, was she?

Hold on. Don't leave. We're coming for you, to help you.

The voice in her mind that had plagued her for hours was growing stronger now. As much as she wanted to trust it, she couldn't hold on, couldn't wait, had to escape.

"Rebecca!"

Another voice—her radio—telling her to stop, to wait. She couldn't obey John, either. If she tried, she wouldn't be able to resist. She'd turn on him and *feed…*

Stumbling toward the parking lot, her gaze fell on a Land Cruiser: the rangers' vehicle, dusted with snow, window open. The keys were still in the ignition.

"Rebecca, damn it, wait!"

Rebecca, wait!

She ignored the voices in her mind—they were in her mind, weren't they?

Hands grabbed her shoulders from behind. Heat and strength and desire surged up in her so forcefully that she whirled around and aimed a blow directly at John's head. He fell, hard, and didn't move.

Control—must keep control!

She threw open the door of the Land Cruiser and tossed his motionless body across the seat. Climbing inside, she turned the key and wrenched the vehicle into gear. The lights weren't needed; her eyes, or maybe her mind, saw everything.

Don't leave!

Gravel sprayed up behind her as the tires nearly lost their grip. New voices joined the cacophony. More people, more *food*, coming for her. She ripped off the radio and heaved it out of the window, speeding down the dirt road lightly frosted with snow.

They were all around her. Soldiers and Marines, just kids, scattered through the bush, their lives bright and powerful—all right there for her to feed on if she just pulled over. Just one life would be enough.

She stomped down on the accelerator.

Wait!

The snow was getting heavier, the wipers shoving flakes

back and forth on the windshield. She heard shots fired, car horns and a shouted obscenity as she slammed through the flimsy roadblock, manned by more beacons of life shining through the cool darkness, *more food*.

She had to get away, to find a place to hide until the burning need passed. It *had* to pass.

An innate sense compelled her to head north on the main road, then turn left, up into the mountains. Past farms, past still more lives like bright candles burning in the night, all pulling her, imploring her to share in their light, to consume it.

No! She pushed the vehicle harder, climbing higher into the mountains. An orange sign sprang up; she swerved around it, past the barrier. God, she was burning up! What had been done to her? She couldn't see, couldn't—

SLAM!

The vehicle hit a stump or a rock, a minor obstacle that failed to prevent her plunge down a lethally steep embankment. Images of cold and fire surrounded her; her head thrashed back and forth but nothing could dislodge the voices imploring her to wait. She should have felt fear, yet the *need* dominated all. Through the crushed windshield, snow poured in along with branches and rubble, striking her. The view outside spun wildly until everything came to a sudden, crunching stop.

Even in that moment she found no peace. She could hear her breathing, hear her heart pumping life through her veins and out through the gashes across her face and arms. She could smell the sweet, succulent warmth beside her. She released the seatbelt—when had she remembered to buckle her seatbelt?—and fell in a crumpled heap against the inverted roof.

Food. Beside her was food. She simply had to reach across and—

No! Fight it, and we will be there!

She crawled out through the smashed remains of the windshield, ignoring the fresh slices across her hands and knees as she pushed glass aside.

"Re-ecca?"

People will need your help, Rebecca.

John. It was John trapped inside the mangled truck, not some delicacy for her to consume. John—his name was *John* and he was human but more…so very much more, because he carried the blood of Ninlil, who had created them all.

He was talking to her, asking her for something. She could see his lips move in the darkness, see the blood that trickled into his eyes and the unnatural angles of broken bones. It would be so easy to take all that he was, all that he had left, into herself. The desire flowed through her, so overpowering that she screamed in denial. She lurched away from the vehicle and plunged face first into the snow-covered embankment, trying to force the shock of cold into her system, trying to quench the searing demand that she *feed*.

Hold on. We're almost there.

But they weren't. She could feel them miles and miles away, too far to help. Why were her palms burning? *What have you done to me?*

Something, some…vague glimmer of different life pulled her face out of the snow. There—a cow.

Anger surged through her. The animal had fallen down the ravine and the damned farmer hadn't bothered to search for it. Black and white stood out in sharp relief against the dirty snow. Why could she see it in the stygian darkness? Fire… around them was fire, reflecting light from the snow-filled clouds. Lying partly on its side, one leg a shattered mess, the animal bellowed pitifully when it saw her. She could taste its fear and pain, feel it begging her for relief.

Her gun. She could shoot it, put it out of its misery. Her hands, slippery with blood, fumbled the weapon. She opened her palms to find them torn, and a memory of what she was briefly infiltrated her need. If she fired her gun she'd have to fill out a report explaining why.

A bubble of hysterical laughter slipped free at the absurdity. She pulled herself from the rapidly melting snow and staggered across to the cow. Kneeling, she placed a hand on its belly to reassure it and—

A scream tore from her throat. The relief from pain was as devastating as pain itself. Her vision flooded with images connected by a million threads tangling in the forefront of her mind. *What did you do to me? Why now?*

Finally, there was clarity and peace.

The watery snow embraced her, cool and comfortable, the damp ice a welcome friend. Rebecca turned and opened her eyes. Soft flakes danced between ice-rimed splinters that fractured her vision of the sky. Branches, cold and lifeless, and yet she was warm. A face entered her field of vision. Kind eyes, full of love and life and the wisdom of a thousand lifetimes. And something more: joy.

Welcome.

The voice in her mind was that of a young man, speaking with a gentle Midwestern accent. Rebecca pushed herself onto her elbows and looked around. Three more people dressed far too lightly for the weather were seated close by, their faces radiating the same elation as the young man who'd woken her.

And at long last, just before she passed out, Rebecca understood.

CHAPTER TWENTY-SEVEN

"Try it again." Rodney adjusted the gain on the receiver. "I'm getting interference."

Lee crouched down on the floor of Jumper Two in order to move closer to the microphone on the side of the unit. "Senoy, Sansenoy, Semangelof," he recited, enunciating carefully.

"Better." Speed and frequency appeared to have a significant effect on the tonal properties of the ancient Hebrew incantation. For all the readings they'd taken, though, their grand world-saving scheme amounted to nothing more than mysticism. Rodney ran the harmonic analysis, wondering how the thickening smoke in the air would affect the equipment. It sure wasn't helping his sinuses. "Of course, by 'better' I mean that the recording is clearer, not that we're any closer to figuring out how a sonic wave is supposed to ward off genetically modified Wraith in human clothing."

"At least we have a precedent, if not any hard data," Lee pointed out. "It wasn't too long ago that Morgan le Fay's dragon was destroyed by the sound of her name."

"Oh, well, as long as we know how to stop a hologram of a mythological animal, we'll certainly be able to apply that to flesh and blood." Rodney jabbed the 'enter' key on his laptop with slightly more force than might have been necessary.

"Be as sarcastic as you want. We never really did identify the nature of the dragon SG-1 tangled with. I'm not so sure you can tag it with the hologram label." The other scientist gazed off into the middle distance, a sign that he was about to either offer a probably useless idea or wander off on an equally useless tangent. "For a while now, I've been developing a theory about such events. Although we've been calling them holograms, they're not projections of light. Rather, I think they may actually be corporeal; temporary organizations of molecules assembled in the same manner as Dr. Jackson used to create the Sangraal."

Or the bomb that had killed Carson, which was a tangent Rodney could have done without. "Hypothesize to your heart's content when you get back to your cushy lab," he said shortly, trying to rid his mind of the countless and disquieting possibilities such technology might give rise to. "Meanwhile, in the real world, we have some kind of supposed magic spell whose effect, assuming it even *has* an effect, is completely unknown. We're in the unenviable position of holding a key and having no idea what, if anything, it unlocks. Did your degree include any coursework in astrology or alchemy? Because none of mine did."

While he was on the subject, his extensive education had failed to cover topics such as marksmanship, intergalactic diplomacy, and resistance to torture, too. Every so often Rodney was reminded that this wasn't at all the career trajectory he'd planned. He'd expected to have a safe, comfortable research job, like Lee's, except with more grants and awards. Instead, he was doing things most scientists couldn't imagine, working under unrelenting pressure to perform miracles... losing friends to inexcusably senseless acts. If the lunacy of it all occasionally got under his skin, he felt he was damn well entitled to his frustration.

Leaning into the microphone, Lee repeated the three names again, this time singing them instead of speaking. It took Rodney a moment to realize that he'd somehow managed to fit "Senoy, Sansenoy, and Semangelof" into the opening bars of the "Gilligan's Island" theme.

At Rodney's withering look, Lee's smile faded. "Not an appropriate time for levity?"

"It rarely is." A cough prompted by the smoke ruined Rodney's intimidation effect. He glanced down at the frequency graph generated by that last inane attempt and noticed that a couple of the syllables had produced harmonic overtones. Interesting. Not much of a start, but interesting.

A signal from the radio interrupted him. "Jumper Two, this is One." Rodney glanced up. He'd let Lorne handle the previous call, ordering the Marines back to the jumpers due to the advancing fires, but Jackson's tone suggested this call might be of more immediate importance. "Got an update from the home front. I'll put the radio next to the sat-phone and patch you in."

Soon General Landry's voice replaced the archeologist's. "Dr. Lam has reported some unsettling results from Agent Larance's blood tests. It appears our FBI colleague has a number of unique genes, not just the ATA gene. The deviations are so widespread that her DNA barely registered as human."

That was a roadblock Rodney hadn't anticipated at all. "Are you saying she's…" His brain started spinning possibilities. Did Larance know what she was? Had her involvement in this 'case' been a fraud all along? "You may have to subdue her," he warned Jumper One. Suddenly he felt like he was watching a thriller in a movie theater, seeing the danger clearly and yet only able to yell a futile warning to the characters. "Is she listening right now?"

A strangled screech came over the radio, followed by a shout identifiable as Sheppard.

"Not exactly," Jackson said tersely. "Stand by."

Before Rodney could protest, more voices joined the frequency—Marines reporting their progress. Lorne spoke to the sergeant leading the squad that had accompanied them in Jumper Two, looking progressively tenser as the conversation continued.

His throat itching painfully, Rodney suggested, "Can we close the hatch for a while to keep the smoke out?"

The Major shook his head. "Our guys are about a quarter-mile out. By the time they get here, we may not be able to afford the extra seconds it'd take to lower the hatch."

Against his better judgment, Rodney edged toward the open end of the jumper and looked out at the reddened sky. A menacing glow was steadily overtaking a stand of trees in the distance.

More shouts from the radio punctured the air. Something about Larance taking Sheppard captive; Teyla, Ronon, and Jackson were fanning out to track them on foot while the two Marines who'd accompanied them guarded Jumper One. Rodney went forward into his jumper's cockpit and called up the HUD, hoping it would show him the path of the fires. It obliged—and what it displayed was terrifying.

He turned to Lorne. "We're going to have to take off the instant those Marines are on board just to get airborne in time to escape this."

Lorne nodded grimly and studied the HUD while Rodney's concerns ran in multiple directions simultaneously. Why—and how—had Larance taken Sheppard? Could she trigger the virus in him? God, the virus would be the least of his problems if they were out in the open when the flames closed in. Without the protection of a jumper...

A pair of Marines came barreling into Jumper Two, narrowly avoiding the acoustic equipment Lee was hastily stowing. "Where are Edwards and Koslov?" Lorne demanded.

"Got cut off, sir." The sergeant's voice was hoarse from sprinting through smoke. "Wind's catching sparks and starting smaller fires all over the place, even where there's snow. They had to detour south to get around. Give 'em five minutes. They'll make it, Major."

A reasoned estimate, or youthful military bravado? Rodney suspected he knew the answer.

To his credit, Lorne didn't hesitate. "Then we'll see 'em in five." He grabbed his radio. "Jumper Two calling all jumpers. Situation report."

"Jumper Three has Alpha team accounted for."

"Jumper Four, same for Bravo."

"Jumper Five, same for Charlie."

That was something, at least. Unfortunately, they already knew the news wasn't as good for Jumper One. Not waiting for a response, Lorne ordered, "All teams withdraw to the alternate landing site and await further instructions. We'll join you ASAP. Jumper One, suggest you continue your search from the air. Ground conditions are deteriorating."

"Would if we could," came the reply from Jackson, shouted over a series of cracks that must have been the result of falling tree limbs. "The fire jumped and blocked my path. I'm going to head upwind and try to outflank it. Snow's not making a damned bit of difference… spot fires breaking out all over."

"Same here," said Ronon, the background noise coming through his radio equally alarming. "Teyla?"

"I believe I am not far from the jumper. It is difficult to see." Teyla sounded barely out of breath. "Sergeant Barnett, are you and the corporal still at your earlier position?"

"Yes, ma'am. I think I see you coming," answered the Marine at Jumper One. "Swing to your left a ways—there you go. Major, unless the Colonel gets back here soon, we're gonna have to hunker down and ride this out in place. He's the only one who can fly us out."

Rodney dug his fingers into the arm of the seat, repressing the temptation to bang his head against something. They hadn't bothered to ensure that there were two gene carriers per crew, because they'd expected to be able to trade personnel between jumpers if backups were needed. No one had anticipated the ferocity of the fires turning each jumper into an island; no one had believed everything could go to hell so quickly. Eucalypt oil, he realized. The tinder-dry brush might as well have been doused in gasoline instead of a thin coating of snow. Idiotic shortsightedness… Or was something more at play? Spot fires breaking out everywhere didn't make sense, unless—

"I'm at the jumper," reported Teyla, her voice finally betraying a hint of tension. "There is not much time left before the blaze will overtake us."

"I'm almost there," Jackson promised.

Ronon cursed viciously. "The wind just shifted and caught

the trees around me. I've got nowhere to go!"

"Sirs, Jumper One's throwing all sorts of warnings at us," said Barnett. "I think it knows the temperature's getting dangerous."

"Jackson, where are you?" Lorne called.

"Still moving." Jackson's voice was starting to give out. "But the fire'll get there before me. Teyla, close the hatch."

"But—"

"Do it," Ronon yelled, "or none of us will get out of this!"

From his marginally safer place inside Jumper Two, Rodney shut his eyes and fought the urge to be sick. Jackson and Ronon had just signed their death warrants. And Sheppard's—if the Colonel was even alive. For all they knew, the virus could be activating in any one of them. Maybe that was the reason the other Marines, Edwards and Koslov, hadn't made it back yet.

Not again. Rodney would be damned if he'd bear witness by radio while more friends died. He launched out of his seat. "We can track them by their locator beacons. If we take off now—"

"Not yet. We've got two men on their way here, and they'll be just as screwed as the others if we leave." Allowing no debate, Lorne tapped his radio. "Edwards, Koslov, sit-rep!"

After a pause, a voice answered, coughing. "Sir…should be only a hundred yards out."

"You waiting for an invitation?" the Major thundered, sounding more like a drill instructor than Rodney had thought him capable of. "Haul ass!"

When he belatedly remembered Lee's presence, Rodney glanced over. Seeing the other scientist all but cowering in a corner of the rear compartment, wide-eyed and close to hyperventilating, almost mitigated some of Rodney's own anxiety. Almost.

"For a while, I considered trying to join an actual SG team," Lee said quietly. "Maybe I'll rethink that."

"You get used to the constant panic," Rodney told him.

Lee met his eyes, curious. "Do you really?"

The sense of utter helplessness was intolerable. This was one time where nothing he did could help a damn. "No."

CHAPTER TWENTY-EIGHT

Pain, along with a chaotic jumble of perceptions, yanked John back to consciousness. He had a disorienting sense of being tossed around inside an enclosed space for what seemed like ages. When everything finally stilled, he closed his eyes against nauseating dizziness and struggled to recall what had happened.

The cave entrance. The jumper. Rebecca freaking out. Memory returned in snatches. They'd just gotten a weather update a few minutes ago, warning of a massive incoming storm. The snowfall was only the edge of a frontal system that would develop into howling northerly winds by dawn, feeding the flames. The change in wind direction had added a new wrinkle to the plan by placing the cave entrances right in the path of the advancing fires. John had ordered the Marines to retreat to their jumpers in case a rapid withdrawal from the area became necessary. The Australian troops had justifiably shifted their priorities to helping local residents evacuate or defend their homes.

Following a pointed comment from Rodney about the obvious effects of global warming, John had glanced at Rebecca and gotten one hell of a scare. She'd been trembling uncontrollably, arms hugged tightly around herself, and the look in her eyes had been almost feral. As soon as he'd touched her shoulder, she'd bolted, and it had taken him a second to shake off his shock and chase her. Jackson had been shouting over the radio at him, telling him that Landry had just checked in with a bizarre report on Rebecca's DNA test, and Teyla's voice had mingled in as well, warning him that she sensed something powerful and unrecognizable but decidedly Wraithlike.

Both calls had only confirmed what John had already

started to suspect; there was no other explanation. Something had just flipped Lilith's modified retrovirus switch in Rebecca, and in a big way.

After that, he remembered nothing until that horrific fall.

He dragged his eyes open, attempting vainly to focus in spite of the pounding in his head. It was dim, and blood obscured his vision, but he was able to make out the shape of a person next to him, shuddering, moaning wordlessly behind tightly closed lips.

"Rebecca?" he tried to say, but the motion radiated agony down his jaw and into his neck. She jerked back and scrambled away from him, climbing out through what looked like a broken car windshield. That explained where they were—sort of. How the hell he'd gotten into the vehicle in the first place was still a major question mark, though it came in a distant second behind figuring out what had triggered the virus.

It took him a while to understand that she must be fighting the urge to feed on him. When that sank in, he recalled the intensity of his own experience in that dark realm and spared a moment's gratitude for her willpower. Then he tried to reach his radio—and, through a haze of pain that threatened to gray his vision completely, it slowly dawned on him that her restraint had only bought him time. His right arm was pinned under the upended seat; his left lay broken and useless next to what was left of the radio. The dashboard pressed insistently against his ribcage, reminding him with every breath that something was very wrong inside. In this temperature, he knew he wouldn't last long without help.

Once the flare of additional pain caused by moving subsided to something marginally more tolerable, a noise outside filtered into his awareness. An animal, sounding about as happy with the world as John was. He managed to turn his head just enough to rest it against the warped doorframe of the vehicle and found the source of the noise: an injured cow.

Under an eerie russet glow that had to be a result of the

approaching fires, John watched Rebecca stagger toward the wretched animal and sink to her knees in front of it. She reached for her holster and then appeared to change her mind, stretching out her hand to touch the cow's flank. Instantly, its cries stopped, its thrashing head falling limp, and its body began to wither in a bizarre, possibly merciful version of a Wraith feeding.

Finally, Rebecca slumped forward over the carcass. Caught between fascination and disgust, John couldn't tell if she was breathing or not. Blood now ran freely into his eyes, and he couldn't clear it. Even if she'd needed to feed on him, there was little left of his life to take.

Time passed; he didn't know how much. It was no longer snowing, and while he still felt the cold—blood loss, no doubt—there was a warm, gritty wind on his face. His team would be looking for him and Rebecca, but if a choice had to be made they'd do their jobs and focus on ending the Lilith threat. He only hoped they wouldn't waste too much of what had to be a limited window of opportunity on a search for him.

A thought struck him, one that he would much rather have avoided. Whatever had triggered the retrovirus in Rebecca might also have triggered it in the population at large. In which case… He didn't want to consider that notion, but his mind insisted on playing all kinds of apocalyptic scenarios, fed by every B-grade sci-fi movie he'd ever seen. The situation was made all the worse by the fact that he was utterly powerless to do anything to stop it.

Motion nearby forced him to open his eyes again. Hands reached toward him and disentangled him from the wreckage, hauling him out. Every part of his body screamed at the torture, and he cried out as he was laid on the muddy ground, damp with melting snow. He wanted to beg for it to end, but the nightmare only deepened. The one horror he'd come to dread more than anything: long, bony fingers shoved against his chest, a brief searing sensation through his ribcage—

—and the pain quickly ebbed. Once he had calmed down enough to realize he could breathe without effort, John instinctively scuttled back and threw a hand up to scrub the blood from his eyes. Aside from the fading echoes of crippling agony, he was whole and healthy again.

Through the light of the fires that seemed to draw closer by the minute, he could see a woman gazing down at him, the reddish glow lending an artificial warmth to her skin. Long-haired and delicate, she could have been the woman in Woolsey's video—except Jackson had met that woman in Iraq. Hanan, he'd called her. How could she have gotten to Tasmania ahead of them?

"Rest your mind, John," she said, helping him to sit up. "The retrovirus remains dormant in the population at large. My name is Anata. We've come to help you both."

Not Hanan after all, then. He didn't like the idea that she'd had an opportunity to rummage around in his brain while he'd been unable to put up a fight. Still, she'd saved his life while she was at it, so he owed her some consideration.

"Okay," he said carefully. "So, can I ask if you're a cambion or a full blood succubus, or is that considered rude?"

Anata smiled and nodded to one of the three people who stood around her, a guy with Ronon's build who scooped up Rebecca easily.

"You don't need to worry about offending me. I've already seen your fears, and I understand them." Anata rose and offered John a hand to pull him to his feet. "I am a succubus. These cambion with me are my children. I'm sorry to rush, but we must hurry now. Don't be fooled by the snow that remains. The fires surround us—fires lit, as you suspect, by those who would hunt us all down—and the wind is only getting worse."

The heat was palpable, and cinders blew across John's field of vision. "How did you get here?"

"The same way we'll leave." Anata was already hurrying along the gully, her wet hair slapping against her back. All

four of them were dripping wet, John noticed. The remains of
the snow? That didn't make much sense.

None of them made any attempt to force him into going
with them, but without a radio he didn't have much in the way
of options. He could actually hear the blaze, a distant roaring
sound that could nearly have been mistaken for a waterfall.
Following Anata, he glanced up and saw the rapid movement
of the clouds. When he returned his attention to the path, he
had to pull up short as a small black shape darted out from
the bushes. About the size of a large housecat, it stopped and
sniffed at the group before loping off with an awkward-look-
ing gait.

"Tasmanian devil," one of the men explained, picking up
the pace.

John frowned. While he hadn't expected the actual animal
to resemble the Warner Brothers cartoon, he hadn't had this
image in mind, either. "I thought they'd be bigger. And nas-
tier."

The man laughed. "Try grabbing hold of one. You'll learn
all about nasty. It'll bite through your arm in one go and tear
it off at the shoulder."

It was hard to tell if that was meant to be a joke or not.
Probably not, John decided. In any case, there were more animals running past now. Dozens of dog-sized kangaroos that
someone identified as pademelons, as well as other things he
couldn't identify, joined them on the trail, heading down the
gulley to…something.

John caught sight of a dark patch like a distorted well at
the bottom of the path. As soon as they reached it, two of the
cambion jumped in. He couldn't see them land but heard the
splashes. Before he could think to object, the man carrying
Rebecca dropped her body in and leaped in after her.

"How long can you hold your breath?" Anata asked
briskly.

Still getting his bearings, John tuned out the panicked
screams of more animals in the distance. "How long do I need

to?"

"Sixty meters underwater."

Sixty yards, farther than the length of an Olympic pool, on one breath. On any other day he would have said that was beyond his capacity. Today, however, the alternative was being charbroiled.

"Through caves," the succubus continued, raising her voice above the alarming crackle of trees being consumed by the flames. "It will be pitch black and there will be some tight turns. If you begin to drown, we should be able to save you, but I need to know if you can do it alone."

With a splintering sound and a shower of sparks, an enormous tree overhanging the gulley went up like a torch. Anata glanced up. "There is insufficient snow to halt the blaze and this spot will be an inferno in less than a minute."

That was all John needed to hear. He jumped in and instantly was assaulted by the icy water, slamming the breath from his chest. Breathing; he had to breathe hard. Hyperventilating would rid his system of as much carbon dioxide as possible before going under. After five or six deep lungfuls, he could feel himself getting lightheaded with excessive oxygen. Good; he'd need it.

Anata surfaced beside him as several animals took the leap as well. "I'll be right behind you," she told him, batting one of the creatures aside as it tried to find purchase on her shoulder. "Swim straight down until you touch the bottom, where you'll see a faint light. Head toward it."

"Got it."

John had never been much of a claustrophobic, and he considered himself to be a pretty good swimmer—he'd even done some SCUBA diving way back when. This experience was very, very different. He ducked under the surface, using his arms and legs at the outset. Almost immediately his ears started to pound. He brought his fingers up, pinched his nose and blew slowly to equalize the air pressure in his Eustachian tubes while continuing to kick. His ears popped right away, but only a few kicks later he had to clear them again. And again.

All around him was darkness, blacker than anything he could have imagined. The water was freezing and Freud must have been out of his mind to equate *this* in any way, shape, or form with returning to the womb. He felt the first tickle of a need to breathe and paused for half a second before something slapped his leg. Anata. It was reassuring to have proof that she was still with him.

Abruptly he hit the bottom, slimy with weeds and silt. The light—where was it? Twisting around, he found a muddy red glow. He turned to head toward it when something caught his leg.

For a brief, terrifying moment, he thought he'd gotten tangled in the weeds. Then he felt Anata's hand on his face, forcing his head around, and a duller greenish light came into view. The magnitude of his near-mistake struck him; he'd been about to head back to the surface.

John's lungs and muscles burned. He battled the instinct to suck in a breath of water, of *anything*. They must have gone down about sixty, maybe seventy feet, which meant the remaining air in his lungs had compressed to…to… He couldn't remember. All he could see, all he could think about, was the light, growing larger and brighter but not quickly enough.

Just focus on the light. Focus…

His vision blurred, and then there was nothing.

CHAPTER TWENTY-NINE

Out of the approaching wall of orange-tinted smoke burst two Marines, coated in ash and diving into the jumper. "Button it up!" Lorne commanded, throwing himself into the pilot's seat. Someone slapped at the hatch controls, and Edwards pounded out a smoldering ember caught in Koslov's sleeve. As Jumper Two lifted off, Rodney could see claws of flame devouring the last few plants that had surrounded their landing zone. The Marines grinned at each other, riding an adrenaline rush even through their wheezing.

Next priority: locator beacons. Rodney returned to the copilot's seat and initialized the sensors while Lorne banked the craft toward the southeast and Jumper One's position. They skimmed over a mountain range whose entire side seemed to be ablaze, long fiery trails snaking all the way down to the coast. The magnitude of it all was astounding. "How the hell does something like this happen?" Rodney had to ask.

"According to that Army captain, State Emergency Services says the northern fires were caused by lightning strikes," Lorne answered, his focus straight ahead. "The way these other small ones started and spread, though…it didn't look natural to him, and I tend to agree. These new outbreaks started miles upwind of the first fires."

If the Lilith were aware the SGC force was there, this might have been the ideal opportunity for them. Flush out the jumper teams, and generate the maximum amount of confusion in the area to divert attention away from their activities. Rodney just wished he knew what their activities might be.

A beep from the sensor screen drew his attention. "Got a signal. It's Sheppard."

"Overlay it on the HUD." When the dot appeared, Lorne

narrowed his eyes. "Crap."

Rodney shifted his gaze from the HUD to the scene beyond the windshield and found it hard to believe what he saw. Flames were leaping from treetop to treetop, even crossing rivers and highways with no sign of slowing down. At the rate it was spreading, there wasn't a creature on the planet that could have outpaced it on foot.

"Damn," muttered Lorne. "Here goes nothing." He lowered the jumper over the road where the locator signal beeped steadily.

Despite being insulated from the heat, Rodney cringed away from the seething curtains of fire that lined the blistering asphalt. The jumper was buffeted by violent updrafts that strained the inertial dampeners. "We have the shield enabled, right?" he asked.

"Do I look that stupid?" The Major guided Jumper Two over the edge of the road and into a ravine, where the distorted wreckage of a Land Cruiser lay—

A fireball erupted, engulfing Rodney's entire field of vision. On instinct, he threw up a hand to shield his face.

From somewhere behind him, he heard Lee murmur, "Oh, no."

"Gas tank must have exploded." Looking shell-shocked, Lorne didn't voice the obvious conclusion. Rodney's brain supplied the details anyway. Even if Sheppard hadn't been within the immediate range of that blast, the air temperature in the whole area had risen far beyond a survivable level.

As Rodney watched, perversely unable to tear his gaze away, the small dot that represented his friend and team leader winked out.

"All right," Lorne said quietly. "Find me Jackson and Ronon."

Rodney reset the search parameters, struggling against a crushing sense of anguish. What good was all the brilliance in the universe if it couldn't keep good people from dying?

His face now schooled into an impassive mask, Lorne

spoke into his radio. "Teyla, have you heard anything from your team?"

"Not since we closed the hatch." Teyla's voice held the same frustration and remorse that Rodney felt. "I believe it has become too loud outside for our calls to be heard."

Two signals appeared, less than a hundred meters apart, and Rodney wasted no time in transferring them to the HUD. "Come left *now*." Ronon and Jackson could still be saved, if the jumper could just get over this ridge and—

At almost the same moment, both signals flickered and vanished.

STARGATE ATLANTIS: BLOOD TIES

CHAPTER THIRTY

Through a gray haze of hypoxia, John felt something grab him by the shoulders and haul him up. The change in pressure re-expanded the air in his lungs, and soon he broke the surface of the water, gasping and choking on his first clean breath in what felt like hours.

"That…" He gagged and spat out a mouthful of water, gulping another huge breath. "You're telling me that was only sixty meters?"

Climbing up onto a rock ledge, Anata gave him a smile that blended apology with approval. "Sixty meters just to the bottom," she amended. "You nearly made it all the way here before starting to black out. Without fins or weights, that was rather impressive, for a human."

She reached down to help him, and he dragged himself out of the water on shaky arms. Shivering in the chill of the underground air, he curled up and waited for his breathing to even out. She'd expected him to die, or at least skirt the ragged edge of drowning. It hadn't mattered, of course, because she'd known she could bring him back if necessary. What a radically different mindset, to be able to risk lives without fear of consequences.

He pushed himself up to his knees and looked around. The pool that had been their entrance was really more of a shallow river, winding through a large cavern. He couldn't tell what was providing the light source, but the place was illuminated much better than the average tourist-traveled cave. The ledge they occupied was a massive piece of flowstone that led up to a relatively flat area, where one of the cambion held a hand over Rebecca's chest—and he wasn't performing CPR.

John got to his feet, instinctively moving toward the profiler's unconscious form. She would have gone without oxygen longer than he had during the swim...

"She'll be fine," Anata assured him, pulling off her soaked jacket as she matched his stride.

When John neared the wider part of the cavern, he was startled to see row after row of automatic weapons and minor artillery pieces. These folks were better equipped than the Atlantis armory. He raised his eyebrows. "Expecting a war?"

The cambion who'd gone ahead of them had now congregated near a group of shelves and were stripping off their wet clothes without a trace of embarrassment. One of them, the big guy who'd carried Rebecca, tossed John a towel and a set of dry clothes: nondescript olive-drab fatigues, probably surplus from one military or another.

"As a matter of fact, yes." Anata wriggled out of her clinging shirt. "But not with the Ori."

Because she seemed as comfortable out of her clothes as in them, John didn't bother to avert his eyes as he pulled his own shirt, ripped and bloodied, over his head. Like the others, Anata's skin was pallid almost to the point of albinism, though not tinted with the sickly teal of a Wraith. Her limbs were exceptionally long and thin—gangly, he might have said had she not moved with such grace. While they honestly did need to get into drier clothes, he nevertheless suspected that this display was a demonstration of sorts; evidence that Anata and her children could pass—outwardly, anyway—as human.

His focus shifted to Rebecca again, and he recalled their conversation in Iraq. Being human now seemed to be more of a sliding scale than an absolute.

"What's going to happen to her?" he asked, nodding in Rebecca's direction. Two women, whose arrival he'd somehow missed, began to rid her of her wet clothes as well. He turned back to Anata and finished dressing.

The smile the succubus wore was warm and genuine. "She will sleep a while longer, and when she wakes she will know that she is the one."

Phrases like that tended to make John nervous. "I don't mean to sound ungrateful for the way you saved us, but just what is she supposed to be 'the one' of?"

Tugging on a soft-looking sweater and freeing her long hair from its collar, Anata met his gaze squarely. "You already have most of the information you need. I felt it in you when I fed you. Come on. We both could use some energy, and there should be hot chocolate brewing." She shot him a disarming grin that almost made him forget how incredibly old she must be. "There's nothing better than chocolate after a cave dive."

John followed her through a narrow gap between two thick stone columns, quickly ducking to avoid an overhanging formation that resembled a side of bacon. The passage opened out into a tall cavern, prompting him to look up. The light barely reached the ceiling, several stories high and covered with clusters of needlelike stalactites, stained dark with soot. On the ground, a campfire was burning low, and a girl of about fifteen was distributing mugs of steaming chocolate complete with marshmallows. John accepted his with a nod and a quiet "thanks." It *was* awfully good, he had to admit. Still, he had priorities.

"If that well is your only way in and out of here," he said to Anata, "how—"

With a laugh, the succubus gestured for him to sit on one of the broken chunks of limestone near the campfire. "The well is one of hundreds of entrances to this cave system. It was merely the closest to where Rebecca's vehicle crashed. I apologize for that, by the way. Normally it takes several more hours for the ginkgo solution to trigger the retrovirus. Like I said, Rebecca is unique."

So the ginkgo theory Atlantis's scientists were following was worthwhile. Even so, John wasn't sure whether that comment had answered more questions than it raised or vice versa. A particular question stood out above the rest, however. "How did you slip her this solution of yours in the first place?"

"Do you remember the water bottle Rebecca had with her in Ramadi?" At John's blank look—Iraq seemed like the distant past by now—Anata elaborated. "The solution is odorless and colorless. Hanan was not far away during your visit. When she realized who Rebecca was, and who you were, she had the water bottle switched. It was a risk, to be sure, especially since our stock of ginkgo on this planet is nearly depleted, but it was necessary. The others, the ones you call the Lilith, were already on her trail because of the investigation. The only way to protect Rebecca was to empower her with her innate abilities."

John decided to skip over the "and who you were" part of what she'd said. He'd long since given up on trying to untangle everyone's various interpretations of his so-called Ancient birthright. "What abilities would those be? The feeding trick?"

"Much more than that. Rebecca is the first among our kind who does not require human life in order to feed."

That explained the cow earlier, which John had been half convinced he'd hallucinated. He took another sip from his mug before responding. "I have a hard time believing you've lived for however many thousands of years and none of you have tried to feed on animals."

"I doubt there's a cambion in existence," replied Anata, unruffled, "except perhaps for those who believe their place is with the Wraith, who hasn't made the attempt. Until now, it's never been successful. It was always Ninlil's intention for animal feeding to be possible, but, as you've learned, her laboratory was destroyed in the great flood five thousand years ago. When the rains ceased and the Tigris and Euphrates finally returned to their riverbanks instead of joining to form a vast inland sea, Ninlil led the survivors north, and we settled in the caves in Germany. They had been used by hunters since Neolithic times and their many passages were well mapped."

Her story made sense, at least in the context of what John already knew. Even so, he had to shake his head. "Hanan could have saved everyone a lot of trouble by telling all this to Daniel Jackson in Iraq, rather than letting us fumble around until we managed to chase you down. If you'd just made yourselves known—"

"Your governments, under the auspices of the International Oversight Authority, would have rounded us up and had us confined to Area 51 for 'study'." Anata fixed him with a knowing look. "You'll forgive me, Colonel, if your organization's previous genetic work on Michael doesn't fill me with confidence."

John winced inwardly. That whole mind-sharing thing had some serious drawbacks.

"Don't misunderstand," she told him, stretching her long legs out in front of her. "We're in no position to claim any kind of moral high ground on such activities. In our own way, we've done much the same, attempting to breed one among us whose blood would permanently adjust the retrovirus to allow all succubi, incubi, and cambion to feed from any form of life. This is the only defense we can offer to protect humans from the Ori—or any new legion the Orici might garner."

Finally beginning to warm up, John edged back from the campfire. He wasn't sure he understood that logic just yet, but he was willing to take what he could get. "And the others—the Lilith?"

With a sigh, Anata said, "Those who worship Ninlil as Lilith consider us to be heretics. In fact it is they who are heretical, although I wouldn't use that term, since they are driven by belief whereas we are driven by biological fact. The active Lilith number in the hundreds, possibly thousands, because they have developed themselves into a religion—one that does not actively seek out followers, I grant you, but it muddles their view of those who carry the bloodline with esoteric nonsense about their rightful place in the universe. We, on the other hand, have no doctrine and take no members beyond those whose genetic memories are lucid enough for them to understand the truth. Those who carry the bloodline unknowingly come under the protection of Watchers like Hanan and me. Rebecca wasn't completely honest with you when she described forming her theories of Ninlil. Most of her knowledge actually came from indistinct glimpses into her own memories, which are now Awakening in full. She will understand that she, like all of us, was bred as an instrument, a means to an end. We are nothing more or less than that."

Having been a lifelong fan of self-determination, John was more than a little skeptical of that assessment. "An instrument? Not the most flattering picture, is it?"

Lifting an eyebrow, Anata sipped her chocolate. "Did you think the second evolution of humanity happened by dumb luck? We're all instruments. Annunaki, Ancients, Others, Lanteans—regardless of what you call them, they created all life in this galaxy and several others. And every single thing they did had a purpose, allowing them to further their ambition."

"To Ascend." The Ancients had been amazingly good at looking out for themselves first and foremost.

Anata shrugged. "Having said that, none of us has any reason to complain. We exist because of them, and we aspire to immortality just as they do. Some of us come closer to the goal than others."

John recalled Rebecca's observation that all belief structures shared certain common themes: namely, the desire for immortality. Under the steady gaze of the succubus, he shifted, wondering how much insight their brief mind-link had given her into his time in the Sanctuary. "That's Daniel Jackson's area of expertise, not mine."

"You're a soldier," said Anata simply. "You made a commitment to defend your people and were trained to do it well. We were created, bred, to do the same. That doesn't prevent either of us from exercising free will, and it doesn't exclude us from Ascension. If the Ori ultimately succeed—"

"The Ori are dead."

"You're not entirely certain of that, and in any case the Orici definitely isn't. She has a ready-made army, an entire galaxy's worth of followers and, if the other Ori are indeed dead, power all to herself."

John didn't want to sound impatient, but so far none of this had gotten him any closer to knowing how to deal with current events. "So what does that mean to us right now?"

Anata finished her chocolate. "We believe that several million, possibly as many as half a billion people carry some trace of the retrovirus. What Rebecca told you is true. The Lilith want to acquire ginkgo from the world you call M1M-316 and seed it across Earth. They also want to bring the Wraith here to assist in the battle against the Ori. Whether or not such a battle will ever actually take place is irrelevant to what will happen should they succeed. The ginkgo will trigger the active retrovirus in human carriers—the Awakening. The Awakened will need the rest of humanity as a source of food." She tossed him a rueful glance. "To quote one of your Talmudic texts, *'The children of Lilith will plague all of mankind for eternity,'* and the Biblical Apocalypse will be here, one way or another."

Cheery thought. "And what's your plan?"

"Acquire the ginkgo without alerting the disastrous experiment known as the Wraith, create a vaccine using the ginkgo and the mutated virus in Rebecca's blood, and slowly and carefully introduce it into the human population so that the Awakening is eased for all concerned. The Awakened will be given live animals to feed upon as soon as the compulsion takes hold. They'll never need to feed from a human—most people are averse to the idea due to deeply ingrained principles of ethical behavior. That's what saved you when Rebecca Awakened."

"Handing them chickens and goats instead will probably piss off a lot of vegetarians," John commented.

Anata's smile returned. "The feeding will be far more merciful than what currently takes place in a slaughterhouse.

More to the point, in the long term you'll have a force capable of going up against the Orici, if necessary, and certainly the Wraith. All the IOA has to do is allow genetic modification on a global scale. Oh, and declassify the Stargate to explain everything while they're at it. Tell me, what do you think the chances are of them going along with that plan?"

Just once, John would really appreciate it if the solution to a problem turned out to be obvious and straightforward.

Before he could answer, the low undercurrent of voices resonating off the cave walls grew louder. He looked up to see people hurrying toward the cavern he thought of as an armory. Abruptly, Anata dropped her mug and ran to join them.

John followed, watching weapons being distributed with alarming speed. "What's going on?" he demanded, afraid he already knew the answer.

"We have guests. The ones you call Lilith know Rebecca is here, and they want her dead. To them she is an abomination. I had hoped we would have more time, but if this is how we are to make our stand, then so be it." Anata snatched up an AK-47. "You can leave through the sinkhole if you choose. This is our fight and—"

From a distance, the first sharp reports of discharging automatic weapons echoed through the caves.

The choices weren't great: take sides in a succubus crusade, or roll the dice and attempt to repeat that marathon swim—this time without help. Of course, if John chose the swim and somehow managed to pull it off, he'd find himself stranded in the middle of an inferno. His teams on the surface must have been either driven back by the fires or overrun by the Lilith. As much as he hoped it was the first option and not the second, the difference didn't change his immediate situation. For now, he was on his own, and he wasn't sure they could afford to let the Lilith win this fight.

"I shoot best with a P-90, if you've got any," he said, reaching for a few spare clips of ammunition. "I think we're all in this together, whether everyone out there knows it or not."

CHAPTER THIRTY-ONE

Years ago, when Ronon's existence had been defined by running and fury and hopelessness, he'd often contemplated the best manner in which to die. All the variations had centered on taking out as many Wraith as possible in the process. None of them had involved burning to death trapped and alone.

For that reason, he didn't plan to burn. Even in the middle of the ever-changing fire, he'd managed to retain his sense of direction, and he knew he was close to the main entrance to the cave. All he had to do was get through the flames that stood between him and that opening.

He sprinted along a creek, the water far too warm as it splashed into his boots. A thermal area, he remembered Rodney saying earlier. In front of him, a huge branch splintered at the point where it joined the tree trunk and started to fall. On instinct, Ronon threw himself into the shallow water on his hands and knees and rolled around to saturate his clothes and hair as best he could.

The branch plummeted to the ground in an explosion of sparks, knocking over a pair of nearby tree ferns as it crashed across his path. The ferns, maybe still damp from the melted snow, didn't ignite right away. They bought him a few seconds, which he used without hesitation.

He took a running start, jumped up onto the shriveling fronds and leapt through the wall of flames. Intense, unimaginable heat assaulted every part of his body, but his coat shielded most of his skin. Emerging on the other side, he found a set of steps and a ramp he recognized as leading to the cave.

At the top of the steps, he caught a quick glimpse of a boot through the smoke. Someone was running ahead of him.

Ronon took the steps three at a time, each breath getting shallower as he felt the heat scorching his lungs.

"Ronon!"

He identified the voice as Daniel Jackson's. Following it, he made for a gray smudge amid the sea of orange. As soon as he crossed into the dark, cool entrance of the cave, the door slammed shut behind him.

Ronon leaned back against a wall and inhaled deeply, tasting the moisture in the air.

Breathing hard, sweat streaking through the soot on his face, Jackson offered, "Fancy meeting you here."

Hands pounding out a lock of hair that had started to smolder, Ronon smirked. The archeologist was just the kind of doctor he could work with.

After taking a few seconds more to recover, Jackson reached for his radio. "Jumper One, this is Daniel Jackson. Ronon and I are safe in the cave for the moment."

No response came. Ronon tried his own radio. "All jumpers, come in. Anyone hear me?" Nothing—not even static. He glanced back at the heavy door separating them from the blaze outside. "Maybe the door's too thick to let the signal through."

"I don't think that's it." Jackson aimed the light affixed to his P-90 down a set of steps. The beam was soon swallowed up by the black void. Changing tactics, he played his light over the nearer walls until he found a rusty box mounted on one side. "Aha. This is a show cave," he explained, opening a panel on the box with one hand while illuminating it with his weapon in the other. "It's been made accessible so tourists can come in and look around."

He flipped a set of switches, and the cave was suddenly awash in light. Looking over the rail, Ronon could see steps descending to an open area.

Bending down, Jackson picked up an abandoned flashlight and handed it to Ronon. He also located a handheld radio and a couple of crumpled pieces of paper advertising some kind of singing concert.

The flashlight and radio served as reminders that others had been here recently, though the warning was unnecessary. The missing park guides and the broken padlock had been clear enough. Ronon drew his blaster and started down the steep steps, listening for any sign of movement or noise in the cave.

At the bottom, a shallow pool, so clear and still that at first he wasn't certain it even contained water, ran alongside a section of flowstone covered in rows of bench seats. While Jackson looked around what he described as pews, Ronon climbed the next set of steps, which had been partially cut into the existing stone and finished with the artificial rock called cement. The cave was large, its layout complex. He was almost to the top step when Jackson said, "They use this place as a concert chamber."

Although he'd used a normal speaking voice, the sound resonated throughout the cavern. Ronon felt the air shift and turned toward a darkened passage off to his left. Was something down there?

He glanced down. Standing motionless at the bottom of the cave, the other man studied the walls with a thoughtful expression. "Sansenoy," Jackson intoned.

The word echoed for some time, reverberating under Ronon's feet and even through his hand where he grasped the guardrail. He watched Jackson as he spoke again, understanding the idea. As weapons went, it didn't seem like much, but it might be better than nothing.

Jackson took the steps returning to the entrance at a run. Ronon hurried down from his position and lengthened his stride to catch up, wondering what the plan was. He considered asking but decided to wait until he was closer and could do so quietly. Not far away, he suspected, someone—or something—was waiting.

Back at the entrance, Jackson put his hand on the door and instantly jerked it back with a grimace. The heat outside had to have been intense to penetrate the thickness of the metal. "I think something in the cave system is interfering with our radios," he said. "If we can stand to open this door even for a short while, we should be able to call Jumper Two. They need to bring their amplifier and speakers in here and set them up inside the cave. It shouldn't be long before the worst of the fire has passed through."

The idea of subduing a Wraithlike mutation with sound still seemed crazy. Even so, Ronon had to admit that the acoustic power in that cavern was remarkable.

Using the sleeves of his coat to protect his hands from the hot metal, he carefully pulled the door ajar, instantly feeling the wave of heat that forced its way inside. It was strong, though not unbearable. The shelter that had been built over the entrance had largely burned down, sparks whipping through the air. The uncontrollable walls of flame had given way to individual burning trees, still deadly but possibly manageable in a jumper.

"Jumpers One and Two," Jackson called into his radio, his head ducked low to protect his face, "how do you read?"

"This is Jumper One," Teyla replied instantly, relief evident in her voice. "Do you know if—"

"I'm here, too," Ronon put in, anticipating her question. "We're inside the main entrance to the cave."

"Nice of you to let us know!" Rodney shouted from Jumper Two. "Your beacons disappeared off our screen ages ago."

"Couldn't get through on the radios earlier. You find Sheppard?"

There was a pause, and the voice that answered was Lorne's. "There was an explosion right on top of his last known position. It's hard to see how he or Agent Larance could have survived."

Sorrow flickered in Jackson's eyes, but Ronon allowed himself only concern. He knew his team leader, and he wasn't about to grieve until he saw a body.

"McKay and Lee, get your equipment down here," Jackson said, lifting his jacket up over his face as a gust blew a curtain of sparks toward them. "I have an idea, and we're going to need the amplifier."

When he explained the properties of the concert chamber, Rodney started to object. "Whoa, wait a minute. We're going to risk going out in the firestorm to play this ridiculous chant through the caves in the hopes it'll reach the bad guys?"

"They're in here somewhere," Ronon said with certainty. "Can you amplify the words enough or not?"

Rodney heaved a sigh. "With enough power, I suppose we could set up a resonance that would transmit through most of the immediate area of the cave system."

"Which would achieve what?" Lorne asked.

Jackson shrugged. "Don't know until we try. If you have any better ideas, we're listening."

"Fine," snapped Rodney. "How close can the jumper get to the cave entrance?"

"Close enough. The shelter's been pretty much destroyed by the fire. Just be ready to offload as quickly as possible. We'll hold the door open for you."

Ronon raised his voice over the crackle of a disintegrating tree in the distance. "If Teyla could come as well to sense the Wraith—or whatever they are…"

"I can," Teyla responded, "but Jumper Two will have to transport me. We have no one to fly Jumper One. Most of the brush in our immediate vicinity has been consumed, so the fire has receded somewhat, at least in the area visible through the windshield. We should be able to open the jumpers' hatches long enough for me to board."

Before Rodney could make much more than a sound of protest, Lorne said, "All right, we're on our way."

His back against the wall of the cave, using the tip of his boot to keep the door open just enough to maintain radio contact, Ronon slid down to a sitting position and waited.

Less than a minute passed, and then Lorne's voice

returned. "Teyla, the fire hasn't receded all that much near the back of your jumper, although the flames are only about four feet high. We can land, but if we open the hatch—"

"Then do not land," said Teyla. "Hover above the flames and open your hatch. We will open ours only as far as necessary, and I will run up the ramp and leap across into Jumper Two."

The image her description created in Ronon's mind was worrying. If the ramps were not perfectly lined up, she risked a fall into the blaze below. He said nothing. If Teyla believed she could do it, he did not doubt her.

"Okay, here goes." Lorne sounded less confident. "We're at six feet and rotating to align the hatches. Edwards, stand by the hatch and be ready to catch her if she needs you. Open the hatches in three, two, one—now!"

Ronon closed his eyes.

"Close 'em up!" In the background, coughing could be heard from several people. Above it, Lorne announced, "Passenger's aboard. We're heading for the entrance."

"That was one hell of a jump," said one of the Marines, sounding awed.

Blowing out a held breath, Ronon stood up and pushed the door open to see Jumper Two rise up out of the still-burning forest and head toward the cave. "We'll lose radio contact as soon as we close the doors," Jackson told Lorne. "Just join the other jumpers and wait for a call."

"Understood," replied Lorne. "Good luck."

The hatch descended, and Teyla ran along the ramp, jumping the last three feet to the ground and sprinting into the cave. Rodney was next, flinching as a tree branch crashed to the smoldering ground a few feet away. Throwing himself through the doorway, he turned and yelled into the jumper, "Get your ass down here, Lee! If Teyla can impersonate the Flying Wallendas, you can handle a damned ramp!"

After another second of hesitation, Lee made an awkward jump, followed closely by two Marines carrying the equipment. The moment everyone was safely inside the cave, Ronon and Jackson swung the door shut.

"Well, I feel extra crispy," grumbled Rodney, examining a singe mark on his sleeve. "Now what?"

"I sense a presence." Teyla sent a wary look in the direction of the steps. "Like before, it is not Wraith, but similar."

"We'd better get moving." Jackson led them down the stairway and into the chamber. No sooner had Ronon's foot hit the last step than a rumble sounded in the distance.

The Marines tensed. "That's an AK-47," one said. "Actually, it sounds like a whole bunch of AK-47s, and maybe a couple of P-90s."

Ronon crossed over to the set of steps he'd climbed before, hoping to gain more information from the noise. "Might be a good sign." The look Rodney threw him made it clear his sanity was being questioned. "Sheppard would be firing a P-90, remember?" he pointed out.

"His signal went missing in the vicinity of a number of sinkholes," Rodney admitted. "And your signals did disappear when you entered the caves." He ducked his head, as if reluctant to show too much hope, and bent down to help Lee connect a bundle of wires to the amplifier.

The weapons-fire grew in volume. Was it getting closer, or more fierce? Perhaps both? "Hurry up!" Ronon told the scientists.

Lee slapped at a row of switches on the amplifier and detached a small microphone from the side. "Testing," he said, an anxious waver in his voice. "Testing, one, two—"

Impatiently snatching the microphone from his hand, Rodney shouted, "Senoy, Sansenoy, Semangelof!"

The vibrations that instantly dominated the chamber were painful. Ronon clapped his hands over his ears, watching the others do the same. As the echoes died down, he listened for the gunfire and found it absent—but only for a moment. Soon the abrasive clatter began again with renewed enthusiasm.

Rodney opened his mouth to try again and was halted by

Jackson's hand on his shoulder. "It's not just the words," the archeologist said, his eyes rounded in sudden realization. "It's a cantillation! I remember running across it in some Hebrew folklore—I heard the melody once at a conference…" He closed his eyes, brow creased in concentration, and started to sing a tentative tune.

Once he'd completed the refrain, he went back to repeat it from the beginning. Teyla quickly picked up on the melody and joined in with a strong, pure tone. Rodney wasted no time in shoving the microphone at her.

The words, and an unsettling harmonic undercurrent, reverberated through the caverns. Although he couldn't have explained it, Ronon got the sense that something very primitive and powerful was happening. He tightened his grip on his weapon and waited.

CHAPTER THIRTY-TWO

The echoes of gunfire reflecting off stone created a continuous roar in the caverns, while countless muzzle flashes gave the area a strobe effect. John had no idea who was winning and could barely bring himself to care anymore. All he could think was that he'd survived Afghanistan, Iraq, and the Pegasus Galaxy only to bleed out in a damned tourist attraction in the most benign place on Earth.

The first bullet had destroyed his shoulder, shattering bones and rendering his shooting arm useless. As he'd attempted to orient himself through a haze of blinding pain, he'd left himself open to another, more critical strike. It had slammed him against the cave wall, folding his legs underneath him before he could even react.

Staring up at the jagged ceiling, he came to the realization that each breath he pulled in brought more searing agony and progressively less air. He choked on a cough, and the sharp, metallic taste in his mouth confirmed what he already feared. He'd flown enough med-evac missions to recognize a lung shot.

Almost as a formality, he raised a shaky hand to his side, knowing he couldn't get enough pressure to do any good.

Dimly he heard a voice shout his name over the clamor, and suddenly Rebecca was leaning over him with a horrified, conflicted expression. "God," she whispered, ineffectually lifting her hands toward the first wound and then the second.

John wanted to tell her not to waste her time, but all he could force out was "Don't…"

"I can heal this," she said with a determined tone, nevertheless looking utterly overwhelmed. "I—I'm not sure how, but I know I can."

His vision dimming around the edges, he could only lie

there as she centered her hand on his chest and closed her eyes.

Abruptly, she was shoved aside, and Anata dropped to her knees beside John. "Not you," the Watcher shouted at Rebecca. "You must live—everything depends on it. Run!"

"I…" Rebecca looked down at John again, and some of the indecision seemed to clear from her face. "This is who I am," she said quietly, to herself as much as to him. "This is what I'm meant to do."

"I know," he managed to say, using what little air he could draw in. "It's okay. Go."

Touching his uninjured shoulder briefly, she rose, and soon she had disappeared from view. John exhaled on a pathetic, rasping groan and let consciousness drift.

He barely felt Anata's hand on his chest. Within moments, though, a flood of adrenaline and endorphins snapped his eyes open. His lungs suddenly clear and whole, he sucked in an unsteady breath. To his dismay, Anata's hair had faded to snow-white in a matter of seconds, and her features began to wither as she channeled her life into him.

She couldn't keep this up; he could sense her weariness. She'd given much of what she had to spare the first time she'd saved him, and this time he was worse off. If she stopped now—if she only healed him *most* of the way—she might live long enough for one of the others to restore her. But she wasn't stopping.

John couldn't let her make that sacrifice. He gathered every scrap of his renewed strength and pushed her away. The force hardly budged her, but it was enough to break the connection. He rolled onto his side and spat the residual blood that had coated his throat onto the cave floor. Even that small motion took a concerted effort, and he lay back, panting.

Anata shook her head, her ageless gaze making it clear that she knew what he'd been trying to do. "Foolish child," she said, looking at him almost fondly. "Be still."

"Why?" he asked simply, certain she'd understand the

question. *Out of all the people dying in this place, why save me?*

Without answering, she reached for him again. The fire in his shoulder cooled, and he felt almost—

An AK-47 report sounded, close by, and Anata slumped forward over him.

No, damn it!

John scrambled up onto his elbows as an incubus stalked toward him, gun raised.

Just then a lyrical, familiar voice reverberated through the chamber, cutting through the weapons fire.

Teyla?

Strangely enough, the haunting melody seemed to be having an effect on the battle. All around, cambion—followers of Lilith and Ninlil alike—began to collapse. The incubus who had shot Anata reared back, as if someone had buried a knife between his shoulder blades, and dropped to the floor. Scattered screams split the air, quickly dissolving into feeble moans.

After a grisly few moments had passed, Teyla's voice was the sole remaining sound. John pulled himself fully upright, moved Anata's body gently to the floor, and did a quick self-check. The Watcher, for whatever inexplicable reason, had done what she'd set out to do; he was fine. He was also—as far as he could tell—the only person still alive in the cavern.

CHAPTER THIRTY-THREE

As the melody traveled throughout the underground system, the gunfire trailed off and eventually ceased. Upon Daniel's gesture of encouragement, Teyla continued to sing, and he found himself entranced by the ethereal beauty of her voice.

At last, she fell silent, and they waited for the final echoes to die away.

"Music soothes the savage breast, or so someone once said," Daniel commented quietly. If this really had worked, it opened up countless possibilities for research in so many areas.

"I thought it was beast?" said one of the two Marines, unable to tear his eyes from Teyla.

Straining to listen to for any distant sounds, Daniel replied, "A common misconception."

"For want of a consonant," McKay muttered. "In either case, I hope whoever it was meant it literally."

They stared at each other, hesitant to do much more than breathe. After a few long, tense minutes, Ronon abruptly spun toward a darkened passage on the perimeter of the chamber. "I heard something," he warned the group, bringing his weapon to bear on the opening.

For a long time, there was only silence. Then, finally, a solitary figure slowly emerged into the light.

"Hey, guys."

Sheppard held a P-90 loosely in one hand. He was dressed in different fatigues than the ones he'd disappeared in, the fabric torn and stained dark in multiple places. A drying smear down one side of his neck could only be blood.

"Holy—" McKay darted forward, only to halt at the foot of the steps. "You look like Victim Number Three in every horror movie ever made. That blood isn't yours, is it?"

"No." Sheppard waved a hand. "I mean, yeah, but it's not a problem anymore."

Since the Colonel seemed unhurt, Daniel chose not to press the issue. He'd been down that path too many times not to intuit what had happened. "What happened to the Lilith?"

Sheppard hitched his shoulder in the direction from which he'd come. "Probably ought to see for yourself. It's not pretty."

Daniel started up the steps to join him and was beaten there by the rest of Atlantis's primary offworld team, unconsciously closing ranks with their leader.

"Uh, if it's all the same to you folks, I'd rather hang out here." Lee shifted his weight from one foot to the other. "To pack up the equipment and all."

Giving him a nod, Sheppard told the Marines, "Stay with him, and check in with Lorne and the others. Let them know they can stand down."

"Aye, sir."

Sheppard led the group through the winding passages, using his P-90 only as a flashlight. He'd even put the safety on. While Daniel trusted the man's judgment, he kept his own weapon ready, as did the others. There was always the possibility that a few remote areas of the cave system hadn't been penetrated by Teyla's amplified voice.

When they arrived at the inner chambers, however, all thoughts of lingering dangers vanished.

"Good God," breathed McKay, his features slack with disbelief.

"According to many ancient religious texts, the invocation of a chant or a cantillation is supposed to be one of the most effective techniques for exorcizing demons." Daniel had witnessed some stunningly lethal results from the use of acoustics in the past. Even so, he never would have believed that something so graceful and delicate as Teyla's rendition of the hymn could produce such a violent outcome.

But the proof lay scattered everywhere. As the group explored the cave, stepping carefully over and around scores of bodies, it became clear that not a single succubus, incubus, or cambion had survived. They lay in tangled heaps, some sprawled over rocks—all with weapons in their hands, although the assorted gunshot wounds were secondary. Every last one had bled copiously from the ears, nose and, in some cases, eyes.

Daniel pulled his gaze from the carnage and noticed a vast network of symbols and drawings covering the dolomite walls. Some were etched into the living rock; most were neatly painted. He felt around in his tac vest until he found his palm-sized digital camera and moved closer to the nearest set of markings.

"This is unnervingly similar to a couple of hive ships we've known and hated," observed McKay. Daniel looked over to see the scientist peering distastefully into an alcove stacked with partially cocooned bodies. Under the wispy membranes, this particular collection of victims clearly had been fed upon and appeared to be dressed for hiking. The Tasmanian authorities probably could call off the search for those who had recently gone missing. The Lilith must have gathered and stored them in order to fuel themselves for the battle.

"I didn't know you could sing like that," he heard Ronon tell Teyla. "What you said a while ago, about not letting fear and war rule every part of life…I think I get it."

"I have always used my voice only to honor my people and the Ancients," the Athosian answered, sounding stunned and not a little disturbed. "To know that it can also be an instrument of such destruction…"

"You honored them both today," Ronon said, resolute.

When Daniel sneaked a glance at Teyla, he could see that she was far from convinced.

Returning to where Sheppard waited, expressionless, McKay asked, "Not that I'm unimpressed by your phoenix imitation, but how exactly did you get down here—and, while you're at it, what the hell happened?"

"Anata happened." The pilot had adopted a thousand-yard stare that Daniel recognized all too well. Jack had pulled the same maneuver plenty of times: compartmentalizing emotions, closing off the parts of himself that couldn't afford to waste time being traumatized. What had transpired over the last few hours to bring Sheppard to that point, Daniel doubted they would learn anytime soon.

"Anata?" asked Ronon in a tone that said he already understood.

"A Ninlil succubus. She and her cambion got Rebecca and me out of the crashed truck and brought us in here. Her people came here to stop the Lilith, to protect someone whose bloodline might have given us a shot at saving humanity."

McKay's face fell. "I'm not thrilled with your use of the past tense just then."

"They're dead." Sheppard gestured with a listless hand at the surrounding massacre. "All of them."

Hearing the Colonel explain the details of the Ninlil plan, Daniel felt the weight of his actions settle over him. Although no one could say here and now whether the people of Earth would need the Ninlil's brand of protection in the future—to say nothing of whether they would *want* it—the odds were good that something fundamental had just been lost to them. In his experience, potential threats like the Orici never merely went away.

Too often, what seemed like a necessary choice in the midst of a crisis ended up difficult to accept when the smoke cleared. He could still recall the anger and bitterness that had fueled him when Jack had shot the android Reese, betraying the trust Daniel had earned from her, ending any chance of learning from her the weaknesses of her replicators. Time and subsequent events hadn't completely eroded his belief that killing her had been a profound mistake. The replicators might have since been destroyed, but their Pegasus counterparts were an entirely different matter. He could only hope that, by acting on his insight into how to take down the Ancient Ninlil's chimeras, he hadn't just committed the same error.

"We didn't know the Ninlil were here," he said simply, the statement sounding weak and ineffectual. "It wasn't our intention to… We didn't know." The useless mantra of the ill informed.

So many deaths here—it would take days, if not weeks, for the caves to be scoured and every last body located. Teyla had pressed her hands to her mouth, her dark eyes broadcasting her dismay and sorrow like a beacon. Daniel wanted to tell her that it wasn't her fault, that it had been his idea more than her voice that had condemned both the Lilith and Ninlil. He knew, though, that it was all a matter of perspective. He might have been the trigger. Her voice had been the silver bullet.

While McKay's shock was obvious as well, Ronon appeared indifferent. Daniel suspected that the Satedan didn't draw much of a distinction between the succubus factions. They were too close to being Wraith to garner any sympathy from him.

Sheppard had been silent for some time when Teyla reached out to grasp his sleeve. "John," she whispered. "I cannot express…"

Her misery seemed to jar him back to the present. "You're not responsible," he told her, sliding his hand up to clasp hers before releasing it. "I'm not explaining this very well. Anata and her people were losing the battle before the sound even reached us. The group who had followed through on the Ancient Ninlil's original intentions had a code of conduct; they only allowed themselves to feed minimally on any one person, usually just the dying. Because of that, they weren't as strong or resilient as the Lilith." He rubbed distractedly at a bloodstain on his shoulder. "I took a couple of hits during the attack, and Anata healed me. One of the Lilith incubi had just gotten the drop on her when we heard the first notes of the song."

Teyla nodded, clearly still conflicted. In the quiet that followed, McKay asked, "I can already guess that the answer isn't good, but where's Agent Larance?"

"I think we'll find her in here." With his weapon dangling from one hand, Sheppard cupped the other around the back of his neck, looking tired beyond measure. "The Ninlil used the ginkgo to trigger the retrovirus in her, so she'd understand her role in all this."

Her role? Comprehension flooded Daniel. "She was the one they were trying to protect," he said suddenly. "She was the evolution Ninlil had been aiming for all along."

And now she was dead, either by the Lilith or the hymn. It didn't matter which—except in the sense that knowing for sure might keep everyone standing here from wondering if they'd done as much damage as they'd prevented.

"At least the Lilith worshippers didn't succeed in whatever it was they were trying to do," said Ronon.

"Not yet." Daniel gave the wall writing another glance. "A lot of them, probably the majority, died here, but more are still out there. Remember, another group was on its way here from Germany."

"The Australians will catch them," suggested McKay, sounding more hopeful than certain.

"Unlikely." Teyla had pulled herself together as well as could be expected. "They share a mind-link. They will have realized what has happened here and will make every attempt to disappear."

"Then we'll do what we have to do to find them." Sheppard turned toward the entrance and abruptly thrust out a hand to steady himself on the wall. In the uneven light provided by a handful of lamps, it was hard to tell, but to Daniel he looked pale.

McKay frowned fiercely, as if unsure how to convey the right amount of concern. "Are you sure this Anata healed you all the way?"

"I'm okay." The Colonel straightened, not without effort. "I think I might not have gotten every last drop of my blood back, that's all."

"Oh, that's all, is it?" Rolling his eyes, McKay dug into his pockets until he came up with a somewhat battered Snickers bar. He slapped it into his teammate's palm. "It might be a bit melted, what with the raging forest fire I had to negotiate earlier."

The corner of Sheppard's mouth quirked up as he looked down at the candy. "Thanks," he said quietly.

"Yes, well, now we're even. Don't say I never gave you anything."

Sheppard scanned the room once more before squaring his shoulders. "Let's get out of here."

When they emerged, the sun was beginning to rise. The fire had taken what it could and moved on, leaving behind a barren world that resembled a forest of spent matchsticks. The sky was bilious and unwelcoming, the air tasting of ashes in the increasingly strong wind, smelling of cinders and death. Daniel scrubbed at gritty eyes, feeling the complete absence of moisture in the air. He'd seen his fair share of post-apocalyptic scenes, but never before had one forewarned of a future their own planet might no longer be able to avoid.

Jumper Two had landed near the cave entrance, and through the devastated foliage it was now easy to see Jumper One parked a few hundred yards away. Marines were loading the acoustic equipment onto Jumper Two under Lee's supervision.

"Damn good to see you, Colonel," Lorne greeted his CO with a relieved smile. As soon as he picked up on the look in Sheppard's eyes, however, his tone and bearing became rigidly professional. "Sir, General Landry's ordered us to remain in place for the time being. We're to secure the cave and help sanitize the area. Local teams will be arriving shortly to assist. The General assumed there would be a number of bodies in need of disposal."

"The General's a smart man," Sheppard said, his voice flat. "We need to make him aware that the last contingent of Lilith followers is probably going to ground as we speak. He'll pass the information to the Australians so they can decide how to mount a search. Can you get him on the sat-link?"

"Will do, sir."

Daniel barely paid attention as the two officers went into the jumper to make the call. As grisly as their duty would be, he was glad of the chance to stay in Tasmania. It would take him a quite a while to document the extensive collection of markings on the cave walls. With any luck, the symbols would give him some indication of what the Lilith had been searching for, either in the caves or in Antarctica.

If their murders and influence could be ended, maybe the recriminations wouldn't remain so long in the back of his mind, mocking him with the torturous beauty of that hymn.

His equipment safely stowed on the jumper, Lee approached the others with an expression of frank curiosity. "I presume the acoustic effect worked," he commented brightly. "Remarkable. Can you describe how?"

McKay's answer was terse and accurate. "Efficiently."

Glancing around at bleak faces, Lee's enthusiasm faltered. "Have I missed something? Shouldn't we consider this a win for our side?"

Under Daniel's boot, a branch crumbled to ash. Between his surroundings and what had transpired over the past few hours, he couldn't avoid thinking of the words of King Pyrrhus. "One more such victory," he mused, "could utterly undo us."

CHAPTER THIRTY-FOUR

The bustling Salamanca markets in the city of Hobart held endless fascination for Teyla. She absorbed all the sights and sounds—more varied, more exuberant, and simply *more* than any trading world she had ever come across. Her teammates had been surprisingly tolerant of her curiosity, showing no impatience as she inspected every stall, marveling at the craftsmanship of each piece of spun glass and sculpted wood. The fragrant scent of lavender began to erase the disturbing odors that had clung to her memory over the past few days. John had managed to procure some local currency for them, and she planned to bring many items home.

They had needed this escape, Teyla was sure. The worst of the fires had been brought under control, and she had been eager to leave the cave area behind as soon as the last of the bodies had been removed. She was not yet certain she had fully accepted the notion that her singing had caused such devastation. Even so, she had begun to understand that the incantation had been intended, in fact programmed, by the Ancient Lilith—or Ninlil, as they had come to think of her—into her creations.

According to the autopsies Dr. Lam had performed, the activated virus caused marked changes in the brain. Exposure to a particular pattern of frequencies—namely, the specific sequence of tonal variations in the cantillation—triggered the rupture of blood vessels. While Teyla didn't pretend to comprehend Lam's detailed explanation, she recognized the results of a massive hemorrhage.

Prompted by the knowledge that Teyla, who carried Wraith DNA fragments, and John, who'd once been infected with the *iratus* virus, had been unaffected by the melody, the doctor had looked further into the neurological differences found in the activated followers. She'd concluded that, despite her presumed insanity, Ninlil had most likely engineered the acoustic trigger as an inbuilt failsafe—a kill switch, John had called it—for her creations. The chances of it having an impact on Wraith, or on humans carrying the inactive retrovirus, were slim.

John had just received a call from General Landry, and the whereabouts of the remaining group of Lilith worshippers had become the subject of discussion.

"So the FBI and Interpol tracked the last group that fled Germany to…where?" Rodney prompted.

After paying for a cup of steaming chestnuts, which the vendor handed to Ronon, John pocketed the change and replied, "Argentina."

For reasons that escaped Teyla, Rodney rolled his eyes and tossed his hands up in the air. "Of *course* they fled to Argentina. Where else would they go?"

With the activity and noise in the crowded market, there was little chance of anyone paying attention to the conversation. Nevertheless, John dropped his voice so that Teyla had to lean in to hear his next words. "They tracked them to the town of Ushuaia, near Cape Horn."

Noticing Rodney's pointed interest in the chestnuts, Ronon tossed him one. Juggling the hot nut between his hands, Rodney said, "Ushuaia. Isn't that where the tourist cruises to Antarctica depart?"

John nodded. "They boarded a Scandinavian-built ice ship, the *Verreisen Sie Heim,* on a chartered cruise that's been planned for months. The ship only carries a hundred and ten people, and it's owned by—"

"Let me guess," said Rodney around a mouthful of chestnut. "Goeldi. So the last group never intended to come to Tasmania in the first place, which leads me to conclude that the other groups intended to acquire information from the caves and then transmit it to their pals."

"Either that or they're not completely sure of the location

of whatever it is they're searching for, so they decided to split up."

Swallowing, Rodney asked, "I'm assuming the General has dispatched a squadron of F-302s down there to engage in a judicious round of target practice?"

"As we speak."

Rodney looked somewhat reassured by that prospect. "May I make a suggestion? As much as I'm enjoying the stroll, can we get some actual food in the near future?"

"Actual food," Ronon said, cocking a disbelieving eyebrow at the scientist, "as opposed to this?" With a half-eaten chestnut skewered atop one of the many thin blades he normally kept in his hair, her Satedan teammate gestured to the rows of fresh fruits and vegetables surrounding them.

"Hey, do I critique your unorthodox choices in utensils?" Rodney shot back. "Believe it or not, most of us periodically require something more substantial than complex carbohydrates. A little protein wouldn't go amiss, and considering we are on the waterfront—"

"You can all have treats if you behave, kids," John cut in good-naturedly. Seeing his faint smirk warmed Teyla, even if she could still detect in it a hint of artificiality. What he had witnessed—no, more than that. What he had experienced in the caves was unspeakable, and for the past few days he had been forced to remain at the scene of the horror. Perhaps, now that this saga was at last nearing an end, he was finally beginning to break free.

"What happened to the Ancient Ninlil anyway?" Ronon pulled the last of the chestnut off the knife with his teeth, garbling his question. "Did she die, or Ascend, or what?"

"Jackson thinks he might have a lead on figuring that out," said John as the group walked north along the waterfront. "The writing on the cave walls ties in with some of the information he got from the tablets in Iraq. He's not sure, but it looks like Ninlil was eventually killed by one of her children, named Nirrti."

Rodney's head swiveled rapidly at the name, which was unfamiliar to Teyla. "Did you just say *Nirrti*? As in the all-time Goa'uld champion of genetic atrocities?"

"Small universe, huh?" John gave a shrug. "Assuming it's the same Nirrti, and the odds of that kind of coincidence are slim, she couldn't actually have been related to Ninlil. Jackson's theory is that she was either a protégé of Ninlil or else took her as a host at some point to get hold of her knowledge. Whatever the story is, putting a cold-blooded Goa'uld and an off-her-rocker Ancient together must have resulted in some fireworks."

"Now there's a notion I could live quite happily without ever contemplating." Rodney seemed to repress a shudder. "As I was saying before: food?"

The waterfront was a much cleaner and more affluent-looking area than most fishing villages Teyla had visited. Boats with polished hulls offered sailing tours, and an enticing array of smells spilled out of a number of restaurants, around which many people were clustered, laughing.

"Let's try this place." John steered the team toward a restaurant that appeared to be built on a ship permanently moored to the wharf. On its lower deck, a man was selling large paper cones filled with seafood delicacies and potato pieces called chips. Patrons seated at nearby tables shooed away noisy seagulls begging for morsels of food. Most of the conversations seemed to focus on a boat race of some sort scheduled for the following week. No mention was made of the devastating fires that had taken so many lives—which was the official explanation for the deaths of the hikers found cocooned in the caves. The humans of Earth were resilient, determined to continue on with their lives despite their losses. Teyla was once again reminded why she admired them and their conviction to grasp life and enjoy it to the fullest.

"I'm entirely serious. If a lemon has been anywhere near that fryer, my resulting anaphylactic reaction will be spectacular and probably worthy of legal action."

The restaurant's owner merely handed Ronon a paper cone, giving only the barest indication that he'd heard Rodney's warning. "So who's your pick to get line honors next week?" he asked cheerfully.

Blinking at him, Ronon was rescued from having to answer when a nearby patron called out a name. An animated debate about yacht racing ensued, quickly lapsing into a language Teyla couldn't follow. She smiled as the owner presented her food to her and turned her attention to the television mounted behind the counter, a common enough sight in many of the stalls and shops she had visited. Currently it was displaying what she had learned was a news broadcast. The screen projected an image of two oceangoing ships floating side by side, the smaller one marked with the word 'Greenpeace' across its hull.

The restaurant's patrons must have noticed the broadcast as well, because one of them commented that the Greenpeace ship had left Hobart soon after the bush fires had passed through. Apparently some of its crewmembers, mainly biologists and doctors, had remained in Tasmania to assist with the wildlife crisis following the blaze. The ship had taken on board unskilled volunteers, some obviously known to the patrons, prompting one of them to declare, "Bloody whalers. Told Davo they'd be more of a worry than icebergs."

His comment was incomprehensible to Teyla until the owner of the restaurant, while pouring battered seafood into a cone, told one of his assistants, "Turn that up." The young man pulled a thin transparent glove from his hand, tossed it into a refuse bin and moved to adjust the volume.

"…a Japanese whaling factory ship," the reporter was saying. "Greenpeace and Sea Shepherd vessels tracking the whalers reported seeing smoke originating from the ship early this morning. Mirroring an incident last year in which one crewman died, both organizations offered assistance and received no response. Greenpeace, fearing an ecological disaster if the ship foundered so close to a major penguin rookery, sent its helicopter to investigate. We warn our viewers now that the images we are about to show are of a graphic and disturbing nature."

An overhead perspective that must have been provided by the helicopter magnified the deck of the larger ship, where dozens of bodies lay scattered. Every one, it appeared, had been fed upon in a Wraithlike manner, and many of them had suffered extreme burns.

To Teyla's right, Rodney made an agonized sound. John's radio, or rather the device called a cell phone, signaled then, and he casually withdrew from the crowd. Rodney's gaze darted back and forth between his team leader and the television.

In that moment, Teyla felt a sense of terrible foreboding. The remaining followers of Lilith had not abandoned their goal. In the background of the picture, she could see the majestic ice cliffs that had been described to her as a feature of Antarctica.

The news broadcast shifted to the deck of the Greenpeace ship, where a grim-faced captain was vehemently denying accusations from the Japanese government that protesters were responsible for the mass murders. "That's just the sort of insane reaction I'd expect," said the bearded man dismissively, radio in hand. "We've just had word from the team we sent across in a Zodiac to the ship. The *Nishin Maru*'s logbook confirms that they responded to calls from an Argentinean-registered cruise ship, the *Verreisen Sie Heim*, which we also picked up last night. The *Verreisen* reported they'd been holed and were taking on water. The *Nishin Maru*'s final log entry reports that the *Verreisen* was in visual range and that the Argentinean ship had sent three tenders full of tourists across to the *Nishin*." The camera followed the captain's gestures out to sea as he added, "The *Verreisen* drifted toward the ice pack and vanished off our radar in the early hours of this morning."

"Since then, there has been no visual or radar sighting of

the *Verreisen*," said the reporter. "The nature of the deaths has raised questions about a connection to recent worldwide reports of a new progeria-like virus. However, of more immediate concern is the large storm system now building in the area. For the second year running, the Japanese fleet is abandoning its…"

As the restaurant owner handed Rodney his cone and John's, Rodney checked the screen again and nearly dropped the food. "Look," he gasped.

In confusion, the man glanced over at the television and furrowed his brow. "What?"

Teyla stared at the image, which now showed many of the crew of the Greenpeace vessel on deck, looking out across the unsettled waters. Behind her, John finished his phone conversation with a "Yes, sir" that suggested the caller had been General Landry. He came up to stand at her shoulder, seemingly at a loss for words.

Dressed in the bright orange survival suit worn by all the ship's crewmen, Rebecca Larance had turned her head to stare directly into the camera. Standing with her were two other people, one a woman with distinctively elongated features. All three wore expressions as grim as that of the ship's captain.

"I'll be damned," John said under his breath. "Hanan and Baqir."

CHAPTER THIRTY-FIVE

"This decision came from the highest levels, Dr. Weir." Woolsey folded his arms. "M1M-316 is the sole source of the plant life that can be used to trigger the Wraith genes in humans on Earth. Eliminating the risk requires that 316's biosphere be neutralized."

Elizabeth sat back in her chair, looking at him with appalled disbelief. John wished he could be as surprised. The cynical part of his brain had suspected something like this was coming. "Wipe out everything on that planet," she said bluntly. "Just like that?"

"As you're aware," Woolsey replied, standing stiffly near the head of the SGC briefing room table, "DNA analysis has confirmed that several IOA representatives, and of course members of their families, are also burdened with fragments of the genes."

Analysis, my ass. John knew damn well the bottom-feeding bureaucrat had gone into panic mode as soon as he'd realized that his late cousin's connection to Hanan implicated his gene pool.

Woolsey continued, "Since the SGC failed to end the threat on Earth—"

"That's going too far, Woolsey." Landry's tone was icy.

"Is it?" Woolsey was undeterred by the General's ire. "Your people were unable—"

"Our people?" Jackson raised his eyebrows. "Wasn't it your idea for us to work with the FBI profiler?"

"Be that as it may. Your top Wraith hunters were unable to prevent Hanan and a group of her cambion followers from escaping."

"Escaping to what? Death by hypothermia or drowning? You know the timeline of events. Less than an hour after the

Greenpeace ship reported one of their Zodiac boats missing, along with a group of eight crewmembers that included Agent Larance, Hanan, and Baqir, a massive storm blew through the area. An inflatable wouldn't have stood a chance in those seas, and there's no way they could have escaped on foot through the ice pack."

With a gesture in John's direction, Jackson stood and activated the viewscreen, which displayed a grid map of Antarctica. "Over the last week, we've performed a comprehensive aerial survey of the entire continent. The deep-look scans indicated nothing beneath the polar ice cap except a surprising quantity of fresh water—enough to fill the Great Lakes a few times over, I'm told. The IOA might be better served to worry about the risk of mass drowning from an abrupt rise in sea levels if the ice shelves damming the water give way. It's far higher than the risk of a mass gene activation."

Woolsey shook his head, not reacting to the implied challenge in Jackson's tone. "You can't be absolutely certain on either aspect of that. For one thing, I've read the reports on global warming, and the conclusions are ambiguous to say the least."

Why the man had chosen to nitpick that particular issue, John had no idea, but he had to acknowledge Woolsey's first point—in spite of that 'Wraith hunter' comment earlier, which might have been aimed at any or all of them and had sounded an awful lot like a pejorative.

John had led the flight of jumpers that had crisscrossed the frozen continent with sensors tuned to maximum settings. As powerful as the scans were, they'd barely managed to get a ping even from the already known Ancient base—and to achieve even that much he'd had to make use of a direct sightline through the tunnel dug by the Goa'uld Al'kesh during the Battle of Antarctica. All things considered, he wouldn't be surprised if Jimmy Hoffa were under that ice cap. More to the point, since a cloaking system wasn't out of the question, it was still wholly possible that another Stargate or even a city-ship like Atlantis waited below the surface.

Then there was the matter of Rebecca's new talent for sucking life from animals. He didn't want to hazard a guess as to how the remaining Lilith contingent from the *Verreisen Sie Heim* had fared in that monster storm, but if Rebecca's group had somehow managed to make landfall, the penguins and seals down that way would allow her to keep her Ninlil cohorts alive. A little cold probably wouldn't bother them too much.

Of course, John had no plans to voice those opinions in this forum. He wasn't about to give the IOA any further ammunition. The rest of his team had spent a fair bit of time on M1M-316 and was adamant that the planet should be left in peace. Jackson had taken up the cause without being asked, pointing out that his standing with the IOA was more secure than that of anyone else involved. John, and to a lesser extent Elizabeth and Rodney, still had to make up lost ground after their unauthorized defense of their city, while Teyla and Ronon, being 'alien,' hardly counted to the unashamedly xenophobic committee.

Although John didn't like having to hide behind a member of SG-1 to get things done, he'd seen the logic. Rodney, however, had never learned about the better part of valor. "Does it strike you as ironic at all that these cambion of which you're so terrified have the same genetic makeup you do?" He snapped his fingers. "Wait, I misspoke. I confused irony with hypocrisy. Subtle difference in this case."

John could practically hear Woolsey's teeth grinding. "If the creatures that escaped find a way to reach 316—"

"They're human beings," Jackson countered. "Not 'creatures'."

"If they've got Wraith genes, they're not human," stated Ronon.

So much for presenting a united front behind Jackson. John would have reined Ronon in, but Teyla beat him to it, spinning her chair sharply toward him. "Go ahead and kill me now, then. If that is the definition by which you view humanity, you must kill all of us." Her cool gaze swept from Ronon to John and then Woolsey. "Every one of us who harbors genes other than those you consider to be purely human."

"That's not what I said," Ronon backpedaled. "Just that they aren't the same as…" Failing to find an appropriate description, he trailed off, looking troubled.

"It might be time for you to rethink that perspective, Ronon." Elizabeth spoke up, her voice resolute but not without compassion. "I would never ask you, of all people, to stop hating the Wraith. The fact is, though, you're immune to their feeding because of a gene that originated from the *iratus* bug. Does that make you less than human? Or more?" She leaned forward, placing her forearms on the table. "The point of all this, and what many of us seem to be missing, is that not one person in this room, or anywhere else for that matter, has a 'perfect' set of genes that's completely free of any trace of other life forms. We evolved from life that came before us. Because of that, we're all linked, not just between our two galaxies but across all others as well, because ultimately we're all made from the same building blocks of life."

For a moment, no one spoke, acknowledging her statement. His gaze downcast, Rodney said quietly, "That sounds like Carson talking."

Elizabeth gave him a wistful half-smile and a nod. "I remember him quoting Sagan once or twice. 'For we are all star stuff.'"

"Exactly," said Jackson. "If the IOA is willing to sanction genocide—"

"It is *not* genocide," Woolsey argued. "M1M-316 has no human inhabitants."

Well, that brief truce hadn't lasted very long.

"Are we really going to have a semantic debate about what to call this particular form of mass murder?" Apparently it was Rodney's turn to be impassioned. "It's utterly insane, the idea of wiping out all life on an entire planet based on nothing more than the off chance that one of its plants might trigger an unwanted gene *if* it ever reached Earth. And it *won't* reach Earth, because its Stargate is sealed off to incoming travelers."

"You've limited your thinking to the Stargate," said Woolsey primly. "Other methods of access are possible. It's not as if the Trust hasn't found its way onto spaceships in the past."

Rodney's eyes narrowed. Someone should have warned the IOA weasel about daring to question Rodney McKay's thought processes, John thought with a flicker of spiteful amusement. Sometimes he really enjoyed watching Rodney tear into someone.

"And *you've* limited your thinking to this one gene," the scientist returned, his tone heavy with scorn. "As Dr. Lam pointed out at the beginning of this saga, the known genetic disorders in the human genome number in the tens of thousands. How do you compare them? Are you absolutely certain that one of those genes won't suddenly switch on and wipe out a sizable chunk of the human population? I would love to see the experimental results you've managed to conjure up within the last few days on that subject. You *have* extensively researched all of them, right? You can say with confidence that French fries don't contain even more dioxins and triggers for cancer than the ones we already know about? What about the observed link between soy sauce and breast cancer? Should we send the Air Force off to blow up all the soybean fields on Earth? Show me the research that says the Wraith gene is the biggest threat we face, please. I'm on the edge of my seat. If the IOA would occasionally extract its collective head from points south and *listen* to the scientists it employs, it's possible we would be able to avoid half the problems we face on a daily basis!"

Performances like that had been known to send Rodney's subordinates cowering into corners. Amazingly, and infuriatingly, Woolsey didn't react. "This is a wholly different situation. We're talking about a known connection between the 316 ginkgoes and the gene that could turn half the human race into monsters able to feed on the other half. We have the capacity to eliminate that threat in a single operation. Dinosaurs, Dr. McKay, are not human. They became extinct sixty-five million years ago, an event which allowed humanity to be present here today. We want to ensure that remains the case."

Jackson, it seemed, wasn't ready to roll over just yet. "Has the IOA fully considered the idea that activating the gene, like the Ninlil intended, might make the human race stronger, more able to defend itself against a global attack from, say, the Orici?"

Woolsey's lips pressed together in a thin line. "It was discussed," he replied finally. "Leaving aside the risks, the logistics are too complicated. How could we even begin to prepare the public for such a massive change, both physiologically and socially?"

"Maybe now isn't the time," Jackson admitted, "but if we destroy 316, we're eliminating the possibility of ever activating the gene in the future. The risks you cite could be managed."

With a short laugh, Woolsey repeated, "Managed? We would have people turning on each other—*feeding* on each other."

"Do you really think the human race would descend into cannibalism just because it could?" Rodney demanded.

"You'd be surprised, and horrified, at some of the things people can and will do," Woolsey said mildly.

On that point, John couldn't dispute him.

The bureaucrat stood up. "The factors have been weighed, and the decision is final. I have a flight back to D.C."

As he strode out of the room, back rigidly straight, everyone else turned to the head of the table, their last hope for a reprieve. Landry shook his head. "This isn't something we can fight," he said simply. "You heard the man. Destroy M1M-316."

The preparations for their return to Atlantis were predictably subdued. Daniel Jackson had said his farewells to the team with an apology in his eyes. It hadn't been necessary—none of them were shortsighted enough to lump him in with the IOA simply by virtue of him being stationed on Earth—but it made John realize that his respect for the archeologist had taken a leap upward in recent weeks.

Rodney had been too despondent to bother going back to his locker for the stash of Starbucks beans left there weeks ago…until about five minutes before they were set to leave, when he abruptly changed his mind. "I'm going to need something to keep me from contemplating the futility of existence while I work on this monstrosity," he muttered, performing an about-face in the corridor. "Don't leave without me…as if you would."

John hadn't paid much attention to the IOA's specific instructions for carrying out their world-killing plan. Essentially, he'd gathered, Rodney was to use a variation on the paired Stargates and black hole trick used in this galaxy once before. The end result would be the explosion of M1M-316's sun. Just like that, they'd be the executioners of countless species—sentient species, if Teyla's report was anything to go by. Getting to sleep at night was about to become a lot tougher.

As the group continued toward the jumper bay, Teyla asked Landry, "General, with the greatest respect, how can your IOA be sure that 316 is the only planet in the Pegasus Galaxy where such an ecosystem can be found?"

Fair question. John checked Landry's expression from the corner of his eye and watched the General's features harden.

"We'll deal with that problem if and when it arises."

The other jumpers had returned to Atlantis at the conclusion of their survey duties, leaving only Jumper One waiting for them in the preflight area. John settled into the pilot's seat and made it about halfway through his checklist before Rodney came running up the ramp, his arms full of coffee and chocolate. Dumping the goods into a mesh cargo pocket affixed to one bulkhead and closing the hatch, the scientist all but threw himself into his seat.

"Let's get this the hell over with," he said shortly. "The sooner I finish doing the IOA's dirty work for them, the sooner I can take a dangerously hot shower and attempt to scrub my soul."

After checking to see that Elizabeth, Teyla, and Ronon had taken their seats, John eased the jumper up from the floor of the bay and aimed it toward the gate room. Normally he couldn't wait to get back to Atlantis after a visit to Earth, which probably said something about him that he didn't really care to contemplate too hard. Today, however, it was difficult not to approach the gate with a sense of reluctance.

"On top of being morally repugnant, this action is serving as yet another distraction from my current projects, not the least of which is my work on the city's star drive systems." Rodney drummed his fingers on the console in front of him. "While I don't have any expectation that we're actually going to need them in the near future, it's a worthwhile precaution to take, considering the fact that the Asurans are still skulking around out there. Also, I'm becoming increasingly convinced that we may run into other similar cities. Thanks to Dr. Jackson's discovery that several Babylonian cities may in fact have been named after cities in the Pegasus Gal—"

The event horizon swallowed them before he could finish, giving John a few prized moments of relative peace. When the puddle jumper emerged at the midway station of the gate bridge between the Milky Way and Pegasus, Rodney paused, momentarily disoriented. With a shudder, he said, "I am never going to get used to the sensation of being demolecularized for that long."

Outside the spartan frame of the station was the utterly

barren void between galaxies, but ahead of them was the unbroken field of stars that was their destination. "I've come to enjoy this stop a bit," commented Elizabeth from behind John's seat. "Absolutely nothing else around for light years, like we're on a balance beam between two immense havens of life."

"Pretty mind-blowing to think that the light we're seeing from Pegasus actually originated at those stars over a million years ago." John sat back and took his hands off the controls for a moment. "With a strong enough telescope, we could park here and watch history unfold in both galaxies. We'd see Atlantis in its heyday, and the first humans figuring out the concept of tools…"

Catching himself, John shook off the philosophical reverie. He reached over to input the next gate address with one hand and initiated the multi-gate autodial program with the other. Waxing lyrical wasn't usually his style. Being yanked back from the edge of death twice in one day had brought him more up close and personal with the idea of mortality than he'd bargained for. As for Rebecca… He couldn't decide whether to pity her or be in awe of her existence. In either case, she was no longer the woman he'd thought he'd come to know.

After all that had happened and all that was still to come, maybe he'd just needed to find a little perspective.

Rodney suddenly turned toward him, his grin so blinding and out of place that John was instantly wary.

"You're freaking me out. What is it?"

The grin became calculating. "You've just given me an idea."

CHAPTER THIRTY-SIX

Elizabeth stood up from her desk and stretched, in a vain attempt to chase out the tension in her shoulders. Across the walkway in the control room, Woolsey was standing at the railing with Rodney, apparently trying to ignore the resentment of the technicians around him. She hadn't been surprised by the IOA's insistence on having one of their representatives witness the neutralization of M1M-316, but she had felt compelled to warn Woolsey that the expedition was unanimous in its vehement opposition to the action. All of them had been touched in some small way by the empathy of the microceratops during their brief visit, and no one wanted to see the animals summarily killed.

Rodney had written a persuasive—and detailed, at two hundred pages—report on the impracticality of using a pair of Stargates to link 316's sun to the nearest black hole. Firstly, they would have to deposit a gate close enough to the black hole for the link to work. Even supposing that such a highly dangerous mission could be undertaken successfully, the resultant supernova would not only destroy M1M-316 but also emit an extraordinary amount of the plutonium isotope Pu-244, coincidentally annihilating all life on every planet of a neighboring star system just one hundred and fifty light-years away.

The report had been worded with such a liberal—even by Rodney's usual standards—amount of hyperbole that the IOA, accustomed to almost instantaneous travel across millions of light years, had failed to note a minor element: the light from the supernova would take one hundred and fifty years to reach the unsuspecting and very human inhabitants of that system, and the dangerous isotope, considerably longer. In Elizabeth's eyes, genocide was genocide regardless of how long it took, and since the IOA's definition of that term seemed to hinge on the victims being human, Rodney had made sure to imply that the committee members would be risking a trip to the Hague if they ordered such an action. Lest anyone accuse the expedition of stalling the inevitable, he'd smoothly offered a counterproposal involving a naquadah-enhanced nuclear bomb.

And now the IOA had taken them up on that, even suggesting that this act would cement the expedition's role as a critical component of Earth's homeworld defense. How quickly some things changed.

Here goes. Elizabeth strode across the walkway to join Rodney and Woolsey.

"How did this alternative proposal come about?" Woolsey was asking, as he feigned obliviousness at the frost in the room.

"Actually, it was the result of a failed test undertaken by Colonel Carter back in 2001, during General Bauer's brief tenure in command of the SGC." While Rodney was at least willing to speak to their visitor, his features were set in hard, sharp lines. "A naquadah-lithium hydride enhanced nuclear weapon set up a chain reaction on a planet whose surface held traces of naquadah in about the same proportion as the soil samples we took from M1M-316. The bomb you're about to send will make the surface of 316 completely uninhabitable for the next eighty-one million years."

Woolsey gave a weak, false-sounding chuckle. "You say that as if you're expecting me to push the button myself."

Elizabeth folded her arms. "We've made our position clear on this matter," she told him. "If the IOA wants to turn 316 into a giant ball of superheated plasma, that's certainly their prerogative. But we're not going to do it for you." She favored him with an equally false expression of innocence. "Besides, I assume you'll want to report back that you personally confirmed the elimination of the threat. What better way to do that than to send the weapon and check the results for yourself?"

Backed into a figurative corner, Woolsey looked uneasy. Still, he lifted his chin and nodded, stepping up to the dialing computer. "Give me the address of the planet, please."

With a glare that could have melted steel, Radek tapped a command into the computer, and the requested address appeared on the screen. Woolsey input each symbol in careful succession, and the gate opened. Mounted on a MALP, looking far too small and simple for a weapon of such magnitude, the bomb trundled through the event horizon.

On the control room screen, the now-familiar landscape of M1M-316 appeared. After a few seconds, a slight bluish shimmer signaled the MALP's passage through the force field surrounding the gate. A massive torosaurus lumbered past the camera, and a pair of childlike microceratops ran up to the MALP, inspecting it curiously. In the distance, Elizabeth could see a group of quetzalcoatlus flying past a breathtaking waterfall. It was the very picture of tranquility, and the very antithesis of the sleek silver weapon that now lay in its midst. How had the sentient raptors described manufactured objects? Dead things? And the bringer of death…

Summoning her resolve, Elizabeth turned to Woolsey. "Is there something you're waiting for?" she asked coldly.

Woolsey glanced around. A crowd had gathered in and around the gate room, in alcoves and on balconies. Everyone stared at him with open hostility. John, Ronon, and Teyla had appeared on the walkway, their expressions only marginally less scathing than that of Dr. Geisler, who'd arrived with them. In the control room, many of the technicians were holding back tears.

His jaw flexing, Woolsey pressed the button.

The MALP's onboard camera swiveled to face the bomb's digital timer, which began a countdown sequence. When the timer reached the final second, the gate shut down.

From the back of the control room, a murmured prayer could be heard.

Before a startled Woolsey could ask about the shutdown,

Rodney said, "Safety measure. The last time we used a bomb like this, the Stargate on the planet in question wasn't destroyed, and the feedback through the wormhole almost blew up Earth's gate, titanium iris and all. Atlantis's shield is considerably stronger, but all the same it's not really worth the risk. We'll dial back to make our confirmation in an hour."

"Just as well," Woolsey said quietly. "No one should have to bear witness to what we just did."

Elizabeth supposed she shouldn't have been surprised to hear his remorse. It wasn't as if he was truly heartless—merely caught in a difficult position and doing what he felt was necessary.

Woolsey raised his voice to address the assembled crowd. "I understand your strong feelings on this matter. This decision wasn't made without difficulty or conflict, but it was determined to be the best option to protect our world. I hope that one day you'll be able to believe that."

As expedition members began to disperse back to their duty stations, he turned to Elizabeth. "I believe it would be best if I return to Earth as soon as possible to deliver my report."

"I think that's a terrific idea," John said, his voice deadly serious. "Why don't you go wait in the briefing room until it's time to dial 316 and check on your handiwork?"

Looking a little pale, Woolsey all but fled the room. Elizabeth motioned John's team, Radek, and Geisler into her office. It was something of a tight squeeze; all of them huddled in a circle in front of her desk like they were setting up a football play. The last one in, Radek closed the door behind him, and all the angry tension seemed to leach out of their bodies.

John bounced on the balls of his feet. "I couldn't see the screen. How did it look?"

"How do you think it looked?" Rodney looked faintly affronted. "The hologram worked brilliantly."

"And so did you and your team, Rodney." Elizabeth sat

on a corner of her desk, feeling drained but elated. "You all deserve Academy Awards for that performance, to say nothing of the technical aspects."

The scientist gave a satisfied smirk. "It was simply a matter of manipulating the dialing crystals. Instead of M1M-316, Woolsey sent the bomb to a thoroughly barren chunk of rock that happened to contain trace amounts of naquadah. I'm sure the fireworks were impressive."

"And M1M-316?" Geisler asked.

"Once Mr. Woolsey confirms that the planet's surface has been completely destroyed," answered Elizabeth, "I'll stall him with a few final reports from the botany department on the properties of the ginkgo while Rodney changes the crystals back. He'll march off to Earth and tell the IOA members the threat's been eliminated."

Rodney added, "I'll also update the database at that time to lock 316 out of the system. The records will show that it won't be safe to visit for eighty-one million years, give or take a few millennia."

Geisler's broad smile turned wistful. "I can only imagine the heights its extraordinary residents will have achieved by then."

"Nice work, everyone. Really. Now get back into character in case Woolsey gets up the courage to stick his head out of the briefing room." Elizabeth watched the others leave, taking her brief euphoria with them. She looked up at John, who'd hung back in the doorway.

"Did we do the right thing here?" she asked simply.

John returned and perched on the opposite corner of the desk. "No question about it."

"If the Lilith, or even the Ninlil, ever find a way off Earth—"

"Let's not worry about that unless we have a reason to. They're pretty decimated, and the SGC's got a good handle on homeworld defense."

Elizabeth accepted that response, weaving her fingers

together in her lap. Decimated. She resisted the urge to press her military commander for details about what had happened on Earth, knowing he would only recite the facts, never explaining the reasons behind the distant expression she'd seen flicker across his features.

"We have a secret now," she said softly, "one we have no choice but to keep. The instant anyone from the SGC or the IOA learns that M1M-316 was spared, every last one of us will be recalled to Earth, and the expedition, if it continues at all, will go forward with new leadership that will finish the job. While I know we all agreed on this course of action, I can't help feeling like I've put a lot of people in a very difficult position."

With a purposely cavalier shrug, John replied, "I can't speak for anyone else, but I've built up something of a name for myself in the business of following my instincts and risking the wrath of superiors. It'd be a shame to break my streak now. I just wish we could tell Jackson how we flipped the IOA the bird." Sobering, he cast a sidelong glance at her. "Don't put this on yourself, Elizabeth. Like you said, we all agreed. We're in this together, just like we always have been."

It was surprisingly comforting, that last phrase, amid all the uncertainty that seemed to define the Atlantis expedition. This time around, they'd managed to circumvent a militaristic preemptive action toward a perceived threat. Between the dangers posed by the Wraith and the Asurans, however, she feared that such actions might become increasingly attractive, possibly even advisable under some circumstances. Where that would leave her, professionally and personally, she couldn't be sure.

But John was right. They'd figure it out together, as always.

"Thank you," she told him, reaching out to touch his shoulder before standing up. "Shall we go mope and glare at Woolsey until he gets out of our hair?"

"Sounds like a plan." John held out a hand in an 'after you' gesture.

Sunlight played over the gate room floor as they crossed the walkway, and Elizabeth felt some of her confidence return. As she'd vowed to herself at the start of this journey, nearly three years ago, she would take each day as it came.

ABOUT THE AUTHORS

With a degree in geomorphology and anthropology, **Sonny Whitelaw** decided that a career in academia wouldn't be as much fun as running a dive charter yacht and adventure tourism business in the South Pacific. Photojournalism came as a natural extension to her travels, and Sonny's work has been featured in numerous international publications, including *National Geographic*.

Sonny is also the author of *Stargate SG-1: City of the Gods*, *The Rhesus Factor*, *Ark Ship*, and *Chimera*. She has coauthored *Stargate Atlantis: The Chosen* and *Stargate Atlantis: Exogenesis* with Elizabeth Christensen and *Stargate SG-1: Roswell* with Jennifer Fallon. She currently resides in Brisbane with her two children.

• For more information, visit www.sonnywhitelaw.com

Elizabeth Christensen owns a T-shirt that says "Actually, I AM a rocket scientist." In her defense, it was a gift from her parents. A civilian engineer at Wright-Patterson Air Force Base, she endures daily the burden of being a University of Michigan alum in the heart of Ohio State territory. She is a native of the Detroit area and misses her hometown hockey team. Alongside her husband, she flies a 1979 Grumman Tiger airplane with a terrific engine and a paint job only a mother could love.

Beth has written three previous Stargate Atlantis novels: *The Chosen* and *Exogenesis*, both coauthored with Sonny Whitelaw, as well as *Casualties of War*. She also has contributed short stories to *Stargate: The Official Magazine*.

• For more information, visit www.elizabethchristensen.com

SNEAK PREVIEW

STARGATE SG-1: DO NO HARM

by Karen Miller

"There was nothing else we could've done, Janet," said Bill afterwards, once the machines were switched off and the carnage was decently shrouded beneath a green sheet. "He was dead before he stepped into the wormhole."

She nodded, vaguely aware of a crushing headache happening to someone else, somewhere else. "Yeah. I know."

He was a good man, Bill Warner. A lot of people would've transferred to Outer Mongolia rather than continue in Stargate Command if they'd been him, the last couple of years. But Bill just shrugged, and smiled, and put in another I/V. Splinted a couple more fractured fingers. Refused to give up no matter how desperate the odds.

He squeezed her shoulder, giving comfort. Getting it. "You going to see Hammond?"

"After I'm done here and I've checked on the others." She glanced at the wall clock. "Your shift ended an hour ago. You should head home."

"Yeah," he said, nodding. "I will."

But she knew he wouldn't. At least not until, like her, he was certain the rest of SG-8 was dealt with.

"I'll finish up," he added. "Don't keep the general waiting."

By 'finish up' he meant stitch together Jake Andrews' gaping wounds. Do his best to return the major to a semblance of wholeness. So that when his team-mates came to say goodbye they'd take away with them an image not entirely horrific.

Throat aching, eyes burning, she managed a brief, small smile. "Okay, Bill. Thanks. I appreciate it."

His own smile was half-hearted. Sad. Resigned. She left him with Jake in the silent operating room and went to see how Ariel Lee had come through her surgery.

"She'll be fine. Eventually," said Kate Dokic, who was still new enough to the SGC after four and a half months to be visibly rattled by what came back through the wormhole. "No arterial damage. The arrowhead nicked the femur, though. She'll be out of rotation for a while."

Still stupored by anesthetic, Ariel snored softly in the recovery room. Under the light blankets, the bandage on her wounded thigh was bulky.

Janet pressed her fingertips to the captain's wrist, feeling for the blessed reassurance of a pulse. *I'm sorry, Ariel. I'm sorry I couldn't save him for you.*

"I guess things didn't go so well for you," said Kate.

The pounding in her head was vicious. "No. No, they didn't."

"Damn," said Kate, and dragged long fingers through her short red hair. "That sucks."

Ya think?

But she didn't say so aloud. Flippancy was Kate's armor of choice, just like it was Jack O'Neill's. People coped how they coped. There was no one right way.

"Janet, I'm sorry," Kate added. "It's been a rough few weeks."

That was one way of putting it. Two fatalities. No – Jake made three. Four near-misses. Two significant spinal injuries, one almost certainly due to end in paraplegia. A broken arm. A broken pelvis. A compound fracture of the clavicle. One whole team down with hemorrhagic dysentery. Three-quarters of another team laid low with some weird alien 'flu. Altogether, five team leaders lost or out of action.

Come on already, universe. Cut us some slack. Anyone would think we'd smashed a dozen mirrors or tripped over a whole herd of black cats.

"Is it always this bad?" said Kate. Her eyes were apprehensive, as though she was having second thoughts about accepting this job.

"No. Not always. Actually, not ever." Janet patted her arm. "Not since I started here. Like you say. It's just a rough patch."

In the same way that the Great Depression was a minor financial inconvenience.

"Okay," said Kate, not sounding convinced. "If you say so."

"I say so. Now, I have to see Hammond," she said. "We'll debrief with Bill in the morning before writing our reports. Okay?"

Outside in the main infirmary Lieutenants Esposito and Brackley sat side by side, Tweedledum and Tweedledee. Their cuts and bruises had been seen to. They'd only be walking wounded for a few days. They looked at her face and knew they'd lost their team leader.

"What about Ariel?" said Jenny Brackley, her eyes too bright and her breathing uneven. "Can we go and sit with her until she wakes up?"

Strictly speaking it was against the regs but right now she didn't care. And anyway, seeing as how the redoubtable Jack O'Neill couldn't be prized from one of his injured team with a Jaffa fire-brand, forget the crowbar, and vice versa when he was the one wounded, it seemed a tad hypocritical for her to say no.

She nodded, gravely. "Sure. Just be nice and quiet."

"And Jake?" said Esposito. His dark eyes were somber. "What about Jake?"

She rested her hand briefly on his tense shoulder. "You can see him a little later. Doctor Warner will tell you when."

"Okay," he said. "Thanks, Doctor Fraiser."

"Yeah. Thanks," said Jenny.

"You're welcome," she told them, though why they should feel grateful when she'd failed to save Jake Andrews for them she couldn't begin to explain.

She left them still sitting there, Tweedledum and Tweedledee, looking for a way to summon the strength to move. Changed out of her blood-stained scrubs into a neat and tidy uniform and took herself off to see General Hammond.

He was in his office, talking with Jack. "Come on in, Doctor," he said, seeing her hesitate in the doorway.

"Screw it. We lost Andrews, didn't we?" Jack demanded, as though he didn't know the answer. His voice was ugly. Loss always did that to him. Made him angry. Unpleasant.

She stepped over the threshold, looking at Hammond. "I'm sorry, sir. It wasn't just the traumatic near-amputation. His liver was cut to pieces." And his upper intestine, and his spleen, but they didn't need to know every last grisly detail. "If he'd had access to surgery within ten minutes of the injury…"

"I'm not blaming you, Doctor," said the general. His voice was tired, his eyes glazed with grief. "What about the rest of SG-8?"

"They'll make a full recovery, sir. Captain Lee won't be fit for duty for a few weeks, though."

"Crap," said Jack and scrubbed his hands across his face. "General…"

"I know, Colonel," said Hammond. "You don't need to tell me."

"This brings us down to eight functioning teams," said Jack, not listening. "With not enough team leaders to go around."

"I know," said Hammond, an edge to his voice. "Are you under the impression I've been asleep at the wheel?"

"Sorry, sir," Jack muttered. "Of course not. I know you know. And you know that I know that—" He stopped. Sighed. "I'm just going to quit while I'm ahead, if that's all right with you."

"It's more than all right. In fact, I insist," said Hammond, glaring. Then he shifted his gaze. "Was there anything else, Doctor?"

"Nothing that can't keep for the moment, General," said Janet, shaking her head. "If you wanted to stop in and see Captain Lee, she should be alert enough to talk by 2100."

Hammond glanced at his watch. "Good. I'll do that. In the meantime, don't let me keep you. You either, Colonel. We'll finish that mission debrief at 0830 tomorrow. For now, I've got some phone-calls to make."

Jack pushed to his feet. "Of course, General. I'll see you in the morning."

"You certainly will."

Janet nodded, in lieu of a salute. "Thank you, sir. I'll be in my office if there's anything else you need to know." Or if you need to talk. Or share a fortified coffee. It wouldn't be the first time, after someone had died.

A little of the bleakness eased from Hammond's eyes. "Thank you, Doctor. Close the door behind you on your way out."

She and Jack retreated to the briefing room, quietly, exchanging a look as she pulled the office door shut.

"This is crap," he said, staring in through the glass map-panel at the general. Hammond hadn't reached for the phone, he was just sitting, motionless, staring at his clasped hands.

"So you said," she replied. "Colonel, I'm sorry. About Jake. Major Andrews."

Jack shoved his hands in his fatigue pockets. His face looked pinched. Pressured. Secretive with feelings he rarely expressed. He and Andrews had bonded over The Simpsons. Drove the base half-nuts with their Marge-and-Homer routines.

God, I'm going to miss that.

"Yeah," he said. "Me too."

His voice sounded indifferent but by now she knew better. "He was a good guy."

"Everyone here's a good guy," said Jack, edgily. He hated platitudes as much as clichés. "Even when they're a pain in the ass they're still a good guy." He looked away, pretending sudden interest in the clock on the wall. "We've lost too many good guys lately, Janet."

"We certainly have," she agreed… and was angry to hear her own voice cracking round the edges, like lake-ice that proved too brittle to bear the weight of more sorrow.

Jack heard it, of course. "Hey…" He looked back at her, his expression softening. "You okay?"

She nodded. "I'm fine. I have to go. I'll see you and the rest of SG-1 tomorrow at 1700 for your pre-flight physical."

"Ah. Yes. I can hardly wait."

She gave him a look. "If memory serves, PX8-050 has a gravity fifteen percent above Earth normal, yes?"

Jack rolled his eyes. "Yes."

"Then you'd better pray that knee of yours is behaving itself or this is one mission you'll be sitting out. Okay?"

"Oh, come on…"

She managed a tight smile. "Don't even think you can charm me, Colonel. Or bully me. Or cajole. I am impervious to your machinations. At 1700 sharp tomorrow I'll be stress-testing your sorry joints and that's the end of the discussion. Get a decent night's sleep, sir. You're going to need it."

She could feel his chagrin behind her, like heat from a glowing fire. "You know what you are, Doc?" he called after her.

"A damn fine physician and a superior chef," she called in reply as she reached the briefing room door. "And don't you forget it. 1700—don't be late!"

AVAILABLE
MARCH 2008

**For more information,
visit <u>www.stargatenovels.com</u>**

STARGATE
SG·1™

STARGATE
ATLANTIS™

**Original novels based on
the hit TV shows,
STARGATE SG-1 and
STARGATE ATLANTIS**

AVAILABLE NOW

**For more information, visit
www.stargatenovels.com**

Series number: SGA-7

STARGATE ATLANTIS: CASUALTIES OF WAR

by Elizabeth Christensen
Price: £6.99 UK | $7.95 US
ISBN-10: 1-905586-06-X
ISBN-13: 978-1-905586-06-6

It is a dark time for Atlantis. In the wake of the Asuran takeover, Colonel Sheppard is buckling under the strain of command. When his team discover Ancient technology which can defeat the Asuran menace, he is determined that Atlantis must possess it — at all costs.

But the involvement of Atlantis heightens local suspicions and brings two peoples to the point of war. Elizabeth Weir believes only her negotiating skills can hope to prevent the carnage, but when her diplomatic mission is attacked — and two of Sheppard's team are lost — both Weir and Sheppard must question their decisions. And their abilities to command.

As the first shots are fired, the Atlantis team must find a way to end the conflict — or live with the blood of innocents on their hands…

STARGATE ATLANTIS: ENTANGLEMENT

by **Martha Wells**
Price: £6.99 UK | $7.95 US
ISBN-10: 1-905586-03-5
ISBN-13: 978-1-905586-03-5

When Dr. Rodney McKay unlocks an Ancient mystery on a distant moon, he discovers a terrifying threat to the Pegasus galaxy.

Determined to disable the device before it's discovered by the Wraith, Colonel John Sheppard and his team navigate the treacherous ruins of an Ancient outpost. But attempts to destroy the technology are complicated by the arrival of a stranger — a stranger who can't be trusted, a stranger who needs the Ancient device to return home. Cut off from backup, under attack from the Wraith, and with the future of the universe hanging in the balance, Sheppard's team must put aside their doubts and step into the unknown.

However, when your mortal enemy is your only ally, betrayal is just a heartbeat away…

STARGATE ATLANTIS: EXOGENESIS

**by Sonny Whitelaw &
Elizabeth Christensen**
Price: £6.99 UK | $7.95 US
ISBN-10: 1-905586-02-7
ISBN-13: 978-1-905586-02-8

When Dr. Carson Beckett disturbs the rest of two long-dead Ancients, he unleashes devastating consequences of global proportions.

With the very existence of Lantea at risk, Colonel John Sheppard leads his team on a desperate search for the long lost Ancient device that could save Atlantis. While Teyla Emmagan and Dr. Elizabeth Weir battle the ecological meltdown consuming their world, Colonel Sheppard, Dr. Rodney McKay and Dr. Zelenka travel to a world created by the Ancients themselves. There they discover a human experiment that could mean their salvation...

But the truth is never as simple as it seems, and the team's prejudices lead them to make a fatal error — an error that could slaughter thousands, including their own Dr. McKay.

STARGATE ATLANTIS: HALCYON

by James Swallow
Price: £6.99 UK | $7.95 US
ISBN-10: 1-905586-01-9
ISBN-13: 978-1-905586-01-1

The team battles the Hounds of Hell

STARGATE ATLANTIS

HALCYON
James Swallow

Based on the hit television series created by
Brad Wright and Robert C. Cooper

Series number: SGA-4

In their ongoing quest for new allies, Atlantis's flagship team travel to Halcyon, a grim industrial world where the Wraith are no longer feared—they are hunted.

Horrified by the brutality of Halcyon's warlike people, Lieutenant Colonel John Sheppard soon becomes caught in the political machinations of Halcyon's aristocracy. In a feudal society where strength means power, he realizes the nobles will stop at nothing to ensure victory over their rivals. Meanwhile, Dr. Rodney McKay enlists the aid of the ruler's daughter to investigate a powerful Ancient structure, but McKay's scientific brilliance has aroused the interest of the planet's most powerful man—a man with a problem he desperately needs McKay to solve.

As Halcyon plunges into a catastrophe of its own making the team must join forces with the warlords—or die at the hands of their bitterest enemy…

Order your copy directly from the publisher today by going to www.stargatenovels.com or send a check or money order made payable to "Fandemonium" to:

<u>USA orders</u>: $10.82 ($7.95 + $2.87 P&P). Send payment to: Fandemonium Books, PO Box 2178, Decatur, GA 30031-2178.

<u>UK orders</u>: £8.30 (£6.99 + £1.31 P&P). <u>Rest of the World orders</u>: £9.70 (£6.99 + £2.71 P&P). Send payment to: Fandemonium Books, PO Box 795A, Surbiton KT5 8YB, United Kingdom.

Or check your local bookshop – available on special order if they are out of stock (quote the ISBN number listed above).

STARGATE ATLANTIS: THE CHOSEN

by Sonny Whitelaw & Elizabeth Christensen

Price: £6.99 UK | $7.95 US

ISBN-10: 0-9547343-8-6

ISBN-13: 978-0-9547343-8-1

With Ancient technology scattered across the Pegasus galaxy, the Atlantis team is not surprised to find it in use on a world once defended by Dalera, an Ancient who was cast out of her society for falling in love with a human.

But in the millennia since Dalera's departure much has changed. Her strict rules have been broken, leaving her people open to Wraith attack. Only a few of the Chosen remain to operate Ancient technology vital to their defense and tensions are running high. Revolution simmers close to the surface.

When Major Sheppard and Rodney McKay are revealed as members of the Chosen, Daleran society convulses into chaos. Wanting to help resolve the crisis and yet refusing to prop up an autocratic regime, Sheppard is forced to act when Teyla and Lieutenant Ford are taken hostage by the rebels…

STARGATE ATLANTIS: RELIQUARY

by Martha Wells
Price: £6.99 UK | $7.95 US
ISBN-10: 0-9547343-7-8
ISBN-13: 978-0-9547343-7-4

Series number: SGA-2

While exploring the unused sections of the Ancient city of Atlantis, Major John Sheppard and Dr. Rodney McKay stumble on a recording device that reveals a mysterious new Stargate address. Believing that the address may lead them to a vast repository of Ancient knowledge, the team embarks on a mission to this uncharted world.

There they discover a ruined city, full of whispered secrets and dark shadows. As tempers fray and trust breaks down, the team uncovers the truth at the heart of the city. A truth that spells their destruction.

With half their people compromised, it falls to Major John Sheppard and Dr. Rodney McKay to risk everything in a deadly game of bluff with the enemy. To fail would mean the fall of Atlantis itself—and, for Sheppard, the annihilation of his very humanity…

Order your copy directly from the publisher today by going to www.stargatenovels.com or send a check or money order made payable to "Fandemonium" to:

USA orders: $10.82 ($7.95 + $2.87 P&P). Send payment to: Fandemonium Books, PO Box 2178, Decatur, GA 30031-2178.

UK orders: £8.30 (£6.99 + £1.31 P&P). Rest of the World orders: £9.70 (£6.99 + £2.71 P&P). Send payment to: Fandemonium Books, PO Box 795A, Surbiton KT5 8YB, United Kingdom.

Or check your local bookshop – available on special order if they are out of stock (quote the ISBN number listed above).

The past comes back to haunt Jack

STARGATE SG·1

RELATIVITY

James Swallow

Based on the hit television series developed by
Brad Wright and Jonathan Glassner

Series number: SG1-10

STARGATE SG-1: RELATIVITY

by James Swallow
Price: $7.95 US | $9.95 Canada |
£6.99 UK
ISBN-10: 1-905586-07-8
ISBN-13: 978-1-905586-07-3

When SG-1 encounter the Pack—a nomadic space-faring people who have fled Goa'uld domination for generations—it seems as though a trade of technologies will benefit both sides.

But someone is determined to derail the deal. With the SGC under attack, and Vice President Kinsey breathing down their necks, it's up to Colonel Jack O'Neill and his team to uncover the saboteur and save the fledgling alliance. But unbeknownst to SG-1 there are far greater forces at work—a calculating revenge that spans decades, and a desperate gambit to prevent a cataclysm of epic proportions.

When the identity of the saboteur is revealed, O'Neill is faced with a horrifying truth and is forced into an unlikely alliance in order to fight for Earth's future.

Order your copy directly from the publisher today by going to www.stargatenovels.com or send a check or money order made payable to "Fandemonium" to:

USA orders: $10.82 ($7.95 + $2.87 P&P). Send payment to: Fandemonium Books, PO Box 2178, Decatur, GA 30031-2178.

UK orders: £8.30 (£6.99 + £1.31 P&P). Rest of the World orders: £9.70 (£6.99 + £2.71 P&P). Send payment to: Fandemonium Books, PO Box 795A, Surbiton KT5 8YB, United Kingdom.

Or check your local bookshop – available on special order if they are out of stock (quote the ISBN number listed above).

STARGATE SG-1: ROSWELL

**by Sonny Whitelaw &
Jennifer Fallon**
Price: $7.95 US | $9.95 Canada |
£6.99 UK
ISBN-10: 1-905586-04-3
ISBN-13: 978-1-905586-04-2

When a Stargate malfunction throws
Colonel Cameron Mitchell, Dr. Daniel Jackson, and Colonel Sam Carter
back in time, they only have minutes
to live.

But their rescue, by an unlikely
duo — General Jack O'Neill and Vala Mal Doran — is only the
beginning of their problems. Ordered to rescue an Asgard also
marooned in 1947, SG-1 find themselves at the mercy of history. While Jack, Daniel, Sam and Teal'c become embroiled in the
Roswell aliens conspiracy, Cam and Vala are stranded in another
timeline, desperately searching for a way home.

As the effects of their interference ripple through time,
the consequences for the future are catastrophic. Trapped in the
past, SG-1 can only watch as their world is overrun by a terrible
invader…

STARGATE SG-1: ALLIANCES

A failed mission leaves O'Neill dealing with the fallout

STARGATE SG·1

ALLIANCES
Karen Miller

Based on the hit television series developed by
Brad Wright and Jonathan Glassner

Series number: SG1-8

by Karen Miller

Price: $7.95 US | $9.95 Canada |
£6.99 UK
ISBN-10: 1-905586-00-0
ISBN-13: 978-1-905586-00-4

All SG-1 wanted was technology to save Earth from the Goa'uld ... but the mission to Euronda was a terrible failure. Now the dogs of Washington are baying for Jack O'Neill's blood—and Senator Robert Kinsey is leading the pack.

When Jacob Carter asks General Hammond for SG-1's participation in mission for the Tok'ra, it seems like the answer to O'Neill's dilemma. The secretive Tok'ra are running out of hosts. Jacob believes he's found the answer—but it means O'Neill and his team must risk their lives infiltrating a Goa'uld slave breeding farm to recruit humans willing to join the Tok'ra.

It's a risky proposition ... especially since the fallout from Euronda has strained the team's bond almost to breaking. If they can't find a way to put their differences behind them, they might not make it home alive ...

STARGATE SG-1: SURVIVAL OF THE FITTEST

by Sabine C. Bauer
Price: $7.95 US | $9.95 Canada |
£6.99 UK
ISBN-10: 0-9547343-9-4
ISBN-13: 978-0-9547343-9-8

Colonel Frank Simmons has never been a friend to SG-1. Working for the shadowy government organisation, the NID, he has hatched a horrifying plan to create an army as devastatingly effective as that of any Goa'uld.

And he will stop at nothing to fulfil his ruthless ambition, even if that means forfeiting the life of the SGC's Chief Medical Officer, Dr. Janet Fraiser. But Simmons underestimates the bond between Stargate Command's officers. When Fraiser, Major Samantha Carter and Teal'c disappear, Colonel Jack O'Neill and Dr. Daniel Jackson are forced to put aside personal differences to follow their trail into a world of savagery and death.

In this complex story of revenge, sacrifice and betrayal, SG-1 must endure their greatest ordeal…

Order your copy directly from the publisher today by going to www.stargatenovels.com or send a check or money order made payable to "Fandemonium" to:

<u>USA orders:</u> **$10.82 ($7.95 + $2.87 P&P). Send payment to: Fandemonium Books, PO Box 2178, Decatur, GA 30031-2178.**

<u>UK orders:</u> **£8.30 (£6.99 + £1.31 P&P). <u>Rest of the World orders:</u> £9.70 (£6.99 + £2.71 P&P). Send payment to: Fandemonium Books, PO Box 795A, Surbiton KT5 8YB, United Kingdom.**

Or check your local bookshop – available on special order if they are out of stock (quote the ISBN number listed above).

STARGATE SG-1: SIREN SONG

Holly Scott and Jaimie Duncan
Price: $7.95 US | $9.95 Canada |
£6.99 UK
ISBN-10: 0-9547343-6-X
ISBN-13: 978-0-9547343-6-7

Bounty-hunter, Aris Boch, once more has his sights on SG-1. But this time Boch isn't interested in trading them for cash. He needs the unique talents of Dr. Daniel Jackson — and he'll do anything to get them.

Taken to Boch's ravaged home-world, Atropos, Colonel Jack O'Neill and his team are handed over to insane Goa'uld, Sebek. Obsessed with opening a mysterious subterranean vault, Sebek demands that Jackson translate the arcane writing on the doors. When Jackson refuses, the Goa'uld resorts to devastating measures to ensure his cooperation.

With the vault exerting a malign influence on all who draw near, Sebek compels Jackson and O'Neill toward a horror that threatens both their sanity and their lives. Meanwhile, Carter and Teal'c struggle to persuade the starving people of Atropos to risk everything they have to save SG-1 — and free their desolate world of the Goa'uld, forever.

Order your copy directly from the publisher today by going to **www.stargatenovels.com** or send a check or money order made payable to "Fandemonium" to:

USA orders: $10.82 ($7.95 + $2.87 P&P). Send payment to: Fandemonium Books, PO Box 2178, Decatur, GA 30031-2178.

UK orders: £8.30 (£6.99 + £1.31 P&P). Rest of the World orders: £9.70 (£6.99 + £2.71 P&P). Send payment to: Fandemonium Books, PO Box 795A, Surbiton KT5 8YB, United Kingdom.

Or check your local bookshop — available on special order if they are out of stock (quote the ISBN number listed above).

STARGATE SG-1: CITY OF THE GODS

The team is stranded on a doomed world

STARGATE SG·1

CITY OF THE GODS
Sonny Whitelaw
Based on the hit television series developed by
Brad Wright and Jonathan Glassner

Series number: SG1-4

by Sonny Whitelaw
Price: $7.95 US | $9.95 Canada |
£6.99 UK
ISBN-10: 0-9547343-3-5
ISBN-13: 978-0-9547343-3-6

When a Crystal Skull is discovered beneath the Pyramid of the Sun in Mexico, it ignites a cataclysmic chain of events that maroons SG-1 on a dying world.

Xalótcan is a brutal society, steeped in death and sacrifice, where the bloody gods of the Aztecs demand tribute from a fearful and superstitious population. But that's the least of Colonel Jack O'Neill's problems. With Xalótcan on the brink of catastrophe, Dr. Daniel Jackson insists that O'Neill must fulfil an ancient prophesy and lead its people to salvation. But with the world tearing itself apart, can anyone survive?

As fear and despair plunge Xalótcan into chaos, SG-1 find themselves with ringside seats at the end of the world...

• *Special section: Excerpts from Dr. Daniel Jackson's mission journal.*

STARGATE SG-1: A MATTER OF HONOR

Part one of two parts
by Sally Malcolm
Price: $7.95 US | $9.95 Canada |
£6.99 UK
ISBN-10: 0-9547343-2-7
ISBN-13: 978-0-9547343-2-9

Five years after Major Henry Boyd
and his team, SG-10, were trapped on
the edge of a black hole, Colonel Jack
O'Neill discovers a device that could
bring them home.

But it's owned by the Kinahhi, an advanced and paranoid people, besieged by a ruthless foe. Unwilling to share the technology, the Kinahhi are pursuing their own agenda in the negotia-
tions with Earth's diplomatic delegation. Maneuvering through a
maze of tyranny, terrorism and deceit, Dr. Daniel Jackson, Major
Samantha Carter and Teal'c unravel a startling truth — a revelation that throws the team into chaos and forces O'Neill to face
a nightmare he is determined to forget.

Resolved to rescue Boyd, O'Neill marches back into the hell he
swore never to revisit. Only this time, he's taking SG-1 with him…

**Order your copy directly from the publisher today by going
to www.stargatenovels.com or send a check or money order
made payable to "Fandemonium" to:**

USA orders: $10.82 ($7.95 + $2.87 P&P). Send payment to:
Fandemonium Books, PO Box 2178, Decatur, GA 30031-2178.

UK orders: £8.30 (£6.99 + £1.31 P&P). **Rest of the World
orders:** £9.70 (£6.99 + £2.71 P&P). Send payment to:
Fandemonium Books, PO Box 795A, Surbiton KT5 8YB,
United Kingdom.

Or check your local bookshop – available on special order if they are
out of stock (quote the ISBN number listed above).

STARGATE SG-1: THE COST OF HONOR

**Part two of two parts
by Sally Malcolm**
Price: $7.95 US | $9.95 Canada |
£6.99 UK
ISBN-10: 0-9547343-4-3
ISBN-13: 978-0-9547343-4-3

In the action-packed sequel to *A Matter of Honor*, SG-1 embark on a desperate mission to save SG-10 from the edge of a black hole. But the price of heroism may be more than they can pay...

Returning to Stargate Command, Colonel Jack O'Neill and his team find more has changed in their absence than they had expected. Nonetheless, O'Neill is determined to face the consequences of their unauthorized activities, only to discover the penalty is far worse than anything he could have imagined.

With the fate of Colonel O'Neill and Major Samantha Carter unknown, and the very survival of the SGC threatened, Dr. Daniel Jackson and Teal'c mount a rescue mission to free their team-mates and reclaim the SGC. Yet returning to the Kinahhi homeworld, they learn a startling truth about its ancient foe. And uncover a horrifying secret...

Order your copy directly from the publisher today by going to www.stargatenovels.com or send a check or money order made payable to "Fandemonium" to:

USA orders: $10.82 ($7.95 + $2.87 P&P). Send payment to: Fandemonium Books, PO Box 2178, Decatur, GA 30031-2178.

UK orders: £8.30 (£6.99 + £1.31 P&P). **Rest of the World orders:** £9.70 (£6.99 + £2.71 P&P). Send payment to: Fandemonium Books, PO Box 795A, Surbiton KT5 8YB, United Kingdom.

Or check your local bookshop – available on special order if they are out of stock (quote the ISBN number listed above).

STARGATE SG-1: SACRIFICE MOON

Terror stalks the team at night

STARGATE SG·1

SACRIFICE MOON

Julie Fortune

Based on the hit television series developed by Brad Wright and Jonathan Glassner

Series number: SG1-2

By Julie Fortune
Price: $7.95 US | $9.95 Canada | £6.99 UK
ISBN-10: 0-9547343-1-9
ISBN-13: 978-0-9547343-1-2

Sacrifice Moon follows the newly commissioned SG-1 on their first mission through the Stargate.

Their destination is Chalcis, a peaceful society at the heart of the Helos Confederacy of planets. But Chalcis harbors a dark secret, one that pitches SG-1 into a world of bloody chaos, betrayal and madness. Battling to escape the living nightmare, Dr. Daniel Jackson and Captain Samantha Carter soon begin to realize that more than their lives are at stake. They are fighting for their very souls.

But while Col Jack O'Neill and Teal'c struggle to keep the team together, Daniel·is hatching a desperate plan that will test SG-1's fledgling bonds of trust and friendship to the limit…

STARGATE SG-1: TRIAL BY FIRE

By Sabine C. Bauer
Price: $7.95 US | $9.95 Canada |
£6.99 UK
ISBN-10: 0-9547343-0-0
ISBN-13: 978-0-9547343-0-5

Trial by Fire follows the team as they embark on a mission to Tyros, an ancient society teetering on the brink of war.

A pious people, the Tyreans are devoted to the Canaanite deity, Meleq. When their spiritual leader is savagely murdered during a mission of peace, they beg SG-1 for help against their sworn enemies, the Phrygians.

Initially reluctant to get involved, the team has no choice when Colonel Jack O'Neill is abducted. O'Neill soon discovers his only hope of escape is to join the ruthless Phrygians — if he can survive their barbaric initiation rite.

As Major Samantha Carter, Dr. Daniel Jackson and Teal'c race to his rescue, they find themselves embroiled in a war of shifting allegiances, where truth has many shades and nothing is as it seems.

And, unbeknownst to them all, an old enemy is hiding in the shadows...

Order your copy directly from the publisher today by going to www.stargatenovels.com or send a check or money order made payable to "Fandemonium" to:

USA orders: $10.82 ($7.95 + $2.87 P&P). Send payment to: Fandemonium Books, PO Box 2178, Decatur, GA 30031-2178.

UK orders: £8.30 (£6.99 + £1.31 P&P). Rest of the World orders: £9.70 (£6.99 + £2.71 P&P). Send payment to: Fandemonium Books, PO Box 795A, Surbiton KT5 8YB, United Kingdom.

Or check your local bookshop – available on special order if they are out of stock (quote the ISBN number listed above).